KU-080-226

I've travelled the world twice over,
Met the famous: saints and sinners,
Poets and artists, kings and queens,
Old stars and hopeful beginners,
I've been where no-one's been before,
Learned secrets from writers and cooks
All with one library ticket
To the wonderful world of books.

© Janice James.

The wisdom of the ages
Is there for you and me,
The wisdom of the ages,
In your local library.

There's large print books
And talking books,
For those who cannot see,
The wisdom of the ages,
It's fantastic, and it's free.

Written by Sam Wood, aged 92

I SPY . . .

Carol Halstead is only eight years old when she is a hidden, terrified witness to the brutal murder of her parents by four teenagers. These killers, whose faces continue to haunt her mind fifteen years later, still walk free. But now Carol looks set to put the past behind her; she begins her first teaching job. Then she sees one of her new infant pupils, Ben, about whom there is something faintly familiar . . . Carol becomes prey to a deepening suspicion. Her fondness for Ben, and her growing friendship with his mother, lead her to a place of terror — and to a dreadful secret.

Books by Tim Wilson
Published by The House of Ulverscroft:

MASTER OF MORHOLM
PURGATORY
CLOSE TO YOU

AS T. R. WILSON:
ROSES IN DECEMBER
HESTER VERNEY
HEARTSEASE
A GREEN HILL FAR AWAY

TIM WILSON

I SPY . . .

Complete and Unabridged

ULVERSCROFT
Leicester

First published in Great Britain in 1996 by
Headline Book Publishing
London

First Large Print Edition
published 1997
by arrangement with
Headline Book Publishing Limited
a division of
Hodder Headline Plc
London

British Library CIP Data

Wilson, Tim, *1962 –*
    I spy . . .—Large print ed.—
    Ulverscroft large print series: mystery
    1. Thrillers
    2. Large type books
    I. Title
    823.9'14 [F]

    ISBN 0–7089–3874–4

Published by
F. A. Thorpe (Publishing) Ltd.
Anstey, Leicestershire
Set by Words & Graphics Ltd.
Anstey, Leicestershire
Printed and bound in Great Britain by
T. J. International Ltd., Padstow, Cornwall

This book is printed on acid-free paper

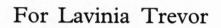

For Lavinia Trevor

*T*HE WPC has never seen anything like it.

The phrase should be meaningless. She has been with the Metropolitan Police for five years, and after that time you've always seen something like it. You're not blasé; just prepared.

But the WPC was not prepared for this, and she has never seen anything like it.

She and her patrol colleague — who is male and in defiance of sexual stereotyping has gone out of the way somewhere to be sick — were the first ones to go into the house. A marital bust-up was the expectation. The little girl who made the 999 call would only say, "It's my mummy and daddy," and wouldn't stay on the line. But she gave the address clearly enough and seemed quite calm. The WPC now knows that that calm was unnatural, the calm of an animal snared and quietly panting; but

1

she did not know that when the patrol car pulled up outside the house. She did not know it until she and her colleague had given up hammering on the front door and gone round to the rear of the house and found the back door forced open, gaping. And had gone inside.

But at least she is outside, now. The plain-clothes crew have descended and taken over the show. A whole section of the street has been cordoned off — with the lights and the activity it looks oddly festive, and the WPC recalls with a dull effort that in a few days it will be Christmas — and of course bods are needed to man the cordon and keep off the goggling neighbours and the press people, yet to get here but surely on their way. The WPC is glad to be one of these bods to stand with her back to the place and breathe fresh clean air while Divisional CID acquaint themselves with what is inside that house.

She notices that most of the residents of the street who are clustering and rubbernecking on the other side of the cordon are fully dressed, despite the fact that it's three thirty-five a.m.

and they must have been in bed when the commotion started. Instinct, she supposes: get dressed, put the kettle on, something big's happened. They still keep plying her and the other uniforms on the scene with questions, some frank, some sly but they'll get no answers.

The police photographer has arrived and a DC takes him swiftly into the house through the front door, hustling him, almost shielding him, as if he were a suspect.

SLAYING.

That's the word the tabloids always use in cases like this. Easy to see why: it does carry a certain unique charge. No doubt they'll be using it for this case. Certainly the WPC can't think of any word more apt to what she has just seen. No, there is a word, similar, usually used in connection with livestock, but she puts the word from her mind, cordons it off.

The DC is at her elbow. For a moment she doesn't understand him.

"She still won't come out."

"Why me?"

"She said something about the police lady. She saw you first. Maybe the

uniform. She doesn't trust us."

"But she wouldn't come out for me when I found her, she — "

"Just come, will you?"

The WPC's reluctance is so great that it must surely show — and show her as unprofessional. But the DC doesn't take much notice of her — his own face is dark and grim enough — and simply steers her up the steps to the front door, and in.

Better now, a little better, the WPC tells herself, trying to control her rapid breathing. Now it's a crime scene, a site of official investigation, no longer the private home with a faint smell of cooking and other people.

The sticky red graffiti, a foot high, is still there on the wall of the first landing, but now it is evidence being examined by an officer from the Metropolitan Police Forensic Science Laboratory and that makes it better, a little better.

Her head lately has been full of her brother's wedding, which is in two days' time. As she climbs the stairs she finds herself thinking for a moment that it will have to be put off now — before she

4

remembers that what has happened in this house will not bring everything to a halt, even though it feels as if it should. This incident — this crime — will be limited in its effects, for all the horror of it. The public will be affected via the media, very fleetingly. Relatives, if any, surely.

The little girl, most certainly. In fact, beyond imagining.

Glimpse into the first-floor living room, with the Christmas tree knocked over, baubles shattered. More bright red graffiti. The WPC keeps a stern eyes-front as they come to the top landing of the three-storey house. The woman's body is in the bedroom to the left, out of sight. But the man must have fought, and got as far as the landing before he was finished off. Not that they had finished with him even then. Anyhow the WPC has seen already, and though a bending pathologist makes a partial screen, she doesn't want to see again.

She has seen this room too, the little girl's room. It was empty and silent then, when the WPC and her colleague made their first exploration, and you wouldn't have supposed that there was anyone here at all. But a little girl had definitely made the 999 call and at last the WPC, whose senses are very acute, located her by the sound of her tiny sobs. And she is still in that same hiding place, except now the room is full, too full. There is DI Lennard whom she knows and a doctor she doesn't know and an ambulancewoman, all gathered round that hiding place, and the little girl isn't coming out.

It occurs to the WPC for the first time, as the DI makes way for her, that the little girl must have crept out to make that phone call. Must have passed that grotesquely positioned body on the stairs. Must have seen, indeed, what the WPC has seen. And then gone back to her hiding place. A child's logic. But an understandable logic, the WPC thinks. She's not sure that she wouldn't have done the same.

And what else did the little girl see?

The house is an old one, Victorian, with deep skirting boards and high moulded ceilings and bulky bedroom chimneypieces. Not much renovated, but in the process of it. As here, where the chimneypiece has been boxed in with sheets of plyboard. An intermediary stage, the WPC guesses: the fireplace probably bricked up behind it, the plyboard covering the unsightliness until redecoration, maybe after the Christmas break. But two important things. The mantelshelf has been retained (books and teddies all along it) and so the sheets of plyboard are flush with the edge of it, leaving a gap just large enough for a small child to crawl into. And as this is a child's bedroom, the plyboard has become covered with pinned-up drawings and posters, disguising it most effectively. Coming into the room, you don't suspect the existence of that hidey-hole at all. And it is plain that whoever ran amok in the house did come into this room, not only from the ransacked wardrobe but from the hamster cage standing open on a table by the bed. Presumably the little girl saw what has been done to her pet too. The WPC remembers stepping on ants as a child, and wishes she had not.

Logical, the WPC thinks, kneeling down by the chimneypiece. Logical to get back in and not come out.

"Listen, sweetheart, it's me again, do you remember?"

Peering into the narrow gap, the WPC sees an oval face, the blink of a large eye amongst tousled hair. And she notices the little bar of illumination laid across that shadowed face. A tiny crack or slit in the plyboard. A peephole: perhaps she made it herself, naughtily, used to hide in here as a game, I can see you Mummy.

Still the little sobbing breaths, but no tears on the lit curve of cheek. All used up by now. All gone.

"Will you come out now, poppet? It's all right to come out. I'm a police lady. Will you come out with me? It'll be all right. It'll be all right, pet, I promise you."

Blink of the round blue eye, fixed on her. The others in the room are silent, waiting at a distance.

"Come on, pet, you come out now and I'll look after you. You don't want to stay squeezed up in there, do you? It's not very comfy." Helplessly the WPC searches her mind: then realizes, from the little frill visible below the child's

8

chin, that she must be in her nightdress. Memory and instinct prompt her. "You'll get cold. You'll get cold if you stop there, now you don't want to get cold, do you?"

And it works. The round eye gives another blink and then, obedient to a formula that must have been often used by the woman who lies hacked and spreadeagled in the next room, the child begins to edge out of her hiding place.

"That's it, pet. Good girl. Come here."

The ambulancewoman is on hand with a blanket, but it is the WPC who takes it and wraps the little girl in it and it is she who carries her downstairs, swathed to the eyes so that she shall not see. The child's body is rigid and her hair smells sweetly of shampoo.

The ambulance has been brought right to the front door. More uniforms are clustered around the steps, screening the little blanket-wrapped figure from any telephoto lens that might be trained on the house. The cold air, the blue lights, cause the girl to squirm a little in the WPC's arms, and cast a timid peep over the top of the blanket; but she makes no sound.

"We're just going to take you to the hospital, pet. Make sure you're all right." Make sure nothing has been done to her. Physically, at any rate. "I'll come with you," she adds, meeting the eyes of DI Lennard over the girl's head, getting a quick nod in reply. And as she steps up into the brightly lit interior of the ambulance, the WPC notices something that of all the things she has seen tonight seems somehow the most terrible and the least likely ever to fade from her mind.

It is the little girl's slippers. They are furry slippers with dog faces on them and, as children will do, she has put them on the wrong feet. Also she has had to walk through her parents' blood in them.

1

"OH God, I don't want to go," Carol said, looking at her watch. "I really do not want to go."

"You'll get used to that," Diane said, chuckling. "I still get that after ten years. Every morning, every breaktime, every lunchtime."

Carol looked at her watch again, as if in hopes that it might start ticking backwards. Rooted to the spot: how vivid and fresh these old phrases came up when you really experienced them. Just now it seemed an impossibility that she would ever be able to get out of this chair. One of those low chairs with knobbly upholstery and wooden arms that you only ever seemed to see in school staff rooms. She had glimpsed the teachers sitting in chairs exactly like this one when she was a schoolchild and it added to her sense of being somehow an imposter here.

Which she wasn't, she reminded herself.

11

She was qualified. She was a Bachelor of Education, and her photograph had been newly placed in the framed montage of teacher mug shots that greeted the visitor on entering Templeton Junior School. And she did very much want to go and meet her class and commence what was, after all, the career that she had set her heart on and that she would have moved mountains to pursue.

If only she could get out of this chair.

"Just remember they're new too," Diane said. "Fresh from infants' school and not knowing what to expect. I've got a horribly knowing bunch of fourth-years this time round. Practically teenagers. Give me the little rug-rats any day."

"Morning, everyone. Hope you're all full of the joys and so on."

A courtier-like murmur of reply went round the staff room as the headmaster breezed in on spongy soles, tie artfully placed over his left shoulder. Bob Macleish, an unctuous silver-haired Scot with reptilian eyes, sharp-nosed and thin-lipped, did not appear to Carol to be overwhelmingly popular with his staff.

12

"Watch him," she had been told, "he's a pure bastard." She understood that it was common practice to say this of heads to probationers, but the warnings seemed to go beyond the conventional.

Macleish stalked over to Carol, rubbing his hands together. It made a sound like two lizards mating.

"Now then, our Miss Halstead looks ready for the fray. I'm sure we all wish her the best of British and so on. No nerves this morning?"

"Just a few," Carol said.

"Well, I'm not in the habit of giving advice, and I'm sure you're not in the habit of taking it," he said, with more scaly rubbings.

"Only if it's good," Carol said, wishing at once that she hadn't said it. Pump-priming was not her strong point, as her tutors at training college had sometimes tried to point out to her.

"Very wise," he said, giving her his alligator smile. "What it is to be young, eh, Diane?"

"I remember," said Diane, who was thirtyish, plump, spectacled, and clearly accustomed to rather than reconciled to the head's patronage.

"You'll find it tough," Macleish went on. "Nothing in your training can prepare you for it. But I don't suppose you went into teaching looking for an easy time. Isn't that so, Martin?" he said, addressing a shambling man-mountain in an unseasonal overcoat who had just come in.

"I went into *life* looking for an easy time," the man-mountain said through the back of his head, shucking off the overcoat, "but I never got it."

"You've remembered where the school is, at any rate," the head said. "Just in time to meet your next-door neighbour. Carol, this is Martin Culler, who'll also be teaching first-years."

Without the overcoat he was less gigantic, but there was still a good deal of the man who stomped over and thrust a hand at Carol, ignoring the acidly hovering Macleish. Well over six feet tall, big-bodied, with huge feet and a schoolboyish fringe of thick black hair that dangled into a pair of eyes Slavic in their darkness, Martin Culler looked more like an eccentric shot-putter than a schoolteacher. But then, Carol thought, people you had known only by name never looked the way you had pictured them. She had known that a Mr Culler was to have the classroom next to hers, but he had never seemed to be around either during her informal visits to the school or during setting-up week. By hints from the other staff she gathered that he was a bit of a black sheep in what Macleish called their big happy family, his devotion to Templeton Junior School somewhat less than total.

"How d'you do?" Martin said, in a faintly Northern voice like soft gravel. "So, what's the current gospel in the College of Eds? Pastoral care, or thrash the three Rs into the little buggers? I incline to the latter myself. Never did me any harm, except turn me into a resentful psychotic, of course. Where are you from?"

"Well, I trained at Lincoln. But I'm from London."

"Good God. What on earth made you come to Dunmarket?"

She shrugged, laughed. "What made you?"

"Oh, I was sent here as a punishment for my sins. Karma, you know. I was a complete bastard in a previous life. It was a choice between schoolteaching in deepest Suffolk or being a dung beetle."

"Ties can be washed, you know, Martin," Macleish said, with a disdainful look at the stained rag round Martin's neck; then, rubbing, "Well now, we have a lot of little newcomers waiting, shall we go and greet them?"

"Prepare to meet thy doom," Martin said to Carol, quite deadpan.

"I'd like to have a word at break, by the by," the head told him.

"Did you say Lincoln? Bishop Grosse-teste?"

"That's right," Carol said, with a nervous glance at Macleish. Plainly treating the head as if he didn't exist was a favourite winding-up tactic of Martin's, and it just as plainly worked.

"Diane, didn't Chris Bryce train there?" Martin said, and then to Carol, "I should think you've met Chris, haven't you? Sole surviving member of the Green Party. Like the Last of the Mohicans. He recycles his beard, you know. Quite human underneath though — "

"Carol's met the whole cast now," Macleish said, "including the clown. So I suggest we get the show on the road."

Carol found she could get out of her chair quite easily after all. Inwardly amused but wary too, she followed the strutting headmaster and the ambling Martin and thought that thirty of the most unruly children were easier on the brain than a handful of adults who didn't like each other.

2

THE new intake of first-years, glum, small, achingly neat and combed, reminded Carol, as they gathered in the hall, of old newsreels of evacuees.

Compassion quietened her own apprehension, without entirely overcoming it. These mites had come from a place that was built to their scale. In comparison this school must look like Rugby. The corridors were loud with hulking boys, effing like convicts, and droopy girls who wore bras beneath the Aertex. Shuffling, finger-sucking, the newcomers eyed the wall bars as if expecting at any moment to be driven up them with whips.

Mrs Juby, the other first-year teacher besides Carol and Martin, certainly looked as if she were capable of it. A steely, crisp-moustached throwback to the days of slapped legs and ounces per pound, she inspected her new class as their names were called out like a sergeant major with a draft of weaklings. The relief on the faces of the others, billeted either on Martin or Carol, was plain to see and gave Carol's confidence a boost, even though it was one she knew she hadn't earned. She was a lesser evil and even she didn't know by how much. This was her first day as a teacher and it was impossible to overstate the utter, uncharted newness of it.

She had taken charge of classes as a student teacher, of course, and she knew she had made a good fist at it. But that meant next to nothing. Kids always loved a student teacher. You were a young kindly novelty and you weren't wise to them, unlike their real teacher, who had to carry the responsibility as well as appearing a pedantic spoilsport in comparison. Macleish, slimy but no fool, was right when he said training couldn't prepare you for this day. Today there was no safety net.

Mrs Juby, having drilled her recruits into a precise double-column, led them off at a quick march. Martin Culler, with clappings of his giant hands, hustled his lot haphazardly before him, looking like

19

a bear driving a flock of nervous geese. Carol got her new charges into twos, didn't fuss when a few threes refused to be separated, and led them with a massed squeaking of plimsolls down the parqueted corridor to the classroom that, unbelievably still, had her name on its bright orange safety door.

"All right, everyone. We'll stop here a minute. Now gather round me — shuffle a bit closer, that's it. Can everyone hear me and see me?" She scanned faces, looking for signs of inattention. Further along the corridor Martin and Mrs Juby were mustering their classes in similar fashion, and she made sure her voice was pitched above them. "Now this is your classroom. See the number one there? That's you — Class one, Miss Halstead's class. I'm Miss Halstead, in case you were wondering." Nervous giggles. "So if anyone asks you what class you're in, you say, 'Class one, Miss Halstead's class.' Let's all say it." They chanted it, obedient and despondent. "That's good. Now this is your classroom, the room that you'll be in every day, just like you had a classroom in your old school." She thought back quickly to the pupil lists, with a sudden apprehension that some might have come from infants' schools with an open-plan setup. No, of course: Dunmarket and its hinterland was all trad. "All right, so this is your special door. Number one written on it, and it's — what colour?"

"Orange." Obedient but not so despondent: this was a breeze.

"Right. Easy. Now everybody look that way, where my finger's pointing. That glass door, see it? That's where we came in, isn't it? And that's the way you go out to the playground at break and to the gate when it's home-time. Now everybody keep having a good look at that glass door so you'll remember it."

It didn't matter if she was overdoing it: a cardinal error with young primary children was to assume that anything was self-evident. They needed, in the most literal sense, to know where they were. Disorientation was, besides, something she understood very well, as her own sense of direction was appalling, indeed semi-legendary amongst her friends. She wished someone had done this for her at training college, where throughout her first term she would regularly walk into boiler rooms and emerge on rooftops.

Mrs Juby and Martin having preceded her, she next acquainted her class with the cloakroom at the other end of the corridor, carefully pointed out the toilets alongside, and then led them back to the orange door. "Now this is where you come every morning. If I'm already in the classroom, the door will be open and you just walk in. If the door's closed, you wait here quietly for me. Then I'll open the door — " she did so — "and in you go, *quietly*. That's it." She didn't believe in children lining up to enter their classroom: it gave a dismal square-bashing air to the whole day.

She had arranged the classroom tables into five groups, and she invited the class to sit wherever they wished. This question of seating was one which training couldn't resolve for you, chiefly because there was no easy answer. You didn't want to break up any friendship groups that existed, but that left the possibility of children without friends from infants' school feeling isolated, not to mention the tendency of the sexes to stick together. Seating by ability wasn't viable with a new class, even supposing you approved of it, which Carol didn't. Then there was the matter of sightlines: she had gone through the children's medical reports and found no serious difficulties of hearing or vision amongst them, but it wasn't unknown for such things to go unnoticed to junior level. She had decided to steer a pragmatic course and let them settle where they wanted for now. As term went on she intended to do plenty of mixing and matching for group work, and anything was to be preferred to the regimented layout she had once seen on teaching practice, with thirty eight-year-olds seated alphabetically in rows at single desks like something from *Hard Times*.

'MISS HALSTEAD.' She wrote it on the blackboard and had them repeat it, recalling at the same time a fellow student at training college who had rejoiced in the name Mr I. Lovett and who had brushed aside all advice that he should change his name before qualifying as a primary school teacher. "Oh, the children would soon get over the joke," he had said, apparently never having noticed that with children, the reverse was true. They were addictive gigglers, and anything remotely ludicrous would set them going. Fortunately there were no mirth-inducers amongst the names on the register. The whole complement was here too, from Joanne Adamson to Ben Yeomans: no one absent with a tummy-bug, real or feigned. As for giggling, the newness of the classroom had turned them all preternaturally solemn. They gazed, and Carol could only hope they liked what they saw. She had spent all the time she could on it in the previous week, and had come in early this morning to add some finishing touches. Eventually, of course, the walls would be covered with the children's own displays, but for now Carol's main concern had been to cover up the glaring spaces, which she had done with as many cheap and colourful posters as she could lay her hands on, as well as a large cut-out in sugar paper which had taken her several laborious evenings to make. It was in the shape of a house, which would tie in with her proposed term topic of Homes, and contained thirty cut-out windows, each with a pupil's name underneath. She had thought at first of photographing them all and placing the snaps in the windows, but it had come to her last night that it might be more fun and involving to fill the spaces with the children's hand-prints.

"All right, everyone. I see you're having a good look at your classroom, so let's get to know it." She made a circuit, pointing out the sink, the unit where the painting equipment was kept and the apron rack next to it, the shelving stack for their exercise books, the computer worktops, the nature worktops, and the book corner. This was her baby: she had made it with a right-angled arrangement of bookcases and a hanging rug. She had wanted beanbags to complete it, but Macleish had responded to the word with a heavy-lidded smile. Presumably if he had his way he would have the children standing up to read, like medieval monks.

"OK, let's see if we know where everything is. I'll go to a place, and you call out where I am." She darted about the classroom, putting in a few hitch steps as she went. It was meant to make them chuckle and relax them: it was also, as Carol admitted to herself, a little piece of ingratiation on her part. Solemn educators might disapprove, but in essence she wanted them to look on this classroom as a place they didn't dread going back to after assembly, the time for which was fast approaching.

She needn't have worried. They positively clung to her as she led them to the hall, and their eyes kept swivelling to her, stationed by the wall bars, throughout the assembly, which was conducted by Macleish in a half-heartedly traditional fashion with a non-denominational prayer about being good and kind to everyone and a non-denominational song along the same lines. It was, of course, a bond like that of newly hatched chicks to the first creature they saw. Carol was their landmark in an unfamiliar world. But then, so was Mrs Juby to her class, and Carol allowed herself the satisfaction of noting that her own lot looked a lot happier about things already than those poor little tykes.

She could comprehend her class's

feelings all the more because she shared them a little herself. Throughout assembly she was aware of the scrutiny of the older years, to whom the school was a drearily known quantity and she, as the only new member of staff this year, an item of unique interest. To these three-quarters of the student body she stood at a distinct disadvantage. They knew the ropes: they were veterans. About the fourth-years especially, as Diane Hollins had said, there was a knowingness which one could easily find intimidating. Pubescence was stirring among those awkwardly squatting back rows. Boys studied her beneath their ruthless haircuts: girls gave her a look which a couple of years' practice would turn into that terrifying once-over that could kill at twenty paces. Carol found the loyalty cutting both ways, and warmed to her ducklings.

The warming continued after assembly when she took them back to the class, where awed eyes watched her every move. Of course they couldn't know that Carol was studying them with the same intensity of speculation: nor that she had her own small share of fear. Over the next year she would be spending as much time with these thirty individuals as many people spent with their families or partners. What would they be like? Old teaching hands loved to make the flesh of probationers creep with tales of legendary classes entirely composed of rotten apples, uncontrollable, heartbreaking, leaving a trail of nervous breakdowns in their wake. Hogwash, of course. But just for a moment, with the toilet episode, it seemed about to come true. One girl plucked up the courage to ask to go to the toilet, which started a stampede. Presumably until then everyone had been crossing their legs under the impression that the incessant piddling of the infants school was a thing of the past and in the stern world of juniors you had to wait until break: whatever, suddenly they all wanted to go at once, and Carol briefly found herself wondering if the probationer's nightmare was about to come true and all semblance of control was going to slip swiftly and for ever from her fingers, with the caretaker scooping up her liquefied remains in a bucket when three o'clock came around . . .

"All right, everyone: listen." She gave three sharp claps. "And that *means* listen. We'll start as we mean to go on. Dos and don'ts. There aren't many, but the ones there are you must stick to because I won't have it any other way." She slowed her speech for emphasis, reminding herself to resist the temptation to get behind her desk and play the heavy from there. That was a crucial mistake for novices: children soon spotted that you were hiding, and drew the appropriate conclusions. "Now when I say *Listen* and clap my hands that means you stop whatever you're doing, you stop talking and you look at me. At me, please. That's it. Another thing you don't do is shout out unless I tell you to. If you want to say something to me in class, you put your hand up. Now if I'm busy at the desk, or at another table, and I can't see you with your hand up, you come up and ask me one at a time. Now one more don't. If I'm talking to the whole class, like I am now, you don't talk amongst yourselves. That doesn't mean you can't ever talk to each other. But it means when I speak up, you shush. That's easy enough, isn't it? All right. Now, anyone who *needs* to go to the toilet, put up your hands."

The waterworks crisis over, it was moderately smooth sailing till break. She distributed exercise books, jotters and pencils, choosing not to relay the memo from Macleish to the effect that these items must be guarded with their young lives. Any child of school age knew how things were nowadays. Carol had made an inventory of her store cupboard, or resources centre, last week and had been pleasantly surprised at the bounty until she learnt that the contents were to last her not until half term but for the rest of the year. She was glad that, anticipating scant materials, she had spent a lot of time since moving to Dunmarket two months ago pestering every office she could find for scrap computer paper.

However, as she had been told with a certain desperate frequency during training, it was human resources that were the most precious, and the thirty specimens of the commodity gathered around her seemed promising enough. Dunmarket was no inner-city melting pot: the names on the register and the faces that regarded her were all thoroughly Anglo-Saxon; but the modest size and moderate means of the town meant that the school intake was well mixed. Templeton avoided the pitfalls of a district school because its catchment area was the whole town: the entire social range came here, except for the very top, which was creamed off by the private sector. Some of the children were economically, but none badly, dressed: skins were clear and hair cared for. Nearly all spoke with the Suffolk burr, which was classless in itself. They were an average bunch of eight-year-olds — in other words, as various as life itself. The prospect of getting to know them, of helping them to learn and learning with them, exhilarated Carol. She was glad she had not acted on the impulse of last night, when in a fit of panic she had decided that her choice of teaching as a career was a disastrous mistake and that her only possible option was to pile everything into the car, light out for the coast, disguise herself as a man, join a tramp steamer as a deckhand and never be heard of again.

At break she entered the staff room to a round of applause.

"She's alive," Martin Culler said wonderingly. "And there's no blood . . . Sorry," he added at her look; plainly he was afraid he had been condescending, though it was not that.

"Well done," Diane said. "Only another forty years to go now."

"Here, drink this while it's lukewarm," Martin said, handing her coffee. He was already on his second mug, which he drank in the abstracted, fist-clenched way of a man to whom coffee is only a pale substitute for a real drink and a cigarette. The former was naturally out of the question during school hours, though Carol had heard it rumoured that these were the only hours that Martin didn't drink in; the latter was forbidden too now, by headmasterly decree. Carol, a non-smoker, wasn't directly affected by this, but she found it oddly disappointing. A staff room that wasn't filled with blue smoke seemed to lack the last degree of authenticity.

"What are yours like?" Carol asked Martin.

"Six bright, six average, six below average, six morons, and six potential bank clerks. And oh God, I've got a Chantelle. I mean, I've had it now, I'm sorry, I've tried to be tolerant but there's only one thing to do and that is prosecute the parents who do this. Just let it be known that anyone who saddles their child with a ludicrous name is liable to a heavy fine or preferably a prison sentence. You can imagine the old lags, can't you? Comparing notes. 'What are you in for?' 'Shannon.' 'Cor, that's nothing. I'm in for Hogan.' No, I'm making that one up, but you wait and see . . . "

"I say, Dennis is *not* best pleased this morning." Jill, the deputy head and school workhorse, breezed in from an encounter with the caretaker. "Says the toilets are a disgrace, piddle all over, don't these kids know how to use the toilet properly, the whole bit."

"Do we?" It was Chris Bryce who spoke, appearing between Carol and Martin and accompanying his enigmatic question with a mystic flourish of his mineral water.

"Do we what?" Martin said.

"Know how to use the toilet properly." Chris presented his beard to each of them in turn. He was a young forty-year-old, of the type, Carol suspected, who will try also to be a young fifty-year-old. The tan leather blouson was the giveaway, an article of clothing chosen for its youthful properties, though it was something no young person would ever have worn. Carol's acquaintance with Chris was short, but as he was far from shy of talking about himself she felt she knew him pretty well. He had been born in India, where his family were leftovers from the Raj like something out of Paul Scott. This apparently gave him a different perspective on the West, which he liked to make you a present of. "The Western way of using the toilet is really unhealthy for the bowels. I climb up on the seat and squat, always have. It's your body's natural position. Clears the waste out much more efficiently. This is quite symbolic of Western attitudes really. We dump toxic fill but we hang on to our own shit."

"Chris," Martin said with a puzzled

34

look, "if you talk like this when you're sober, what do you talk like when you're pissed?"

"I don't drink. So, you were at Lincoln, I hear. Crazy place, isn't it?"

Carol couldn't think of anything about the cathedral city of Lincoln that could be called crazy, and came out lamely with, "Well, it's not like any other place."

"I couldn't handle it," Chris Bryce said. "I respond more to places with some industrial background, you know, urban, funky."

"Whatever made you choose Dunmarket?" she said.

"Oh, well, I was teaching in London, Hounslow actually, but I couldn't reconcile the contradictions of what I was doing. I was teaching a class of thirty-six Muslim kids. Inevitably you end up imposing a different value-system on them in spite of your best intentions. To try to add to a self-sufficient culture is like polluting a clear stream. Multiculturalism itself is a piece of Western fudge."

"Is that anything like Turkish delight?" Martin said.

"Anyhow, I had to get out of London,

the air's become literally poisonous. You're from London, right? Whereabouts?"

"Kennington," Carol said. "The one without the S." It was Aunt Jean's perennial joke. As always when talk began to touch on the past, Carol moved smoothly on: it was a habit so ingrained she had ceased to be aware of it. "I don't know Dunmarket very well yet. But I fell in love with Suffolk when I visited a college friend down here, and I went straight for Suffolk LEA when I qualified. Though I'm afraid I hadn't actually heard of Dunmarket when they mentioned the vacancy."

"It's the one that neither Gainsborough nor Constable was born in," Martin said. "They were thinking of putting that on the town sign. Ah God," as the bell rang, "condemned by the bell." He lifted the net curtain at the window and peeped out at the playground. "Dear dear, you can spot our lot. Wandering around on their own, poor sods. Like new arrivals in Cell Block H."

Carol looked out. Small neat figures, hands glumly in pockets, were conspicuous amongst the whirling boisterousness.

"How does it stand with bullying here?" she asked. Her views on this were strong, and she intended to descend like a fiery angel on the first sign.

"Sporadic," Martin said. "Macleish gave me a Chinese burn once. Right, better be off."

Visiting the staff toilet before returning to her class, Carol checked her appearance. Very fair and blue-eyed, slim to the point of thinness, she was liable to darkness under the orbits of the eyes, and stress and fatigue wrote themselves on her appearance like banner headlines; but the face looked to be holding up all right. It was pride more than vanity that made her concerned about this. She didn't want her body to betray her, giving the other staff the opportunity to nod at each other knowingly: *she's finding it tough*. It was as well to start off with a touch of paranoia, because she knew that the staff room crackled with it. Not this staff room: any staff room. What training couldn't teach you — what you had to grasp yourself, instinctively — was that the profession trod an unusually narrow line between backbiting and loyalty. It wasn't only with the kids that you had to have your wits about you.

Well, she had met all of the dozen other members of staff now, and while she felt a little shy and still could not rid herself of that feeling of being an imposter among them, she was not intimidated: she could picture herself working here. Diane had at once put out a gentle and undemanding hand of friendship: Jill, the deputy head, was jolly and open and quite obviously the person to go to when there was a problem. Mrs Juby knitted ferociously in a corner of the staff room during break: very much a case of Here Be Dragons. Near retirement, she must be frustrated that government educational policy, with its Ragged-School nostalgia, was catching up with her just as she was about to depart. Chris Bryce, to someone fresh out of college, was a yawningly familiar figure: she had met junior replicas of him in a hundred study-bedrooms and digs, right down to the drowsy catarrhal voice. As for Martin Culler, she didn't know what to make of him; except that she liked him a good deal, enough to hope that he had not taken a conscious decision to be eccentric and life-enhancing after too many viewings of *Dead Poets Society*. The others all seemed pleasant enough, and having a head like Macleish was by no means a disadvantage: someone so universally mistrusted was a powerful force for staff solidarity.

Carol wondered about her hair. She had put it up, to look older and brisker, which was fine: the problems would start if she ever wanted to have it down. It was naturally curly, and *Peanuts* notwithstanding, having naturally curly hair was not an unmixed blessing. As soon as you gave up on the crimpers and grips and just let it bubble out, people immediately assumed you'd had a perm, and said so. What she resented was the implication that she was the sort of person who had nothing better to do with her time, money and energy than that.

She was getting worked up thinking about it: she found also, as she tucked up some stray strands of hair, that she was counting. She remembered Dr Kaufman's advice: whenever it comes back, whenever little things start niggling you, whenever you start counting and making lists, remember the word *serendipity*. Defined as the knack of making happy discoveries by accident. Chance can be good; leave things to chance. You don't have to be minutely prepared for everything. Life will not hurl sudden disaster at you if you're not standing to attention. Serendipity rules.

It worked, and she spared a fond thought for Dr Kaufman as she hurried back to her class. That she was here at all, beginning her cherished career, was due in large part to him. It was odd that though he was now friend and confidant to her rather than doctor, she still couldn't think of him as John. He had promised her a visit next weekend, though with some half-serious grumblings about how he was going to bear the ghastliness of the country, and she reminded herself that she must get things ready for him. That didn't count as excessive preparation: the progress of his illness required it. "Yes, it's getting worse and worse," he'd said robustly last time they spoke on the phone. "Nature's efficient. If we can ever get it to do all our work for us, technology will seem as absurd and archaic as fortune-telling." He refused self-pity and pity equally.

The children looked glad to be back in class after the unfriendly playground. A slight brouhaha at the back alerted her to the possibility that her contingent contained at least one Little Sod, which was after all to be expected. "Miss, him's pushen me out of my seat!" came the mournful cry when she investigated. 'Him' was a stocky high-coloured boy named Stephen Stone, who was stubborn innocence for a few moments and then slunk away to his own seat, smirking. He got a giggle from one or two of the girls, which was presumably the intention. Carol told Stephen to choose a seat and keep to it, and left it at that. It was important to keep plenty in reserve. Teachers who were always comparing themselves to a descending ton of bricks were on a hiding to nothing. It was the poacher in Carol rather than the gamekeeper that knew this. She vividly recalled from her own school years the indignities inflicted on a certain Mr Harbottle, who announced himself a pushover by continually asserting that he wasn't. "I warn you, I shall take very severe action if there's any more of this," he would shout, purple-faced. "You won't know what's hit you, I promise you." Meanwhile the class threw things at him.

"All right now. I want to introduce you to Myrtle."

Myrtle was a stuffed toy elephant who acted as a kind of mascot for the three first-year classes. Each class had her for one term. She accompanied them on school trips, had eccentric outfits made for her, and generally presided like a household god over their progress. Also she had a collective story written about her each term, composed and illustrated by the class she was living with: it would be progressively displayed, like the Bayeux Tapestry, on one of the classroom walls, and then transferred to the hall at the end of the year. It was a fun project that had been instituted by Macleish's predecessor, and it was always popular. Macleish didn't like it, perhaps for that reason, perhaps because it was fun and fostered creativity and imagination. Certainly Carol's class immediately responded: in fact there was a sort of hilarious relief about them, as if a dentist's appointment had been cancelled and replaced with a trip to the cinema. She guessed why. They had probably picked up an impression, from older siblings and friends, that junior school meant multiplication tables. No more guinea pigs and wax crayons: it was hard, stern, inky stuff from here on in. Well, it was true that there was going to be a lot more to this term's work than Myrtle the Elephant, and the old integrated approach to primary school work had to give way to the iron-rations nonsense of the National Curriculum to some degree whether the teacher liked it or not. But Myrtle was a gentle way of easing them into the new regime. Mrs Juby was probably already socking her nurselings with long division, but Carol believed in the softly-softly approach.

The theme she had chosen for their instalment of Myrtle's adventures was the letter B. Everyone had to think of something beginning with B, write it down, and draw it. Myrtle's story would be built round these things, with as many other uses of the initial B as possible. Alliteration was a great greaser of the wheels of invention.

"I want you all to write your name at the top of the sheet of paper before you start. Now if you get stuck or can't think of anything, put your hand up and I'll see if I can help. And if you finish your thing beginning with B, carry on and do another, as many as you can think of."

Making the circuit of the class, looking over intent shoulders, she felt encouraged. She saw no handwriting below standard and plenty of confidence in the drawing. Originality too: whoever would have thought of a black pudding? There were a few timid arm-wavers, pink-cheeked, apparently fearful of being sent into the corner with a dunce's cap. She set them going by asking them to describe in detail what they had done at the weekend. Gone out to play? What with? Football. What did they use for goalposts? Coats. How do you do up a coat? Buttons.

"Oh, yes. I like him," Carol said, looking over one boy's shoulder at a very proficient drawing of a badger.

The boy tipped his head up to look at

her. "It was in the paper this morning about them," he said, quietly and shyly, but with distinct articulation.

"Oh, yes? What did it say?"

"It was about these people who bait them with dogs. And — and they take videos of it." He spoke solemnly. He was a dark little boy with a slender, expressive face. There was a touch of Just William about him with his shirt collar sticking up and the fringe of his newly barbered hair already tangled beyond the capabilities of a mere comb.

"Ah, yes. I know. They're very cruel, aren't they? They should be stopped."

Reading the newspaper at eight was pretty unusual. His writing was particularly well-formed too. Bright. His name was at the top of the sheet of paper: Ben Yeomans. The last on the register, she remembered.

"I've never seen a live badger, have you?"

"No. I saw a weasel."

"Really? Where was that?"

"Hoxham Woods."

She didn't know where Hoxham Woods was: presumably it was local, but she had only been living in Dunmarket for a couple of months and hadn't explored.

"Whereabouts . . . " she began, and then a curious thing happened. She found herself drying like an actress forgetting her lines. It was almost as if she were the one suddenly paralysed by childlike shyness.

Ben Yeomans continued to look up into her face. Then as if deciding she simply hadn't heard him, he repeated, "Hoxham Woods."

It was alarming. She couldn't remember where Hoxham Woods came into the conversation at all. She must have been staring, staring right into Ben's brown eyes, because he shifted awkwardly in his seat and then turned his attention back to his drawing.

"Miss, we went for a picnic there once," said the little girl seated beside Ben. "Sheppy, that's our dog, he got stung by a bee."

"Oh, did he? Was he all right?"

Carol came to herself. That peculiar sensation passed as quickly as it had come. The only comparison she could think of was hypnosis — which was odd in itself, as she had never been a good hypnotic subject, though they had tried it with her for months.

"He had to go to the vet," the girl said, "and he had an injection in his bottom."

"Ooh, ouch."

The others at the table chortled, Ben included. Carol moved on to the next table.

A momentary loss of concentration in a high-pressure situation: that was all. The analogy with the actor, in fact, was pretty well exact. It was nothing to worry about. In her teens she had been subject to infrequent but abrupt and shattering losses of self-confidence: she had mentally labelled it the Trapdoor. Determination and the help of Dr Kaufman had got rid of it, but she remembered well what it felt like and this sensation didn't resemble it at all. Carol had long ago become accustomed to as brisk and practical a self-monitoring as a diabetic, and she did not linger over this. Shyness, too, might not be such an unlikely explanation as it at first appeared. They were as new to her as she to them: thirty new people, albeit small ones. The world's greatest extrovert could be forgiven a tongue-tied moment in such a situation.

"All right, pass your papers to this end of your tables. Let's see what we've got." Sitting on the edge of her desk, she went through them. "So. We've got a ball, a beefburger, a bed, a bear — oh, hello, we've got Blur as well, that can't be bad . . . a banana, a badger . . . "

Instinctively she glanced in Ben Yeomans' direction, and met his attentive brown eyes fixed on her. Looking again at his drawing, she saw that he had shown an elementary grasp of perspective, the legs on the further side of the animal's body being appreciably smaller, and also shaded.

Bright, definitely. Bright and dark: his colouring stood out amongst the many fair and mousy heads. That must be why she felt so intensely aware of his presence in the classroom; that must be why his individuality thrust itself upon her out of so many.

"Right, it looks as if Myrtle's got a very interesting collection of things for her story. Let's start with Myrtle's bed . . . "

The story had a lively beginning. Using the letter B got their imaginations working: Myrtle did not simply get out of bed but bounced out of it, buzzed into the bathroom, had a bubble bath and, naturally, blew bubbles, brushed her back teeth, bumped down the stairs for breakfast . . . Carol wrote it all up on the blackboard and, calling a halt at Myrtle's breakfast of burgers and baked beans, had them copy it down in their books. When she spoke of continuing the story next week she saw some dismayed looks. They had been enjoying this, and wanted it to go on. But the Adventures of Myrtle could only be a weekly diversion. It *was* going to be different from infants' school. The recognition was on their faces, and some looked at her as if she were a betrayer. She was going to set them long sums, give them spelling tests, and make them do joined-up writing.

Well, yes, Carol thought, in a way that's exactly what I am going to do. But I'm also going to do my darnedest to make sure you enjoy it.

There was a knock at the classroom door. She called, "Come in!" but no one did. She went and opened it, and found a small boy nervously holding out a folded-up note.

"Mr Culler said give you this, miss," he said, with such a highpitched babble that there was a laugh of collusion from the class behind her. *Esprit de corps* didn't take long in establishing itself.

"Thank you very much. If you have to take a note to class again, just knock and then walk in, OK . . . ? And you can all remember that," she said, turning to her chuckling class.

She opened the note: *You're doing great. You must be, if you're reading this.*

She slipped it into her desk drawer. She was busy, and she would have to decide later whether she found it condescending or thoughtful.

3

'FRAZZLED' was a word they had used a lot at training college in connection with your first day's teaching. To go home from that first day feeling frazzled was, apparently, par for the course. The word suggested shredded nerves and traumatized emotions, and on that score at least Carol, getting into her car and driving away from Templeton Juniors, felt entitled to congratulate herself. It wasn't *that* bad. But what she hadn't been prepared for was the sheer physical exhaustion. She felt as if she had just done a twelve-hour shift in a quarry.

How could this be? The teaching day wasn't long, there were substantial breaks in it, and she had had to lift nothing heavier than a blackboard rubber. She supposed it would get better with use; but just now all she knew was that when the final bell had rung she had watched the kids haring out of the classroom with the wistful envy of a bedridden old lady. Perhaps, like little vampires, they had simply sucked the energy out of her. It was certainly a struggle to drag herself down to the headmaster's office, where Macleish was waiting to enquire after her progress and, as it turned out, give her a pep talk full of illustrations from his own exemplary teaching career. She had blinked and nodded through it, casting the odd resentful glance round the office. There was a thick carpet and a coffee machine in there. There weren't thirty children who grew in confidence as the day went on and who by the time three o'clock came were making a noise like a street market. Being a head was a doddle. All you had to do was run a school.

Carol drove carefully through the school gates. A couple of children lingering there waved to her. Not from her own class: that was nice. She waved back and smiled.

Of course, of course it would get easier. She had been wound up for this day like a runner for the race of her life, and it was inevitable that once over the finish line you would collapse in a heap. The rhythm of routine would work wonders. She would cope: she was positive that she would cope. But one thing was for sure. Though until now she had shrugged off the customary jokes aimed at teachers and would-be teachers — 'Long holidays and home by four, very nice, I can see why you went in for that' — Carol felt that from this moment on she could never let such a quip pass. At the first suggestion that she was on to a cushy number she would rise up, roaring.

Professional touchiness: I really am a teacher, thought Carol. That was something else the exhausting day had done for her: the feeling of being an imposter that had afflicted her in the staff room had wholly disappeared by the time she dragged herself in there to say her goodbyes at the end of the day. As if to underline the point, she had found herself being politely pestered by Tony Plumb. Tony was a scholastic Renaissance man who besides teaching, playing the piano, directing the school play and coaching the school football team also acted as a representative for the largest of the teachers' unions, and he wanted to enlist Carol. Though she fully intended joining, she was too weary to give him much response, and he had looked disappointed. Now as she drove home she hoped she hadn't given him the wrong impression. Perhaps he suspected her of already belonging to that bizarre minority union made up of born-again Christians and masochists which periodically campaigned for longer hours, less pay and the introduction of the cat-o'-nine-tails into kindergartens.

Time enough to worry about that later. Just now she couldn't worry about anything beyond getting home and getting rested. It occurred to her that this pure, incontrovertible tiredness was precisely what she used to try to induce in herself years ago, when she had suffered from insomnia. The frantic activity had only made it worse, as Dr Kaufman had told her it would, but she was a teenager then and knew everything.

About to take the turning for home, she remembered food, or rather the food she didn't have. Shopping had gone by the board in the hectic past few days: the fish and chip shop just round the corner from her flat had sustained her through them, but a moment's visualization convinced her that she couldn't face another grease supper.

She made a last-second indicator change, expecting horn-blasts of fury from the car behind her. But of course, this was Dunmarket: driving here was not like participating in the chariot race from *Ben Hur*. Heading for the town centre, she spared an appreciative thought for her surroundings, which without being in any way a planned environment might have been designed to minimize stress at the end of a working day, especially a day such as she had had. Dunmarket had imperfections aplenty, and no doubt as she settled down here she would become more aware of them, but it didn't matter. She already felt something of the same bond with the town that she had formed with her class: whilst she still tended to think of London as home, she did not think the transfer of loyalties would take long.

The town was small, with less than fifteen thousand people, but she had noted none of the dismal stifling qualities that she associated with the words 'small town'. Perhaps this was partly because in the seventies London overspill had spiced and stirred the ethnographic recipe: perhaps partly because there were no large towns nearby. A big brother ten miles down the A road was a great sapper of a place's vitality. Dunmarket had to supply everything its inhabitants needed, and from what Carol had seen it did so pretty well. She had overheard some culture-vulture sighings in the staff room at lunchtime, but for her own part she didn't expect a small Suffolk town to mount productions of the lesser-known operas of Donizetti or stage a Hockney retrospective in the town hall. She expected it to offer attractions peculiar to it, such as clean air, accessible genuine countryside, buildings on a human scale, and an amiable atmosphere. These Dunmarket possessed; fortunately it did not possess too much distinction either. It had not been seized on by neo-Georgians and placed under glass like a civic museum: you could walk down the High Street without feeling that you were the only person in sight who did not own the complete works of E. F. Benson. The town had no famous son to burden it: as Martin had said, Gainsborough and Constable had chosen other Suffolk towns to be born in, and it had never been the stamping ground of Benjamin Britten and his Art-Deco hair. There were teashops but there were fast-food franchises too: there were little arid bay-windowed shops selling nothing but expensive greetings cards and scented pincushions, but serving behind their mahogany repro counters was not the only chance of employment the place offered, for books were made here. Paper-milling, printing and binding — just about everything that went into the physical production of a book happened in the unassuming industrial buildings scattered around the outskirts of Dunmarket. There were newer factory units too, their flat roofs and service bays looking straight out on to green Suffolk meadows. Deploring these seemed to Carol quite beside the point. Life went on here, instead of stopping and facing the other way.

She parked her car close to the top

of Mill Hill. The mill was still here, a Victorian pile converted into the most chichi of the town's hotels: the others were the standard provincial Trust House Pickwickian. The hill, though gentle, was real enough too, as was Market Hill opposite, the two holding the old streets of the town centre between them like a cat's cradle. The impression that the whole of Suffolk was as flat as a football field had been corrected by Carol's first visits to the county with Emma, the friend from college who was a native (but now teaching in London — they had moved in opposite directions), yet she still experienced moments of surprise like this, walking down Mill Hill and feeling her calf muscles twanging a little at the steepness of the gradient, with the town spread out below her.

And it was at moments like this too that Carol became aware of something in her feeling for the town that made absolutely no sense and yet was perhaps the strongest element in her attraction to it. The feeling could only be called nostalgia, even though she had never lived in such a place before now. It was a feeling of which she had first had an inkling on long train journeys home from college in Lincoln. She vividly remembered the train halting at places like this, presenting her from her railway embankment vantage with slices of townscape that fascinated her beyond their intrinsic interest: the back gardens of plain bright brick houses, children cycling, a van unloading at the rear of a shopping parade, amateur footballers gamely trudging about a bumpy playing field, birch trees between red rooftops, all revealed in a seemingly unlikely L. S. Lowry perspective. And absurd as it was, as she looked something called to her like a voice from long ago. It was as if a place like this constituted part of her birthright and she were now, at last, claiming it.

Carol waited to cross the street in front of the old Corn Exchange, a florid Victorian building that now housed a very acceptable library. Macleish and the library authorities permitting, she wanted to bring her class here at some time in the term. Knowing your way around books, rather than just knowing how to read them, was a skill that she believed wasn't given its full value. That old school-project bromide, *now find out about such-and-such*, was meaningless if you didn't know where to look. If you were an ignoramus about flowers, as Carol was, no one would expect you to be able to go out in the garden and pick out a periwinkle; but many otherwise sympathetic teachers thought nothing of pointing children at a stack of books and telling them to find out about the Vikings.

Thinking of her class, Carol suffered a flush of anxiety. Tiredness aside, had she really performed satisfactorily today? The afternoon session had been more ragged: the children had worked well on the number cards but they were unruly when it came to her reading aloud to them and she had always understood that reading aloud was the one part of the day when you could guarantee that the kids would shut up and be good . . . Perhaps what she had dared to think was a reasonable effort for an NQT on her first day was really a ground-breaking shambles and a scandalized whisper was going round the other staff and her class were running home to tell their parents that this lady took charge of them who wasn't like a teacher at all . . .

Suddenly one of those very children was in front of her eyes, four feet away, and waving at her.

Ben Yeomans: in the back seat of a passing car, waving and smiling for all he was worth. Just in time Carol collected herself and waved back as the car rounded the next turning and moved out of sight. It was unmistakably Ben, with his parents presumably, though she only glimpsed the backs of two heads in the front seats of the car.

Well, he would hardly have waved like that if she had made a complete ass of herself as a teacher. Which of course she hadn't: the self-doubt came from fatigue, that was all. It gave her a nice feeling, seeing him like that. Miss Halstead, that's our teacher. Nice.

It gave her another feeling too: something like a recurrence of that mental pause she had experienced in the classroom with him this morning. Freer now to analyse it, Carol could only call it familiarity. As far as she knew she hadn't seen Ben before today, but it was possible that she had without knowing it. Her flat was in a single-person block but it adjoined a small estate full of young families and overlooked an adventure playground. That was probably it — he must look familiar because she had simply seen him around a lot since moving here. She would have to look up his home address in the class file some time.

Still it niggled at her; longer, she thought as she entered the supermarket, than it should. The self-scrutiny in which she had been coached came sternly into play. Worrying needlessly over a small detail? Yes. Anything to be done about it now? Not really. Then drop it. Let serendipity rule. The process took a couple of seconds of mental effort, like flexing a muscle, and then she concentrated on her shopping. This, like cooking and indeed eating, was a matter about which she was briskly impatient: anything that could be boiled or grilled in about five minutes, or preferably eaten straight from the packet, went into her basket. Her idea of hell was the dinner party — not the people but the palaver.

Turning a corner, she clashed baskets with Chris Bryce.

"They keep saying fresh," he announced, too laid back for greetings. He pointed to a display of eggs. "But none of it's fresh really. It's all old. And this crazy thing." He indicated a price tag. "I mean, wouldn't it make more sense to offer the vendor what you think the goods are worth? But no, we've got it all arse-forwards. So, everything go OK today, yeah?"

She had made only a brief appearance in the staff room after school, feeling somehow unequal to congratulations or enquiries. "Well, I think so," she said. "Hope so anyway. I'm looking forward to going back again tomorrow, rather than wanting to jump in the river, so I suppose that's something."

The conversational convention that required you to answer a weak joke and a nervous laugh with a sympathetic nervous laugh of your own was obviously not acknowledged by Chris Bryce. He only nodded, intently blinking, and said, "It's one of the very few jobs worth doing. I actually do honestly believe that. You know, there's . . . " He waved his arm, clicking his fingers, oblivious of the affronted shoppers trying to get past him. "There's a lot of bullshit, do you see what I'm saying? Teaching's supposed to be this and it's supposed to be that. A whole lot of bullshit, but it can't destroy the, you know, the . . . " He resorted to an expressive gesture, which looked like a mime of someone pulling open a packet of crisps. "It can't destroy it. Never. You feel the same?"

"Oh, yes," she said agreeably, not having the faintest idea what he was talking about, "that's just what I think. I don't know if teaching's going to destroy me, though. I feel done in already, so God knows what I'll be like at the end of the week."

"What do you sleep on?"

" . . . A bed."

"Sprung mattress?"

"Yes."

Chris Bryce shook his heavy head. "You're going to cripple yourself. You should try something like, hey I don't mean futons or that trendy rubbish, but

64

it's got to be something really flat and hard. Like a palliasse. Even just a mat on the floor."

Carol nodded, registering a moment of charmed surprise: she had never in her life heard anyone actually use the word palliasse.

"Trish and I have always slept on mats. Alcohol is actually a depressant," he added, fingering the bottle of wine in her basket. "You know, in the West we treat our pets better than our own bodies. Hey, speaking of which, you met Martin, yeah? Had quite a run-in with old Macleish today, apparently."

"Why?"

"Oh, attitude, timekeeping, you know the stuff. I like the guy, you know. I'm not into judging, I mean he's doing himself no good with the booze and everything but that's his business, and I think the divorce hit him hard and a lot of it's down to that, you know?"

"Oh, when was that?"

"Last year, I think. She moved away with the kid. He wasn't left with a lot. Lives in this little flat which is kind of, you know, not good. Trish and I have tried, you know, having him round, extending the hand, whatever. I mean he is basically a good guy, it's just . . . he . . . it's . . . " Chris fell back on another mime, this one suggestive of squeezing the juice out of two lemons.

"The kids seem to like him," Carol said, recalling the sight of Martin in the playground on lunch duty, hung about with children like a bulky Pied Piper.

"Kids have understanding. Wisdom even. Have you read Kohlberg on moral reasoning?"

She shook her head.

"You should."

She hated it when people said that. Your immediate impulse was to vow never to look at the book even if offered a million pounds to do so.

"Martin's not in danger of losing his job, is he?"

"Macleish would do it if he could, but he needs a lot more than he's got. Listen, you must come and have a meal with us some time. If you're seeing anybody, with anybody, you know, bring him or her."

"Thanks, that's kind of you, I'd like that."

"I'll talk to Trish and we'll see what we can fix up," Chris said. "What do you eat?"

"Oh, whatever's put in front of me." Which would be what? she wondered. She imagined the Bryces as vegetarian, but on second thoughts it was possible they were the sterner sort of eco-freaks who slaughtered their own pigs.

Chris gave up on some vague patting motions suggestive of searching for a pocket diary. "Listen, I'd better make a move. Got Trish's parents coming over tonight. God. I mean they're basically good people, you know, and Trish really loves them even though she feels like murdering them sometimes. It's just . . . What's that poem that goes, 'They fuck you up, your mum and dad'?"

"Larkin. I'd better get going too."

"Catch you later," he said, but she was already hurrying towards the checkout.

It was just because she was tired, she thought as she paid for her purchases and hastily scrabbled them into bags. And too damned hot in here: the cashiers must be stifling in those overalls and tabards. She wanted air.

Tired, that was all, she thought, as she got outside at last and filled her lungs. The nerve that had been touched was not usually so sensitive: in fact she had trained herself to deal with such difficult moments so well that most of the time it was possible to forget the nerve existed at all, like an operation scar that had faded almost to invisibility. But just as a scar might become livid when you were overheated or ill, so fatigue occasionally did this to her — brought the old pain shooting to the surface, beyond her power to control.

Well, she had controlled it now, and she doubted if Chris Bryce had noticed anything beyond a sudden shortness, if even that. The days when such references could emotionally immobilize her were long gone, thankfully, and she was quite calm again by the time she had loaded her bags into her car and started for home. She was even able to think over Chris's invitation with a mixture of apprehension and amusement, and to wonder what Trish was like. They had two teenage children, she knew: did they have to sleep on palliasses as well?

Somehow she couldn't imagine teenagers taking to that. She also caught herself in a little pedantic and, she supposed, schoolmistressy deprecation of Chris's use of that phrase 'Catch you later.' This 'later' business was everywhere now. People said 'See you later' when they weren't going to see you again till next week; and yes, of course, that was 'later' in time but properly speaking "later" meant later in the day. With teenagers the phrase had become 'Slater', and a universal substitution for 'Goodbye'. But then 'Goodbye' was itself a contraction of 'God be with you', so probably this was only the natural process of a living language and in a couple of hundred years 'Slater' would appear unreproved in dictionaries. Still, she didn't like the sloppiness of it.

Dear God, she thought, one day's teaching and already I've turned into Miss Jean Brodie. She glimpsed herself in the driving mirror slightly smiling. Well, that was better. Definitely tired, though: hell, look at those eyes.

She thought too about Martin Culler, and what Chris had told her. She hadn't seen him in the staff room at the end of school, and had felt a faint indefinable disappointment; there was no doubt that as a person he interested her. What she hoped was that he wasn't a person who set out to be Interesting, with a parade of self-destruction as part of the performance. There had been an element of that in Paul, the man with whom she had had her one serious relationship. For serious, read intense. Carol was the first to admit that she was not a person to do things by halves, and at college in Lincoln, where the two of them had met, their unbroken two-year relationship had attained a certain mild fame, or notoriety, among their contemporaries, who generally took such things more lightly (and they were probably right, she thought now). When it had ended, Paul's increasing tendency to regard life as a stage and himself as the tragic hero striding across it to a fascinating doom had had much to do with the break-up. It was from this that she had formed a suspicion of men going conspicuously downhill, mainly because it involved doing things they liked doing, only more so. You could claim you were dying inside while you lived it up. Being Byronic was all right if you were Byron, but she thought that lesser mortals shouldn't try it. The trouble was that some women had a corresponding fantasy, and wanted to play the redeemer to his Flying Dutchman. She had done it herself with Paul, until she got tired — not body-tired but heart-tired, a complaint with only one remedy.

Not that Martin Culler was any of her business. But she liked him, and didn't like the idea of Macleish hovering over him and waiting for his moment to swoop. A teacher who got the chuck really was finished. Even a suggestion from the head and governors that a move to another school might provide refreshing benefits to both parties was likely to break your career in two.

Probationer's smugness, she admonished herself. She had been warned against it at college: don't go marching into your first staff room spouting educational theory and thinking you know it all. And whatever you do, leave your teacher persona behind when you go home at

71

the end of the day, else you'll find yourself with no friends and a permanent headache. Well, Carol thought, that was one prescription she was happy to follow. All she wanted just now was to get home and feed her face whilst staring at the least demanding TV she could find.

Home was in the Meadows, the old suburb of Dunmarket, a tidy cluster of tree-lined streets on the other side of the river. Here a council estate and an 'executive development' coexisted in unusual harmony; but then the council estate had been built way back in the days of duffle coats and optimism, before public housing was seen as a punishment for indolence, and actually looked rather more solidly made than its executive neighbour. Carol, as a key worker coming to the area, had landed a one-bedroomed flat belonging to a housing association in an L-shaped block designed, fancifully but not unpleasantly, in a sort of Mediterranean style with cream cladding and red tiles and arched access doors. She had been prepared, seeing this whimsical exterior, to find a shambles inside — doors opening the wrong way, kitchen three foot square — but in fact the flat was a gem, practical and attractive. Its only drawback was being on the second floor. Stairs, stairs. She expected her legs to be muscled like a footballer's by the end of term and today it was all she could do to ram her key in the lock and crash in before they gave way.

Someone else had made the knee-racking ascent today while she was out: two letters had arrived with the second post. She scooped them up and sank into the first chair that offered itself.

She recognized Aunt Jean's handwriting on the first. Opening it, she found a Good Luck card. *Not that you'll need it*, Jean had written inside. *You'll be great.* Carol smiled. It was the latest in a line of such cards and letters: graduation, passing her driving test, job interview, landing her job. When she was living at home with Jean they would appear on her bedside table; when she moved away they arrived unerringly on the appropriate day, Aunt Jean being one of those people who seem to have a supernatural judgement of the vagaries of the post. Some might dismiss it as a mere social skill — in fact it was Aunt Jean's kindness taking typically practical form.

The address on the other envelope was anonymously typewritten, but as soon as she opened it and saw the letterhead Carol knew what this was about. Yes: here it was.

She glanced through it, then folded the letter up and placed it carefully in a drawer. She stood Aunt Jean's card on her desk, then went through to the kitchen to unpack her shopping and make something to eat.

There ought to be a lot to think about, a lot to feel, in response to the news in the letter; but there was only a blankness inside her. Perhaps that was not so surprising. The sale of the house really made no difference. She had had nothing to do with it since that time, had never even been near it; all it meant was that the severance was formally complete. But then it had felt complete for a long time.

Or had it? This numbness in itself must mean some sort of reaction to the news, some change in her. She supposed that a part of her mind must always have been aware of her name on the deeds of that house, though she had kept it at a good distance from her everyday consciousness. Now the name would be removed, and the last link to that past broken.

An event.

Yet that past didn't exist for her any more — of necessity. Because to be able to live at all she had had to relinquish it. And now to be told in legalistic terms that it was finally gone was a strange experience, with no sense of relief or release about it. If anything it brought things back rather than burying them. It was a little like hearing of the death of someone you hadn't seen for years: instantly they became more real to you than they had been during those years when you neglected to think about them.

Some property developer had finally put in an offer for the house. Her solicitor said it was a good offer and urged her to accept. All that was needed was her consent. A short letter would suffice. She could write it after she had eaten. It would take a matter of moments. There was no reason why she should hesitate.

No reason except for the fact that any sort of finality had something awful about it. And the fact that whilst the house couldn't be sold, while it was let as bedsits to transient tenants, while it lacked an identity as a house, then at least it wasn't *normal*: it retained something of the characteristics of a monument.

And now it would be sold, made over, shorn of its associations, and would become a house like any other. What had happened there was old news now and if the purchasers knew of it they evidently weren't bothered by it. Normal.

Maybe it was right that it should be so, in fact she was sure it was. But something would be obliterated all the same, like the lettering on an old gravestone finally fading out of recognition.

Her kitchen window was the one overlooking the playing field, and while she waited for the burgers to cook Carol gazed at the small figures milling about down there. Boys absorbed in one of those incomprehensible football games with only three players and one goal.

Girls spinning round and round to make themselves dizzy, toppling over and squealing with laughter. (No Ben Yeomans there, incidentally. Still, she was sure she knew him from somewhere.) She had the window open in the warm September dusk, and the voices of the children reached her, faint and sweet.

A reassuring sound. Carol remembered a time when such sounds had not had that effect on her. They had seemed wrong. All such evidences of the world proceeding normally had seemed wrong, wrong with the ghastly skewed inappropriateness of a dream. A seagull perched on the apex of a roof opposite, its breast brilliant white in the late sun. That would have seemed wrong too, once, the flash of beauty a grotesque obscenity. Back then it had seemed to her wounded young mind that the continued existence of good things after what had happened was the ultimate cruelty. Hurt beyond her own comprehension, she had wanted the world to empty itself and stop.

Time, Dr Kaufman and his colleagues, and perhaps her own strength of will had brought her out of that long ago. If anything Carol possessed an exceptionally sharp appetite for life, eagerly pursuing what she wanted, sometimes with an impatient disregard for the limits of her capacities: last weekend just before the shops closed she had spotted a tin of paint of the exact shade she wanted for her living room, and had worked at it all night, squinting at the results in the artificial light and finishing hollow-eyed and thirsty at three in the morning. Relish, not rejection, was her approach to the world now.

And yet, she thought, wasn't her hesitation over this matter of the house a manifestation of that old childish denial? If she could accept that the laughter of children in the sun and the beauty of living creatures did not constitute a blasphemous insult to the dead, then she should follow that acceptance through to its conclusion. The house *wasn't* a monument. Let the house go. Let it rejoin the turning world.

She ate without tasting and watched TV without understanding. When the phone rang she knew whose voice she wanted to hear more than anything in the world and when the voice spoke from the receiver she felt both delighted and unsurprised. That was the way it was with Aunt Jean: she seemed to have some seventh sense that mingled empathy and telepathy.

"So, how was your day? Feel free to say, 'Don't ask,' if it was like that."

"No, no, not that bad. I enjoyed it, I actually did enjoy it. I just feel so tired, like I've run a marathon or something. Thanks so much for your card, by the way. How's things with you?"

"Pretty much as usual. Got this new secretary at work who's very, very nice but frightened of the telephone. Someone rang me when I was at lunch and that's all I know. Did he leave a number? Well — no — didn't ask him. A name? No — didn't ask him. Going to ring back?
Don't know . . . but he *rang* anyway. What can you do? Anyhow, away with that, come on, I want all the details. What was it like? I think you've got a heart like a lion, standing up in front of however many kids it is."

"Thirty. Well, they're as new to

the school as me, so I've got an advantage . . . " Carol gave an account of her day, finding herself brightening as she did so, her tiredness falling away. There was nothing like this: being able to talk freely in the knowledge of complete understanding and sympathy. She realized now that she had been a little lonely since moving to Dunmarket, and that the hectic activity had been both compensation and disguise.

"So I *think* I did all right. I just can't believe that was only one day. Looking back it seems to stretch back to the beginning of time. I suppose eventually it'll just settle into routine."

"I don't think a job like that would ever just become routine. And knowing you I'm sure it won't. I wish I could have gone to school in this day and age, if you see what I mean. It really was dismal in my time, or so I remember it. Having to sit up straight while some old battleaxe chalked up endless sums. I remember one weird woman who would get carried away talking about the Battle of Hastings or something and start stroking her own boobs, right in front of the class."

"Oh my God, I hope I don't end up doing that!" Carol laughed.

"Looks like they're trying to bring those days back, anyway."

"They're trying. It still partly depends on the individual teacher's co-operation, but you do have to spend a certain amount of time on these core subjects whether you like it or not. There's this awful phrase 'the delivered curriculum', which basically means hurling a set number of facts at the kids and then sitting back thinking you've done your job. But don't get me started on that. How's Brendan?"

"Lopping and felling. We made the big decision, by the way. You know I told you we were thinking about living together? Well, we took the leap. Three days now and we're not at each other's throats yet, so it can't be bad. Well, more of a little step than a leap — I mean he's moved in here with me but he hasn't given his flat up yet. I wasn't too sure how it would be, living with someone again after all this time. I don't know whether I'm right for it. Except with you, of course, that's different. But it seems to be going OK, anyway. Brendan doesn't whistle and doesn't leave hairs in the bath, which counts for a lot. Oh dear, sound very unromantic, don't I?"

"No, no, that's great, Jean. I'm really happy for you." In fact Carol had felt a slight jolt at the news, even though she had been expecting it. She examined her own reaction with interest. Jean had acted *in loco parentis* but had been Carol's best friend too. Jean was unconventional, independent, young for her age (which was an ageist concept anyhow) and had her head firmly screwed on. Carol was a grown woman with her own home and had strong convictions about the rights of everyone to live as they pleased without having to conform to any sort of role. So all in all, the idea of her aunt's having a live-in boyfriend shouldn't have fazed her in the slightest.

And yet, unmistakably, a worm of suspicion and jealousy had moved in her, just for a moment. *Hey, Aunt Jean, don't go thinking you can have a life of your own. You have to consult me first. You belong to me, you know.*

Despicable, even if it was interesting.

"Whenever you get a free weekend, please come down," Jean was saying. "It seems ages since I saw you. You know you're welcome, don't you? A moment's notice, or no notice at all."

"Oh, thanks, it'd be lovely to see you again." Carol felt like a rat.

"I'd like you to meet Brendan, and he's longing to meet you."

Perhaps that was it: she hadn't met Brendan yet. All she knew was that he was in his thirties and worked as a tree surgeon, which for no reason at all had a faintly ludicrous sound.

"I'll be down as soon as I get the chance, and bore you both to tears about the problems of a primary school probationer. Won't be this weekend, because Dr Kaufman's coming up, did I tell you?"

"No, how's he doing?"

"Well, it's got worse. He's . . . well, how you'd expect him to be. Tough."

"Is he going to make the journey on his own?"

"Determined to. Apparently he still travels by train regularly. He says it means relying on the goodwill of strangers, but so does living in the world at all, so it doesn't bother him."

"That sounds like him. Well, I hope you have a nice time. What is it like up there? How are you taking to Suffolk? Or how's Suffolk taking to you, more importantly?"

"Well, no one's given me the evil eye, at least I don't think so. No, honestly, it's a very nice place, I'm sure you'd like it."

"Mm, maybe." Raised with grim gentility in a leafy Surrey no-man's-land, Jean had embraced the city at the first opportunity and retained a strong scepticism about the country and all its works. And then, displaying that seventh sense again, she said, "Listen, did you hear any more from the solicitors? I remember you saying something about there being a possible buyer for the house."

"Yes." Carol couldn't prevent a quick intake of breath. "Yes, actually I had a letter from them today. The buyer's made an offer and . . . well, looks like it's going to be sold, if I agree to it."

"Right. Oh well, that's promising."

The alteration in Aunt Jean's voice would have been imperceptible to anyone less close to her than Carol. An undertone of TV had been audible at Jean's end, but now it diminished as if a remote control had been pressed. "So, how do you feel about it?"

"Ah — not quite the way I'd expected to feel," Carol said after a fractional hesitation.

"Mm-hm?" Jean didn't hurry her. Carol pictured her aunt's face, the strong-cheekboned paleness and elegance that reflected composure but never complacence, the large grey worldly eyes that spoke of things seen and felt and stored away, the generous mouth full of tolerant humour. Friends of Carol's teenage years, coming back with her to the flamboyant house in Kennington, had been wonderfully struck by Aunt Jean and more than one had been convinced that she must have been on intimate terms with rock stars in her youth. Jean had shouted with laughter when Carol told her. Uncle Keith had once appeared playing the piano in the background of a TV commercial and Jean could lay claim to having had as an overnight guest the bass player of an obscure seventies group named Witch Hazel, but that was as far as it went. There was no denying, however, that she had that look. Carol sometimes felt that her mother, Jean's sister, had had it too; but she wasn't sure how far she could trust her memories of her mother. Occasionally she would look at an old photograph of her parents and see only strangers.

"Well — I suppose I should feel relieved and free and all the rest of it. And I do in a way. But it feels like — like giving into something as well, if that makes any sense."

"You know you don't have to sell, Carol. It's your choice."

"That's just it. I've got to make this choice and — and I wish somehow it was out of my hands. I know it's just a matter of signing my name, no big deal, but it . . . it's not easy."

"I know. I know, love. I suppose it might have been easier if it had been sold straight away, back then, but — "

"But no one would live in it." Carol said it for her.

"No." Jean's voice was quiet, thoughtful. "And what with the solicitor being your father's friend and offering to handle all the letting arrangements and everything it seemed — well, the best way. It was being taken care of and we could both forget about it until you came of age."

"Oh, it was the best way. I'm sure of that. But maybe that's it — what you said about forgetting about it. Because I could put it out of my mind without ever really feeling that it was forgotten. It wasn't like washing my hands of it. But now once it's sold I won't ever have anything to do with it again, and that . . . that really means forgetting."

Jean was silent a moment, and then took from Carol's shoulders the burden of which she had only just become aware.

"It doesn't mean forgetting them, Carol," she said.

Relief that the subject had been broached seemed to burst inside Carol like a held-in sob. It made her a little childlike in her desperation as she said, "Doesn't it?"

"No, it doesn't. Oh, I understand that

it feels that way. God, I couldn't honestly promise you that it won't go on feeling that way for a while. It was their house and the house where you lived with them. Now it's an estate agent's des res. It would be more worrying if you *didn't* feel anything."

"I suppose that's true . . . Well, it *is* true. You're right. I'll write back to the solicitors straight away."

"Whoa, don't do anything because of what I've said. I never give advice — that way you don't get blamed afterwards."

"That's great coming from the manager of a Citizens' Advice Bureau," Carol said, managing a laugh.

"Oh, I don't advise any more, not from my great eminence. Like Walt Disney not being able to draw Mickey Mouse. Seriously, you've got to be sure. I know this has been in the wind since you formally inherited, but there's no rush if you're not sure. I mean, is it something about having to take the money . . . ?"

"Oh, I'm not bothered about that." This was entirely true: she had already decided that if the house were sold she would split the proceeds down the middle with her aunt whether Jean liked it or not. Her own share, she supposed, would go in the bank: she couldn't have been less interested.

"You're allowed to have new beginnings, Carol. You wouldn't have worked so hard to be a teacher if that wasn't so. Think of this as another."

"They would have wanted it — wouldn't they?"

"I haven't got any doubt about that at all."

Carol agreed, whilst a part of her experienced a moment of niggling doubt. It was so easy to hypothesize about what the dead would have wanted. People could comfort themselves with it, knowing there was no possibility of the truth ever being put to the test. *Great-uncle Walter would have wanted you to have that*. Maybe. But surely what Great-uncle Walter would really have wanted was not to die at all.

And the shades of her own parents would surely want one thing above all — and that thing had never transpired. Carol, Jean, Dr Kaufman, the police, and everyone involved had long ago acknowledged that it never would now. But maybe the sale of the house represented a further acknowledgement of that fact, and so it stung.

They weren't saying that nothing had ever happened in that house, but they were saying that nothing could be done about what had happened. There, Carol realized, was where the feeling of wrongness and betrayal came in.

As so often, talking to Aunt Jean had helped her see her own conclusions more clearly.

"Has this been on your mind all day? Your first day teaching?"

"No, no. The letter was here when I got home."

"Well, that's something. Because there's one thing I can swear to about what your mother and father would have wanted." Somehow she must have sensed Carol's doubts on this point. "Of course we can't ever know, but I would swear that they wouldn't want *anything* to stand in the way of that. Your teaching — everything you've set your heart on. They'd say that comes first. Every time. You know that, don't you?"

"Yes. I think I do. Damn, isn't it always the most annoying, clichéd old chestnuts that are the most true? Like 'Life goes on.' You can hate it all you like but — it's still true."

"Life goes on. That's it."

Life goes on: it had been the hardest lesson and the one that Aunt Jean above all had laboured to teach Carol as she grew out of her shattered childhood. A true labour of love that had involved convincing someone whose mind had been blasted with powerful evidence to the contrary that the world was a good place and worth living in. It hadn't been a simple matter of loving Carol and doing nice things for her. It had meant demonstrating something to her that Carol had later found, in Camus, a perfect phrase for: *happiness, too, is inevitable*.

And here was Jean still having to do it and still not shirking the task. Carol apologized. "It's making a mountain out of a molehill, I know. God, I'm sorry. I've been bending your ear. Give me a couple of months up here and I shall be different. I shall be all Suffolky and reserved. 'Ah, I'm a-doing,' I shall say and that'll be it."

"I'll believe *that* when I see it. And don't be sorry. Listen, ring me any time and I mean any time, do you see what I'm saying? Nothing's changed. Don't think that."

"No, of course not." Carol remembered her jealous tingle and felt ashamed of it. "I'm going to write to the solicitors now."

"You're sure?"

"I'm sure. Thanks, Jean. You're a . . . you're the best."

"D'you know, I always had a feeling I was, I was waiting for someone else to spot it . . . You take care now."

Carol did exactly what she had said. As soon as she put down the phone she sat at her desk and wrote to the solicitors in Clapham, instructing them to accept the offer for the house.

And though she had no religious faith to speak of, when she had sealed and stamped the letter she found her mind murmuring something like a prayer. Not for departed souls, but to them.

I'm sorry. But you know I could never

live there. And it can't stay the same for ever. So it has to be let go. It doesn't mean anything's changed, not inside me.

She could only hope they would understand.

4

CAROL woke to find herself being pinned down to the bed.

She couldn't move her arms or legs: literally, couldn't move them. And she couldn't turn her head either — though her eyes were shifting in their sockets as she gazed round the room, and that one piece of movement had as strongly physical a feel as if she were straining every muscle in her body.

Wait, though. This wasn't waking at all. It was a dream, and this illusion of being unable to move your limbs was common in dreams — a classic feature, in fact. In a moment she would wake with a start and with that sensation of breaking upwards through some viscid veil like the surface of a pond.

In a moment . . . if she just tried.

Come on . . .

Carol suffered several moments of terror as she realized that she wasn't dreaming. She was awake all right: the blinking of her eyelids confirmed it. They felt like grainy shutters coming down over the orbits of her eyes. And the sight of the room confirmed it. This wasn't a dreamscape full of Dali distortions. It was her own bedroom, lit by a pre-dawn glimmer and by the slice of sharper light from the hall: she always slept with the bedroom door ajar and the hall light on. Every realistic detail was in place — the clothes slung over the back of the wicker chair, the copper mobile hanging from the ceiling, the fringed rug she had put down to brighten the dullness of the carpet tiles, even the half-drunk glass of milk by the bed with a furrowed skin beginning to form on its surface in the warmth. It was all real and it was all hers and it was all perfectly normal and everyday.

And she didn't recognize any of it.

She lay unable to move, her eyes circling and circling the room, trying to cut through the smothering fear with a blade of logic. Of course she recognized this place, she could put a name to everything in it, none of it was strange in itself . . . And yet none of it made any sense, she was lost, a spot of helpless consciousness in an alien environment, unable to *connect* with anything her roaming eyes saw. Perhaps this was madness — perhaps this was what it actually felt like to go mad . . .

And then she moved. It didn't feel like the result of voluntary action on her part — more as if some capacity had been magically restored to her, a wave of a fairy wand — but still the movement cost her an enormous wrench that left her gasping, not dissimilar from the wrench that brought you out of a bad dream but ten times more powerful. For a few moments she writhed like a landed fish and then sat bolt upright, rubbing her face.

Suddenly, the room was her bedroom again and the very idea of its being unfamiliar seemed ridiculous. This was her own bedroom in her own small flat in a block called Stour Court in the town of Dunmarket and she had slept here every night for the past two months. As for moving, of course she could move: it was just a thing you did. Your brain said move and you moved.

Still, she was aware of a sort of

shift having taken place. It was a little reminiscent of those computer-generated optical illusions that were popular just now: you could stare at them for ages seeing nothing and convinced the whole thing was a hoax and then all at once the 3-D image was there, right in front of your eyes, and it was impossible *not* to see it.

Carol went into the bathroom and wiped her perspiring face with a flannel. She felt not just better but even a little smug because she knew now what this was, thank God. There were plenty of natural bodily phenomena that were alarming if you didn't know what they were. Look at those poor Victorian maidens who had never been told about menstruation, fainting at the sight of their first period. She remembered a friend at college being thrown into panic and convinced she was going blind by the symptoms of a migraine; she had never suffered one before and didn't know what was happening to her.

This thing had never happened to Carol before as far as she was aware, but she had heard about it. Dr Kaufman had once told her about it in passing and, in the coincidental way of such things, she had come across a newspaper article about it shortly afterwards. It was called sleep paralysis. She couldn't remember the precise physiological explanation behind it or even whether the scientists had one: she fancied it was something like a neurological lag, with the brain still being asleep while the senses were awake. But the symptoms were exactly as she had just experienced them and as a lot of other people had experienced them, apparently, often to their considerable alarm. It could happen to anyone and it was nothing to worry about.

In fact it was rather interesting once you were detached from it: not on a level with having an out-of-body experience or spotting a UFO but still quite a fascinating glimpse into mystery. The only thing that faintly troubled her was whether you would know it for what it was if it happened again — or whether you would have the same reaction of terrified bewilderment. After all, everyone had more than one nightmare in their lives, but each one that came along seemed like the real thing.

Was this a thing to worry about? she silently interrogated herself in the bathroom mirror. Was the possible return of sleep paralysis at some point in her life a thing to worry about?

Surely not. It was just that disturbances in her sleeping patterns — not of this curious kind, but insomnia, nightmares, sleepwalking — had been such a feature of her younger years that any sign in that direction was to be viewed with suspicion.

But not dread, she told herself, because the nightmares and sleepwalking had stopped years ago, and such bouts of insomnia as she had suffered as an adult had been at least partly self-inflicted — she was physically incapable, for instance, of going to bed leaving an interesting book unfinished. It was more of an unpleasant reminder than a threat. Like someone whose teenage years had been plagued with an acne finding a spot on their grown-up nose.

And speaking of reminders, it was worth reminding herself that it was past four in the morning and she had a class to teach in a few hours' time and if she was going to be fit to do so she had better fill those few hours with as much rest as possible.

She gave her reflection a last displeased look. White as the tiles, and downright haggard. Perhaps there had been some sort of bad dream after all, and that was what had started the whole thing off. But she couldn't remember any dreams.

She lay down, trying to relocate the comfortable shape that her body had made in the bedclothes, and searching her mind for dream-fragments. As she relaxed and inclined towards sleep the search became pleasantly unnecessary: her mind did its own drowsy housekeeping, shaking out and rearranging bits and pieces: Aunt Jean's voice on the phone, her classroom, Chris Bryce stroking his beard, Myrtle the Elephant, Ben Yeomans waving from the back of a car, Martin, the letter . . .

She started up. That noise.

There *was* a dream, now or earlier, the old dream, its horror was on her — the bird, the bird at the window tapping and fluttering and trying to get in . . .

God not that dream not after all this

100

time anything but that . . .

A breeze touched her face. She looked over at the window, where the curtains were stirring.

She sighed.

She had left the window open on the first latch, but it had come loose and was swinging to and fro, occasionally shutting against the casement with a tap before swinging out again.

She got up and closed the window, and as she did so the arm of the latch came off in her hand. The screw fastening it to the windowsill had worn away. Hence the looseness. She would have to get it fixed. Her rent included a service charge, though another tenant in the block had warned her that their landlords played a long game when it came to repairs.

Carol darted back to the bed. No nightmare. No bird. The tapping sound had been very like the one that used to bring her screaming out of sleep night after night — but that was all. There were no inexplicably terrifying feathery images imprinted on her mind's eye: it was in fact difficult to recall the visual details of that old phantasm. Thank God, she thought, for adulthood, its rationality, its deadened imagination.

Because one thing was for sure: she couldn't remember the details of that old dream, couldn't even understand precisely why it used to terrify her to such an extent — but she knew that she didn't want it to come back, ever.

★ ★ ★

She has never been in a hospital before. Not to stay. She went once to visit Grandma, when Grandma was having one of her operations. She didn't like it very much, the funny smell, the corridors, the wheelchairs, the nurses in their uniforms: it was all a bit frightening, and Grandma was a bit frightening too, sitting up in bed with her hair all over the pillow and red lipstick on. She hoped then she would never have to stay in a hospital herself, but it didn't seem likely to happen. Her daddy was a doctor, and he would always take care of her if she was poorly.

Now she knows that her daddy won't be able to take care of her any more.

And here she is in hospital. So the two things must be connected somehow. She can't work it out any further than that. Her head is funny, not right, and she keeps wanting to go to sleep even when she's not tired — can't be tired, because she hasn't really done anything except lie in bed.

This is very strange to her because she has never been very good at going to sleep. She has never liked the feeling of having to stop the day and curl up and shut her eyes. It's so boring when you want to carry on and do other things. A late bedtime has always been her favourite treat. She would try anything to be allowed to stay up late.

"I shall come and make sure you're in bed," Mummy would say. "Five minutes." And sometimes — since they put the boards round the old fireplace in her bedroom — she wouldn't be able to resist playing a little game with Mummy. She would wriggle in behind the boards and hide there. There was just room for her, and she was completely invisible. But she could see Mummy when she came in, because there was a tiny crack in the

boards that made a peephole. She had widened it a bit with her fingernail.

Of course it was only the first time she did it that Mummy didn't really know where she was; and she didn't stay behind there long because it was mean. But afterwards Mummy would make a joke of it too. "Where on earth is she?" she would say, coming into the bedroom and scratching her head. "Have you seen her, Harry?" That was to the hamster. And Mummy would do her Harry voice, which she knew always made her giggle because it made Harry sound American. "No, ma'am. Ain't seen her all night." "Oh, well," Mummy would say, "in that case, I'll have a look and see if she's got any sweets I can pinch . . . " And that would bring her running out, laughing.

Then last week Mummy was in a bad mood one night and didn't bother with the joke. Mummy just said, "Come out of there. It's dangerous, you'll get stuck if you're not careful," and so she came out and didn't do it any more. She knew she wouldn't get stuck, and Mummy hadn't thought about it before; but she knew also that when grown-ups were in a bad mood, things changed. There was a radiator in the hall that didn't work and most of the time Daddy didn't take any notice of it. But when he was in a bad mood — which wasn't often — he would hammer at it and then swear and say that nothing in this damned house worked. Which wasn't true. Everything worked except that radiator.

She understands this, and understands that when grown-ups are in that mood it's best not to push them. So she didn't play the game of hiding behind the boards any more. The game was getting boring anyway.

When she did hide there again (last night? the night before? she's not sure) it wasn't a game.

And now all she wants to do is keep going to sleep. The bed isn't comfy like her bed at home and it's not even dark or quiet in this place. But she snuggles up in it all the same and closes her eyes and sleep just comes. Perhaps it's the medicine they gave her.

Or perhaps it's dying. She feels as if she's going far away when she sleeps and when she wakes up she wants to go back there, and perhaps that's dying. She doesn't really mind if it is.

(Her bed at home. One of the boys weed on it. She saw him through the peephole. She remembers telling that to the police lady when they brought her here. She isn't sure, but she thought the police lady cried. She hasn't seen the police lady any more. After she said about seeing the boy weeing on her bed there was a policeman who kept asking her questions, but she wanted to go to sleep by then and he went away.)

Perhaps she's in a hospital because she's dying. She puts these two thoughts together for the first time as she lies on her side with her head buried in the pillow and one eye blinking at the nurse. The nurse is doing something with the bedclothes and smiling at her. The smile is nice but not quite real. It's like she's trying too hard. She thinks of asking the nurse something, she's not sure what: there's a question inside her that's something to do with what's going to happen to her and why she's here and something too about her Mummy and Daddy, but she can't make the question come right. In fact she doesn't think she's said anything at all since she told the police lady about the boy weeing on her bed and she's not sure she knows how. When she was a baby she couldn't talk: perhaps she's gone back to that somehow. She has a shameful memory of wetting the bed when they first put her here too, and she hasn't done that since she was a baby.

Chatterbox. That's what Daddy would call her sometimes. And sometimes, at the breakfast table or when they were on a train, he would look at his watch and bet her that she couldn't keep completely quiet for five minutes. She never could do it. He didn't really seem to mind her chattering, though. And now and then the things she said would make him laugh till there were tears in his eyes. Daddy had a great big laugh, though he wasn't very big. He was thin and he wasn't really tall like some of her friends' fathers. He was strong, though. Like a Scots terrier, Mummy would sometimes say, giving him a smile and a sort of secret look. (Daddy was from Scotland, but she still didn't quite understand.)

Daddy was strong: he fought those boys. She heard it. She saw it too, at the end, through the peephole. Her bedroom door was open where one of the boys had come in and got Harry, and she could see out on to the landing. That was where they got her daddy in the end. He was in his pyjamas and the pyjamas were all covered in blood but she saw him, he was on his feet and fighting them. But there were four of them and it wasn't fair. Four of them, she saw them and they had knives. One of the knives was still sticking out of Daddy, they left it sticking out of —

Fighting, fighting. She is fighting the nurse who is trying to hold her arms down with her hands, warm hands and a bit rough. It's bad to fight the nurse but she's bad anyway, really bad: she knows that. She heard the noises and the screaming and she hid. The boys did those things to Mummy and Daddy while she hid. She didn't help them, she didn't do anything, and that means she is really bad, bad enough for any punishment.

They're sticking a needle in her arm now. It hurts, but not much, not enough.

She bites the pillow and keeps hitting out, not seeing, and then all at once turns to sleep. Sleep is what she has now instead of Mummy and Daddy.

"Feeling a bit better, poppet?"

That's the nurse, bending over her and brushing her hair out of her eyes. She remembers the fighting, and feels ashamed, but the nurse is smiling and doesn't seem to mind.

"Feeling any better?"

She is, sort of. Just dozy and comfy and like her head's full of cotton wool. She sees faces. First the faces of a teddy bear and a rag doll, by the pillow. Nice faces but quite new to her. She has a bear and a doll very similar to these at home, but these are definitely not the ones.

And then faces of people sitting by the bed. Grandma and Grandad. Grandma has a black coat on and that red lipstick. She looks ill. She often looks ill, but not like this. Her face is so thin and white and the lipstick looks like blood. Grandad just looks old. His eyes are yellowy and he keeps squeezing Grandma's hand, or trying to. It has a black shiny glove on it and the fingers are clenched tight.

And there's Auntie Jean, with Uncle Keith standing behind her. They both give her a smile. Uncle Keith is wearing his funny green jacket and Auntie Jean those big bangles. There's a gap between Grandma's chair and hers. Grandma doesn't like Auntie Jean and Uncle Keith. She doesn't seem to like anyone very much, and Daddy sometimes swears about her. It upsets Mummy, who's Grandma's daughter, but it's as if he can't help it. "Bloody woman," he'll say about Grandma when she's not there, though he's never nasty to her.

Well, she is in hospital, and Grandma and Grandad and Auntie Jean and Uncle Keith have all come to see her. She must have been ill: or knocked down by a car. She can't remember anything, but then she's seen that on TV — people who've had an accident not being able to remember it afterwards. So that's easy enough. But where are Mummy and Daddy?

"She had to have a sedative," the nurse is saying, "so she's a bit dopey."

She hears that, and the word 'dopey' makes her think of the Seven Dwarfs and she wants to laugh. And then she sees a tear running down Grandpa's cheek and suddenly Grandma is crying too.

What . . . ?

"Hello, sweetheart." It's Auntie Jean speaking, while Grandma and Grandpa cry. Auntie Jean, leaning forward, shows her the teddy bear and the doll. "What do you think of these? They haven't got names yet. I thought you could think of some names for them. What about that? Could you think of some names?"

She nods, and looks around for her mummy and daddy. She feels funny. The cotton wool is still in her head but she has a feeling like something's going to happen, or she's going to fall off something.

Turning her head, she sees for the first time a man on the other side of the bed.

"Hello there," he says. "Remember me?"

She shakes her head, no. But she finds that she does remember him. He's the policeman. You can tell he's a policeman somehow even though he hasn't got a uniform and he's quite old. He's the *policeman who kept asking her questions about something.*

She feels funny. She's going to fall. She turns her head into the pillow and starts to cry. She feels Auntie Jean's hand stroking her hair.

"It's all right, sweetheart. It's all right."

"I want to go to sleep."

"You can, my love. In a minute." *That's the policeman.* "Can we just have a chat for a minute? We'll just have a chat for a minute and then you go back to sleep, all right? Look over here, my love. That's it. Do you remember you said something about those boys? Do you remember that? Oh, you do. I'm sure you do. I just want you to tell me about those boys. Anything you can think of. Anything at all."

No, no. She is acting like a baby, she knows, but she can't help it. Her hands go up as if she's going to start hitting out again. But something about Auntie Jean's cool hand slowly stroking her hair stops her, at least, from doing that.

"Did you see the boys?" *The policeman is leaning forward, frowning, breathing* heavily. "Did you see what the boys looked like?"

No, no.

"Try and remember, love. Anything at all."

Auntie Jean's hand keeps stroking and soothing. It makes her feel a bit better and it is somehow in gratitude for that, rather than as an answer to the policeman, that she speaks, her voice cracking as if she has a cold and sounding strange to her own ears.

"There was four," she says.

5

"WHO knows?" Dr Kaufman said. "It may level out or there may be improvement. Even my specialist doesn't pretend to know. Medicine is very respectful nowadays. Bends the knee before nature where it used to try and conquer it. I'm quite fond of the old days myself. The days of 'heroic treatments', as they used to call them. I was talking to a chemotherapy patient the last time I was at the hospital and it occurred to me that perhaps chemotherapy is the last of the heroic treatments. Maybe future ages will look on it as we look on massive purges and operations without anaesthetic. Though I'm not sure about future ages and how futuristic they'll be. There are things given serious attention now which to a man of the eighteenth-century Enlightenment would have seemed sheer superstition and barbarism. Crystals with magical properties. These 'ancient arts' that keep turning up out of nowhere. Nostradamus, who was a joke for centuries and now has more books written about him than Newton. Natural this and natural that. Of course one sympathizes. In the fifties we had public information films saying nukes are good for you, nowadays Chernobyl: so there's a backlash. A plague on your rational science and so on. It's the overlap that worries me. Birth control was fought for as a human right. It freed people. It stopped women becoming used-up rags by the time they were forty. Now we have these *nouveau* hippies who have kids by the dozen because it's natural and birth control equals mind control and all the rest of it. They're well meaning, sure, but they end up with one foot in the same camp as some very ill-meaning people, pro-lifers and so on."

"Now that's odd," Carol said, teasing, "I'd always thought New Age travellers would be right up your street."

"Pah! Even when I read *The Wind in the Willows* as a child I didn't like the idea of that caravan on the open road. I thought Toad Hall was much nicer.

Oh, I've nothing against them. It's their choice and they're entitled to it. As long as they realize that it depends on other people *not* making that choice, and that their whole philosophy depends on their being a minority. The man who drives the machine that lays the tarmac can't come and join them, nor the man in the Dagenham factory who makes their car engines, nor the farm worker who cuts the wheat that makes the bread that they buy on the way — or makes the flour, if they bake their own bread. The industrial society they despise has made their choice possible."

"Well, they might answer that they don't ask for these things. They happen to be there, and they use them, but they'd carry on without if not."

"Well, that's fine if they want to follow it to those lengths. But if no one's out in the fields growing crops, then ultimately they'll have to be prepared to hunt and gather, specifically hunt. Vegetarianism isn't an option with a gathered diet, there isn't enough wild protein." He laughed. "And now I'm painting myself into a corner with people *I* disagree with, like pro-hunters. That's you, that is."

"Me?"

"Playing devil's advocate. I remember you when you were no more than thirteen or fourteen attacking me on Freud. Don't we need to have a Freudian analysis of Freud's psyche before we can trust anything he says, or something like that. How do we know that 'ego' isn't a Freudian slip for 'egg'. I actually found myself defending Freud . . . This is pretty."

They had been walking along the river bank, and now Dr Kaufman stopped, turning his face towards the river. Sunlight was sparkling on the ripples, and dancing amongst the yellowing leaves of the trees on the other side. Tiny glints were reflected in the matt surface of his dark glasses.

"How much?" she said.

"Of this? Actually, quite a lot. The sunlight's giving me the shapes of the trees, and light on water always communicates, though of course your other senses fill in a lot and may convince you that you're seeing more than you are. Dusk is bad. It's like nothing."

Dr Kaufman spoke as usual with ready incisiveness. If anything the onset of partial blindness had sharpened the liveliness and decision in his manner. Words had always been vital to him, to be handled with love and respect. Now as the light faded on him it was as if words had become physical and tangible, the most concrete aspect of reality. There had been much talk over the weekend and now, half-jokingly, he began to apologize.

"I dare say you expected a visit from me to be wearing, but not this much. I cheerfully admit to having a big mouth and this little development — " he touched the glasses — "has made it bigger. Given me an excuse, too. I never know the time, hence I never know when to shut up and go to bed. That's why I'm putting off getting one of those damn watches you can read with your fingers."

"There's a seat here. Let's sit down."

She guided him to the timber bench. These were set out all along that portion of the river bank known as The Leas, which lay directly below the suburb of the town where she lived. It was a favourite recreational spot but today there weren't many people around: an old lady reading, a couple of children fishing. There was a great Sunday peace everywhere. Even the twittering of birds was drowsy and low-key.

Dr Kaufman didn't appear to have aged at all in the fifteen years she had known him, which made the signs of his illness all the more disorienting for her. He was a short spry stocky man, with boyish dimples when he smiled, and thick black hair that was untouched by grey, though she reckoned his age to be well over fifty. He had always worn thick spectacles, so the dark glasses with dark side-wings did not change his appearance very much; and he had always been a careless and even eccentric dresser, so the baseball cap he wore to give extra protection to his suffering eyes was as unremarkable to her as the rest of his outfit of green tennis shoes, white slacks and hound's-tooth-check jacket. To Carol he was simply Dr Kaufman, who was her long-time friend and had been at one point in her life — she quietly and firmly believed it — her saviour. She had readied herself for many emotions when she had first heard of his illness, but what she had not expected was to find him so unchanged. Would it be the same with the total blindness for which he had been told to prepare himself?

"It's been wonderful seeing you," she told him. "And I can take any amount of talk. It's chatter I can't stand." She wasn't being polite. Conversation with Dr Kaufman was an entertainment in itself, and they'd hardly stopped except for an hour or so last night when she'd taken him to a piano recital in Dunmarket town hall, partly to stymie any suggestion (which he mischievously made anyway) that she was living in a cultural desert. Afterwards they'd gone to a pub where he'd drunk vodka like water and still run verbal rings round her.

"So, how do you sleep nowadays?" he asked her.

"Pretty good. Well, like a log this past week, but I suppose that's plain exhaustion."

"That'll pass."

"That's what I keep telling myself: I'll get tougher. But on the other hand my class are getting more and more lively as they're losing their inhibitions and settling in, so that takes more out of you. The other day they were making such a racket that I — well, I know now that there's a truth behind that phrase 'to see red'. I literally did. And I *screamed* at them to shut up. I'd never heard my own voice that loud. They looked at me like I was a monster."

He laughed. "But did they shut up?"

"Oh, yes. Not a peep out of them. But I felt I'd let them and myself down a bit. I mean, I should have got them to shut up some other way."

"Oh, I don't know. Most of the time you do, don't you? It's only if you're permanently at the end of your tether that it's anything to worry about. There aren't any 'No Smoking' notices around here, are there?" he said, taking out his cigarettes. "It wouldn't surprise me. They have no-smoking beaches now. When smoking is finally stamped out altogether, who are self-righteous people going to hate instead, I wonder? Have to be something visible. Like skin colour, maybe. First-year juniors they'd be eight-year-olds, yes?"

"Yes. A few are turned eight already, some won't be eight till next summer, end of the school year. It makes a fair difference at that age, which isn't always taken into account."

"How do you feel? Thirty eight-year-olds looking at you. You were eight when it happened."

She could cope with this sort of directness from Dr Kaufman: the subject belonged at least partly to him.

"Well. They don't seem like I was when I was eight. I mean, quite regardless of the — of those circumstances. They seem younger. But it's difficult to tell. When you're eight you don't really think of yourself as young and small. You're bigger than a seven-year-old. You're older and bigger than you've ever been."

"Top of the tree. True stuff. You were advanced for your age, though, when I first met you. Regardless of those circumstances."

"You could tell?"

"Oh, sure. The Carol who existed

before that event still existed after it. The intelligence was the same though the responses were inevitably conditioned by what had happened, and would be for a long time."

"Still?" she said.

He cocked his head: he was already learning to interpret tone without facial expression. "Does it feel like it?"

"Oh, no. Not really. I just wonder sometimes. Is the person I am determined by what happened that night?"

"No. You're the sum of every moment that has passed in your life, as I am. There's nothing that affects an individual *wholly* just as there's nothing that doesn't affect an individual at all. You're running your fingertips over the rough wood of this seat. You won't even remember doing that, it's a tiny insignificant moment amongst millions. But it adds to the sum. It adds an infinitesimal amount to your experience of tactile sensation. Possibly some day you'll have a garden and buy a seat for it and your choice will be influenced by which timber pleases you, and *that's* conditioned by the total of all the wood textures your senses have experienced in your life. Of course experience differs widely in intensity. There are big numbers in the sum. What you went through is vastly bigger than most. There won't be much it leaves untouched. Which is partly why I asked you about the eight-year-olds."

"I suppose I feel a strong empathy with them. Want the best for them, want them to reach their full potential. But that's teaching. I do feel very protective. There was a hell of a yelp in class the other day — someone trapped their finger in a drawer — and my heart was in my mouth, the sound of it, the idea of a kid in my charge being hurt . . . I almost feel I want to protect them from life."

"Which you can't do if they're to reach their full potential."

"Right. Oh, I know it's highly unlikely that anything's going to happen in their lives like what happened to me. Or part of me knows that."

"And the other part?"

"Well, the other part says, who knows? Such things do still happen. You only have to read the newspapers." The face of Ben Yeomans, looking up from his drawing of a badger and telling her what he had read in the paper, flashed on her mind. "They happen."

"Do you think that would occur to you less if those youths had ever been caught?"

She felt an inward flinch, the mental equivalent of an old sprain playing up, but answered promptly, "I think so, yes. I mean, they're still walking around, aren't they? The people who did that are walking around scot-free. So I can't look at my kids and honestly tell myself they're going to be safe out there in the big world."

Across the other side of the river a small black dog was running ahead of its owner. In its excitement it darted about in wild zigzags, yapping, which gave it the appearance of being relentlessly pursued by something.

"Was that part of your reason for moving out of London?"

It was Dr Kaufman's habit to probe: it had been part of their personal as well as their professional relationship and she usually found it stimulating. Just now he was shining his light on some very dark places, but the day was beautiful and peaceful and Carol felt strong.

"Maybe at some level," she said. "London was where it happened and it's where . . . that side of life shows itself most, maybe. Really it was a couple of little things that made me decide that London wasn't a place where I wanted to spend my life. It was the summer before I qualified and I was walking down Streatham High Street one day and suddenly this old Asian man shouted out across the other side of the street. He was sort of sitting down on the pavement — I suppose people thought he was drunk and it went through my mind at first. Anyway I went to see if I could help and so did one or two other people. He was all right, but very shaken up and — well, ashamed, humiliated really. He'd been roughed up and had his tobacco tin and a few pound coins taken off him. It was a couple of teenage girls that had done it, which seemed to be the thing that he couldn't get over. And they actually rode past on their bikes while we were helping him — did a bit of cat-calling and what have you. Somehow it was the . . . the everydayness, the triviality almost that was so horrible. There were people coming out of the shops with carrier bags and a traffic warden writing tickets and here's this poor old guy struggling on the pavement wondering what he's done to deserve it. That was one thing that set me thinking . . . But I think it was the man with the duck that clinched it for me."

Dr Kaufman raised his eyebrows, but he didn't laugh.

"Not a real duck. It was . . . Well, it sounds ridiculous when you talk about it. I was meeting Aunt Jean for lunch, outside the CAB where she works, and this man walked past. Good-looking sort of man, forties, smart business suit, well-groomed — you could imagine that he worked in a solicitor's or an accountant's around there somewhere and was on his way to lunch. Except that behind him he was pulling along a little wooden duck on wheels, on a string, you know, the sort that very small children have. And being very careful with it, just as you would if you had a little nervy dog on a lead, talking to it when he stopped at the kerb to cross the road . . . Jean says he's a familiar figure around there. Even been into the CAB once or twice, and with some perfectly sensible enquiry about consumer rights or whatever, not loony ramblings. Nothing loony about him at all, except that he walks the streets with a pull-along duck on wheels. Apparently there are the usual rumours to explain it all — how he was a successful businessman until he just flipped one day, or his wife left him and that's what sent him over the edge. Maybe true — it doesn't really matter, I suppose. Something did it. And I couldn't get it out of my mind. Well, no — I *could* get it out of my mind, quite easily, if I kept making the necessary effort. But that was just the prospect I didn't like — having to train myself to continually block things out, push them away. And inevitably you're going to have to do that in a big city. I can't say that that's what decided it for me, but it — it tipped the balance." She tapped his hand. "And now you can accuse me of falling for the myth of rural innocence and tell me I'll be begging to come back to London in six months."

"It's a myth all right," Dr Kaufman said chuckling, "but I've never known you repent of any of your decisions. Anyway, it's not as if you're in retreat from anything. Strictly speaking, you're entering the real world coming here. This is where eighty-five per cent of the population live. And it *is* completely different. Our capital is undoubtedly weird in its separation from the rest of the national life. Like a gigantic Versailles. There's a lot to be said for not having a metropolis at all, like the old West Germany — every town and city the thriving centre of its own hinterland. It can't be coincidence that West Germany was probably the most politically mature, prosperous and well-educated state of the twentieth century. Pour your whole country's resources into one massive conurbation, and of course you're going to end up with a nation of village idiots." Dr Kaufman smiled ruefully: he could often argue himself into a corner completely opposite to his own views. "Of course, having said that, I wouldn't live out here if you paid me a fortune to do it."

"Elitist," she said, lightly punching his shoulder.

"Unashamedly. That's the trouble — the good things in life are precisely the things I like. I just haven't got any simple tastes. Some wretched pretentious chef was on the radio the other day claiming that he likes nothing better than to sit down to a plate of baked beans on toast at the end of a hard day's creation in the kitchen. Such balls. I suppose it's time for us to be moving, is it? Better not miss that train."

"Yes, it's past three, I'm afraid."

They got up. Dr Kaufman's conversation had been so bracingly typical of the man she had known for fifteen years that the fact of his going blind had gone completely out of her head for a while. Now as he stood up and turned himself around, groping out for her arm and looking momentarily lost and helpless, the fact came brutally back to her. In his refusal to feel sorry for himself there was a strong admonition to others not to do so, but the pity hit her without warning and she must have expressed it in the sudden tight squeeze she gave his hand.

"They're not all gone, you know," he said, a faint smile on his lips while his eyes remained unreadable. "Those pleasures I was talking about. Was that what you were thinking?"

"Something like that."

They began to walk. A swan gracefully approached the bank and swam along close beside them, but Dr Kaufman's head didn't turn towards it.

"No, there's a lot left, and there still will be if and when the process completes itself, which seems likely. Not one hundred per cent likely, I gather it's more like eighty, and there's an operation they can try — but that has to wait until the process *is* complete, for some reason. No, print's gone, but I've read pretty well everything worth reading anyhow. Oh, yes — I'm not going to get in a tizzy because I didn't find time to read the minor novels of Balzac. Come to think of it, I have anyway. And technology can keep you abreast of things. Even esoteric psychology journals are becoming available in aural digests. Music remains, of course. Talk. Food. Knowledge and understanding. I've never contemplated sunsets, in fact I would have been quite at home with those eighteenth-century gentlemen who pulled down their carriage blinds when crossing the Alps because mountains were vulgar. And I shall continue to practise as long as I'm permitted, at least in a consultative capacity. Child psychiatry needs ears not eyes — but child patients would probably find a blind man frightening in a one-to-one situation."

Still moved, Carol tightened her grip on his arm and said, "I don't think I would have."

"When I first treated you, you were frightened of everything and frightened of nothing. Because you'd seen it all," Dr Kaufman said quietly. "I thought about that when they told me about my eyes. Yes, I'll tell you this, because it's not sentimental, just a fact: I put the whole thing into perspective by thinking about what happened to you. You survived that. You came through, and you were easily the most traumatized case in my experience. So what had I got to be afraid of?" In spite of his words, he seemed to feel that he had let sentiment creep in, because he went on briskly, "Anyhow, the most important thing of all remains — Smirnoff. Imagine if there were a disease that took away your ability to enjoy alcohol. Then I really would shake my fist at the heavens. Speaking of which, will we have time for one before I get that train?"

There was just time, after they had collected Dr Kaufman's overnight bag from her flat, for a drink in the King Leopold Hotel next to the station. Carol was glad of one, because partings of any kind were her weak point. This was something that wasn't going to change: saying goodbye to someone always raised a stupid atavistic fear that she would never see them again and all she could do was recognize it and live with it.

The drink also had the effect of unlocking something inside her and she found herself saying, "Why did you ask whether I'd been sleeping all right?"

"Grey area between nosiness and affection," Dr Kaufman said. "Sleep was always the great indicator with you."

"Yes . . . " She was going to say something about the episode of sleep paralysis, but again the words that came out surprised her. "*Déjà vu*," she said. "There's a scientific explanation for that, isn't there?"

"Sort of. Really psychology's about as scientific as water-divining, but we pretend. Have you been experiencing it? Feel like you've lived in a one-horse town before?"

"You'll get lynched if you're not careful. No, it's not the place, it's . . . well, it's probably nothing. It's just so convincing when you do get that feeling, I wonder exactly where it comes from."

"Neurophysiology would give you chapter and verse. Basically it's crossed wires. Normally your brain makes a clear distinction between memory and perception. Now and then it gets mixed up and paramnesia is the result. 'I remember this,' you say, when what's really happening is, 'I am perceiving this.' It's a blip in function, though I must admit that seems to beg the question of why it happens and why nearly everyone experiences it at some time. But it beats falling back on previous lives and psychic powers and all that junk. The other explanation is that it's not false memory at all but true memory — a reminder of something you've forgotten. It's the French tag that makes it sound romantic and mystical. They always do."

It was the sort of dogmatic pronouncement he loved to be challenged on, and she took him up. "What about *mal de mer*?"

"Well, it sounds better than seasick. A traveller would have *mal de mer*, a day tripper would get seasick."

They continued to wrangle good-humouredly over this until his train came, and it helped draw the sting of parting. Carol guided him to a seat on the train, hugged him, and then as the whistle blew was smitten by a horrible image of herself waving from the platform, and he unable to see her.

But she was going to have to toughen up about such things — she knew it, and Dr Kaufman, without saying it in so many words, positively insisted on it. He wouldn't have much patience with her if she didn't.

And besides, there wasn't much that he didn't see one way or another. As she left him, squeezing his hand, he smiled and said, "Phone me any time, Carol. Tell me about this *déjà vu*."

6

DÉJÀ vu.

It wasn't important, but it nagged at her. There was just something so familiar about the face of young Ben Yeomans that she was driven to unlikely lengths in her efforts to explain it to herself. Perhaps, she thought, Ben had been amongst the pupils she had taken charge of as a trainee. This soon fell apart, of course, under the pressure of various undeniable facts. She had done her training a hundred miles away. If he had been taught by her previously, there would surely have been recollection on his own part, and he was not too shy a child to mention it. And besides, there was nothing in Ben's records to indicate that he had moved from Lincolnshire to Dunmarket at precisely the same time as herself. In fact it was there in black and white that he had spent the past three years at a Dunmarket infants' school. So, that was that. But it was a sign of how much the question bugged her that she had to go so thoroughly into it before she could drop it. And even then, couldn't drop it, not entirely.

Déjà vu.

Then it occurred to her that she was possibly giving a fancy name and a fancy explanation to something that wasn't fancy at all and was really rather deplorable. Maybe it was all an excuse to disguise from herself the fact that Ben was a favourite of hers and she paid him a lot of attention.

Deplorable, of course, in theory, and all the more so for a NQT who should be on her guard against such habits. The fiery baptism of her first few weeks' teaching had already shown her that a great deal of theory simply had to stay behind in the training college where it belonged, and she recognized that you would have to be superhuman not to prefer, secretly, some pupils to others. They were human beings, and no one but a saint or an idiot liked all human beings equally. Which wasn't to say that you didn't try to give all the children the same sympathy, care and understanding. She was quite prepared to make the effort to discover hidden depths in Stephen Stone, for instance, and to make every possible allowance for the effects of an unsatisfactory home life; prepared to accept too that viewing him as a smug, untrustworthy little sadist who would grow up to be a smug, untrustworthy big sadist represented a failure on her part. It didn't alter the feeling. And nor did ticking herself off for warming to Ben Yeomans. In theory he was simply one of thirty pupils: in practice she had a definite soft spot for him.

And that could account for the sensation of familiarity. After all, a common feature of a new friendship or love affair was the feeling that you had known each other for years. The comparison was not so outlandish. She felt with Ben a rapport of a sort that was usually experienced between adults. When the class watched a nature television programme presented by an unctuous American who kept pronouncing the word 'tadpoles' with goofy emphasis, it was Ben's eye that she caught registering an amusement like her own, and after that she couldn't look at him for fear of bursting out laughing.

Also, he was bright. His language and visual skills were highly developed, and he was scarcely less quick at mathematics. He had a surprising conceptual grasp: in their project work on Homes and Houses he had raised the idea of a home country, a topic which she hadn't thought to include and which might lead to some deeper political waters than were normally entered in primary education. His was not a neat intelligence; his work was sometimes messy and rambling, he would get absorbed in detail at the expense of form, and he was very shaky on time — an exercise in which he had to fill in clock faces with the various stages of the school day left him floundering.

But he was always surprising her. To take away the nasty taste of spelling tests she followed them with a group game inspired by a TV panel show, and which she called Something That. Each table had their own game in progress while she acted as a mobile referee. Turns were taken to draw something that . . . flew, was red, made a noise — initially the suggestions were hers, but the children were soon thinking of their own categories — while the others tried to guess the object. She found Ben one day challenged to draw something that you opened. He had come up with a can of worms. Only one of the group had guessed it: the rest didn't know the phrase, but he had drawn the worms so amusingly wriggly and creepy that there were no groans or puzzled protests. This was encouraging in itself, Carol thought: there was always the possibility that cleverness would provoke resentment, later in his school career if not now, and humour was as effective a shield as any.

Understanding of the figurative: that was unusual. That he did understand it as a concept was made clear to her at home-time that day. Often he lingered after the bell to chat to her, and she made a joke about planning to have spaghetti tonight but being put off by his can of worms.

"Was that cheating?" he said suddenly.

"I don't think so, why?"

"Well, you don't really have a can of worms. It's just a thing you say when

141

you do something that starts a lot of trouble."

"That's right. But a fisherman might have a real can of worms. And when it's opened they all come wriggling out. That must be where the phrase comes from."

"My dad goes fishing. But he uses flies. He makes them himself. It's really fiddly."

"Do you go fishing with him?"

Ben shook his head. "I did once or twice. Thass really, really boring."

He spoke with solemnity and evident sincerity, but lowered his voice as if to say he respected his father's preferences, then went off in his slightly dreamy absent-minded fashion to get his coat from the cloakroom. He waved to her as he passed the classroom door again on his way out, his coat wrongly buttoned and lopsided. Not for the first time Carol found herself both amused and touched. And tantalized by that fleeting, unplaceable sensation of recognition.

She knew she must not allow any of this to make a teacher's pet out of him. But she was flattered and pleased to find that he was not the only one to seek her company after the bell had rung. Often she had a whole cluster of chatterers gathered round her as she cleared her desk: she was invited to view new bicycles, shown photographs of baby siblings, and coached in the latest dances by a precocious girl named Sarah Murkett who looked like a miniature Madonna and had an irresistible kookaburra laugh that could reduce the class to hysterics if it were not held in check.

They were her lot: she liked them and was proud of them. Mrs Juby's class might be better drilled, maybe even better behaved as far as talking in assembly and running down the corridors were concerned, but Carol didn't much care about that. What mattered to her was that after three or four weeks of term her class had lost their fears and inhibitions and were as lively and responsive as eight-year-olds could be. She kept this knowledge steadily before her as an aid to her confidence, because inevitably there were moments aplenty when she regretted her decision ever to be a teacher or doubted her ability to be a successful one. She found consistent discipline tricky and sometimes when the class were in an excitable mood there seemed to be a hundred children in the room with her rather than thirty. She found she hadn't catered for the sheer messiness of a modelling project, which usurped a whole day because of the cleaning-up involved; nor sufficiently taken into account the quickness of some children, who finished a piece of work long before the others and then were disruptive simply because they had nothing to do. She scrapped a carefully garnered collection of poems which she had thought would appeal to eight-year-olds and which left them not only cold and uncomprehending but bored to the point of scratchiness. Handwriting lessons were a struggle because she found it difficult to keep her own examples to the school's prescribed style, which Macleish was strict about: it was a script that managed to be both utterly devoid of character and awkward to form. And she seriously lost her cool with Stephen Stone when she tripped over his ever-restless legs and nearly went flat on her face. She was sure on that occasion that she breathed a four-letter word and wasn't sure, from the expression on their faces, that the children hadn't heard it.

There were enough such moments, in fact, to make the probationer's bugbear, a visit from an LEA adviser, a very real terror. Because it was axiomatic that these detested snoopers always descended on you on your very worst days and stood beadily watching whilst the children tied you to the radiator and threw paintballs at you. Macleish, too, provided his share of spirit-breakers, including a miserably carping inspection of her wall display which caused her to spend a fuming two hours after school ripping at sugar paper and thumping staples into the boards whilst a kindly cleaner looked on, remarking that it looked all right to her.

She was often disheartened — but never disheartened for long. Carol found that though she was the only probationer at Templeton Juniors, she was still not alone. It took her about ten days to discover the force behind this truism, ten days of resolutely maintaining to the staff room that she hadn't a single problem worth mentioning. Then she suddenly stopped pretending, and her colleagues, who surely hadn't been fooled for a moment, responded with a flood of encouraging anecdotes. Everyone had their own probationary horror story. They were probably exaggerated, but there was a sufficient core of truth in them to reassure her that what she was going through had been gone through by everyone in their time. As soon as she stopped being strong and silent, distances closed up. She was one of them.

She had previously declined an invitation to join an after-school session in the pub. For some reason, a chance remark by a college lecturer that being roped into staff drinking-clubs was the surest road to perdition for probationers had stuck with Carol. When she did go, it was a month into term. She had been collecting money that day for the year's first school trip, scheduled for next week. The first years, and their class teachers, were to be treated to a modest day out at a place called Collingham Gardens, twenty miles away.

"Collingham Gardens, Steam Museum

and Wildfowl Sanctuary," Martin said, bringing a tray of drinks to the table. "There's not a whole lot there. Couple of old locomotives and some ducks. Kids seem to like it, though."

"Talking of ducks," Diane Hollins said, "I had one of my lot come back after lunch in a terrible state. Apparently on the way back to school she'd seen a dove get run over by a car. You know those really dopey doves you get in the market square. It just didn't get out of the way and the wheel went right over it. Poor Karen couldn't get it out of her mind — the noise, she said. Like a football bursting. And she said it was still, you know, alive for a bit afterwards."

"Vestigial movement," Tony Plumb said. "It wouldn't have been feeling anything."

"Well, that's what I tried to tell her, but it was a hell of a job to calm her down. And I felt a bit of a fraud, really. Saying never mind and don't think about it. But how can you tell kids that horrible things are going to happen and they're going to see them all their lives and there's nothing you can do about it?"

"It's a tricky one," Martin said. "Maybe the royals have got the right idea. As soon as their kids are old enough to walk they shove a freshly killed fox in their faces. Good strong dose of unthinkable cruelty straight off, works wonders. Never be troubled with normal human feelings again." He took a pull at his beer, which was a dark potent Suffolk ale and the universal Dunmarket tipple. Only Chris Bryce, who completed the group, was not drinking it: he was nursing some sort of non-alcoholic punch. "You know, when I first went to senior school there was a big framed photograph of the Queen in the lobby. And it was in *black and white*. Let's see, I'm thirty-two, that would be . . . 1975. What a place. You expected to see Alastair Sim taking assembly. We sang Christmas carols in Latin. I mean . . . *why*? And what certifiable old fart had the bright idea of taking a book of Christmas carols and translating them into Latin in the first place? Piddling provincial grammar school, of course. They made it go comprehensive a couple of years later.

Half the teachers left. 'I'm not going to teach wogs,' one confided in me. Old pet who looked like Mr Pickwick. Anyway. Give me a punchline, somebody."

"That bird," said Chris Bryce, his mind moving along slow grooves of its own. "Karen wouldn't have had to see that if we hadn't invented the car. Maybe you should have brought that up."

"Well, I could have done, yes," said Diane. She was the essence of gentleness: her clothes were like a statement against power-dressing, and her voice was as soft as her habitual cashmere. But she could be pleasantly stubborn too. "But I don't suppose that would have made her feel any better."

"Maybe she could have gone to Dagenham and firebombed Ford's," Martin said.

"It would have given her something to, you know, bite on," Chris said. "The kid's thinking, why do horrible things have to happen? Answer, they don't have to, but we in the West make machines that make them more likely."

"Do my eyes deceive me, Chris, or

is that your Nissan parked out there?" Martin said.

"I admit it, I have a car," Chris said imperturbably. "Unfortunately I can't fully live in Western society without one. But I recognize that it's an environmental poison and use my bike whenever possible."

"How green was my Raleigh," Martin said.

"You can't protect them," Tony Plumb said, "even if you were to get rid of cars and guns and whatever else. If she'd seen a hawk catch the dove it would have looked just as horrible. All you can do is try to teach them not to be cruel themselves, and subtract from the sum a bit." Tony was a boyish forty, who with his unbarbered fringe and fatless body looked as if he should have been presenting nature programmes in a safari shirt. Diane had a special sad-happy covert look for him which Carol, at least, had no difficulty reading.

"Doesn't need teaching," Chris said, propping up his feet on the seat in an uncomfortably laid-back position. Carol noticed the thick climbing socks and remembered them from her college days. Chrises always wore them and it had always puzzled her. "It's there to begin with."

"What is?" Carol said.

Chris did one of his agonized searching-for-words mimes, then fell back on language. "Innocence."

"Oh, come on," Martin said. "I've known some right little sods and the big bad world didn't make them that way. It was just in them."

"Bastards!" An old man seated alone at a nearby table bellowed it out. He was a well-known drunk, or local character if you preferred, with a dewlapped face like a bloodhound. This pub, a dark-beamed catty-cornered shoebox called the Dragonfly, was one of the few to allow him in for more than half an hour. Like most town drunks, he was smartly dressed in suit and tie. "Bloody muppets," he added. "German bastards."

"That's right, sir," Martin called out.

"It's in them?" Chris said. He performed a street-theatre shrug. "Are we talking Original Sin here?"

"Sure, why not?" Martin said. His

pint was gone and he was ready, Carol could see, to fight any corner. "Good a concept as any, even if you don't want the theology. Maybe we've been getting it wrong all these years, ever since Rousseau and Blake and all that *Songs of Innocence* stuff — people aren't nasty, they just get made that way by the world. Criminology's helped us carry on the delusion. Every serial killer profile turns up some awful warped childhood that explains everything. Some day soon there's going to be a serial killer who's very nice and well-adjusted and no skeletons in his cupboard. Just likes doing it."

Carol stood up and went to get more drinks, though only Martin had finished his. When she came back Martin and Chris were still locking horns.

"You're taking an exclusively Western view," Chris said. "Children in a Third World country just wouldn't have that mind-set. They would be attuned to nature and so respectful of life."

"Oh, which particular Third World country is this? You mean a kid in Mexico City, the largest urban area in the world? What would they have to do with nature? And what's so kindly about nature anyway? What's Mother Nature cooking up in her kitchen today, children? Well, she's making two diseases called cancer and multiple sclerosis and when she's finished that she's going to make a spider that lays its eggs in the live body of a wasp."

"So you're saying every individual has this innate capacity for evil?" Chris said.

"Yes!"

"You'd include Lucy in that, then? You'd include your own little daughter?"

"You're kidding. With my ex-wife's genes, she'll probably grow up to be Countess Dracula."

Martin had turned the point with a laugh, but there had been a moment's hesitation in which Carol had seen hurt and bewilderment. The discussion touched on matters she had trained herself to avoid, but Chris's unwarranted descent into the personal prompted her to throw down the mental barrier and join in.

"Not everything that's good comes naturally," she said. "Language is good but children don't just have it. They learn it socially. It's the same with a moral sense. It has to be acquired. If there is something there to begin with, something like a conscience, it still has to be developed like a weak muscle."

"It's an evolutionary thing," Tony said. "Our brains have got so large that we can envisage practically anything. A cat or a dog hasn't got the mental capacity to invent a gas chamber. We have, so we do. The human brain has never thought of anything so horrible that it won't try it out."

"Look at the National Lottery," Martin said.

"How is Lucy, by the way?" Diane said. "I suppose she'll have started infants now?"

"Yep, fine, loves it apparently." Martin jiggled his glass, making the beer foam. "I'm taking her out next weekend."

"German bastards." The drunk, after a period of brooding, began shouting again. "Muppets. Bloody DJs."

"Shut it," the barmaid told him casually.

"At least the poor kid's spared having

another teacher at home when she comes back from school," Martin said. "Teachers shouldn't breed really. They start cross-examining their own offspring. 'Would you like chips for tea? Do you know what chips are made from? Potatoes, very good. And do you know where potatoes come from?'" He looked across at Carol and caught himself up. "Sorry, your parents aren't teachers, by any chance?"

"No, no." She smiled. Fielding questions like these was an inevitable consequence of getting to know new people. She was used to it. But there was always the fear that someone would press: if they did, only the truth was available to her. In her teens, when the question seemed to come up most frequently, she had invented a car crash, but in the end the lie had hurt her too much.

Martin didn't press, though. "I thought you seemed pretty sane," was all he said. He didn't, Carol noticed, meet her eyes much. His own eyes were a very dark brown. His thick dark hair was of the sort that would only go bald from the crown, if it ever did at all. For all his bear-like size and eccentricity of dress there was something dapper and old-fashioned about him: he had deftly pulled out Carol and Diane's chairs for them when they came to sit down, and he used his long-fingered hands with the delicacy of a silver-service waiter.

"My dear old grandma lays out the red carpet when I visit her," Diane said. "She still thinks it's posh to be a teacher."

"It would be in her day," Tony said. "The profession used to be a highly respected one. Strange to think of, isn't it? A teacher's name on your references was like having a clergyman's or a Justice of the Peace and now — well, we've been governed by supreme image-makers for a long time, and the image they've created for us is probably one of the most harmful things they've done. Well, anyway . . . " Tony got down off his union hobby-horse apologetically.

"Of course," Martin said, "that's why I went into it. I thought it was the only chance I stood of anyone ever calling me sir. Why'd you go into it, Carol?"

"I — wanted to make a difference,

I suppose," she said after a moment's surprise.

"Do you think we can?"

"Oh, I wouldn't be doing it otherwise."

"What if it's a myth, though? Maybe there are too many other things in the world now. Too many other influences. You used to get these scholarship boys who escaped the pit and grew up to be famous writers and they owed it all to one idealistic teacher in the village school. But that was when there was only the pit and the school and nothing else to choose from. Kids now have got lots of escape routes. They can go and have sex and take crack and watch Sky and not feel they're missing out."

"Martin, you're really quite puritanical at heart, aren't you?" Chris said. Despite the laid-back posture, he had his eye on Martin; he wasn't, Carol saw, going to drop it, for whatever reason — maybe just a pure chalk-and-cheese antipathy.

"Some kids might not want those things," Carol said.

"Prefer knowledge, you mean? They're crazy if they do."

"You don't mean that," Carol said.

Martin held up his hands. "OK. But the brainy ones are going to follow that path anyway, regardless of what we do. But if a kid's got real tossers for parents and a hopeless setup at home then we're not going to turn him on to English lit. no matter what we do."

"All right, maybe not. But we can add to the sum. Every experience counts, it's cumulative. If we add to that kid's total experience of interesting and fulfilling things then we've done some good." It was partly Dr Kaufman's argument, but she was so pleased with its aptness that she didn't mind passing it off as her own.

"It depends what the teacher's got inside him," Chris said. "If he has a negative attitude then he's probably going to communicate that to his students. It's not only the kids' private lives that are a factor in the equation."

"So what are you saying, exactly, Chris?" Martin turned to face him. "Unless you've got a home life that's like a scene from *The Sound of Music*, you can't teach?"

"Listen, why be confrontational about

this?" Chris said, back-pedalling a little. "We're just talking about lifestyles."

"Everyone's different," Diane put in rather desperately.

"Exactly, Diane. Everyone's different," Martin said. His jaw had tightened, and Carol saw that the interruption had not worked. "You believe in alternative lifestyles, don't you, Chris? Well, my alternative includes booze and a big fry-up on a Saturday while I watch the racing results and it doesn't include being some kind of bloody pious earth-father."

"Maybe that's why you go home to an empty house," Chris said with a shrug.

"Now, now, I think this one should go to arbitration," Tony said loudly, with a forced laugh, and began to say something about a game of darts; but Carol found herself saying before he could finish, "I go home to an empty house, or flat anyway. So where does that put me?"

"That's different, Carol," Martin said, with a sort of courtliness. "You have yet to embark on family life and then screw it up, which I think is what our friend is getting at."

"Hey, I didn't mean that," Chris said,

"peace, peace." But he gave Carol a speculative look, and she saw something of the same kind in Diane's eyes. She had taken sides, and they found it significant.

Perhaps it was, but she didn't have time to reflect on it just yet, because Tony almost physically forced them to the dartboard. Hopeless at games, she volunteered after the first few wild throws to be scorer; and only then was she able to look into herself with surprise.

She hadn't really agreed with anything Martin had said. In many ways the man was a bull artist. But at some deeper level she was on his side. Watching him play — Tony with astute diplomacy had teamed him with Chris, and they were showing each other that exaggerated politeness of people who have said things they are sorry for — Carol wondered if it came down to the simple fact that Martin did not believe in the essential goodness of people. And she didn't believe in that either.

She believed in the potential of goodness, she believed in education and mutual understanding and tolerance, she was as liberal as could be and would confidently have described herself as an optimist: a long hard road had brought her to this position and she was sure of her footing upon it.

And yet she knew there was a night side to human beings. The knowledge was more fundamental to her than her own name.

* * *

The doctor's office has a nice smell.

It comes from the coffee machine in the corner. She doesn't much like the taste of coffee, preferring the orange juice that he gives her in a beaker with a picture of the Smurfs on it, but the smell is a nice one and comforting.

She doesn't know whether she likes the doctor or not. She is not really afraid of him as she was at the beginning — though everything makes her a little afraid, now, because she doesn't know how it will turn out. She doesn't mind his eyes as she did at first — they looked so big behind the thick glasses. In fact she thinks they are quite kind eyes. But she isn't sure whether she really likes coming here.

Not because it's a doctor's. Daddy was a doctor so she never minded that, and anyway this place isn't at all like a surgery: there are no medical things, no sink or stethoscope or that thing you put round your arm and blow up like a tyre. Sphyg-mo-man-o-meter. It used to make Daddy laugh when she tried to pronounce it. In the end she learnt it, but she would get it wrong on purpose because it was nice to make Daddy laugh.

(Laughing. She doesn't do it any more and she doesn't like it. Sometimes Uncle Keith laughs and she has to go quietly out of the room. Those boys laughed when they were doing things to Daddy. She knows Uncle Keith's laugh is different. Yet it's the same really.)

No, this place doesn't look like a doctor's surgery at all, and really it's very nice. Full of books and papers, with big squidgy armchairs with brightly coloured quilts thrown over them. The window looks out on a lovely garden and sometimes you can see a squirrel go bobbing across the lawn. And through an archway there's another sort of room with beanbags and lots of toys and games, and she's allowed to go in there whenever she wants. If she wants to stop, walk in there and play, she can.

In spite of all this, she's not sure about coming here. She knows it's supposed to help her and make her better. But when she's here, she has to talk about Mummy and Daddy and what happened to them, and she'd rather not.

Or she has to talk about herself. And she'd rather not do that either. She knows all about herself: she's just a very bad girl and that's it.

The doctor doesn't seem to see that. He puts a Rubik cube in her hands and while she's trying to do it he asks her about the nightmares.

"Can you tell me about them? Tell me what it was you dreamt about?"

She tells him, but she can't see the point of it. She has the nightmares because she's being punished. It's quite right that she should have nightmares. Otherwise she would be forgetting what she did.

She tells him: about the bird at the window, trying to get in. The way its beak and claws scratch at the glass. The panicky flapping sound of its wings.

"Why is the bird trying to get in, do you think?"

She shakes her head, her fingers working at the Rubik cube.

"Do you feel it wants to get to you, hurt you?"

She shakes her head, then nods.

"Why should it do that?"

"Because." She knows that sounds like a stubborn cheeky answer, but she doesn't mean it that way. She just means it: because.

"What about the other dreams?"

Her eyes stray upwards a little, take in his crossed legs, off-white trousers and suede shoes and funny-coloured socks. He is a bit scruffy, the doctor, which she quite likes. Daddy was scruffy like that. But he could be very smart too, when him and Mummy were going out. "I like you in a suit," Mummy would say, and pull him towards her by his tie and give him a kiss.

They used Daddy's ties on Mummy's

ankles. One on each bedpost.

"What else do you dream of?"

"Those boys."

Oh yes, she dreams about them, of course. She dreams about them coming back to get her the way they got Mummy and Daddy. And this time she can't hide from them. But though the dream's horrible, it's somehow not as frightening as the bird dream. Because it's only what should have happened, after all.

"Do you want the dreams to go away?"

"No."

"Why not?"

She shrugs.

"They don't sound very nice dreams. It would be better not to have them, wouldn't it?"

"No." The Rubik cube turns and crunches. "It was my fault."

"What happened to Mummy and Daddy?"

She nods.

"Did you let the boys into the house?"

"No."

"Did you help the boys?"

She puts her head on one side, struggling. For a moment she hates

165

the doctor. She doesn't want to be here any more. She doesn't want to be anywhere.

"You're stupid," she bursts out.

She is rather shocked at herself, and expects to be told off. But the doctor just says, "Yes, probably. There are a lot of things I don't understand."

Ashamed, she makes an effort. It hurts, but she says it.

"I didn't help Mummy and Daddy, I hid. I heard the noises of the people in the house and then Mummy screaming out and I went and hid and so it's my fault."

"I see." The doctor sips his coffee. "Yes, I see."

Good. Perhaps now he won't talk about it any more. Perhaps now . . .

"What would you have done, then? Suppose you hadn't gone and hid. What would you have done?"

There. One face of the Rubik cube is all orange. Now the white squares . . .

"There were four boys, weren't there? You told me there were four — you saw them through your peephole. And they were big boys — teenagers."

166

White. White. Wait, can't turn it that way, because it would break up the oranges . . .

"What could you have done? Do you think you could have fought four big teenage boys, and stopped them?"

She glares at him. She hates him.

"Or do you think you could have run out and got help? But they were upstairs. They would have seen you and stopped you, wouldn't they?"

She feels her lower lip go out. "So what?" she says.

"Oh, you mean you should have tried it anyway? Is that what you mean?"

She frowns down at the Rubik cube.

"Well, let's think about that. Suppose there was a tiger in this room with us now. And we couldn't get to the door. What do you think I would do? Expect you to fight the tiger? No. I'd pop you in the cupboard or lift you up on that high shelf where you'd be safe."

"A tiger could reach up there," she says, her imagination picturing the scene in spite of herself.

"A leopard then. Small but fierce. That's what I'd do. And I think Mummy and Daddy would have done the same. In fact I'm sure of it." Suddenly the doctor bends forward and looks into her face. "They always wanted you to be safe. Isn't that right? Do you think Mummy and Daddy would have wanted the boys to find you? I don't. I think they would have wanted you to hide and be safe. And that's what you did. You did what Mummy and Daddy would have wanted. That means you're a good girl, not a bad one."

Suddenly, she doesn't know why, she hurls the Rubik cube down on the floor. She wants to break it but it doesn't break, just bounces, and so she jumps up and runs through the arch and grabs something else, a doll, perhaps that will break, but its face is pretty and she can't bear to smash it and so she sits down on the floor, crying loudly and babyishly, feeling she has made a fool of herself.

After a while she looks up to find the doctor sitting on the floor near her. He looks funny and awkward sitting like that. She thinks she was mean to hate him.

"Will they catch those boys?" she says.

"Do you want them to?"

She nods, and feels something hard and cold inside her: something, she guesses, like the feelings grown-ups have, which have always seemed so strange and difficult.

"Good. Because it's their fault, isn't it? What happened. Nobody else's."

"I hid because I was scared."

"That's right. Anyone would have been scared."

"But . . . " She wipes her eyes and nose, trying to think of words. It's as if she's fighting something inside her own chest. "Why did they do it?"

The doctor looks as if he's thinking.

"We don't know," he said at last. "When people do very bad things, we usually try to find a reason. Sometimes it's because they're ill in their minds."

"Like Grandma."

He looks at her with a little bit of a smile. "Is your Grandma ill in her mind?"

"Well, Daddy used to say that. She'd always be poorly and complaining about it and Daddy said it was all in her mind."

169

"Well, that is like being ill, really. That's why your Grandma can't look after you. She's not really well enough. But her mind hasn't got something wrong with it. Some people who do very bad things have something wrong with their minds, just like some people who've got something wrong with their legs can't walk."

"Were those boys like that?"

"Maybe. We don't know. They might have taken some drugs that made them behave that way. We'll only know when the police find them."

"When?"

"It might take some time."

She stares at him.

"I should think you'll have seen how they do these things on the TV. When the police want to find someone and don't know who they are, they have to use clues and evidence, to try — "

"Witnesses," she says.

He nods. "That's right. Sometimes they have witnesses, who can tell them what the people looked like, perhaps what their car looked like, things like that."

"I saw them. I saw the boys. I know

170

what they look like." She is breathing fast, probably because she's been crying.

"I know. And you told the police what you saw. But that doesn't necessarily mean they can find them. There are lots of teenage boys in London. Nobody else saw them, nobody saw a car. I would think there must have been clues left behind in the house, but it's still very difficult and takes time."

"Will I have to see them if the police get them?"

"I don't know. You might. It depends."

"What on?"

"Would you know the boys if you saw them again?"

She nods. Yes.

"Suppose those four boys were lined up with a lot of others, like a football team. Would you be able to pick them out?"

She nods again; but her lips tighten and she looks away from the doctor's kind magnified eyes.

"Do you see their faces when you dream? See them clearly?"

She picks up the doll and straightens its dress, trying to think, trying to stop the terrible babyish feeling coming over her and making her silly. The boys' faces . . . she knows them, and yet when she tries to picture them something in her mind pulls away, the way your hand pulls away from a fire. One, two, three, four. Hair. Laughing faces. Some spots. A nose and eyebrows, a throaty voice. Not really boys but not men. Youths, the policeman kept saying when he talked to her. White skins. One, two, three, four. One smaller than the others, younger. The one who stamped on Harry. Another in a leather jacket, shining. One, two, three, four . . .

"Don't know," she says. "I think about it and then it goes."

"It doesn't matter then. Let it go."

"Will they go to prison?"

"Yes. Or to a special sort of hospital, if they're ill in their minds."

"What if they're just bad?"

"Well . . . then they would go to prison."

"No." Again she fights for words to express a harsh, difficult, grown-up feeling. "I know, but I mean — what if they're just bad?"

She looks into the doctor's face, and sees him hesitating.

"When you're a doctor like me," he says, "a doctor who looks after people's minds, you look for a reason behind things. The way people think and why they do the things they do. There has to be a reason behind it. There has to be a because. If people do bad things, it's up to us doctors to learn about them and find out why."

She stares at him again, because she does not think this is really an answer, and when he does not say anything more she lowers her eyes and holding the doll to her chest begins rocking.

"They stuck a bottle in my Mummy's thing and a knife in my Daddy's bottom," she says, and rocks faster, and though the doctor tries to say something she pretends he isn't there.

7

IT was all going well until the episode of the swan's nest.

"Swimmingly, in fact," Martin said later, when they were on their way back to Dunmarket.

"You said it was all going well until the swan thing, and I said swimmingly. Swan, swimming, oh please yourself . . . "

She was able to laugh then, but her sense of humour definitely hadn't been working when it happened. In fact she felt she had made rather a spectacle of herself and the reasons for it bothered her. At the time she had angrily demanded of young Ben Yeomans just what the hell had got into him; but she might just as appropriately have asked it of herself.

Setting out that morning for Collingham Gardens she had felt not unlike one of the children herself: excited and with a delightful sense of not being at work.

"Skiving," said Martin, who was seated next to her at the front of the coach.

"Best feeling in the world. Actually it isn't, there are quite a few that are nicer. That's a piece of social hyperbole there, and do you know I was twenty-five years old before I discovered that that word wasn't pronounced hyperbowl?"

"How do you know you were twenty-five?"

"Wrote it down in my diary. 'Today made an interesting discovery. All my life I have been mispronouncing hyperbole. Now I know why Sharon Coolidge wouldn't go out with me.'"

"I always thought awry rhymed with Tory. Can everybody quieten down, please?" she added, showing her face over the top of the seat. Sitting down, she noticed a couple of pink-cheeked whispering faces, and guessed what was being said. "They've got the giggles because we're sitting next to each other."

"Ah, innocence! I want it back, Carol. I want to feel again the scandalous thrill of saying the word *bra*."

"God, yes, that was really, really rude. And the *pictures* of bras in mail-order catalogues. You didn't know where to put your face."

"Doesn't fade, you know. When my wife had a catalogue I was still actually embarrassed if it opened at the bra pages. And as for the men in Y-fronts showing each other cricket bats — "

"Ugh!"

"Exactly. Think what untold damage they've done to the nation's psyche. Girls have grown up with an image of the male body as a sort of strong-tea brown all over. Boys have grown up wondering why they don't stick out at the front like that." He stood up and addressed a screeching girl in the back seat. "Jacqueline, did you know I can hear your voice right at the front of the coach?"

"Yes, sir."

"Well, that's all right then. As long as you know." He sat down. "You forget what a buzz everything is when you're a kid. I used to get excited about just going on a bus when I was small. I'd be chuffed if my dad's car broke down because it meant going on a bus. Of course, we had conductors on buses then. Toscanini, Karajan, André Previn, we had them all. Now, here, tell me something. Have you ever in your life heard anyone refer to a bus conductor as a 'clippie'? You're from London, maybe they do it there."

"Never," she said laughing. "Never once."

"Well, then, my case rests. That's another great canard of modern life. You get these old gits who write reminiscing articles in local papers and they go on about the old days when you had clippies. Like going scrumping apples. The said old gits always go on about scrumping apples when they were boys but that's a lie too because *no one ever did*. What kid gives a stuff about apples? You like sweets and chips, maybe. Apples, no. And they all reckon they had Mickey Mouse gas masks in the war but the fact is there were very few of those issued and if you were a kid in the war you just had an ordinary gas mask and it makes me so *angry* . . . Calm down. Calm down, Martin."

"You remind me of a friend of mine. He can't bear anything that's not strictly the truth. When I was in my teens and going through a stage of thinking I was Rosa Luxemburg I used to rant and rave at him about Fascism. There were a lot of far-right skinhead groups round our way then. That's not Fascism, he would say. Fascism didn't have a racialist aspect. It's neo-nazism. Oh, it's all the same, I would shout, but he wouldn't budge. I seem to remember getting so worked up I ended up calling him a Fascist. Which was a teensy bit out of place as he's Jewish."

"Ouch. I don't think I ever thought I was Rosa Luxemburg. I thought I was Radio Luxembourg for a few years, you know. I kept repeating adverts for spot cream and then going all cracky, but they cured me of that . . . No, I was very CND at that time. Pacifism was my bag. Or badge. I remember writing this very biting and satirical poem for the school magazine in which I proved to my satisfaction that the First World War was a Bad Thing. You know the sort of stuff, men dying in the trenches while the generals quaffed port. My teachers were too kind to point out to me that the First World War had been over for sixty years and I might as well have got on my high horse about Mr Gladstone."

A girl in the seat across the aisle began trying to get his attention. "Mister Cullerrrr . . . "

"Ah no, Helen, don't do the whine, for God's sake don't do the whine . . . "

Thus encouraged, she did it. "*Mis*-ter Cullerrrr . . . "

Martin howled and grimaced. "I hear that in my dreams. Dreams, did I say? Nightmares. What do you want, you horrible child?"

"Mister Culler, are we nearly there?"

"Nearly there, good Lord no, there's another hundred and fifty miles yet."

"But I need to go to the to-i-lerrrt . . . "

There were groans from Helen's companions.

"We'll be there in a few minutes, Helen," Martin said. "Now how badly do you need to go? Can you wait?"

"I think so-ooo."

"Well, I suppose we'll all know about it if you can't." He turned back to Carol. "Where would we be without toilet humour?"

"Up shit creek without a paddle," she whispered, sending him into snorts of smothered laughter.

"You whispered in my ear. You'll *have* to marry me now."

"Oh no, I'm a probationer. At college probationers are strongly discouraged from entering into relationships with other staff members."

"Is that right?"

"No, I made it up."

"Eileen Juby's old man's a teacher, did you know?"

"No, I didn't know that." Mrs Juby, who was in the other coach and had been infected by the holiday spirit to the extent of donning an incongruous pair of Ray-Bans, did not speak of her private life to Carol: in fact she seemed to regard her as little more than an overgrown pupil.

"Teaches maths at a comp in Ipswich. Probably the best arrangement, actually. They can mutually bore each other with school talk when they get home. It doesn't work too well one way."

"Oh dear. Is that the voice of experience?" She felt comfortable enough with him to ask.

"Yes and no. I mean, yes, my ex-wife wasn't thrilled by teaching, but it wasn't just that. I wish I could say we were very young and foolish, but we weren't. Just foolish. To get married, I mean. Sue's far from foolish. She's a brilliant lady. Works in educational publishing."

"She lives in London?"

"Yep. She used to commute when we were together. No limits to her energy. Picked up her work not long after Lucy was born. Same after the divorce, up and running. She combines a demanding job with excellent childcare, just like one of those women in an American self-help book. Damn it, I've gone and said something bitter after all. Basically she didn't like Dunmarket or anything about it. She thought Chris Bryce was a prat, for example, and didn't hesitate to say so."

"I thought he seemed to dig you a lot. And that night in the Dragonfly . . . "

"Oh, we just wind each other up, always have. Friends again now, sort of. A little bird told me, by the way, that his wife clobbers him."

"No!"

"Uh-huh. I said, how do you know this, little bird? It said I'm a little bird, it's my job to know things . . . "

For a wonder, no one had been sick by the time they arrived at Collingham Gardens: once the children had descended from the coach, Carol checked all along the seats to make absolutely sure. She found Stephen Stone hiding under one of the seats, and ticked him off more in weariness than anger. Continual attention-seeking of his sort was sometimes a diversion from difficulty with work, but Stephen's work was good when he wasn't writing *Bum* all over it. Her hope was that it was just a phase of silliness. One girl in her class currently had a giggly thing about willies. Any word that might possibly be a term for the male member and any object that even faintly resembled it sent her off. She was either going to shed it or grow up to write situation comedy.

The Railway Museum was a hit with the children, which rather surprised Carol. It was housed in an old stone tithe barn and it seemed to her that more care had been lavished on restoring the exterior than making the interior interesting: a couple of steam locos and a lot of sepia photographs was as far as it went, and the guide was a droning bore. But the children gave him a silent attention he didn't deserve and clamoured to buy postcards. She envied them the receptivity of their young minds, and was proud of them.

Next was a ride on a working steam train: this was more her idea of fun, and the gardens that the train circled were still beautiful despite the lateness of the year, with the glorious autumn colours of the trees contrasting with the cold blue sky to soul-lifting effect. The smell of the steam was as wonderful as she had always heard, and it was Ben Yeomans who asked her the question she was wondering herself.

"Miss Halstead, why don't they have steam trains any more?"

"Well, I think the newer type of trains, that run on diesel or electricity, cost a lot less to run, and they're faster and cleaner." She spoke confidently, but she wasn't sure it was really true. It wasn't as if trains were either cheap, fast or clean nowadays. And there was coal in the ground. When they disembarked at the little platform by the museum she sidelined Martin and said, "Why *don't* they have steam trains any more?"

"They do in Poland," he said. "Don't know why. Maybe to slow the Germans down next time round."

There was a picnic area in the gardens, where the children ate their packed lunches before moving on to the wildfowl park. The usual instructions not to bring anything squashable had as usual been disregarded: everywhere bags dripped and seeped.

"Mis-ter Cullerrr . . . "

"Ye-ees, Helerrrn."

"My sandwiches have got all tri-ifle on them."

"Well, that'll save you time, won't it? Main course and pudding all in one go. Here, have mine."

"What's in them?"

"Helen, do you know the expression, 'Never look gift horse in the mouth'?"

"Par-don?"

"Just eat the sandwiches, Helen."

Execpt for Helen, however, no one made a fuss. Everybody was in a good mood, and even Stephen Stone had stopped playing the fool: he sat quietly by Carol eating his lunch and occasionally pointing out flights of birds overhead and asking what they were. Something about the open air seemed to change him.

It seemed, in view of what happened in the wildfowl park, that the same applied to Ben Yeomans, with the change in his case being for the worse. But afterwards Carol had to admit that even his behaviour there was more characteristic than deliberately naughty. She knew his capacity for absorption, his forgetfulness of time and place and everything else once his interest was engaged. Unfortunately what engaged his interest was that swan's nest.

Probably the wildfowl park had made her a little highly strung to begin with. It was laid out around a natural watercourse, which had been diverted in places to make freshwater ponds, each cultivated to provide a habitat for various native and exotic species, with here and there a tiny artificial island — a feature which enchanted the children, as did the charm of the little mandarin ducks with their bright cartoon faces. But Carol couldn't relax with so much water around. The banks were well fenced and she trusted her class to be sensible — but she had never been responsible for them outside the school before and she couldn't help thinking of awful scenarios and counting their heads every few minutes. She counted them so many times that when the number finally came to twenty-nine instead of thirty she didn't trust her addition. She made herself count again, and then she panicked.

"Everybody stand still! Everybody in my class stay where you are! Who's not here?" A ridiculous thing to say. What should she do? She knew the register by heart, maybe she should call it . . .

A voice piped up. "Miss, Ben's not here, I don't think . . . "

She ran back down the path, remembering now the swan that had fascinated him and how she had warned him not to get too close because they could be fierce. She hadn't heard any splash but then the kids had been making such a racket . . . Oh God . . .

A few feet ahead of her there was

movement in the thick bulrushes by the bank. Before she could open her mouth to call out Ben Yeomans lurched up out of the rushes and scrambled on to the bank. He was upright for a few moments, looking open-mouthed straight at her, and then his feet slipped from under him and he fell on his behind.

"I wanted to try and see the swan's nest," he burbled, picking himself up. "It went in there in them rushes and I thought I could creep up and . . . "

He looked at himself. From the chest downwards he was a mess of reedy, black, stinking mud.

And that was when he started giggling. He was not a boy who laughed a great deal and the sound of it, high, girlish and abandoned, surprised Carol at first. Then something about it incensed her. Quite irrationally, she felt hatred and felt that it was mutual.

She darted forward and grabbed him by the arm and brought her face close to his.

"You ever pull a stunt like that again and there'll be no more school trips for you! Just what the hell do you think you're playing at? Look at you! I'd send you back to the infants' except I don't think they'd have anybody so stupid and childish!"

The words and the tone were unheard of, coming from Miss Halstead; but more frightening yet must have been the expression on her face. Ben's head went back and his eyes filled. The other children, who had started laughing when he did, fell silent.

"Hey. Go easy on him." Martin had appeared at her side and spoke the words quietly. She turned, glaring: it was bad enough failing in her responsibility without him patronizing and undermining her . . .

But all at once the fury died. She *was* being excessive. All right, it wasn't easy to see the funny side of this and his parents certainly wouldn't when he got home — but screaming and bawling weren't going to do any good.

"I — I'm sorry I shouted, Ben," she said, trying to turn her grip on his arm into a pat. "But that was a very silly thing to do and dangerous."

"I thought that was just like firm muck

and I could walk on it," he said, his lip wobbling.

The tremulous Suffolk accent was a great turner away of wrath. "Yes, well," she said, "it wasn't, was it? You're lucky you didn't get sucked under like in those Tarzan films."

He chuckled obligingly: the willingness made her feel worse. But it was different, not that wild high-pitched laughter. There had been something loathsome about that.

Or maybe she was just an old sourpuss before her time. She noticed Mrs Juby give her a grim satisfied look, as if to say that was the right stuff. If I'd gone the whole hog and slapped his legs, Carol thought, she'd probably have given me a round of applause.

The giggles were gone now, anyhow; and with the other children gathering round and craning their necks to gape at him Ben began to look wretchedly ashamed and embarrassed. Carol checked him over for damage. "There wouldn't have been anything in the nest anyway. No eggs at this time of year," she said, wondering what she was going to do and feeling a little of her anger return. She was supposed to be competent to be in charge of these children, and here was damning evidence to the contrary — suppose it got back to Macleish? And the boy's parents wouldn't be best pleased either . . . There was nothing to be done with his clothes except thoroughly wash them, and there was no chance of that out here. He was damp with mud if not thoroughly wet, and might catch cold. And the schedule of their trip wasn't complete yet; there was an indoor visitors' centre in the park and she doubted if he would even be allowed in there, smelly and squelching as he was. Damn, damn . . .

Ben's eyes looked into hers.

"Sorry," he said. And then in a whisper, "I've spoilt it all, haven't I?"

She half shook her head; and remembering the wild rage that had filled her, could not escape a feeling that it was she who had done that.

8

WELL, things could have been worse, Carol told herself when she got home that evening.

At the wildfowl park's visitors' centre a kindly guide had done wonders with paper towels, dried Ben's trainers on a radiator, and generally made both Ben and his teacher feel better — perhaps chiefly by conveying that what had happened was not so unusual. And back at school she had managed to find some tracksuit bottoms and a sweatshirt in the PE cupboard and had Ben change into them while she scraped off the worst of the now dried mud from his clothes and packed them in a carrier bag for him to take home together with a note to his parents from herself. She had phrased it carefully, at once apologizing, explaining exactly what had happened, and skirting the question of blame for Ben's sake. From what she had heard of his home life, it seemed quite happy; but you could never be sure that there wasn't some tyrannical belt-wielding parent who would make a child's life hell if he came home bearing a reproof from the school. And she had only met a few of her class's parents as yet: the children were of an age to go home by themselves rather than being collected at the gate, and thankfully the fashion for having parents help in the classroom had not reached Dunmarket. She hoped it never would. It was very nice in theory, but on a practical level she thought it was about as sensible as having your relatives assisting the surgeon while you had your appendix out.

Best of all, Macleish hadn't been around when they got back to Templeton Juniors, being closeted with a school supplier, an exercise which engaged all his penny-pinching attention. The story would probably come to his ears, but it would be second-hand, and that was a lot better than having him see one of her class returning from a school trip looking as if he had just completed an assault course.

So all in all it was probably best to

forget about it. But as she roamed about her flat doing some more than usually distracted tidying-up Carol found that that was exactly what she couldn't do. There was the memory of her strange lapse, when the sight of Ben's giggling face had made something snap inside her. That was disturbing indeed, all the more so because there was nothing to be done about it; it had come over her entirely without warning and she could see no way of preparing herself for its happening again. And beyond that there was the consciousness of not having done her job properly. She was a perfectionist, and the more she thought about it the more it seemed to her that sending Ben home with his clothes in a bag and an apologetic note was simply not good enough. Either she accepted her responsibilities or she didn't.

She was aware that her inability to let things lie had cost her some pains in the past. At college she would retype an entire essay because she had missed out one minor point in the middle and would not countenance the expedient of scribbling it in the margin with an arrow.

She had once very nearly got her arm stuck fast inside a postbox, trying to retrieve a Christmas card — moments after posting it she had realized that she had omitted one member of the family from her greeting. It was a problem she had, fair enough: something to do with a need for control, all right. But she couldn't help it. And she couldn't settle, thinking of what had happened today. Ben seemed to have got over his upset, his parents would probably cluck their tongues or even laugh it off, and her professional competence was not really at issue. But none of this was sure enough, not for her.

She picked up the phone book. There was only one Yeomans listed, and the address was definitely his — she had looked it up in her class records when trying to establish where she had seen him before. (It wasn't nearby — the other side of the town.) She got as far as dialling the number before realizing that this wasn't good enough either.

Carol threw her half-cooked supper in the bin and went out.

Visiting parents at home was all right,

but she knew that strictly you were supposed to phone first. But that was precisely what she wanted to avoid. If they were all sweet reason on the phone, they would surely say she needn't bother to call round — which would be letting her off the hook again. Ditto if they wanted to bawl her out — the phone would be her shield. It was face to face or nothing. Driving over the river bridge, Carol recalled Aunt Jean's amused reaction to her conscientious fits: "Have you robbed a bank?" she'd say. "I just wondered. You must have done something to deserve such punishment."

It was a cold evening of smoky shadows: a greenish brightness was still visible on the skyline but in the hollow of the town, mist was already forming and the lights of the centre were like hazy blooms. The Yeomans' home was down near the railway station, in a little dead-end street of terraced late-Victorian houses with slate roofs and miniature bay windows, the sort that were originally run up to accommodate railway workers. In a more chic place than Dunmarket they would have been snapped up and gentrified, but here they remained pretty much as they had always been, modestly comfortable housing for the modestly comfortable. One or two were run-down: one looked to have been renovated a good deal. The roof slates were new and there were new double-glazed windows: the front door had been stripped for repainting. The number had been removed in the process, and it was only by looking at the numbers of the adjoining houses that Carol worked out that this was the Yeomanses' house.

Now that she was here she wondered what she would say. "I'm Carol Halstead, Ben's teacher." That was all very well for a start, except that once outside the school — in civvies, as it were — she didn't feel much like a teacher. Not with the authority and solidity of identity that that implied. She felt more conscious in this situation of being young — almost certainly younger than Ben's parents — and inexperienced, to say nothing of being a stranger to Dunmarket and not very tall. More like a negligent babysitter than a teacher.

Not very tall — where had that come

from? It was years since she had let that get to her. There were limits to self-deprecation. She parked her car behind a white Transit van, stepped out and went briskly up to the stripped front door.

"Hello!"

It was none other than Ben himself who opened the door to her knock — a simple unsurprising fact which none the less found her totally unprepared. He in turn looked amazed to see her on his own doorstep, but pleased too.

"Hello, Ben. Are your mum and dad at home?"

"Who is it, Benny?" a woman's voice called from somewhere inside the house.

"It's my teacher from school!" he hollered out, smiling shyly at Carol.

She braced herself as there were footsteps down the hall and a woman appeared behind Ben wiping her hands on a tea towel.

"Well, don't let her stand out there in the cold," the woman said, ruffling Ben's hair and offering Carol a smile. "Come in, will you? Come through to the kitchen. Geoff's making a racket in the front."

She led Carol down the hall to a large, warm kitchen, cluttered and oddly shaped but with new pine units and a bright colour scheme of yellow and Wedgwood blue. A canary hopped about a hanging cage and there was a large bowl of goldfishes. Drawings instantly recognizable as Ben's covered the refrigerator and had overflowed on to the walls.

"I'm sorry to spring up on you like this," Carol said, "and I hope I haven't come at an awkward time. My name's Carol Halstead, by the way. If you're having your tea — "

"Oh, this isn't ready yet," Ben's mother said, turning down the flame under a bubbling pan. "I don't know if it'll be fit to eat when it is, I mean I followed the recipe but somehow these things never . . . Geoff!" She darted into the hall and threw open a door from behind which there came sounds of hammering. "Geoff, knock it off a minute, will you? There's Ben's teacher here. Listen," she said coming back, "I'm sorry if he spoilt things today. I mean all I can say is I don't think he meant any harm, but obviously we do need to talk about it if he is acting up a lot, and thanks ever so much for finding him some britches and that, I'll wash and iron them and have him bring them back — "

"No, no," Carol said, "it's not that at all, I came because I wanted to apologize, you know, for sending him home in that state. I thought I ought to come and — "

"God, no," Ben's mother said with a shout of laughter, before Carol could finish. "He's come home in a worse mess than that many a time. Like I say, he doesn't mean any harm — at least, I *think* he doesn't. He just gets so wrapped up in things. Not that that's any excuse, is it, Ben?"

"No, Mum," Ben said, seemingly not at all put out.

"No, Mum. That's right." Ben's mother investigated the bubbling pot, made a dubious face. "I don't know about this. You're welcome to stay and have some but I can't swear you won't end up poisoned."

"Oh, that's kind of you, I've eaten, thanks. I don't want to keep you. I just wanted to — well, come and see you . . . "

"I'm glad you did. My name's Elaine, by the way. No, it's nice to meet you at last. I feel like I half know you anyway. Ben's always talking about you. Have a job to shut him up sometimes. I said to him tonight, this teacher you're so stuck on isn't going to be too keen on you if you mess her about like this."

"Oh no," Carol said, feeling absurdly pleased and shy, "it was just an accident. Ben's never given any trouble before, in fact he's a pleasure to teach."

"We can't be talking about the same Ben."

The words came from behind Carol and she jumped a little, turning. The man who spoke them gave a broad grin, as if to say he was only teasing. "This is the famous Miss Halstead, is it?" he went on. He was holding a hammer in his right hand and he switched it to the left before shaking hands with her.

"Carol."

"So, what's the story? What else has he done that he hasn't told us about?"

"Nothing at all. I just wanted to

apologize, because it must have been worrying, him coming back like that. You must have wondered what the teacher was playing at."

"Nah. Don't get me wrong, I'd be the first to complain if I thought my lad wasn't being taken proper care of when he's at school. But I get the picture all right in this case. Ben playing silly beggars. Right, Ben?"

Ben nodded. Carol studied him covertly. He looked abashed, but not frightened.

"Sit down, sit down," Ben's mother said, "we'll have a cup of tea."

"Well, I don't want to intrude . . . "

"That's not likely — like I say, Ben's always full of you."

"Yes, come on, have a seat." Ben's father motioned her to a chair at the kitchen table with a sort of old-fashioned courtliness that reminded her a little of Martin. He was a big man too, but rather gaunt and stooped: though only ten years her senior at the most, there was a heavy, man-of-the-house deliberateness about him. Still curiously shy, Carol did not look into his face much, but she fleetingly traced a resemblance to

Ben despite the neatly trimmed beard and light receding hair: something in the darkness of the eyes, and maybe the smile.

Elaine was recognizably Ben's mother too, though family resemblances were mysterious and elusive things, often difficult to pin down to a single feature. She was tall and thirtyish too, but quick and mercurial where her husband was deliberate. The check workshirt and the hammer and the weighty manner gave the impression that Geoff Yeomans was a man very comfortable with traditional sex roles, but there was nothing of the Stepford Wife about Elaine. Her reddish hair was cut in a no-frills bob and she had a lively, narrow, mobile face with a touch of devilment about the bright kohl-rimmed eyes. Her skin was noticeably pale and tender-looking, as if she were prone to eczema. Slender and loose-limbed in jeans and a vast pullover, large earrings swinging, she clattered deftly about the kitchen, singing out for Ben to help her in an unselfconscious comic falsetto. Carol tried not to be nosy but it was natural to measure up the home of one of your pupils, and everything she saw fitted. Ben was interested in a lot of things, and plainly that was an attitude fostered here: the kitchen surfaces were covered with everything from model aeroplanes to birdseed to 78 rpm records. But there was a feeling of security too amongst the chaos.

"So he's doing all right at school, then, this one?" Ben's father said, hand-rolling a cigarette.

"Yes, Ben's adapted to the junior curriculum very well. I'm very pleased with his project work. There'll be a parents' evening in December, and hopefully you'll see it then."

"Oh yes, we'll be there."

"Give us a date for that," Elaine said, hunting for a piece of paper. "I'll make sure I'm not working. I'm on nights, you see. At Buddleigh Lodge."

"Oh, where's that?"

"Just the other side of the bridge. Old folks' home. Three nights a week I have the pleasure of mopping up wee and making sure they don't set fire to themselves."

"It's not ideal," Geoff Yeomans said,

with a little constraint. "Won't be for ever. I'm a painter and decorator," he told Carol. "Ipswich firm. They're not the best. It'll be better when I start up on my own."

"Right, what's that date?"

"Tuesday the tenth. Seven o'clock," Carol said.

"I think I'll be free. We're on rotation, see, I'll have to check. You must be new to Dunmarket, then?"

"Yes. I only moved here just before term started." Apologetically she added, perhaps because her presence here seemed to need some further explanation, "It's my first teaching post, actually. So it's all as new to me as to Ben in a way."

"Everyone has to start somewhere," Geoff said seriously, his heavy brows knitted. "I'd sooner trust my kid with somebody young and up to date than these old fogies you get in some places. Some of the teachers I had when I was a nipper just weren't fit for the job, do you know what I'm saying? Just old bullies who'd lost their marbles. Mind you, I'm not saying you should treat kids too soft. Only there's different ways of doing it.

So where are you from, then?"

"London originally."

"Snap," Elaine said. "Oh, I know Ben's got the local accent, but he was born here. We came here when we were first married. My uncle moved out here with the overspill thing years ago and he talked us into it."

"Best move we ever made," Geoff said. "I wouldn't bring up a kid in London nowadays."

"No," Carol said, "I know what you mean."

"I wouldn't mind seeing that Collingham place myself," he went on. "The steam museum, I mean. I'm into old machines and things like that. Military history — that's my thing. Read up on it a fair bit, you know. I've got a fair little collection now. Have a look."

He took her with a sort of cumbrous eagerness into the living room, where a small collection of books, chiefly on the world wars, was neatly shelved in an alcove. "Learn a lot from these," he said, taking volumes out and leafing through them and then carefully replacing them. "Not a lot of practical use, you know, but still . . . the way things happened and everything . . . "

There was something oddly touching about this big dour man inarticulately trying to express his enthusiasm: perhaps it reminded her of Ben. In the opposite alcove there was evidence of another of his enthusiasms, a half-finished bar, which he had been working on when she called.

"Yes, I've done most of the work on this place myself," he said, solemn and sheepish.

"That's why we have to put the washing in the toilet and wear rubber gloves when we switch the lights on," Elaine said, slipping her arm round his waist.

He gripped her to him, laughing. It was a low metallic laugh, a little harsh. Ben, squatting on the floor, chuckled too and aimed the remote at the TV. "There was that time when the lawnmower blew up, Dad," he said.

"Ah, that was the parts," Geoff said. "Only a tiny part about the size of your finger. Couldn't get the right one, so I tried something that was near enough. It *wasn't* enough, though. Nearly blew me — me wig off with that one. Wouldn't believe it, would you?"

"Well, I've got something like that with my flat. A window-catch came off. It doesn't look like the landlords will ever get round to repairing it so I've been trying to find a replacement catch. I've tried the big DIY stores in Ipswich, builders' merchants. And no one's ever seen anything like it."

"Who's your landlords?" Geoff said.

"Axton Housing."

Geoff grimaced. "Cowboys. We did a painting job for them once. They skimp on everything. So you can't have the window open?"

"No, but the cold weather's setting in now anyway, so — "

"I'll have a look at that for you."

"Oh, no, I — I couldn't let you do that — "

"Nah, no trouble. I'm not promising, but I can fix most things, can't I, love?"

"It's true," Elaine said. "I hate to admit it, but it's true."

"Soon as I get a free day. Will you be

here this weekend?"

"No, I'm going to be in London this weekend, but really, you don't have to — "

"Next weekend then. Yeah?"

"Well . . . it's very kind of you. If you're sure it's no trouble . . . "

"Course not. Give us a note of where you live. That's the thing about living in a place like Dunmarket, you see. People help each other out more. It's the way it should be. Anyway, it's the least I can do to make up for Benny here and his shenanigans. What are you like, Ben, eh? What are you like?" He bent to tickle his son's ribs, and Ben yelped with laughter.

Carol gave them her address. "Well, I'd better not keep you from your tea any longer," she said, making ready to go.

"Oh, no, I'm just putting off the awful moment," Elaine said. "Well, it was nice meeting you at last."

"Yes, thanks for taking the trouble to come, that was good of you," Geoff said, looming over Carol with his hard smile and shaking her hand again. His teeth were large and a little stained from tobacco.

"It was right what Ben was saying," Elaine said, studying her. "He kept going on about how pretty his new teacher is. And it's true as well, you cow."

"Oh — dear," Carol said laughing in confusion. "Well, he's normally very good with words, but I think he's got the wrong one there."

They saw her out at the door and watched her to her car, Ben waving and Geoff calling out, "Weekend after next, then?" Nice people, she thought; and everything had turned out better than she had hoped. Geoff's offer to fix her window had made her a little uncomfortable — she hoped to God it hadn't seemed as if she were fishing for it; but as he said, that was the sort of place Dunmarket was.

And it was good to make contact with parents. She certainly felt like a grown-up person again, instead of that cringing babysitter. The tight-wound tension of this long day seemed finally to leave her.

It might have been something to

do with that, or it might have been something to do with the combination of an empty stomach and the smell of cooking at the Yeomanses', which had been highly spicy. Something, at any rate, made her begin to feel queasy. By the time she parked outside Stour Court, the feeling had gone beyond queasiness, and she only just made it to her bathroom.

After being sick she washed her face, then made herself eat some dry toast to settle her stomach. It stayed down, which was promising. She didn't fancy TV tonight, and sat down to listen to some music. Her record collection was extremely eclectic — jazz was her only blind spot — but tonight after hunting through a stack of CDs she found she couldn't decide on anything.

She sat back, knees up, head against the sofa, and interrogated herself. She had suffered from frequent migraines in her teens: they had become rare occurences now but she still knew the symptoms, and wondered if this was behind it. Nausea was a classic indication. So was photophobia, which was maybe why she hadn't wanted to look at TV. And so was a generalized, unplaceable feeling of malaise and unease.

And she had that: she definitely had that. A headache would complete the classic pattern, but there was no sign of it.

What about *déjà vu*? she wondered. Could that figure amongst the symptoms of migraine? Maybe. Dr Kaufman would probably know. She could call him, but it was a trivial thing to ask about; and she didn't feel up to talking any more. That short visit to the Yeomanses' seemed to have exhausted her.

After another three-quarters of an hour, during which she couldn't settle to anything and the feeling of unease continued to crawl over her skin like a slow cloud-shadow, she took two aspirins and went to bed. There was still no headache, but it was best to be on the safe side, and she was doing herself no good being up.

She had no trouble sleeping: it came with wonderful limb-lifting swiftness, as if she were a small child after a day at the seaside.

But at three-fifteen in the morning she woke up screaming, and as she lay back panting against the crushed pillows Carol realized that she had had the bird dream for the first time in her adult life.

9

GOING from the country to London for the weekend was not the traditional restorative of health. It was supposed to work the other way. But Carol, setting out on Saturday morning to visit Aunt Jean, had hopes of it.

She had, after all, had an exhausting few months, exhausting in their intensity as well as in their physical demands. Not only the job was new but the place too: the two were intertwined. A change of scene was needed. Soldiers didn't take R and R at the front, she reasoned.

The analogy was far-fetched, she realized, but the need was real. The malaise that had come over her the night after the school trip did not develop into any illness disabling enough to keep her from work, but an oppressive feeling of unease lingered through the following days. And then there was the bird dream. It only occurred once, but that once was enough profoundly to trouble if not alarm her. As Dr Kaufman had said, sleep was her litmus paper, an infallible indicator of her mental and emotional state. Throughout her younger years equilibrium had been for Carol the distant goal, the Celestial City that she must overcome toil and trouble to reach. It was precious and any threat to it was not to be lightly dismissed. Constant interior watchfulness: that was the way she lived.

And so though there was no more nausea and no more nightmares, and even the lurking feeling of distress and unresolved tension might well be no more than the onset of her period, Carol did not try to put the whole thing out of her mind. She acknowledged it and accommodated it and looked on the visit to Aunt Jean not only as a positive pleasure but an opportunity, perhaps the very safety valve her body and mind were demanding. Serendipity.

She also hoped, time permitting, to drop in on Dr Kaufman while she was in London. But she didn't intend speaking to him about what had happened the other night. Though he had treated her as a child and as an adolescent and had informally counselled her all her life, she wanted to think of him as a friend, not use him as a continual sounding-board for her passing frailties. She guessed that he probably wouldn't mind that a bit, but she found it distasteful all the same. Taking the other night's episode seriously was different from blowing it out of proportion. The sweetest thing about living in the Celestial City was being a person instead of a patient.

London hit her with its usual mix of sensations. Until she had gone away to college, she had never been aware of the city as an entity at all: it was just life. Residence away confirmed its brilliant oddness, which struck her again as the train laboriously penetrated to the heart of it. Even a few months in Dunmarket had accustomed her to a different scale. Really this place was like a small nation-state. It was a place that you could get lost in and never be found.

She began her visit with rituals, perhaps because she was seeking to establish as much familiarity as possible, knowing that she might find things changed at Aunt Jean's. At Liverpool Street she bought flowers, as she always used to when visiting from college: coming out of the Tube at the Oval, she made a diversion to a nearby store where they sold Asian snack foods by weight and, as she always used to, bought Aunt Jean a pound of the special hot gram that she liked to nibble while she watched TV.

Going home. There was something different about your gait as you approached an old home, Carol thought, even if it was one you had left. Somehow you walked as if you had a right to be there. Sometimes too, as now, you got a lump in your throat.

This old home was special, of course: it had been made for her. She had not been born into it and grown up in it as of right. It was a testament to Aunt Jean's own special qualities that Carol had never been conscious of that.

Uncle Keith too, of course. Carol wondered how he was doing and reproached herself for not writing recently. Jean and Keith's had been on the whole a happy marriage with at the end of it a divorce that was as near to happy as such a thing could be. Perhaps their managing to marry at all was such an achievement that everything afterwards was a bonus. Carol's maternal grandparents had been appallingly prim and conventional people. They wanted the best for their daughters — meaning, Aunt Jean once said, that they would have sold them to the devil if he lived in Reigate and dressed nicely. Aunt Jean had disappointed them by rebelling, or doing what she wanted to do rather than what they wanted her to do. They had sent her to college as a sort of time-filler before fulfilling her destiny by marrying a right-thinking man with lots of money, and having babies. Instead Jean had walked out of college into the arms of Keith Halstead, who was wrong-thinking, had no money, and was a musician who played the sort of instruments you plugged in rather than treated with resin. He was nobody's idea of a wild man — a little fey and eccentric was as far as it went — and as time went on he made a reasonable living as a session musician: he was even the composer of an advertising jingle that everyone knew and that yielded enough royalties to pay the bills for the house in Kennington that they moved into after a succession of bedsits and flats. Jean meanwhile took correspondence courses, did volunteer work for the Citizens' Advice Bureau, and eventually worked her way up to fully paid-up manageress. It made no difference: her parents didn't uncurl their lips for a moment. Even the Citizens' Advice Bureau, with its reputation for genteel busybodying, did not please because of its clientele — people with problems were sure to be not nice.

Jean never made a big issue of this parental disdain. But Carol knew that it was a source of unhappiness to her, right up until the time her grandparents fastidiously died within a few weeks of each other, when she was twelve; and probably beyond. Straightforward guilt, Jean said; but it couldn't be entirely straightforward, as she once tentatively admitted, because of Jean's sister, Carol's mother. She was the younger sister, and the pressure on her to turn out well was all the greater once they had washed thei hands of Jean. "Of course I couldn't have known what was going to happen," Jean said. "But there's no getting away from it, I made life tougher on her. And her life was short. That's not a thing you can shrug off."

At any rate the marriage that had caused so much grief was more successful than most. When Carol was orphaned as a child there was immediate agreement between Jean and Keith that they would adopt their niece: they were comfortably circumstanced by then, they had no children of their own, and Carol's grandparents were too frail and self-absorbed to look after her. The home they gave her was a harmonious one, and when Uncle Keith moved out when she was fourteen the event was not traumatic. They had decided to call it a day: Keith had realized he was gay, a little later than Jean had realized it, as it happened. "I should have known before," she confided in Carol later. "I always got on so well with him, he could cook and look after himself, he was considerate and he was bloody good-looking. He had gay written all over him." They had considered staying together anyway, then decided they'd better each spread their wings while they were still up to it. Uncle Keith had moved only as far as Chiswick and they still saw a lot of him. Jean had kept her married name, Halstead — the name Carol had taken when they adopted her. Her birth certificate read Carol Mitcheson, but publicity had attached to that name when she was orphaned and there was no knowing at the time how long it would last.

It was only when Carol went to college that she began to lose touch a little with Uncle Keith: he was away touring a lot as an accompanist to cabaret performers, and though their letters and phone calls were warm they were sporadic. But this was a fair reflection of the fact that the greatest influence on Carol's life — or what she thought of as her second life — was Jean alone. Dr Kaufman had done much to refashion the splintered fragments of a personality that had resulted from her orphaning, but he would be the first to understand that in a profound sense she owed Jean everything. And this was not altered by the fact that Jean's creed was that you owed her nothing.

And now Jean had embarked on a new relationship — serious, it seemed. There had been a man-friend or two after the break-up with Keith, but nothing had lasted very long and Jean had seemed to like her life just as it was. Solitude did not trouble her — so she had frequently assured Carol on her departure for educational college, when the thought of leaving her aunt alone had brought Carol quite genuinely to the brink of giving the whole thing up. In the end Jean had had to use a persuasion she plainly did not like using, but which was unanswerable. "Carol," she'd said, taking her hands, "at some point in your life you're going to have to leave someone you love to their own devices, and just trust that they'll be safe." She had squeezed Carol's hands tightly, looking into her eyes. "To live in the world at all, you've got to do that. They would say the same if they were here. I know that for sure."

And Jean had certainly seemed entirely comfortable living alone: she had, as she said, her little ways, such as tightening the taps to snapping point before going to bed in case of a flood and never throwing away a newspaper. "Keith put up with them and you put up with them," she said. "Three would be pushing it."

It was about the time of Carol's graduation that she first heard the name of Brendan, and shortly after she had moved to Dunmarket Jean came clean. "My toyboy," she laughingly referred to him: she was forty-nine and he fifteen years younger. It wasn't much of a gap, as Carol, perceiving a faint anxiety in the way Jean kept repeating the joke, had hastened to reassure her; and then felt a hypocrite. Because she had thought it *was* a large age-gap when Jean first told her; and had found herself mistrusting this Brendan on grounds that were wholly ignoble. Put crudely, she wondered what he was after. Which was contemptible of her: it was wholly understandable for a man of any age to fall in love with Jean, and for her part Jean was the last woman in the world to be vulnerable to a blue-eyed charmer. Carol's reaction, in fact, was an insult to everybody, Jean and Brendan, men and women, young and old. She knew it. She was ashamed; and now that Brendan had moved in she was fiercely vigilant against allowing the thought, *That was fast work*, to enter her head.

It was going to be strange, sure, she thought, as she turned the corner into the street where Jean and now somebody called Brendan lived. But it would be strange for Jean too, and the important thing was that Jean should not be made uncomfortable. Any prejudices still hanging around, Carol told herself, get rid of them right now.

The housing madness of the eighties had passed over the neighbourhood where Jean lived and had departed, leaving an odd assortment of gutted shells, houses converted gorgeously and so beyond their worth as to be unsaleable, and a few homes like Jean's standing untouched like the freak survivors of an earthquake. Probably because of the topiary-fenced rigidity of her suburban upbringing, Jean didn't give a damn for outward show. The front garden was a miniature wilderness of thistles, the window-frames were peeling, the knocker had come off the front door and the bell had stopped working years ago. This latter shouldn't really have mattered because Carol still had her own key; indeed her hand was instinctively feeling for it in her pocket when she suddenly stopped.

Someone else lived here now: she must remember that. Of course, it wasn't a thing she was likely to forget, and it had been in the back of her mind all the way here. But the business of the key reminded her how careful she would have to be.

Home: but not really. She knocked, and wondered for the first time whether this was a good idea.

10

SHE must have taken some prejudices in with her after all, because when Brendan turned out to be nice she was surprised.

And then instantly ashamed again, naturally. Didn't she trust Jean's judgement? Did she suppose Jean would pick anyone who wasn't nice? Of course that argument only went so far. She herself had fallen for a complete rat on first arriving at college. Thankfully she had got out early, but there was no doubt that she would have jumped in the river for him while it lasted.

But Brendan didn't appear to be a rat. Nor did he look much younger than Jean, perhaps because his hair had thinned considerably. With his stocky build and round close-cropped head he might have been taken for a wrestler, but his voice was curiously at odds with his physical presence. It was a soft hesitant tenor, and the effect when he spoke was almost ventriloquial.

Aunt Jean hugged Carol when she answered the door. This was not usual: they didn't normally go in for hugs. She didn't mention Carol not using the key. Other than that, everything was unchanged. A bottle of Niersteiner was produced and the three of them sat in the sitting room and drank it while Jean and Carol talked and Brendan put in the odd word here and there, sitting slightly forward with his elbows on his knees, not shy or bored but with a sort of patient discretion.

"You look well," Aunt Jean said, when the first bubbling spate of talk was over.

"So do you," Carol said.

It was true: always willowy, Jean had put on just a little weight and it suited her. She had lightly crimped her long fine fair hair and that suited her too. She was dressed in her usual style with carved necklaces and bracelets, long tasselled skirt and soft leather boots. Brendan's eyes were often on her, with what seemed an entirely comprehensible warmth and admiration. Every now and then he excused himself to go to the kitchen, and each time there was a waft of rich herby cooking.

"He's a smashing cook," Jean said to her one of these times, dropping her voice. "It's quite exciting wondering what you're going to have for dinner every day. Oh, I know that won't last," she added with a wink. "But it's nice."

"So I hear you're a — a tree surgeon," Carol said when he came back.

"It's all right, you're allowed to laugh," he said smiling. "That's the only trouble with the job, there isn't a reasonable name for it. Arboriculturist is a bit of a mouthful. And if you say tree feller it reminds people of the joke about the two Irishmen who saw an advert saying Tree Fellers Wanted and they said that's a pity, there's only two of us."

There was something almost sleepy about the way he talked, and about his slow nerveless movements: Carol was reminded of a late-summer bee drunk with pollen. Aunt Jean had always had something similar about her, though in her case it took the form of a cool relaxation and poise. Carol had long envied it, knowing she lacked it, and with Brendan there she began to be a little more conscious of the lack, of the contrast between her and this couple.

Couple: that was what they were, of course. It was remarkable how quickly she took it for granted. There was no sign of Brendan's presence in the room except for Brendan himself; none of the crowded, colourful, Portobello Market furnishings were altered; yet it wasn't just Aunt Jean's place any more. The two of them fitted into it.

"So how do you like Suffolk?" he asked.

"I love it. Most of it. I mean, I've only lived there since August, and I don't know what it'll be like to spend a long winter there, say. But it's nice. Friendly. I suppose it wouldn't suit everybody."

"It would suit me," he said.

"Brendan's a country-lover," Jean said. "He's been trying unsuccessfully to convert me to long walks in the freezing cold."

"It's not cold yet," he said. They smiled at each other.

Of course, there was no formula for this, Carol thought. Jean wasn't her mother, though she had acted as such for the last fifteen years; and the love Carol felt for her, though quite as deep, was coloured by mature elements of friendship that she doubted would ever be fully present between a mother and daughter. The house was not her home, though it had been until recently, and there was a bedroom upstairs that was still called hers. A certain confusion was inevitable, not only in her emotions but in the matter of how to behave: she felt like a guest and when she needed to go to the toilet it was actually on her lips to say, "All right if I use the loo?" Instead she found herself getting up and announcing the fact that she was going to the toilet, a compromise that didn't make any sense at all.

Returning past the kitchen door she caught another waft of cooking. For a moment the sensation of nausea she had experienced on leaving the Yeomanses' house hit her again and she wondered if she was going to be able to eat. Or was this another undeveloped migraine? That would be a disaster.

Her glass had been refilled in her

absence. She drank quickly, and the wine helped. She told some stories of her first weeks' teaching, and there was laughter. She was feeling more relaxed when Brendan went to dish up the meal, though she still felt curiously shy of meeting Jean's eyes.

"Oh, how did your school trip go, by the way?"

"Pretty good. Well, there was a bit of a hitch. Ben, that's one of my class, went a bit AWOL in the wildfowl park and ended up covered in mud and nearly giving me a heart attack."

"What, your Ben?" Jean said in surprise.

"Er — Ben Yeomans his name is, yes. One of my lot." Carol looked her puzzlement.

"Oh, it's just that I feel like I know him. He's the one you're always telling me about."

" . . . Am I?"

"You must have a favourite without knowing it. He always sounds a dear kid, which is why I was surprised. Was he all right?"

"Oh, just filthy dirty and a bit sorry

for himself. I don't think he meant any harm. He just gets so wrapped up in things that he doesn't think . . . " The memory of Ben, besmirched and dripping, giggling in that high gleeful way, came to her with an indefinably unpleasant sharpness. She put her wine glass down, suddenly not fancying it. Migraine or period, she thought. Either that or a miraculous conception.

"Well, these things are bound to happen. I can't even begin to imagine ferrying thirty kids around. I think I'd feel I'd done well if I came back with half of them."

"His parents were very understanding about it." Just don't think about being sick, she told herself. Just don't think about it and it won't happen.

"Are you all right, love? You look a bit peaky."

"Oh, I'm fine, thanks. Just the time of the month, I think. That smells good, doesn't it? It must be lovely to be able to cook, I'm still as hopeless at it as ever. He's very nice, isn't he? He reminds me of an actor off the TV, but I can't for the life of me think who . . . "

Aunt Jean gave her a close, kind look. "Thanks, Carol."

"What for?"

"For being good about it. It's awkward — no, no, I don't mean it shows at all, not in you. Brendan's nervous as well, though you might not guess it. He knows where he stands and where you and I stand."

"Does he know about . . . ?"

"Only that they died. That's all he needs to know." The kitchen was at the end of a long passage and Jean's voice was habitually quiet and husky, but she lowered it further. "He knows who comes first, anyway."

"Oh, Jean, that shouldn't be — "

"Maybe. Just is. I can't very well say I don't care what you think when I do. D'you know, when I left home my parents got a dog. Straight away. They hadn't before because I was scared of them. Natural, I suppose. But the phrase that sprang to mind was 'unseemly haste'. And that's what I didn't want you to think, about Brendan moving in here. All I can say is it just seemed the right thing."

"You look happy," Carol said. "That's all that matters."

All of a sudden something — perhaps the reinstated warmth between them — made Carol want to say to Aunt Jean, "I had the bird dream again." Just that: she didn't feel the need for any sort of feedback or reassurance, she didn't even feel that the matter was very important. It was just something that pressed on her, like a finger on a bruise, impossible not to respond to.

She opened her mouth to speak, and then Brendan came in to tell them the meal was ready.

She found to her relief that the queasiness had passed, and she was hungry after all. The food, pasta with meatballs, was good if nothing to get excited about, and the meal passed pleasantly enough. Carol found much to like and nothing to dislike in Brendan, except perhaps when Jean happened to mention Uncle Keith.

"He's abroad again, did you know? Cabaret. He's doing the arrangements for that singer, you know the one, he won the Eurovision thing."

"Christ," Brendan said, "how many ways can you arrange 'You Are The Sunshine of My Life'?"

It seemed subtly wrong that he should speak so familiarly, dismissively even, of a man who as far as Carol knew he had never even met. It was none of her business, she supposed; just as it was none of her business that the rickety shelves with their hoards of knick-knacks that had covered the dining-room wall had been taken down and replaced with a set of dull bird prints.

In the evening the three of them walked down to the local pub. Everyone seemed to know Brendan there. It was a smoky noisy evening and there really wasn't much chance for her to talk to Jean. Feeling out of sorts, she tried with a sort of desperate obviousness to be good company. Soon Brendan, who drank beer with a steady inexcitable relish, began to demonstrate pub tricks with matches and empty glasses. Jean, presumably, had seen them before but made apparently spontaneous responses of amusement. Carol found herself thinking about Martin Culler and the way she found talking with him effortless, as absorbing and entertaining in itself as a good film.

And then she caught herself up sharp and told herself, sternly, that it really *was* none of her business. Brendan was not her type but he was not meant to be her type, he was meant to be Aunt Jean's and there was no doubt that she was enjoying herself. She looked young and animated in his company. This time Carol took the warning to heart, and it prevented her answering him back when Brendan leant over and said in her ear, "Lighten up, Carol. You're not in the classroom now."

The evening seemed to go on for ever, but it ended at last. They walked home, Brendan doing a peg-leg dance along the gutter. Carol felt tired and owl-eyed and wondered if she would be able to slip up to bed without appearing rude. It was not a question that would have occurred to her before, but circumstances had changed. When you were a guest you had obligations.

Brendan seemed to regret his comment in the pub. Back home he whipped up sandwiches and pressed her to eat, fussing over her a bit. Of course, Carol thought, it couldn't be easy for him either. His position was every bit as awkward as hers, perhaps more so: he had to live in the shadow of an older loyalty. But she couldn't help resenting that element of watchfulness about him. It was as if he had her typed from the start as a possessive disapproving daughter, or stepdaughter, and were continually daring her to be a killjoy and confirm it for him. That was why she forced down the sandwiches even though she wasn't hungry. She wasn't going to give him the opportunity to say to Jean later that he had tried everything with that girl but nothing pleased her.

Jean, a little tipsy, lay back on the sitting-room settee and beckoned him to pull off her boots for her. "Come on, slave," she said, looking flushed, supremely relaxed, even radiant. "Chop chop. Do your duties."

Brendan knelt to remove the boots, massaging her feet as he did so. He had large white well-shaped hands, with hair that extended past the knuckles and almost to the cuticles.

"Like blocks of ice," he said, rubbing.

"Always are. Ooh, that's nice." Jean had always had bad circulation. She had a feline love of heat and was comfortable when everyone else sweltered.

"I'm going to get to work on that radiator in the bedroom next weekend. I don't know how you've managed with it so long. I'll tell you another thing: as soon as we get a weekend free I think we should drive up to Suffolk, see Carol. Show you that Watford's not the end of the world." He turned round. "Carol?"

"Oh yes, that'd be great," Carol said. At the last moment she saw that he was actually offering to take her boots off for her, and it was too late now to withdraw her assent. Uncomfortably she extended her feet and he undid the laces, then slowly pulled the boots off. For a moment she was afraid he was going to massage her feet too, but instead he sat back on his haunches, carefully rearranging the tongues, and said, "I'll clean these up for you in the morning."

"Oh no, you don't have to do that . . . "

"No, let him, Carol," Jean said woozily. "Take advantage of it. He's very domesticated. I think he must be this New Man they keep talking about."

"I was wondering where he was," Carol said, and Brendan smiled. He did have an attractive smile. Jean plainly loved him. It was all right.

"If that's OK, I should say," Brendan said. "Coming up to see you in Suffolk, I mean."

"Of course, yes. You're welcome to stay at my place, there's — "

"No, no. We'll stay in a hotel," Brendan said.

"Well, whatever's best for you," Carol said, glancing at Jean; then felt impatient with herself. Yes, it was 'we': of course it was. It was not a big deal. As the kids at her school were always saying, get a life.

A yawn from Brendan gave her the opportunity to do likewise and head for bed. "You two go on up," he said. "I'll just clear away down here." Jean extended a limp hand, and he pulled her half-asleep off the settee and steered her towards the stairs.

Carol followed. "After you," she said to Jean with a smile. "I'll catch you if you fall."

"You might have to," Jean said drowsily, and in the same happy floating way began to ascend.

Living in a contemporary building as she did now, Carol had quickly forgotten how narrow and steep the stairs could be in these older houses, even a roomy place like Jean's. She put her foot on the bottom stair and looked up.

Suddenly she couldn't move. The upward perspective was like a dark funnel and an abrupt terror possessed her, a terror that was inexplicable until a memory suddenly attached itself to it. A memory of her first coming here to live after her parents' death, and how she had been frightened of going up these stairs despite all the gentle urging of Aunt Jean and Uncle Keith. It was something to do with the dark mystery at the top, not being able to see the landing, not knowing what might be there beyond the turning . . .

She passed a hand over her face. What was happening? Her life had been an

exercise in putting the past behind her
— indeed it had been a condition of her
achieving any sort of life at all. To have
it intruding on her mind like this was not
only distressing but ominous.

Not migraine, not period. That was
certain. But nothing else was.

"They're easier on your legs if you take
them at a run," Brendan said, appearing
behind her with a washing-up cloth in
his hand.

I know. I used to live here.

She was glad she managed not to say
it. "Right," she said, and moved with a
wrenching sensation. She made it to the
top by looking down at her feet, then
gave Jean a hasty good night and darted
into her room.

It was the room that had been her
old bedroom. Jean had kept it pretty
much as it had been then, even down
to the dog-eared poster of Klimt's *Kiss*
that had been the favourite acquisition
of her adolescence. A vase of flowers had
been placed on the bedside table, just as
it always had been when she came home
from college. Carol undressed quickly
and got into bed. Everything felt strange

beyond words: her mind was like a mass of interweaved scribblings and she just wanted sleep to come and wipe it all clean.

She lay in darkness listening to the great city all around her — more an aural presence than a sound, like a murmurous roar on the edge of hearing. Its immensity seemed obscurely threatening. Country girl already, she thought: then didn't think any more.

She sat up. She was covered in sweat, and the light was on. She had no consciousness of having slept, but the bedside clock said half-past three, and Aunt Jean was beside her, kneeling by the bed in her dressing gown.

"Are you all right, Carol?"

"What . . . what's the matter?"

"You called out," Jean said. She smoothed out the duvet, stroked Carol's fringe from her forehead. "Nightmares?"

"I don't know . . . I don't remember any." Carol searched her mind. The bird dream again . . . ? But she found no fluttery, panicked images imprinted on her brain. "What did I say?"

Jean hesitated. "I think it was, 'No,

no,' but I couldn't be sure."

"Oh God, I'm sorry, did I wake Brendan?"

"No. He sleeps with earplugs in. I snore, apparently . . . Have you been sleeping OK lately?"

Carol looked at her aunt's face. Naked from sleep and without make-up, it still had a classic fineness. The eyes were naked too in their open love and concern. Jean didn't want to shirk: she wanted to be told, to help if it was possible; she was ready. And it didn't seem fair. She was happy and starting a new chapter.

"Do you think it could be something to do with the house being sold?" Jean said. "Upsetting you — reminding you. You know."

"It could be. Yes, maybe it's that. But I've been sleeping OK, really." She smiled. "Must be that Parmesan."

Again Jean hesitated. "Did you say you were going to see John Kaufman tomorrow?"

"Yes, I thought so. Just to say hello. I'm fine, really. I'd tell him if there was any real problem."

"Well. As long as you're sure."

That's just what I'm not, Carol thought after Jean had said good night again and left her. I'm not sure of anything any more.

★ ★ ★

She wakes from the bird dream and though she has tried so often, so hard not to cry out she can't help herself.

"No! No . . . !"

"Ssh. It's all right. I'm here. It was just a dream."

Auntie Jean, holding her hand tightly.

"I'm sorry." She feels ashamed. She's always doing this.

"There's nothing to be sorry about. Would you like a drink of milk?"

She shakes her head. "No thank you." Though it's so babyish, and it's mean keeping Auntie Jean out of bed, she can't let go of Auntie Jean's hand.

"Shall I stay here a little while?"

She nods.

"All right. Budge up."

Auntie Jean sits on the bed beside her and strokes her hair. Sometimes this is the only thing that can calm her down.

She likes it, but she still feels a bit ashamed: ashamed of being a person who always needs calming down, who's always getting frightened, who doesn't just go to sleep like other children. Dr Kaufman tells her she shouldn't feel that way, but she can't help it sometimes.

She remembers something.

"Auntie, Dr Kaufman got angry today."

"Did he? With you?"

"Oh no. It was about the hypnotist."

"Ah, I see. Yes, he said something to me about that."

"The hypnotist is a doctor as well, isn't he?"

"Well, yes. I think that's partly the trouble. You see, Dr Kaufman is supposed to be the doctor who's helping you. And he said he wouldn't mind hypnotism as part of your therapy — you know, the things to make you feel better? But what he doesn't like is the idea of the police getting involved in it. You know they thought you might remember something more about those boys if you were hypnotized? He thinks that would be wrong."

"I do remember those boys, though. I

told the policemen lots of times."

"I know, love. You helped them all you could."

"But they still haven't got them, have they?"

Auntie Jean shakes her head. She looks pretty, but tired and poorly. It was what happened that night that made her look like this, because Mummy was Auntie Jean's sister. They liked each other and would always ring each other up at weekends and laugh a lot.

"How long is it since Mummy and Daddy died?"

"It's about six months."

She thinks.

"I wish I had like a camera in my head."

"Do you, love?"

"Yes. Then I could show the policemen a picture of those boys."

"That would be good, yes. Never mind."

"I'd have to hurry up, though. The picture would go away after a while, wouldn't it?"

11

'YOU can't go home again': the weekend had certainly demonstrated the truth of that phrase to Carol. But the week that followed demonstrated something else, something that had happened without her being aware of it. In Dunmarket, in Templeton Junior School, in her class and her flat and Martin and Diane and even Chris Bryce, she found precisely that sense of rightness and belonging that had been missing from her visit to Kennington. At some time in the past few months her centre of self had shifted, and she had found a home.

It didn't mean, of course, that Aunt Jean was lost to her or that their relationship was fundamentally altered. But the advent of Brendan meant there had been a similar shifting on Jean's part and it was pointless both to pretend otherwise and to resent it. They were each entering on a new chapter. It was more important to understand, and welcome, this fact than to gnaw over her own feelings about Brendan — which she might not have done so much, she thought, if they had been straightforward either way. Somehow she just couldn't relax with him, without being able to put her finger on why.

But it didn't matter: Jean looked well, in fact never better, and wellbeing was something Carol was in a position to value highly just at the moment. When she had rung Dr Kaufman on Sunday and only got his answering machine, she had felt something akin to relief. The deterioration of his eyesight wouldn't prevent him spotting that something was wrong: he knew her too well.

It wasn't that she was trying to evade the truth. The nightmares, the flashes of memory, the feelings of oppressive unease — these were undeniable facts and not to be dismissed. But Carol had a life, she had fought hard to get it, and she was damned if she was going to let this phase, this episode, this *thing* disable her. She would monitor it, get to the bottom of it with luck, but she was determinded not to let it ride her like a monkey. She was a well person, not an ill one: that was what she must keep steadily before her.

And it was her work that helped her do so. Once back at school, she felt solid rock beneath her feet. She hadn't fully realized until now how complete was her identification with the job at which she was still, officially at least, a novice. At some point in these past weeks, unknown to her, her identity had been confirmed: she had become a teacher.

She wondered if other things were developing without her conscious knowledge. On Wednesday she shared dinner duty with Martin. They got so deep in conversation outside the dining hall that they weren't even aware that Jill, the deputy head, had joined them until she waved a hand in front of their faces. Jolly and equine as Joyce Grenfell, Jill gave them a toothy smile and remarked with a sort of admiring reproach, "You two."

You two . . . Was there, then, an 'us two'? The remark gave them pause, literally; and possibly the fact that neither of them made any comment on it was significant too. Here was something to think about. And yet, not so: Carol didn't find it pressing on her mind with great urgency. Neither of them was going anywhere. The need to be in control was, she knew, her frequent failing, but for once it didn't figure: where Martin was concerned she was content just to go with the flow.

Besides, he made her laugh so much; there didn't seem any need to analyse that.

Curiously, this very theme of unconscious change came up in class that week.

"Miss Halstead, when do we grow?"

"You're growing all the time."

"Why can't we see it?"

"You can." She had them bring in photographs of themselves as babies and toddlers, and they studied the way their faces had changed whilst remaining recognizably the same: she assuaged any embarrassment about this by bringing in a photograph of herself at sixteen with unthinkably sprayed, spiked and maltreated hair, which went down a storm. Thus a mini-topic was born. She made a height chart and measured them all against it: she would do the same at the end of the year, and she reckoned they would be surprised at the results. Other ideas followed naturally — measuring the growth of the plants along the windowsills, measuring where the sun's rays reached across the classroom floor throughout the day; though she had to call a discreet halt when a discussion veered towards the growth of breasts and body hair. That wasn't in her brief, thankfully. She didn't want to be the one to tell them that they all had an appointment with a ghastly monster called puberty.

This, then, was her place. Whatever tricks her mind or her nerves or her hormones got up to, this stood firm. And by Friday she was feeling as strong as she ever had. No nightmares, no flashbacks, no sensation of *déjà vu*. She was riding high.

That was Friday. By Saturday night she had crashed, not just to earth but further, down into darkness and fire.

12

SHE had overslept, and she had just stepped blearily out of the shower when she heard the knocking at the door.

Who the hell — ? she thought, and then remembered. And wondered how she had managed to forget.

She scrambled into some clothes and got to the door at the third knock.

"Oh, no." Elaine Yeomans' bright birdlike eyes met hers. "We've gone and got you out of the bath."

"No, no. Shower. I mean, I've just finished." All three of them were standing outside her door: Geoff, Elaine, and Ben. She hadn't expected that. But then she hadn't really expected anything — somehow she had put Geoff Yeomans' offer out of her mind. "Come in, come in . . ."

"You sure this isn't a bad time or anything?" Elaine said.

"Not at all. I just overslept." She put

a hand nervously to her wet hair and cast a rueful glance around the untidy flat as they trooped in; she hated being unprepared for something like this.

"This one been wearing you out at school, has he?" Geoff Yeomans said.

"No more than usual. Hello, Ben." The boy had gone shy and tongue-tied at being in his teacher's home. He was wearing jeans and trainers, which made him look older. "This is really good of you, you know. I feel a bit ashamed when it's such a small thing . . . "

"You need to be able to have ventilation in a flat like this," Geoff said in his dogged way. He was carrying a toolbox, and looked around with a professional eye. The three of them had brought in a fresh outdoorsy smell, like washing just off the line, that seemed to fill the flat: it was almost overpowering.

"Sorry you've got the whole team crashing in on you, you probably weren't expecting that," Elaine said. "Only we've got something to ask you, or Ben has, haven't you, Benny?"

Ben nodded stiffly, hands stuffed in his pockets.

"Oh well, ask away."

Ben looked up at his mother, pink-cheeked.

"It's your party," Elaine said to him. "It's up to you who you ask."

"Do you want to come to my birthday party next Wednesday?" Ben murmured painfully, with no questioning inflection.

"Oh, you've got a birthday coming? Well, that's very nice of you to ask me," Carol said. She looked quizzially at Elaine. "I'd love to, if — I mean, if it wouldn't put a dampener on it having a teacher there."

Elaine laughed. "Not just any old teacher. Benjamino thinks you're the best thing since sliced bread. Now look, don't worry if you can't make it. He's just had a bee in his bonnet about asking you."

"No, I'd love to come. Thank you for inviting me, Ben. Sorry I look such a state." She rubbed up her hair so it stood out in damp corkscrews. "Think I should come to school like this on Monday?"

She got a little grin from him in return.

"So then, where's this window?" Geoff Yeomans said. He looked very big and cumbrous, and almost gratuitously male, in this small flat. Carol showed him the bedroom window, wishing she had made the bed. Even a bed that you had done nothing but sleep peacefully in looked sleazy.

"I kept trying to find a way of fixing the arm back on," she explained, "but it looks like the screw's actually broken inside."

"It's a shame what they do with these places," Geoff said, kneeling by the window and frowning disdainfully at the broken catch. "They build 'em really nice, and then they skimp on things like this. I've seen it before. You get electrical sockets where you can't use an adaptor because it covers the switch, that kind of nonsense. How do you get on with that?" he added, pointing at the storage heater.

"It's not ideal. Too hot or too cold."

"This is it." He opened his toolbox, breathing heavily. She noticed for the first time a small tattoo on his forearm. It looked like a bird of prey, a hawk or eagle. "They're supposed to be economical, but it's a false economy because they're not

254

controllable. You always get some heat being given out at night, which is when you don't need it. I can do you a bodge on this. What I mean is, you'll be able to open and close it, but it won't be like your landlords' own maintenance people would do it."

"Oh, that shouldn't be a problem, I'll tell them where to get off if they complain."

"He is a very good bodger," Elaine said from the doorway. "If you ever got shipwrecked, Geoff'd be the one to make a raft out of the bits. I should think you want to dry your hair, don't you?"

"Oh, it's all right — "

"You grab your dryer and carry on. It's natural, isn't it, the curl in your hair? I can tell. But I'll bet you get people saying it's a perm."

"You've got it."

At Elaine's insistence she took the dryer into the living room. While Geoff worked and Ben stared and Carol blasted hastily at her hair, Elaine chattered. She was a lively talker, with a droll quickness of expression. "I tried perming mine once. I came out like Shirley Temple.

Then I wanted it mahogany and didn't like it and tried to dye it back and it came out orange. I was pregnant at the time and wearing this smock effort and I looked *exactly* like one of those orang-utans out of *Planet of the Apes*. Here, sit still, fidget. You can wait, can't you?"

"Do you want the toilet, Ben?" Carol said. "It's through there."

"Anyway," Elaine said conspiratorially, when he had gone. "Ben's birthday party. Don't worry about having to, you know, sit down and eat jelly with a paper hat on. It's more of a drop-by sort of thing, do you know what I mean? If the weather's warm enough we'll have a barbecue in the garden and they can all go loony outside. There'll be other adults and we might have a drink later. So, you know. Treat it like that. Tra-la-laaa!" she sang out as Ben returned. "No, Benbow, we haven't been talking about you, whatever makes you think that?"

"Ow!"

It was Geoff. The bedroom door stood open and they could see him, kneeling by the windowsill. He sucked his forefinger, shook his hand in the air and then sucked again.

"Are you all right?" Carol said.

"Little cut," he said, "it's nothing."

"Do you need a plaster?"

"He's always cutting himself," Elaine said. "And he won't wear plasters, and he won't take aspirin either. Some men are funny like that, aren't they?"

Carol went through to see, nevertheless. The cut wasn't deep but when he had shaken his hand in pain a drop of blood had flown off and landed on the curtain. He hadn't seen it, so she didn't say anything.

"You're sure you don't want something on that?" she said: she felt bad that he had hurt himself performing this act of kindness.

"No, no." He looked up at her and smiled. The large size of his teeth gave him a wolfish look. There was a trace of indulgence in the look too: womanly fussing. She noticed the tattoo again. It was definitely meant to be an eagle. The way the hairs on his arm grew through the picture made it look almost three-dimensional.

"Cup of tea, then?"

"Oh, that's very nice of you, thank you very much." Again there was that gruff courtliness about him. It was an odd juxtaposition.

She had just made a move for the kitchen when there was another knock at the door.

"Dear, everybody's descending on you today," Elaine said with a sympathetic look.

"Not to worry," Carol said; but she felt flustered as she went to answer the door, and even more so when she opened it to find Martin standing there.

"Oh, hi," he said. He had a book in his hand, one she'd lent him last week. She saw him glance over her shoulder, observe that she had company. "Sorry to disturb you, I — I was just passing and I thought I'd return this." He held the book out, stiff and awkward.

"Oh, thanks." She took the book, and they exchanged perplexed glances. "Do you want to come in?"

"No, no, I can't stop, like I say I was just passing and I thought — you know, that you might want it back. Very good, by the way."

"Yes. I mean, I'm glad you liked it."

"OK, best be off then."

"Well, thanks anyway. Bye."

She had a consciousness that something had been initiated by Martin's calling round like that, a line stepped over, an admission made; but what she felt about it, whether gladness or surprise or apprehension, would have to be postponed for now, and that added to her state of fluster and confusion.

Elaine was giving her a sly look, one eyebrow raised.

"Wish I had 'em queuing up for me," she said.

"Colleague," Carol said, smiling in spite of herself.

"Oh, I know. Like *him* with that Hayley McBride," Elaine said, giving Ben a nudge. "Just plays out with her now and then, he says. That's all. *We* know."

"Oh, Ben, you never told me," Carol said with mock reproach, while Ben squirmed.

She made tea, forgoing any herself: her

furnishing of the flat had been basic and she only had three mugs. It surprised her when Ben said yes to her offer of tea, thinking he would like Coke or something, but this was, Elaine revealed, not his only idiosyncrasy. "Doesn't like chips either, do you, mate? His favourite food is Brussels sprouts. You can cover his plate with them. Here's me thirty years old and I still have to force 'em down."

Carol took Geoff's tea through to him, and found him just finishing.

"There you go," he said. "It's not a proper job. I've had to make a new screw-hole in the frame and fix it there, so it won't open quite so wide as before." He demonstrated.

"Oh, it's lovely having it open at all. Thanks so much. I'd have been waiting for ever for the damn landlords to shift themselves."

"It's the cowboys they employ," he said, taking the mug of tea in a fleshy fist. "We did a painting job for a new block of flats over Bury St Edmunds. Smashing places, only the electricians had wired the Economy 7 boilers the wrong way, so the tenants would have been paying full rate when they thought they were on cheap rate, you know? They had to rip out the wiring, then replaster, the whole lot. Shocking."

Carol became burningly conscious that a pair of her knickers lay on the bedroom floor: a faint feeling of invasion contended with her genuine gratitude. But Geoff Yeomans seemed more concerned with the delinquencies of cowboy builders and talked on about them while she subtly ushered him back to the living room.

"There's no pride in their work these days." He had swallowed his tea in a few gulps and now stood absently cradling the mug, pursuing his theme with that earnest preoccupied look which reminded her, she realized, of Ben when he was interested in a piece of work. "What I like to see is the old furniture, you know like on that antiques programme on TV, where you can see all the work that went into it, the way the craftsman got this piece of wood and used it . . . "

Very like Ben, in fact, Carol thought, glancing at the boy and then at Elaine, who was giving her husband a look half sceptical, half indulgent. All at once a memory came unbidden: Ben emerging from the reeds at the wildfowl park, filthy and stubborn . . .

A unison laugh made her jump. Woolgathering, she hadn't heard what Geoff had said, and hurried to join in. Her flat seemed to be full of laughing mouths and loud voices, and a feeling of oppression and claustrophobia came over her.

She tried to hide it; but perhaps Elaine picked up on her unease, because she put down her mug and smiled at Carol and said, "Well, we'd better let you get yourself sorted. Come on, boys, let's be having you."

"Thanks again for your help. It was really kind of you, coming all the way over here to do that." Now it was her relief she was trying to hide. "Oh, and by the way, thanks for letting Ben bring the photographs in for the Growing project. Is it all right if I hang on to them for a while yet? I was thinking of making a display with all the kids' photographs, showing them getting older.

We'll be using Blu-Tack, so they won't be damaged."

"Of course, feel free," Elaine said. "We've got stacks of photos. Well, of Ben and me anyway. You can't get a photo of Geoff. He runs away if you point a camera at him."

"Never have liked it," Geoff said, again boyish in his big awkwardness. "Just one of those things."

"Thinks you're going to steal his soul away," Elaine said, propelling them towards the door. "Now remember what I said about the birthday bash, right?"

"Right. Thank you very much for asking me, Ben."

"That's all right," Ben said. "Bye."

It was a noticeable mark of Ben's maturity that he was good at greetings and farewells, acknowledgements, polite replies — things that many children older than he found difficult. It was Geoff who turned out to be the graceless one in this, suddenly turning in the doorway to say goodbye without realizing that Carol was right behind him. Their bodies bumped and she was close to his large-toothed mouth for a moment. "Sorry," they said together. Elaine, already going down the stairs, gave a peal of laughter, and Carol wondered for a second whether he was the sort of man it was wise to laugh at; but then she heard Ben giggling too, which he wouldn't have done if it was that sort of setup.

(Why think that? Because he has a tattoo and can mend things? Stereotyping. Bad.)

"Sorry, what's that?"

Elaine had called something up to her. "I said, he might come back now we've gone." The top of her head was just showing above the landing through the banister, and she winked. "Your admirer."

"Oh, that." Carol laughed weakly.

Geoff, following them down the stairs, put on speed and tried to elbow past them. "And he's coming through on the inside," he said. "Suddenly this race is wide open . . . "

Carol heard them laughing and jostling as they descended, their footsteps echoing loudly up the stairwell.

She turned and closed the door behind her. She found that she was trembling.

She stood rigidly still for some moments, looking round at the flat. She was seeing it but none of it connected. But this couldn't be another episode of sleep paralysis, because she was wide awake.

A wave of pure, unspeakable fear passed over her. It was almost literally a wave, retreating from her as suddenly as it had come and leaving her shivering, gasping, wondering what had hit her.

She searched herself for precedents. Was this the Trapdoor, the bane of her adolescence, the abrupt draining of confidence that had once sent her fleeing and stumbling from a post office queue because it was her turn next and she couldn't face speaking to the cashier?

It didn't feel like that: it felt closer to her, and in a paradoxical way more rational.

"You'll probably always have your bad times," Dr Kaufman had told her once. "Times when you'll feel threatened and insecure for no apparent reason."

No reason. That was how she had coped with those bad times over the years. Knowing that they were just phantom manifestations, like the itching in an amputated limb; that they came from inside her, not from anything outside.

No reason. That was OK. As long as there was no reason, it was OK.

She began to dart about the flat, scooping up the mugs and washing them, stuffing rubbish into the bin and laundry into the basket. Her movements were frantic and when a part of her mind registered this fact she became more frantic yet.

In the bedroom she stopped dead in front of the window.

The spot of blood that had landed on the curtain was already drying and turning brown. It was about the size of a penny and had tiny rays extending from its circumference, like a child's drawing of the sun.

When the nausea hit her she expected to be able to fight it down, the way she had in the car coming back from the Yeomanses'. You weren't just sick for no reason at all, she thought, putting a hand to her mouth.

No reason.

Her gullet burnt as if she had swallowed acid. The stuff came up just before she reached the toilet.

When she had finished retching she sat back against the bathroom wall for a minute, gasping, and then began to clean up. She flung her soiled sweater in the bath and began to rinse it; and then it was as if the exhaustion of the vomiting brought down other defences too and Carol obeyed an impulse that she had been fighting and that she knew might bring a terrible destroying army in its wake.

She went to her desk, and opened the folder that contained the photographs her class had brought in. At the top were those of Ben Yeomans. The first was of him as a toddler of two: woolly-hatted, fat-cheeked, his characteristic features only just beginning to show through the anonymity of babyhood. The other was recent, a school photo taken during his last year at infants': the face narrower, the eyes larger and more expressive, the first shadows of uncertainty and complexity lurking in the corners of his smile. Process, growth, ageing: it was striking to see.

And striking too, more striking than

ever, was that feeling of familiarity and *déjà vu*. She had dismissed it, evaded it, argued it away time and again, simply because it wasn't possible that she had seen Ben before.

"Not Ben."

She said the words aloud, and as she did so the doors of the past opened and its terrors came hurtling at her, fifteen years old and fresh as yesterday.

13

CAROL MITCHESON had been a fortunate child. Carol Halstead knew this with hindsight, but it seemed to her that long-ago little girl had known it too. In the memories of her life as Carol Mitcheson, gratitude and contentment seemed to figure largely.

She had loved the house she lived in. Though she was two when they moved there, it was the only home she remembered and the only one she wanted. She loved the space of the old three-storey Clapham house, the smell of wood and floor polish, the bay windows and the plaster mouldings on the ceiling, the smooth round feel of the big newel posts at the stair turnings. She loved the back garden, though it was shady and mossy and sometimes her mother despaired of anything but a few tough alpines ever growing there. She loved the gnarled feel of the bark of the old crab apple tree, the rockery that looked as if it ought to have pixies living in it even though there were only slugs, and the stone birdbath where once she watched a huge crow perch and linger in apparent fascination with his own reflection. She loved the pleasant street where the house was situated, with her school just round the corner and her father's surgery not far off; a self-contained and reassuring world that also had exciting things close at hand, places that her parents would take her to at weekends and on days off, where you could see animals and shows, dinosaurs and pictures, ride on trains and sail on boats.

She loved her mother and father, of course: and they, of course, loved her; but in this too the older Carol suspected that her younger self was grateful rather than complacent, and that she had not taken it for granted. She could have had no direct experience that it was not so for everyone; but the knowledge must have been there, somewhere, on the edge of her infant consciousness, just as she dimly discerned the vastness of the city in the midst of which she lived, stretching far beyond the view from her bedroom window.

She was spoilt, probably — in as much as her parents were comfortably off and she was an only child; but people were often rather too ready to call a child spoilt when what they really meant was that the child had a pleasanter life than they had had. Carol Mitcheson's life up until her ninth year was certainly pleasant, but Carol Halstead didn't remember it as one long indulgence, and there were plenty of things she couldn't get away with. Her parents were not wishy-washy people: they had both had their struggles, her mother's perhaps less obvious than her father's but no less testing.

Dr Alan Mitcheson had been born in Edinburgh. His father had been a boozer who habitually beat up his mother and finally left, never to be heard of again. In the meantime she had got into habits of her own: one was beating up the boy, the other was heroin. Eventually he was taken away from her, she disappeared down a hole of drugs, and he was fostered. One specially devoted foster family brought him to a stable adolescence, and he was able to climb on their shoulders to a dream of medical school. Whether aptly or ironically in view of his ambition, they were both killed by cancer before he had qualified. He was tough and realistic and he bounced back from this, but his furious scorn for the consolations of religion, for notions of providence and justice, probably dated from that time.

Shortly after qualifying he met Hilary Monk, Carol's mother, and they were married. This simple sequence of events was not simple for Hilary, whose parents, archaically genteel and fragile, had already worked themselves into a tizzy of resentment over the delinquency of their elder daughter, Jean, and who let it be known that they would sink into the grave if their younger daughter proved similarly disappointing. Dr Alan Mitcheson just passed muster because of his profession, but that was as far as it went. He was only a GP, after all, and had set up his practice in an area of London that included what the elderly Monks called 'coloured folk'. His background was apparent in his speech, in his outspoken Scots Labour sympathies, in his impatience with social niceties. He did not get on well with his in-laws, a situation that was made more fraught because Hilary was so desperate to keep them sweet.

Or not too sour: that was as much as she could hope for. Clever and good-looking, Hilary worked from home at secretarial services, typing manuscripts and preparing reports: it was a job she liked and was good at but which she had to pretend to her finicking parents was merely a hobby like macramé, just as their fastidious carping had left her convinced that she was as plain as a pikestaff. Such a sowing of bitter seeds by the old couple should have produced a harvest of resentment between their children, but Hilary and Jean remained close.

It was from Jean that Carol later learnt many of these things about her parents, and they interlocked with things she remembered herself, like the pieces of a jigsaw — with an effect very much like that of a jigsaw, the picture completed but not satisfying in itself because of that network of tiny cracks and joins. Her father: a smallish, wiry man with a sturdy bronze-like head and a low thick crown of dark hair; seldom tired, often talkative, on occasion fiercely vituperative about government and about a woman called Victoria Gillick; good at nippy sports like squash, and games requiring a snappy, almost underhand skill. Fond of a drink, very fond of good food, and almost infatuated with all things French: he had a collection of Asterix books in the original language and sometimes he would look through them with Carol, making her laugh as he pronounced the French cartoon onomatopoeia: *Hips!* and *Tchoc!* and best of all the scream *Hiiiiii!*

(The French version was accurate, at least as far as a man's scream went. She would learn this later.)

Pieces of the jigsaw: her mother working at her desk on the first floor, wearing her glasses on the end of her nose. When Carol came in she would peep at her over the top of those glasses, in a funny way that made her laugh. A fair-skinned, delicate-looking woman, who loved long baths with a book, and scented oils, and soft diaphanous scarves.

She could juggle, and she hated wearing shoes, would kick them off the moment she got inside the front door.

Pieces of the jigsaw. Carol Mitcheson got Harry the hamster for her seventh birthday, waking on the birthday morning to find his cage by her bed and Harry trundling round in his exercise wheel. Her mother liked Harry, but she was nervous of him when he was let out of his cage, because he was a little ratlike; and when he ran up the curtains she couldn't stand it and bolted.

Carol Halstead had read about synaesthesia, a condition in which the senses are confused: you see sounds and hear smells. Carol Mitcheson, and probably most small children, suffered from synaesthesia, or rather gloried in it. Days of the week had colours. Monday was red, Tuesday was yellow, Wednesday was orange, Thursday bluey-grey, Friday white, Saturday a pure sky blue. Sunday was brown: it might be a rich brown or a dingy brown, depending on which Sunday it was. If it was the Sunday when Grandma and Grandad came for lunch, it was a dingy brown.

Carol Halstead knew that the gloom this inspired in little Carol Mitcheson was shared by her parents. At the time she had felt rather ashamed of not wanting Grandma and Grandad to come. If she noticed her father drinking a lot of whisky at these times, she supposed it was simply adult conviviality. Hindsight showed her that her grandparents made prize pains of themselves every time, finding fault with everything, advising her mother at intolerable length on precisely which variety of potatoes to buy in order to achieve the exact balance of crispness and tenderness when roasting. Old Mr Monk would complain about the traffic they had endured on driving here. He made the complaint sound personal: it genuinely irked him that people should be using the roads on a Sunday morning and didn't occur to him that he was doing so himself. Meanwhile old Mrs Monk would move her eyes and her head in slow observant circles while she talked, conning the ceilings for cobwebs and the picture-rails for dust. She couldn't understand why anyone would live in a house like this, and least of all with no daily cleaner.

She would notice anything that was new. Both Carol's father and mother were great magpies and neither of them minded clutter, so anyone else would have been hard put to spot a new arrival amongst the crowds of bric-a-brac and books; but her grandma's eye would always alight on it at once and make a comment.

"My goodness, how much did that cost you, I wonder," she would murmur; or if any of them were wearing an item of clothing she hadn't seen before, "Is that new? Good Lord, you must have more clothes than Marks."

Then there would be her illnesses. These were real enough, but Mrs Monk had pre-empted sympathy by hypochondria when she was perfectly well; and she had an unlovable habit of running down acquaintances who dared to be unwell themselves. She resented them as much as if they had stolen something from her. "Always complaining about her back," she would say, "but she can walk to and from the High Street without a twinge.

I've seen her do it, and she wouldn't be able to do *that* if she suffered from her back the way I do mine."

An extra edge was given to this by the fact that Carol's father was a doctor. Inevitably the inadequacies of doctors in diagnosing and treating Mrs Monk's manifold complaints came up. With hindsight what seemed remarkable to Carol was not the prickly atmosphere of these times but the fact that it never went any further. Her father didn't have much time for neurotic malingerers, and he had a touchy pride about his profession, and he wasn't the world's most patient man. Yet there was never a blow-up. He seemed to have cultivated a special nod for his in-laws, eyes half-closed, head on one side, his mouth set in a straight line; and he would keep this nod steadily going while Mrs Monk informed him that her doctors had told her to take aspirin when she suffered no less than three migraines a day, or Mr Monk stated it as a fact that the coloured folk got everything for free. Possibly Carol's father was practising some sort of self-hypnosis at these times. Whatever it was, it worked, though sometimes after her grandparents had gone Carol's parents would be scratchy with one another, an occurrence that was rare; she wasn't sure, in fact, that it wasn't entirely confined to those dingy brown Sundays.

They might, of course, have rowed without her knowledge, but she didn't think it likely. They were a devoted couple. They had plenty of friends and sometimes went out with them in the evening, leaving Carol with a babysitter, but often they would come back early, seeming simply to prefer each other's company; and often on these occasions, if Carol wasn't asleep yet, they would let her come down in her dressing gown and watch TV with them, placing her between them on the settee. If she brought a doll or a teddy down with her, her mother would take hold of it and make it do a dance to any music that came on the TV, or wag its head and make it imitate whoever was talking. She was an excellent mimic, and Carol had sometimes seen her father literally doubled up, tears streaming down his face, at her mother's impressions of someone they knew.

A fortunate child, yes. Sheltered and protected, maybe; but no more than children ought to be, Carol thought. The world impinged, even if it did not penetrate. Once her father came home from the surgery, gave them cheerful greetings, admired the cornflake box castle she had brought home from school, made a pot of tea, and burst out crying. A patient of his had been diagnosed as having cancer: she was a little girl of Carol's age. Another time a homeless man got into her school during the day, shut himself in the girls' toilets, and slit his wrists: one of Carol's classmates found him.

Bad things happened. Carol Mitcheson knew this. But the knowledge was like having to go to the dentist or being told off: it was part of life. It did not threaten it.

Fortunate, yes; sheltered, maybe. Certainly she didn't lack for anything materially. There were always plans afoot: for next year's holiday, for improvements to the house, for Christmas. The future was a presence, tantalizing indeed, but with nothing of doubt or darkness or menace about it.

Fragments of the jigsaw: Christmas.

As the days of the week had colours, the year had a shape. There was a wonderful long smooth expanse in the middle that was summer. The beginning was dull and rough except for a moderately interesting egg-shape that was Easter. The end mounted upwards through her birthday (September) to a high peak: Christmas.

Her father loved Christmas with a child's intensity, maybe because the Christmases of his childhood had simply been more booze and more fighting. He was not a man to go half-measures with something that engaged him, a characteristic that Carol had inherited; and where other adults went about the business of the tree and the decorations and the presents and the cards with a barely concealed resentment, he gave it the works and enjoyed every moment. He was particular about the tree: only a real Norwegian spruce would do, and it had to be large.

Fragment: her mother pretending to be shocked when he brought it home.

"Alan, that's a *tree*."

"Well, of course it's a tree. A Christmas tree. Gorgeous, isn't it? You smell it. I love that smell."

"But I mean, it's a *tree*. Like a tree you'd have in the garden. How are you going to get it up the stairs?" Their living room was on the first floor.

"Oh, it's not heavy. Or it won't be when I trim the roots."

Trimming the roots turned out to be a lengthy operation, with her father red-faced and sweating as he worked the handsaw and her mother trying to smother her smiles. But he didn't lose patience; and somehow he got the tree up the stairs, emerging triumphant at last with his face and hands covered in tiny red spots where the needles had pricked him.

He let Carol decorate it, of course. But she couldn't do it all, the tree being so big; and so he added his own touches, placing baubles and crackers with an artist's fastidiousness and stepping back to judge the effect. His Christmas was important to him.

And he liked the tree up early — which

called forth the inevitable comments from her grandparents.

"It'll die before Christmas," they griped. "You'll have needles everywhere and a bare tree." And, "We put ours up last thing on Christmas Eve. That's quite soon enough." It was as if Christmas were a punishment, to be got over with as quickly as possible.

The smell of the Christmas tree in the house: it was a wonderful smell and Carol Mitcheson had loved it. It was an essence of Christmas, always in the air when you came down to breakfast in the morning or when you came in from school, always reminding you that the time was special.

It was a smell that Carol Halstead could not abide. It was the smell of the Christmas of her ninth year. It was a smell with blood in it.

Saturday, 19 December. Early hours of the twentieth, to be precise. That was the time of the occurrence, the incident, the crime — whatever word you wanted to use. Carol Halstead had no word for it. It was just what had happened.

Yet she could not think of it as a single

entity. There were two versions of it. There was the objective, factual account, the one that existed for the police and the press and the outer world, with its times and measurements and forensic detail. And then there was her own subjective version, the one that existed for her alone — the one that she experienced. And though they were the same, she could never quite bring them together. They did not so much dovetail as run parallel to one another.

Saturday, 19 December. Dr Alan Mitcheson, thirty-seven years old, a general practitioner with a surgery in nearby Wandsworth, spent a quiet evening at his home in a quiet residential street in Clapham with his thirty-two-year-old wife, Hilary, and his eight-year-old daughter, Carol.

Saturday night, and she had been allowed to stay up late to watch a film. The good films always came on near Christmas. It was cold out but warm and cosy in the living room, with the lights of the Christmas tree winking and the smell of pine needles. They had been shopping that afternoon, and got plenty of food in, including a lot of nuts. They were supposed to be for Christmas but her father couldn't resist eating a few — he was a great nibbler — and by the end of the film he had eaten his way through a whole bag of monkey nuts. She saw him cast a slightly shame-faced glance at the pile of shells by his chair. Her mother had one eye on the film and the other on a manuscript in her lap, and occasionally she would read out some terrible misspelling to her father. Some of them were so obvious that Carol couldn't believe an adult had made them.

The little girl went to bed around ten; Dr and Mrs Mitcheson went to bed about two hours later, after turning out the lights and making sure the front and rear doors were secured.

. . . Carol snuggled down into bed and drowsily asked her mother why there were bits in the film where the words didn't match the actors' mouths when they spoke. Her mother told her that these were probably swearwords originally, but they'd covered them over so that children could watch the film. Drifting off to sleep,

Carol wondered what the swearwords were. She knew plenty: she heard them in the playground all the time, though she didn't know exactly what some of them meant.

At some time around three o'clock in the morning a gang of four youths gained access to the house by forcing the back door using a crowbar. The house was not alarmed and neighbours heard no sounds of disturbance. A night-shift worker who was awake at the time and lived at the other end of the street thought he heard a car at about this time, but could not be sure.

. . . Carol opened her eyes. She could hear people on the landing. Footsteps, and giggling. For a moment her sleepy mind, running on Christmas, thought that it must be Christmas Eve and that her parents were bringing her presents to put by her bed (she knew all about Father Christmas). And then she heard something terrifyingly different about the voices and froze. The single word BURGLARS went through her head. There was something so sinister and horrible about the sound of that word.

The voices and the footsteps were near: she was afraid the burglars were going to come in and find her. And so, hardly daring to breathe, hardly feeling her feet touch the floor, she slipped out of bed and darted across the room into her hiding place — the blocked-in chimney with the little peephole she had made. The burglars wouldn't see her there; maybe they would go away. It was all she could think of.

The four youths made their way to the top floor of the house, where the bedrooms of Dr and Mrs Mitcheson and their daughter were both situated. There they came upon Dr and Mrs Mitcheson in bed, and proceeded to torture and brutally murder them for no apparent motive. Mrs Mitcheson was bound and sexually assaulted though not raped, and died of multiple stab wounds. Dr Mitcheson appeared to have fought his attackers, but was also killed by multiple stab wounds. Both bodies were mutilated after death.

. . . Squeezed into her hiding place, drawing in breath in tiny gasps, silently begging, *Go away go away*. Her eye at the peephole, blinking, her eyelashes feeling like heavy curtains swishing. The bedroom door opening, a figure appearing, lit by the landing light, usually left on because it gave a nice glow over the transom. A youth, looking in. Glimpse of another head behind his. Looking in, peering round, seeing no one. Then going away *yes go away go away* and then noises. Cries. Her mother and father. Doing things to them. Her mother screaming, her father going No no. And Carol paralysed, mute, lips together, eye blinking at the view of her open bedroom door and the landing, feeling small, feeling tiny, just an eye, a little eye blinking in darkness, *I spy*, while the terrible sounds tore at the air. And then her father appearing in that view of the landing, suddenly thrusting himself into it, in pyjamas and bloody, running and struggling, get to the phone perhaps, get help *yes yes* but then figures closing in on him, four of them, getting round him like boys bullying in the playground, her father punching and thrashing and then knives going in. And that giggling, breathless and throaty and sensual, as her father went down, all in a heap with his bottom sticking up. A last thrust of a knife, an abrupt meaty sound. And the little eye blinking and seeing.

The murdered couple's daughter escaped unharmed by hiding in a narrow gap made by a blocked-in fireplace in her bedroom. The youths ransacked the house, daubing obscene graffiti on the walls in their victims' blood. Nothing of value was taken. The motive seemed to be a sheer sick pleasure in random destruction and killing, a savage amusement.

. . . Tiny, blinking eye, knowing it was her turn next. The youths in her bedroom, rummaging round. Those throaty voices. *Fucking kid's room must be a fucking kid where?* Opening her wardrobe, throwing out her clothes. Then the giggling again. The little paralysed creature that was Carol Mitcheson panted like a rabbit trapped in a burrow by ferrets, and watched as the youths amused themselves. One in a leather jacket got out his penis, wagged it around, then urinated on her bed. Another, smaller, more boy than youth, put his hand in the hamster's cage, got Harry out and threw him on the floor and stamped on him. Meanwhile a sob, a sob that was like all the knives and death and screams of the world, formed in her stomach and began to fight its way up. And then *come on must be downstairs* and they were gone, with a thundering of hasty feet. The sob continued to fight its way up as she listened to them smashing things and laughing downstairs and she knew that it would reach her throat any minute and then it would all be over. And then suddenly there was another noise, a noise so achingly friendly and familiar that it seemed to her transfixed, skewered mind that the mere sound of it must undo everything that had happened. It was the boiler, set to a timer and lighting up with a *Whumph* and then that rapid knocking sound that came from the pump and that her father was always saying he was going to have to do something about. And for a moment it seemed that the boiler had changed it all back because the noises of the youths downstairs suddenly stopped. Then they came again, softer, a rapid bundling sound, and turned into noises outside, feet down the passage, speedily dwindling and gone.

The youths made their escape by the same way they had entered the house, probably disturbed by the noise of the water boiler starting up or some other sound. At around three-thirty the little girl made a 999 call, giving the address of the house but apparently unable to give any further details. A patrol car was initially dispatched to the scene, under the impression that what had been reported was a domestic dispute. The officers discovered the truth of the case and detectives and medical teams were called. An investigation was begun at once.

. . . Blank. She knew that she had waited until she was sure the youths were gone, she knew that she had crept out of her hiding place and for some reason put on her slippers and dressing gown. She knew that she had gone to see what had happened to her parents, and seen; and that she had gone to the telephone and called the police and then gone back into her hiding place. She knew what had prompted her to go back there: it was the only safe place in the world, and she had certainly not intended ever coming out of it again. But this knowledge really belonged to the objective account of what had happened, rather than to her subjective experience. She did not have a true visual memory of what her murdered parents had looked like, though she had undoubtedly seen them at close quarters, and her fingerprints found later on her mother's arm suggested that she had shaken it in an attempt to rouse her. In the jigsaw of that night, those were missing pieces.

There always would be gaps: she had learnt that from Dr Kaufman, the child psychiatrist who had been assigned to the task of turning that tiny blinking eye into a human being again. In the trauma of such an event the mind activated its own defence systems, and blocked some things out. There could even be total amnesia, though it was rarer than the movies made out. Carol's memories faded out at about the time she left her hiding place and took shape again only when she was in a hospital bed.

Gaps in the jigsaw.

But there were no gaps where the youths' faces were. She had seen them.

The eye blinking at the peephole had taken those four youths in, their images had been projected on the retina at the back of that eye, and the brain behind it had interpreted the signals sent by the retina, and Carol had seen the murderers of her parents.

Objective version: on the basis of a description given by the Mitchesons' young daughter, police began a hunt for four youths aged between fourteen and twenty. All had shortish to medium-length hair, one was noticeably fair. One was wearing a leather motorcycle jacket, the others dark jackets or coats and jeans. One possibly had an acned face. Footprints at the scene also established that at least one was wearing size eight Adidas trainers, and forensic evidence indicated that all were wearing gloves.

Subjective version: Carol had four people in her head and couldn't get them out. She couldn't get them out to show the police; and even inside her head they were like elusive fish, slippery, revealing a glimpse here, a glimmer there, then twisting away into shadow. Young face and throaty voices, denizens of her mind. What did people look like? They looked like themselves. Young old fat thin fair dark tall short: you could mix and match, draw up categories, but an individual was defined only by his or her self, a sum total beyond computation. Take beauty in a face: everyone could recognize it, but who could isolate and calibrate the exact details of feature that distinguished it from plainness? They had shown her identikits and sketch artists' impressions, hopefully, but they had only been collections of features, figures that didn't make a sum. They were in her head, occasionally in her dreams. And they would stay there — unless the police caught their counterparts out in the world, and showed them to her.

The police never did.

The investigation by the Metropolitan Police into the murders of Alan and Hilary Mitcheson went on for a year, to her knowledge: probably some avenues, or blind alleys, were still being explored after that. As far as she knew the file was never closed. The four youths were just never caught. Every physical trace at the scene was analysed, enquiries were made at every house within five miles, every youth who had shown even the slightest signs of delinquency was pulled in, appeals went out over the excited media, psychologists and graphologists analysed the bloody graffiti on the walls, Dr Mitcheson's files were combed in case they might turn up a patient with a grudge, and his colleagues in the practice put up a reward. And it was all no good. In the middle of London a gang of youths had broken into a house one dark night, killed for fun, and melted away again.

And meanwhile Carol Mitcheson, though physically uninjured, battled for life. Between them Aunt Jean, Dr Kaufman and the police managed to shelter her from the hungry media until another horror story came along to satisfy its greedy but short-lived appetite. What they could not shelter her from was the fact that she was an eight-year-old child who had seen her parents butchered. An infant citizen of a nation at peace in a supposedly civilized age had been confronted with bestial senselessness: here was the conundrum and challenge.

In the course of meeting it, the fact that the perpetrators were still at large was sidelined, if not relegated. In the counselling and psychotherapy she underwent it was a negative aspect without fruitful potential. If Carol were ever to achieve a stable, secure life without irrational fear, this fact had to be accommodated but not emphasized. For her mental health, it was more vital that she realized there were good people in the world than that she thought about those four bad ones still out there.

It worked, and she did. At the back of her mind, as she grew up, there was always the knowledge that those four murderers were still walking around scot-free — the knowledge, indeed, that she might have sat on the same bus as them or passed them in the street. But the knowledge was pretty much a truism, and fundamentally meaningless. That was just the way things were. After all, you could pass *her* in the street and not know, not realize that she was one of those people you read about in the papers and forgot, who had figured in large and terrible events. The knowledge got her nowhere, and getting her somewhere had been the aim and effort of Dr Kaufman and his colleagues and Aunt Jean and Uncle Keith and her teachers and, at last, of herself.

And yet. They never left her, those people in her head. The pool in which the elusive fishes swam grew darker and more shadowy, the glints and glimpses more hazy and infrequent, but they never disappeared. They were part of her experience; part of her selfhood. Beneath the knowledge that they were still at large lay something else, deeper, knottier, more truly a conviction than a knowledge: if she ever saw them again, she would recognize them.

There were things in you that you did not expect ever to use — reserves of strength in extremity, for example — and it was one of those things. Not really to be considered. If there were an earthquake you would heave tons of rubble to dig out your loved ones, but that capacity wasn't a thing you thought about.

And now the earthquake had happened.

No wonder the unease, the nausea,

the panic. The dreams and flashes of memory. The *déjà vu*.

As Dr Kaufman had said, *déjà vu* might not be false memory at all. It might be true memory. It might be recognition.

Sitting on the floor, cradling herself, with Ben Yeomans' photographs in her lap, Carol returned through the doors of the past. As she stepped into the present, she cast a glance back and remembered those photofits that the police had plied her with. It was what her mind had been struggling with these past weeks: unconsciously she had been making a photofit.

And until now she had refused to let herself see what she had come up with. An older Ben Yeomans.

A younger Geoff Yeomans. Fifteen years younger.

14

"TELL me to butt out if I'm being nosy," Martin said, sitting down by her in the staff room at lunchtime, "but you don't seem yourself today."

Carol looked up: she had been so lost in thought that she had forgotten where she was for a moment. "Oh," she said, "I'm fine."

"My God, I actually said 'butt out'. I can't believe I did that. They've got me. American cultural domination is complete. I mean, I would never use the word 'butt' to denote backside, and neither would any British person, which I presume is what the usage signifies. Unless it's meant to be the opposite of 'butt in', of course, but it always sounds as if it's meant to be a mild obscenity. Just as we would never use the word 'fag' as a derogatory term for a homosexual, but we've got the usage 'fag-hag'. This must be the point where an indigenous culture goes under, when it starts to use terms that don't have any meaning to it. Plus you get some very tricky ambiguities. I mean imagine an American reading the sentence, 'He pressed the butt of the fag to his lips.' Say shut up, Martin."

"Shut up, Martin."

"OK." Martin rummaged in a paper bag. "While we're talking in this risqué vein, would you like a banana?"

"I've eaten, thanks."

"Just as well. I've only got one." He took out a banana and then screwed up the paper bag.

"Is that all your lunch?"

"Dieting."

"You're not fat."

"I'm no sylph, or is it nymph. Answer that, Miss Clever Clogs."

"You're just big-boned."

"No bones in my behind, or butt rather," he said, finishing his banana and toying with the skin. "Shall I put this down outside Macleish's office, and then peep round the corner like somebody in the *Beano* going, 'Chortle Chortle'? Or alternatively, shall I purchase a Kalashnikov and cream the bastard?"

"Ssh." Macleish's noiseless spongy shoes seemed to have been chosen for the express purpose of creeping up on you, and she had more than once found him appearing genie-like beside her. She glanced round the staff room, but there was no sign of him, and the only person within earshot was Ernest Robinson, known to pupils and staff alike as Robbo, who was like Mr Chips' older brother and was snoring gently in his armchair.

"Is he still giving you grief?"

"Oh, not really. More a case of, 'I've got my eye on you, laddie,' as he would no doubt say if he were a teacher instead of a — I won't say it." Martin gave her a swift assessing look. "Could you fancy a drink later?"

"I could fancy one now."

"Know what you mean. Not wise though. I did try it once. Going for a drink at lunchtime, a real drink, I mean, not half a shandy and a packet of peanuts. Ended up more stressed out that afternoon than I'd ever been in my life, trying not to show that I'd had a drink. Never tried it again. You know, if you're going to have drink you need to be sure you can fall over at the end of it without exciting comment. Kids notice things like that, little buggers . . . I'm sorry about Saturday."

She looked at him with a start. "Saturday."

"Me springing up on you like that."

"Oh, that." For a moment there it had seemed he was clairvoyant. "No, not at all, I — I'm sorry I couldn't ask you in or anything. Only I had — people there. Ben Yeomans' father, actually, he offered to repair this broken window for me." She didn't know how her voice sounded, whether it gave any indication of the sensation, something like a shadow made physical, that passed over her as she spoke of these things.

"This is my cue to say, I could have done that for you. Except that I couldn't. Incurably cack-handed. I wish the gender debate would throw me a line here. I'm not so bothered about being allowed to cry or express my feelings or take my kid in the father-and-baby room, I just want to be excused not being able to

302

mend things. My first job was working in Gartside's MiniMart in Stockport when I was sixteen. After school and in the holidays. I used to prepare the fruit and veg in a back room. They sold white cabbages in halves. So I had to cut them in half. I cut them against the grain. These poor old dears were taking their half-cabbages home and finding they were all stalk and no leaves. What can you do when you possess that level of practical stupidity? Except be a teacher, of course. Sorry anyway."

"What for?"

"Turning up unannounced."

She shook her head. "You don't have to be."

He was quiet a moment. "Tell me to butt out again, but it's not just Monday morning blues, is it?"

She made an effort to smile. "Probably. Can I take you up on that drink later?"

She didn't know whether drink was any sort of answer; and as the bell rang and she made her way back to her class, she didn't know either whether an urge to confide was what had made her respond to Martin's invitation.

Nor whether that urge was prudent, or even possible to follow.

Listen, Martin, it's like this. When I was eight years old my parents were murdered by four youths who broke into the house, and I saw them. You probably read about the case in the papers. The 'Mitcheson slaying'. It was one of those things that everyone's shocked at and then it fades away. Well, it doesn't of course. Things remain. Those four youths were never caught, for one thing. And the survivors remain, in this case me. And I grew up and ended up a teacher and a reasonably normal human being instead of a basket case because I was lucky and had wonderful family and a wonderful doctor. It was quite a long rocky road from that place to this and I'm so glad to be here and not there. A past like that, you just have to leave it behind you, don't you? As far as you're able, I mean. Of course there are going to be things in your life that are still conditioned by it, like changing the subject when it comes to parents and not being able to stand the smell of a Christmas tree (it happened at Christmas, you see) and maybe less obvious things like needing to be in control and making obsessive lists of things to take with you when you go away and feeling this kind of wall in front of you when you meet new people that you have to make yourself climb over every time . . . But basically you have to cut that past off in order to carry on and it's worked. I've even had some help with it lately, because the house in London where it happened is being sold. It was my inheritance when my parents died, you see, and it was held in trust till I was of age and rented out. And now a developer wants to buy it and I've given the go-ahead and so that really is the last link being broken, wouldn't you say? That past finally, completely gone.

Except it isn't. Because, as I said, they never caught those youths. And all the time I've had this knowledge at the back of my mind that they're still around, grown men of thirty-odd now, of course, changed, but still around somewhere. But very much at the *back* of my mind. You know what the back of your mind's like. All sorts of junk and lumber down there. Stuff you don't touch or bother about. I certainly never went around scrutinizing every man of thirty-odd in case he was one of those youths grown up. That would be crazy.

And now guess what. Ever since I started at Templeton Juniors, ever since I set eyes on Ben Yeomans, I've had these — feelings. Unease. *Déjà vu*. Familiarity. Recognition. How do you define recognition? It's not a straightforward mental activity, really. It's some grey area between memory and perception. You could even call it a gut feeling. "I know this", you say. "I've seen this somewhere before." But you can't for the life of you think where or when.

Well, this weekend I thought it. I thought the where and when. I realized why Ben's face was familiar. Family resemblance. 'Family' and 'familiar' have the same word-root, don't they? Well, that's telling. Recognition: mysterious process. But however it works, it's happened.

Martin, I believe I have recognized one of the killers of my parents.

Now tell me what to do.

Oh, yes, there was no difficulty about what to say. It was quite simple in essence. And amongst the chaos of emotions that had overwhelmed her in the past two days one had predominated: an intense, penetrating, almost cosmic sense of aloneness. She was utterly alone with this thing that had happened and she felt the weight of it would break her back. To speak out, to share it, must offer some relief, like vomiting up a poison.

Yet she knew that the sharing could only be notional. This thing was hers alone. The formula *I know how you feel* was debatable at best, and here it was out of court — even leaving aside the question of who in their right mind would want to be burdened with confidences like these.

And not the least part of the agonized confusion of these past two days was that Carol didn't know how she felt herself. Saturday had seen the crash, and she hadn't slept at all Saturday night, had merely groped around in the mental rubble, dazed and bruised. Early Sunday morning she had dozed, and woken to the sound of church bells and children playing in the field adjoining the flats and her neighbour knocking on the door to ask if she could borrow yet another cup of sugar. And Carol was surprised; perplexed. Life, normal life, was going on. The turmoil and overthrow in her mind had no counterpart outside. Mundanity, hardiest of plants, flourished everywhere. And of course, it was the rule not the exception. In any given situation the dull, harmless, undramatic resolution was the most likely. That was why people drank themselves blotto or yearned for flying saucers to descend from the skies.

And so began doubt.

It wasn't so much herself she doubted: it was the sheer transparency and plainness of the world that thrust itself upon her that day. She went for a walk around Dunmarket, and in spite of the revelation she had undergone, nothing she saw teemed with hidden menace. Everything was what it seemed to be: a provincial town going about its business on a cool mist-wrapped Sunday, people buying newspapers and chocolates, joints roasting in ovens, pubs opening their doors with a waft of beer and warmth and smoky carpets. A sort of vast statistical blankness opposed itself to the feeling at her heart. *Get real*, it said.

But of course it was only a short step from that to *These things don't happen.* And she knew — no one knew better — that they did. Fifteen years ago a gang had slaughtered her parents for the fun of it. It would be great if you could deny that — wave a hand at the ordinariness and predictability of the world and say, "No, no way" — but it wouldn't wash.

And so she was caught: caught between doubt and certainty. From every objective viewpoint her conclusion made no sense. But inside her it was a different matter. There a terrible bell had sounded and its echo trembled through her every moment. It was unbelievable, it was shocking, it threatened to blow her carefully reconstructed world apart, but there was no getting away from it. Nothing else could have caused the feelings she had experienced; nothing else had that much power.

Unless she was cracking up, of course.

That was the alternative explanation. Simply losing her mind.

She had fought hard to keep it, so this was a possibility that was to be both seriously addressed and strongly resisted. But once she had addressed it, she was left with the crucial question: why now? Maybe her mind had something like metal fatigue, which had only just shown itself. Maybe. But she found her self-belief pretty much intact, and her self-belief was firmly against that idea. If she had been a neurotic time-bomb just waiting to explode on the slightest pretext, she would have known it.

And the fact that recognition had been slow and painful in dawning acted on the side of certainty rather than doubt. It was natural that her mind should try to fight off such a conclusion as she had finally come to. She had been in the same room as one of her parents' killers: had even shaken his hand. That was not an easy thing. That was not a thing you could let in your life without much stretching and tearing.

And there, on the side of doubt, rose up the figure of Geoff Yeomans himself. Father and husband. Painter and decorator, householder, resourceful do-it-yourself enthusiast, collector of books on military history. Boyishly polite and clumsily serious and, as far as the window went, genuinely helpful and good-natured.

What to set against that? Maybe that hardness she heard in his laugh, something equivocal in that wide grim-lined smile, like a big slow dog showing its teeth. Something suggestive of the settled-down tearaway about him. And he was from London originally and was thirty-odd. That was the quantifiable stuff, at any rate. It didn't add up to much. But it didn't need to, when her unquantifiable, undeniable feeling was so strong.

And besides, what did happen to criminals who weren't caught? One of two things. Either they carried on committing crimes until they were caught and banged up: or else they took their place in society with the rest of us.

Even murderers.

Such had been Carol's mind since Saturday: something like a thrumming motorway, hectic, garish, thoughts hurtling in opposite directions, overtaking one another and almost colliding, and with no landmarks to it, no still centre — and no possibility of getting off. Coming to work on Monday had merely been a physical action, insignificant beside the internal mayhem — that is, until she entered the class and saw Ben Yeomans. And then the hum of the traffic rose to such a pitch that her desire for a drink at lunchtime was more serious than she let on, and the urge to confide even stronger as the afternoon slowly wore away.

Yet she doubted whether Martin was the right person. She found him more than simpatico: she was drawn to him in a way that was both simple and complex. But some selfish part of her also wanted to guard this secret from him for that very reason. He had no part in that old cruel darkness that seemed to be reaching out to touch her again: he belonged to her new world of hope and strength and light. And what added the final touch to the motorway madness in her head was a guilty wish that this had not happened.

Guilty, because it made it seem as

if she didn't care about finding her parents' killers, preferred peace of mind and a quiet life instead. Not so. It was difficult to think of these things except in melodramatic terms, but nevertheless the fact remained that if she were one hundred per cent certain that she was face to face with one of those killers, Carol would kill in turn and go smiling to whatever punishment came her way. Still, the guilt remained.

Maybe Aunt Jean, who had done so much to build up her new world, would understand that. Maybe Aunt Jean, in fact, was the person to confide in. But that didn't feel right either. Telephone was out of the question, and Carol couldn't even envisage telling it face to face. Jean was starting a new world of her own, and only she could say how much of her old one had been sacrificed to the darkness.

No: Carol was alone with it. She met Martin in the Dragonfly that evening knowing already that she would not say anything.

At least, nothing directly.

He was wearing a big shapeless

fisherman's jersey, and the town drunk, sitting morose and dapper over his umpteenth barley wine, took exception to it. "German bastards," he croaked as they passed him with their drinks. "All our brave lads went to the bottom of the sea for you."

"That's right, sir," Martin said agreeably, turning to Carol with an eyebrow-shrug and murmuring, "Work that one out."

"Thinks you're a U-boat captain, maybe," she said as they sat down.

"Bloody muppets!" the drunk bellowed.

"That or Kermit the Frog. Kermit the Kraut, maybe. Cheers . . . Oh." He looked at her empty gin glass. "You were ready for that. The citizens of tomorrow giving you a hard time?"

"Not really. Some of them are not coping too well with the new number work. I think they stood still a bit in the last year of infants' and they're resisting new ideas."

"My lot are the same. Except for one amazing whiz called Nigel who already looks and talks like a minor Cabinet minister. And probably will be one. They all hate him, poor kid. Maybe that's where Cabinet ministers come from. It's funny, you know. When you're a little kid you don't see the others as having children's faces: you see grown-up faces. Maybe that's why you recognize them years later."

"Do you?"

"Eh?"

"Would you recognize somebody you last saw in infants' school, say?"

"I have done. Little boy who lived next door to me in Stockport. Moved away when I was, oh, no more than six. I met him on a train when I was coming down from college. I knew him straight off and the weird thing was, his *voice* hadn't changed. Still had this same whingey tone."

"You're sure it was him? I mean, you talked to him?"

"I certainly did, he'd still got my Matchbox Lagonda with the opening doors. Front *and* rear. Thieving tyke denied it, of course. What's up, have you got this feeling that Chris Bryce was your childhood sweetheart?"

"Oh no, nothing like that." She

laughed briefly. "I'll get us another drink."

When she came back with the drinks Martin was building a beermat house with that peculiar lightness of touch he had. He did not look up but shifted about in his seat and cleared his throat and finally said gruffly, "It's fine, you know."

"What?"

"If you don't want me to come on heavy, that's fine. I really mean it. I know that counts as one of the great male bullshit lines of all time, and in fact I probably am talking bullshit. But I am enormously happy to be your friend. I will also back off from that if it's causing you grief, as something is."

"You don't have to say any of this, Martin," she said, shaking her head. "You don't have to because — well, it's fine. As long as it's fine with you that I'm not very responsive at the moment, not very — well, not all there, really. I know I'm hard going just now. I don't *want* to be. But there's this problem, and I can't see past it properly, and it's something I'm going to have to sort out

316

myself. And if you think — " she laughed distressfully — "well, sod that for a game of soldiers, then I can't blame you and that's fine too."

They looked at each other for a long moment, and then they both laughed, without awkwardness now.

"We make Mr Muppet over there sound like the essence of lucidity," he said. "But I do know what you mean. Only if this problem turns into something I can help you with — "

"Thanks. But it'll probably sort itself out."

But that, she saw clearly now and perhaps for the first time, was exactly what it would not do. She was going to have to do something, something that would bring her nearer to the truth.

Fortunately, she had an invitation to the Yeomanses' house the day after tomorrow.

15

BEN'S birthday party was a good one and under normal circumstances Carol would have enjoyed it thoroughly. A pity: and again guilt gripped her for thinking it so and wishing that normal circumstances would return. Wishing that she could wake up and it would all be a dream, in other words.

But it wasn't, and normal circumstances weren't operating. She went to the party with a hidden agenda, a spy in the Yeomanses' domestic midst. She wanted to find out everything she could about Geoff Yeomans. And incidentally she would be submitting herself to his sheer presence again, seeing what its effect would be under, as it were, test conditions. She hoped that she was forearmed now against any drastic and uncontrollable reaction — the fear and hysteria and nausea — but if it came, so be it. If some element of choice remained in her actions — she could, possibly, have not gone to the party after all — she could see the time rapidly looming when choice would not be a factor. She was in this now: she must follow it to the end.

There must have been some strength in her that she didn't know she had, because if just a year ago a crystal ball had shown her this situation coming her way, had told her that her nightmare past was waiting to reclaim her, she was sure her response would have been terror and even blank rejection. Yet somehow she was accommodating this ghastly thing that had arisen in her life. She was continuing to function, continuing even to teach a class in which one of the pupils was the son of the man she so dreadfully suspected. Maybe she was running on autopilot: she certainly wasn't cruising; but she was holding herself together. Last night she had found herself making a list of things she had to do tomorrow and then getting up after she had gone to bed and switching on the light and checking the list over again: familiar signs, and they would have to be watched. But she was, she felt, reasonably in control.

As long as she kept her eyes fixed on

her immediate objective: to find out, to be sure. Beyond that was a void, or what her mind preferred to see as a void simply because she knew that it would contain sterner tests than this whichever way the truth lay.

She pushed aside, too, any consideration of the moral dimensions that her suspicions opened up. It had been natural and necessary for her to think of the people who had so savagely amused themselves that December night fifteen years ago as, simply, evil. The evil must run all through them: they must in a very real sense be made of it. To think of such evil coexisting with other elements, the elements that enabled a person to rub along nicely and normally in society, was to open up unbearable perspectives.

Of course you knew it happened; you didn't have to be an aficionado of true-crime stories to know that murder wore a human face, the neighbours never suspected a thing, and the journalist interviewing the monster in his lifer's cell was always struck by his charm. But still she had thought of such creatures as having some definite mark of Cain about them, their very ordinariness creepy and off key. To believe that made it easier on the mind.

But to think of Geoff Yeomans as he was now and as she suspected he was fifteen years ago was not easy on the mind. It meant truly confronting the abyss, and so she averted her eyes.

She was still fond of Ben Yeomans. Doubtless that was extremely odd of her, since she knew now what memory it was that stirred in her when she looked into his smooth open young face. But there it was. Ben was a special child to her, and only the thought that some of his classmates would be at the party and might consider him a teacher's pet prevented her from taking a present along with her.

Wednesday was murky, grey and chill, the dying side of autumn showing itself instead of the crisp appley invigorating side for the first time. Carol had supposed the barbecue idea would be abandoned, but when she arrived at the Yeomanses' house she found a handpainted poster with an arrow and the words 'TO THE PARTY' taped to the brick wall of the passage at the side of the house.

There they were in the garden at the back, the children beetling about in gloves and balaclava helmets, the adults, of whom there were quite a few, gathered round the barbecue like a brazier. The children had even got out a swingball set and some badminton rackets, and were whooping it up, breath steaming, just as if it were a summer's day.

"I know, we're mad," a well-wrapped-up Elaine Yeomans said, handing Carol a plastic cup of soup. "But then you do it on Bonfire Night, don't you? He was so keen on the barbecue idea and, well, we felt rotten that we couldn't get him a bouncy castle like he wanted. There just isn't room in this garden. Unless there's such a thing as a bouncy shed."

It was a small town garden with a high brick wall at the end where the railway ran, and very much a young family's garden: a square of punished lawn, a tree dangling a dilapidated swing, and two large hutches containing rabbits and guinea pigs, together with much evidence of Geoff's do-it-yourself activities, odd lengths of timber and offcuts of melamine. Carol was reminded of those Lowry-like views from the train going to and from college that had called out to her from towns like Dunmarket, showing her places like this and inviting her to live amongst them.

"Thanks ever so much for coming, anyway," Elaine said. "Ben'll be made up when he sees you. We won't be out here for long. Soon as you feel your feet go dead, go in and get warm. God, my nose!" Elaine pressed her cup of soup against the red tip of it, comically grimacing. "Now you'd know this, you tell me, which noses get colder, big ones or small ones?"

"Small ones, I think," Carol said. "They lose the heat quicker."

"So the same goes for small people as well? Aha! See, bighead." Elaine stuck out her tongue at her husband, who was taking charge of the barbecue. "I do feel the cold more than you because shortarses do."

"Or is it that they just moan about it more?" Geoff said with a grin, turning burgers over.

"I hate it when they've got an answer, don't you?" Elaine said, turning back to Carol and crossing her eyes in frustration.

She was a nice person, Carol thought: fun, without making a parade of being a "fun person". For a moment she felt a traitor. What would Elaine think of her if she could know the secret suspicion she brought with her?

Stop, though: to think of that was to look beyond her immediate objective, into the void, and that she must not do. Her feelings about Elaine and Ben and about this apparently innocent happy family must be kept separate from her intentions, or else she would be lost.

She had allowed herself only one brief glance at Geoff, busy with the food. Tall, round-shouldered, strong-jawed, with that heavily brisk look of being a man in control of things. She experienced no lightning flash, but did not expect it. What she felt was rather as if something were slowly setting and hardening within her.

"Benny!" Elaine called out. "Miss Halstead's here."

A bobble-hatted figure disengaged itself

from the mêlée on the lawn and sprinted over to her.

"Happy birthday, Ben," Carol said. "Thanks for asking me to your party. What did you get for your birthday?"

Ben, highly excited, rattled off a list which sounded very generous. All, she noticed, from Mum and Dad.

"Geoff reckons I spoil him," Elaine said when Ben had galumphed back to the swingball. "Probably do, but why not while they're young enough to enjoy it? They'll soon be old and fuddy-duddy like me."

"I wouldn't call you old and fuddy-duddy."

"That's what you're supposed to say. Thank you very much. But you know what I mean. You see kids and you remember what it was like when you had that much energy. Anyway, I'm earning and Geoff's earning, so why not go to the wire, that's what I say. Some kids have got millions of aunties and grannies to buy 'em prezzies, but Ben hasn't, so we make it up."

"Ben hasn't got any grandparents?"

"Well, he has on my side. My mum

and dad are still around. They live in Wimbledon. Ben calls them the Wombles. Bit cheeky but I can't really blame him. To be honest, they're a bit — well . . . " Elaine did a mime, sticking her nose up with her finger. "They weren't too keen on me marrying Geoff," she went on in an undertone. "Not quaite naice enough. Dad's only a pen-pusher in the Inland Revenue but you know how it is. They keep their distance and send Benny a card with a tenner in it at birthdays and Crimbo and that's it really."

"Nobody on Geoff's side?" Carol said, sipping her soup. She had never been a good actor; but it was not too difficult to make this casual and conversational, and it helped that Elaine was so frank and open.

"Not a sausage. He never had a dad and his mum's dead. He doesn't say much, but from what he has said I think he hated her." Elaine glanced over at Geoff to make sure he wasn't hearing her; but the children were making enough noise to prevent that. "Sounds like she was a bit of a cow, and I don't think he had it very nice when he was young. Makes him all the more determined to do right by Ben, I reckon."

"That's nice."

"Oh, he's the original rough diamond, my Geoff," Elaine said. She glanced over at him again, this time meeting his eyes, and there was a teasing affection in her look.

Carol was nerving herself up to ask more about him when Ben reappeared at her side and with the confidence of being on his home ground asked her to have a game of swingball.

"You won't like me any more when you see how bad I am at games," Carol said. "I mean *really* bad." He did seem, if not disappointed, a little surprised at her uncoordinated flailings. But Elaine gave her a clap when she returned puffing and blowing to the patio.

"I don't deserve that — I'm useless!"

"That's why. Thank God I'm not the only one. I can't stand sporty types. I must admit when Ben first talked about you I was afraid you'd be all jolly hockey sticks. It's not fair, I know, but you just expect teachers to be like that, don't you?"

"A lot of them are still. There were plenty of beefy sorts when I was at training college. Always smelt of embrocation. You can't completely avoid it, I mean I have to take PE with Ben's lot, but at least it's not me who has to climb up the wall bars."

"I should think you get plenty of exercise just being in a classroom. Thirty kids, how do you do it? I've only got Benny and he runs rings round me."

"Oh, it's not so bad. I'll bet your job's just as taxing."

"Well, the old grannies don't move so fast. But they can still be a handful. We've got one old dear called May, very active though her marbles are long gone. You never know what she'll come up with next. You'll be ironing in the kitchen and she'll come wandering down fully dressed with her skirt all wrapped round her waist like a nappy. Last week she was swanning about in her nightie with her hat on at two o'clock in the morning, asking when her taxi was coming. You just get her back to bed and settled and go back to the ironing and down she comes again with her knickers on her head."

"It's a wonder you've got any energy left at all!"

"Well, they are long shifts. The pay's not brilliant, either, considering the money they get out of the poor old sticks. D'you know, they charge four hundred quid a week *and* the residents have to pay for their own incontinence pads? Not kidding. They keep a tally and present 'em with a separate bill at the end of the month."

"My God. Who owns that place?"

"Naming no names, but she's a county councillor," Elaine said, lifting one eyebrow. "Getting on a bit now herself. I hope to be nursing her one day. I shall put swarf in *her* incontinence pads."

Carol laughed. Strange: the laugh was genuine, and her ease with Elaine was genuine, even as darkness lurked at her elbow and the terrible question lay coiled like a poisonous snake within her. "How long have you been in that line of work?"

"Oh, since I left school, on and off.

It always appealed to me. My mum and dad would have preferred me to go into something a bit more, well, naice. I think they saw me as the manageress of some posh shop, you know, strutting around being a megabitch in a tight skirt. Not my thing, though. I'll bet you always wanted to be a teacher, didn't you?"

Carol took a deep breath. "Yes. Pretty well."

Elaine gave her a bright friendly look. "It's funny, you know. Ben's last teacher was a right old battleaxe. Well, she wasn't, but you always felt you were talking to a teacher, you know? But it's different with you, it's like you're . . . "

"Human?" Carol said.

Elaine slapped at her hand. "Don't," she said with her big healthy laugh, "you've made me feel awful now."

"No, really," Carol said, "that's the nicest thing anyone's ever said to me." Again she felt a pricking of treachery. And then Geoff's voice broke in on them, calling out that the food was ready.

The children descended like locusts, and the only option was to serve them first. Carol didn't feel like eating, and hoped she would escape it in the hullaballoo; but Geoff beckoned to her over the small munching heads and said punctiliously, "What would you like, Carol? Don't worry, there's plenty left. The anklebiters won't get it all. What do you fancy?"

"The sausages are nice," Ben said, turning a greasy smiling face to her.

"Oh, hang on, you're not veggie, are you?" Geoff said abruptly, frowning.

He must have seen her hesitation: hurriedly she said, "No, no. I feel like I should be, you know, but I just can't help liking meat. Um, the drumsticks look nice."

"It's nature, that's the way I look at it," Geoff said, heaping her plate. "When we were cavemen, we ate meat. It's what our bodies want. Anyway, the animals don't suffer. There you go."

"Thanks." Carol took the plate. She lifted a drumstick to her mouth and felt the hot touch of the flesh against her lips and suddenly it seemed to her she couldn't go on with this. This was beyond her, too much, she was in an impossible position, she was just going to have to run, get away from it . . .

She bit into the meat, aware of his eyes on her. Just hold up, she told herself. You know what this is. It's the Trapdoor, that's all. The old weak spot. It's nothing new, you've experienced it before. You can deal with it.

"Mm," she said, looking up and meeting his eyes. "Done to a turn."

"See, we're not all useless at cooking," he said with a satisfied look. "Had any more trouble with that window?"

"No, it's great, thanks ever so much. Is your finger OK?"

"Had some harder knocks than that in my time." He served himself last, and began to eat with peculiarly delicate mincing bites.

"I can't cook to save my life."

"No? Well, I can manage. I mean, the kitchen tends to be Elaine's department but I suppose I'm a bit old-fashioned like that. Mind you, I'd want Ben to be able to look after himself, because things are changing, aren't they? Not everybody goes straight from home to getting married nowadays."

"Is that what you did?" It was harder

very much harder, to act with him than with Elaine, and she was sure the question came out oddly. She imagined him turning to her in his slow frowning way, demanding, "Why? What's it to you?" and wondered what she would do, how she would keep it up . . .

"Me, no," he said with a slight shrug. "Knocked about a bit before I got married. Calmed me down a bit, actually. I'm hoping Ben'll be as lucky as me. Finding someone like Elaine, I mean."

"She's — great, isn't she?" Carol said, hardly knowing what she was saying.

"She's more than that." He spoke dogmatically, as if she had challenged him. "She's a treasure. I don't know where I'd be without her." He stared across the garden, slowly chewing. Every muscle in his face seemed to flex and stand out as he did so, as if he were performing some violent and taxing exertion.

Where did you meet? The question seemed the nearest and likeliest to the many, more vital ones that she needed to ask; but before she could say it, Elaine began introducing her to the other adults present: a few neighbours, and the parents of Ben's best friend, a well-meaning, thumpingly earnest couple, somewhat of the Chris Bryce type except that they were intense and staring where he was professionally laid back. The woman was so comprehensively dressed in hand-knitted wool that her outline was fuzzy, like a smudged drawing; the man, in a rainbow sweater, dungarees and green Dr Marten boots, looked as if at any moment he might break into street theatre. They quizzed her about the National Curriculum, seizing on her vague replies as if they were Holy Writ. She couldn't shake them off, and once she saw Elaine give her a half-apologetic, half-amused smile from the other side of the patio.

They stuck with her when Geoff called time on the children, dousing the barbecue and ushering them inside. It was quite dark now and the afternoon chill had turned to evening cold. The party continued for a while indoors; there was a cake, and after he had blown out the candles and cringed through a chorus of "Happy Birthday to You" Ben rescued Carol from the increasingly heavy discussion by roping her into a board game he had got for his birthday. It was so complicated she wasn't sure what she was doing, but she couldn't give it her full attention anyhow. She was back here, in the house where she had first seen Geoff Yeomans and which like most homes carried his impress on every square inch.

It was a nest-builder's place; a place too of someone who had been poor and for whom comfort should be expressed in appearance, with pride of place given to a buttony, shiny leather chesterfield. The highest value seemed to be set on newness. Though the living room was filled to the point of clutter, there was little that was old, and she could see no mementoes — no little silver trophies or objects that could have been kept only for sentimental reasons. And no framed photographs. Carol couldn't be sure whether it was her own heightened awareness that marked this absence as significant, but once she had noticed it

she couldn't let go of it, and there was
a renewal of that sensation that was like
a hardening of ice inside her.

The game ended with Ben winning in
some incomprehensible way, and though
he tried to string things out by showing
Carol all his birthday cards, his time had
run out. The other children were collected
by their parents, the woolly couple took
their charge away after plying Carol with
a few last pain-racked questions about
educational standards, and Elaine hustled
Ben off to bed.

The neighbours were staying for a
drink, and Geoff pressed Carol to stay
too. She said she was driving, but it
was only a token protest: she had every
intention of staying.

"One or two won't hurt you," Geoff
said. "We've got to christen this bar,
haven't we? I mean, it's not totally
finished, I've got to get the optics up
yet, but it's near enough."

"That's amazing," Carol said. "It was
nowhere near finished last time I was
here."

"Ah, I don't hang about." He had a
way when pleased with himself of slightly

wagging his large head from side to side, his mouth open and his tongue daintily touching his bottom teeth. It made him look —

Boyish. She made herself acknowledge the word.

"What's your poison? We've got beer, lager, cider, gin, vodka — "

"Just a small vodka would be lovely, thanks."

Accepting hospitality from a killer. From someone she had last seen when she was a terrified eye looking through a peephole at her family being ripped into bloody chaos. The thought entered her mind too swiftly to be prevented. She let it go through and then slammed the gates shut.

Priorities. Find things out. No more.

The neighbours who had stayed for a drink were two youngish couples. Unless it was the distortion of vodka and tension, something odd seemed to be on: each of the women clung to her husband's arm and laughed watchfully at everything he said as if she were afraid of the other one stealing him. They perched around the bar, leaving Carol awkwardly placed on the settee, and she was glad when Elaine came down from seeing Ben off to bed.

"He says he won't sleep, but he will. He's just overtired." Elaine, smiling, came straight over and sat beside her. This was something men didn't seem to have, Carol thought: an instinct that they were going to get on, the readiness to express it. She liked Elaine. The liking shouldn't have been able to persist alongside the monstrous suspicion inside her without tearing her apart, but somehow it did. Almost incidentally Carol was discovering a new side to herself — or rather, discovering how many sides she could contain. She was genuinely appreciative of Elaine's friendliness at the same time as she was prepared to use it.

"Don't I get a drink, then?" Elaine called. "And put some music on."

"What did your last slave die of?" Geoff said. He brought over a brandy in a glass with Elaine's name engraved on it. "What about you, Carol?"

"I'm still on this, thanks."

"Ta, petal." Elaine took hold of his

little finger and squeezed it before he went back to the bar. Rock music started up, seemingly from nowhere. "He's got a tape player rigged up behind the bar," Elaine said at Carol's look. "There's one speaker in the corner, see? And the other one's hidden in that alcove. Oh, he's fiendish. Better turn it down a bit, Geoff! I like it loud myself, but there's Benny up top. Course, he's going to redo it all when he gets this CD player he's always on about. Tapes sound perfectly all right to me, but men are fiddly about those things, aren't they? They sit there with their ear pressed against the speaker saying oh, my tweeters aren't up to scratch or whatever. But if you asked 'em what music they'd just been listening to they'd have no idea. God!" she said, stretching out her legs. "I'm absolutely knackered."

"I should think you are after that," Carol said. "It did go off well, though. Nicest children's party I've been to."

"Well, I remember what they were like when I was a kid. You'd all sit round the table in your best frocks eating little sandwiches and frightened to speak. And

I remember going to one where there was this children's entertainer — a creepy old guy in a clown suit, smelling of booze. There was some awful murderer in America who used to do that, wasn't there?"

"John Wayne Gacy, that's right. Had all these piles of bodies under his house. He threw them through a trapdoor."

"Jesus!" Elaine gave Carol her droll crossed-eyes look. "You know some fascinating facts, don't you? Here, you seen any more of, you know, thingy? Your admirer. The one who came round on Saturday."

"Oh, I — well, I work with him."

"Oh, he's a teacher? I thought I knew him. Well, *that* handy. Sorry, we really cramped your style being there that day, didn't we?"

"It isn't anything like that," Carol said, laughing a little.

"You liar. Big bloke, isn't he? I like big blokes myself. It's unfair, I know, but I can't stand those little pipsqueaks who look like they're standing in a hole, you know? And little ratty hands. Mind you, I suppose it's not ideal, him working in the same place as you. I suppose you'd get a lot of gossip. Plus it'd be awkward if it didn't work out — having to pass him in the corridor every day, you know, looking daggers and grinding your teeth at each other. Sorry, I know, you're just friends." Elaine performed a comically deadpan wink, her eyelid coming smoothly down like a shutter. "Still, you've got to meet Mr Right somewhere, haven't you? You never know where he'll turn up."

"How did you and Geoff meet?"

"Oh, it was the classic crowded room, eyes meeting, the whole bit. I was working in London, Streatham actually, mopping up granny wee as per, and one of the girls I worked with had this party. And there was Geoffrey — hates it if I call him that, by the way. I only found out afterwards that he'd gate-crashed that party. Rough diamond, like I say." The group at the bar were talking loudly and laughing, and this with the taped music meant that Elaine could confide without being heard. "He was just drifting about at the time. Really on a downer. He'd had this decorating job but he'd packed it in for some reason. He can get very low if you don't gee him up, even now. Anyway he really picked himself up, and we got married, and my parents tore their hair out, and then we came out here. There was good work going and we didn't want to bring up a kid in London. Well, Geoff didn't especially. He said he wanted his kid to turn out right and have what he never had. Like I say, it's a bit of a mystery, what he went through when he was younger, and he doesn't seem to like to talk about it. We're his family and that's it kind of thing, which is nice really, even if — "

A huge shout of laughter from the group round the bar cut her off. Geoff was drinking strong lager and there was a whisky chaser at his elbow. Carol didn't catch the joke he had made but he was laughing the loudest, that large metallic laugh, head thrown back and eyes puckered and frowning as if in pain. She tried to study him both covertly and with the dispassion of a witness in court; tried too not to look away quickly when he suddenly stopped laughing and caught her eye.

"That was a mucky one, no doubt,"

Elaine shouted, then turned back to Carol, tucking her legs up on the seat. "I shall have trouble with that one in the morning. Do you smoke? No? Mind if I have one? Don't often get the chance. His lordship doesn't like it when Ben's around — passive smoking and all that. He's got a bit of a thing about it."

Carol found herself unsurprised by this: she could detect a curiously prim element in Geoff alongside the conspicuous manliness.

"I've tried telling him there's an old girl where I work who smokes thirty a day and she's eighty-five, but it's no good. Of course, I wouldn't want Ben to smoke when he grows up, but there we are, I'm just a hypocrite and that's it. Anyway they're going to do as they like whatever you tell 'em, and that's the way it should be as far as I'm concerned. You ever caught any of the kids at it behind the bike sheds at school? Smoking, I mean."

"Not so far. Diane Hollins, she teaches fourth-years, apparently she's had a bit of trouble that way. And dirty magazines floating around the class. But then they're eleven-year-olds, and that's a different ball game."

"They've got it all to come, haven't they? Poor sods. I remember first finding out that men got erections. Stunned, I was. The sheer weirdness of it. I went around looking at the front of men's trousers, thinking, Well, he hasn't got one. And he hasn't. Now he might have . . . More drink, please, slave!"

"What are you two cooking up over here?" He was clearly getting drunk, but Geoff moved with his usual slow, heavy restraint. His face was flushed, which made his eyes look glassy in their lightness.

"Talking about you," Elaine said. "So you can go away again now."

"Hm." He grinned and shook a mock fist. "You don't want to believe everything she tells you," he said to Carol.

"You don't want to believe everything she tells you," Elaine echoed, in a very accurate imitation of his gruffness, and slapped at his behind. "Go on, go and tell some more mucky jokes."

"Is, er . . . " *Is Geoff a violent man?*

Can you do that to him without fear? Do you know why he doesn't talk about his past? Impossible. There was only so much she could ask, only so much she could learn this way. "Where's Geoff working at the moment?"

"He's doing a job just outside Ipswich. New office development. He'll probably be there for another three months. That's what's good about this firm he works for, they get the big jobs. He's not going to get that sort of work if he sets up on his own like he wants to. But I don't say anything. He's got his heart set on it. And he really doesn't like being told what to do, I mean *really* doesn't like it, so it would make sense being his own boss."

There was another roar of laughter from the bar. "Ah, now you're talking," Geoff was saying, his voice booming and expansive. "Now you're talking my kind of comedy. Your pure oldfashioned slapstick. I don't care what anybody says, he's still the best."

"Who is?" Elaine shouted.

"Norman Wisdom, the great Norman. I'm telling you. There's still nothing to beat it for sheer — laughter. It'll never die, that slapstick, because it is just timeless." He wagged his forefinger emphatically: the drink intensified the dogmatic, almost pedantic way he talked. "You show me someone who doesn't laugh at that, and I'll show you someone with no sense of humour."

"Can't stand Norman Wisdom," Elaine hissed through her teeth at Carol, smiling. "Oh no, here he goes."

Geoff began doing an imitation of Norman Wisdom's helpless hysterical laugh. From his deep chest it came out as a yelping, baying noise, like a dog in pain.

"Wait till he starts singing 'Don't Laugh at Me 'Cos I'm a Fool'," Elaine said to Carol. "Or on second thoughts, don't."

"Carol!" Geoff bellowed. "He's the best, isn't he? Norman Wisdom. He's the best."

"He is, he's hilarious," Carol said.

He began doing the laugh again. It unnerved her.

"So what about you?" Elaine said, shrugging. "You fancy having children yourself?"

"I don't know — haven't really thought about it. I do love children, but, er — I don't know about twenty-four hours a day."

"Well, you'll know if the time's right. Oh God, I can't believe I said that, I sound like one of those unbearable women who think they're experts just because they've popped out a kid. And when they say *broody*, don't you just hate that, like you're just this *womb* with a person attached. And it's babies who are supposed to make you like that, I mean what's so great about babies? Kids are different because you can do things with a kid and have fun, but a baby just lies there."

The yelping laugh rang out again. The sound seemed to burrow under Carol's skin like a needle. He had begun repeating it, emptily, to whatever was said whether funny or not. Elaine merely chuckled and clucked her tongue; but Carol was suddenly afraid she couldn't stand it, she was going to have to run, get away, she knew she must control the panic rising in her but it was beyond her, this whole thing was beyond her . . .

She must have unconsciously made a movement to get to her feet, because Elaine said, "Need to go? Upstairs, first on your left."

"Thanks."

Out in the hall she gripped the newel post at the bottom of the stairs and took several deep breaths. All right. Use the loo, then say her goodbyes and leave.

She looked up. The steep perspective of stairs vanishing into darkness confronted her with an old terror just as it had in Aunt Jean's house; but this time it was much worse.

She blinked.

CUNTS.

She blinked again. The memory remained vividly splashed on her mind's eye for several intensely lucid moments, as the flash from a camera lingers on the retinas.

That word, daubed on the landing wall fifteen years ago, written in her parents' blood. It seemed to her that she had just *seen* the memory of it, in a way she hadn't before. Had she? It was difficult to disentangle what she remembered from what she knew of: Dr

Kaufman had told her details like these later in life, when her need to know had been stronger than the danger of knowing.

She put her hand on the banister. Imagined, pictured or remembered her own small eight-year-old hand on the banister of her parents' house. Slippered feet running down to the telephone. And above her, graffiti, smeared and sticky, like gloss paint that hadn't been stirred.

Just open that front door and get away from here. Just go, now.

For a few moments she seriously considered this. But then she knew that she couldn't run away. She might run away physically, never come near the Yeomanses again, leave Dunmarket even: it didn't matter. She would always come back to this — or rather, this would go with her.

She had no choice now.

There was another burst of high yammering laughter from the living room. Almost without volition, but with sudden purpose, Carol moved.

She found the bathroom to her left,

and turned on the light by the cord switch. But she didn't go in.

There were two other doors on the landing. One was nearly closed. A ceramic tile reading 'BEN'S ROOM' was fixed to it: above that, one of Ben's own drawings, a skilfully copied picture of Aladdin on his magic carpet. The light was off inside.

The other door stood half open.

Carol listened over the banister a moment, then stepped softly into the room.

The curtains were open, and the window, at the front of the house, let in a fair light from the streetlamp outside. The room was quite large, but there was a huge white louvred bedroom unit covering one whole wall that restricted the space. In front of the window was a dressing table. On either side of the double bed there were little pine chests of drawers.

She didn't know what she was looking for. Something. The bedroom was the ultimate private place, the place of secrets.

She tried to move carefully, but her

hip brushed something at once. No good: she was going to have to risk putting the light on.

She groped along the wall, found the light switch. The light made her squint, and then her heart hit her throat as she saw that there was someone in the room.

She began backing away, trying to unlock her throat to say something. Then she saw who it was.

Herself. The bedroom unit incorporated a full-length mirror. Carol met her own eyes. She looked guilty, an intruder.

She turned away from her reflection, moved towards the chest of drawers on the near side. Then she noticed the softness of the carpet underfoot. Looking down, she saw that it was such a thick soft pile, like sand, that she was leaving clear footprints in it.

Sorry took the wrong turning went into your bedroom instead.

And started hunting through the drawers, naturally.

Her nerve faltered. Just what the hell was she expecting to find, anyway? Some clinching clue about Geoff Yeomans' past, just lying there in a drawer?

Something. Anything.

She put a hand out to the handle on the top drawer, and then stopped dead, transfixed.

On top of the chest of drawers was a framed photograph. It was at an angle to her, the picture obscured by the light reflecting on the glass.

Carol reached out and turned it so it was facing her.

A wedding photograph. Elaine and Geoff smiling out at her. Veil and suit. Wedding cake. Young faces. Much younger. The smile . . .

Carol's head swam. Her hand shook and the photograph went over on its face with a slap and then she gasped as a hand touched her back.

"Miss Halstead, are you all right?"

She spun round to find Ben, dressed in his pyjamas, looking up at her in surprise.

"Oh! Ben, yes, I — I wanted the loo, I've gone wrong . . . "

She tried to laugh. His face was solemn as he gazed at her; then a smile began to touch the corners of his lips. It was a shy yet somehow adult smile, its amusement wry and secret.

"It's there," he said, turning and pointing.

"Oh, right, thanks." And then, hardly knowing why she did so, she put a finger to her lips and said, "Sssh."

He must have seen her looking at the photograph, and she was trusting him to say nothing of it. And somehow she felt he understood. It was almost as if he understood everything.

"This one, you say? OK. Night night."

She needed it now: to be sick, or so she thought. But there was only a dry retching and heaving that made spots dance before her eyes, the spots mingling with the image of a young face —

no no shut it out

smiling above a wedding cake.

She flushed the toilet, ran cold water over her face. She noticed a shaving brush by the sink, its bristles worn down and splayed so that they looked like a half-shaven beard themselves.

Can't stay here any longer . . .

She hurried downstairs, prepared simply to shout a goodbye and get out of the front door. But she found Elaine waiting in the hall.

"You all right, Carol? I just thought, what with barbecue and cake and then the booze . . . "

Carol snatched at the chance.

"Bit queasy," she said, trying for a smile. "Think I'd better pop off home."

"OK. Don't worry, I'll tell the others."

Elaine didn't fuss. A nice woman — friend even. Could she really be married to . . . ?

Don't think about it. Just get out.

"I've had a lovely time, though. Thanks ever so much," fumbling for the door handle. But there was a draught curtain in the way, she couldn't . . .

"You'll be all right to drive?" Elaine said, opening the door for her.

"Oh, yes, really, I'm fine."

"Have to do it again next week, then."

"What?"

"Another party next week," Elaine said, a little surprised. "Just joking."

"Oh! Of course, yes. I'll — I'll see you."

Next week. The very idea of it was as remote and alien as the mountains of the moon. Something was going to happen before then because of the knowledge inside her, a bomb ticking away, ticking fast like the pattering of a heart in terror.

16

SHE dreamt of the bird. The nightmare was so vivid and present and unshakable, she was in it and of it so profoundly, that it gave her the strange impression that the bird was dreaming of her.

In the morning she dragged herself to school. A cold heavy listless rain was falling over Dunmarket. It made the surrounding perspectives of meadow and wood look misty and unwholesome, as if a poisonous miasma were encircling the town. Bedraggled children trudged through the gates up to the school, faces pinched, like child labourers to a cotton mill.

In so far as she was feeling anything, Carol felt emptiness. Perhaps it was the disturbed night, with scarcely an hour's true sleep in the course of it: perhaps tension had been wrought up to such a pitch within her that she had suffered a kind of emotional short circuit. She knew that she shouldn't be like this, knew that a dilemma which encompassed the whole of her life was closing its jaws around her. Yet she couldn't stir her brain beyond anything but a numbed apprehension, as if each moment were a step in darkness, the light not to be sought but waited for.

She certainly knew that she didn't want to talk to anyone, and when she entered the staff room and Tony Plumb homed in on her with some exhortations about the next union meeting she could only shrug him off and hope he wasn't offended. There was no sign of Martin: he was late as usual. She took the first book that came to hand in her locker and sat down with it.

She meant it merely as a screen, but she found herself turning the pages and reading a passage here and there. It was a selected poems of Hardy. She had brought it in with the idea of using 'The Oxen' as a Christmas recitation for her class, though their lack of response to poetry so far made her doubtful.

She paused at a short poem. It was titled 'Heredity'.

I am the family face;
Flesh perishes, I live on.

"Things must be bad."

It was Diane, bending over her.

"Oh — sorry." Diane indicated the book, which had a black binding. "Thought you'd turned to the Bible for a minute." She retreated, looking perplexed.

The five-minute bell rang. Carol put the book into her bag and made her way to her class.

The first-year corridor was rackety and smelt of wet clothes and hair. Whilst the fourth-years would shelter themselves fastidiously from the merest drop, this lot didn't, literally, have the sense to come in out of the rain. Carol made a mental note to lay down some cardboard on the classroom floor, or there would be muddy footmarks everywhere.

There was a commotion outside her classroom. She was about to signal her presence with a shout when Stephen Stone came pelting down the corridor towards her with Ben Yeomans in pursuit.

Neither of them had seen her. She recognized the object Stephen had tucked under his arm. It was an addictive puzzle toy that had been the hit of Ben's birthday party, a transparent sphere with a smaller ball and a series of cups inside it: you tilted it to make the ball hop from cup to cup.

"Give it back! Give it back!"

That was Ben, screaming, his voice unrecognizable. Stephen was giggling maliciously. Before Carol could step in, Stephen's shoes slipped on the damp floor. He went over, flat on his face, with a loud slap and a louder cracking noise. The toy broke under his weight like an egg.

If she hadn't been in such a state of blank lethargy, she would have acted more quickly. As it was, Ben had pounced on Stephen before she could close up the few paces between them. And then it was sheer shock that immobilized her for several seconds.

"Bastard, bastard, fucking cunt . . . "

Crimson-faced, his mouth a wide savage square spraying saliva, Ben screamed obscenities whilst his arms windmilled, landing wild blows on the cringing Stephen's face and head and back.

"Ben!" She had meant to shout it, but the word came out feebly from her throat, transfixed as she was by the sight of Ben's contorted face and the frantic rain of blows.

The sight frightened her.

The sight terrified her.

"I'll *kill* you! I'll fucking *kill* you . . . !"

Ben drew back his foot and kicked Stephen sharply in the ribs. And then something clicked in Carol and she hurled herself forward, dragging Ben away.

She had to use such force that she ended up pinning him against the wall.

"Ben! Ben, stop it!"

But he wouldn't stop it, cursing and spitting and writhing in her grasp, and he wasn't Ben either, not when he turned his choked face, still alight with brilliant hatred and violence, to stare into her eyes.

He wasn't Ben, but she knew him.

★ ★ ★

"You're not feeling too good today, are you, Carol?"

"I'm all right."

"I wish you'd tell me about it. Maybe I can help."

"I'm all right."

"OK. If you say so, fine. So how's Aunt Jean?"

"She's all right."

"And Uncle Keith?"

"He's all right."

"Apparently he's doing the music for a TV programme soon."

"Yes."

"Do you know which one?"

"Just . . . something on the Open University. Nothing famous."

"Oh. Oh well, it's interesting nevertheless. Do you mind this music being on, by the way?"

"No."

"I find it relaxing. It's by a composer called Roussel. A ballet called The Spider's Feast. Didn't you say your class was going on a school trip to the ballet?"

"Next week."

"Are you looking forward to it?"

Shrug.

Dr Kaufman gets up from his crunchy leather chair and goes to the window. He parts the Venetian blind and peers at the street outside. Men are drilling in the road there and the noise comes through the music. Every now and then it stops for a few moments, then starts again. It's more like a feeling than a noise: it rattles through her head.

Raising her head for the first time since she came in, she looks at Dr Kaufman's back. Something strange happens: she finds that she hates him. She has been coming to see him for something like two years now. It was hard at first, because she had to talk about things that hurt her and sometimes she cried. But then it got better, and in a way she started to like coming to see him. She knew he was kind and clever and trying to help her. She began to think of him as her friend.

She thought so right up until today, and it is a shock to find that she hates him. The big check jacket and pink shirt and baggy corduroys — usually she finds his clothes nice and funny, but now she just thinks they're stupid. And the music he plays: she used to think it was different and interesting, but now it's just stupid and boring. And the pictures on his walls, the one with the room in a crystal ball and the one with a pile of smiling hippos. And the smell of the coffee machine. And the little joined-on room with the toys and books. She hates it all.

She hates everything, but most of all she hates him. And she hates the way he's going to spot it, and want to know about it. What does it matter?

"They seem to have been digging up this road for months now," he says. "It makes me wonder if they keep filling the hole up and then digging it out again." He turns to her, the sunlight flashing off his spectacles. It makes him look bright and cheerful and she hates that too. "So how are you getting on at school?"

"All right." She went to a different school after her mother and father died. It's quite nice, and finding that she hates it too she feels like crying. Except she knows she won't: it's locked up deep inside and won't come out.

"I remember you telling me about the friends you'd made. There was Donna, wasn't there, and — "

"I hate Donna."

She didn't mean to say it. It just came out, and she is angry with herself.

"Do you?" He doesn't look surprised: he never does. He just sits down and says, "That's a shame. Do you want to tell me about it?"

No she doesn't. It's stupid and it doesn't matter. But he goes on looking at her in his stupid kind way and suddenly she can't stand it.

She gets up and walks into the next room where the toys and the books are. She's allowed to do this, of course, if she doesn't want to talk. But she's sure she's not allowed to do what she begins to do next.

She takes hold of the Etch-a-Sketch, the first thing she sees, and throws it on the floor and stamps on it. Then she gets the marionette of a baby dragon and tears off its head and throws it against the wall, and then she picks up a book and rips the pages out of it and scatters them and then she picks up the toy guitar and swings it against the wall so that it breaks with a terrible noise and the strings snap and twang and then she kicks everything she can see so hard that in the end her leg hurts and she has to sit down making a coughing grunting sound. At first she thinks she's crying but she isn't, it's locked away tightly and she's glad of that.

Dr Kaufman is standing a little way away from her, his hands in his pockets.

"You got angry a bit like that once before," he says. "Do you remember? Only it didn't make quite such a mess."

She glances up at his face, but she sees he isn't cross. He's even smiling a bit, which makes her hate him more.

"You're allowed to get angry," he says. "Everyone's allowed to get a bit angry if they're upset. It's the best thing sometimes. And then when you've calmed down a bit, you can think about what it was that made you angry and try and make it better."

She looks away from him, panting, tugging at the strap of her shoe. Her leg's hurting but she's determined not to let on about that.

"Why don't you like Donna any more, Carol? Has she been nasty to you?"

"No." It's no but it's yes, and all at once she wants to stop hating Dr Kaufman because she thinks he would probably understand that. But she won't say it, she can't say it.

It's too rude, too horrible. He'll think she's disgusting.

"How about a cup of coffee?"

She looks up at him in surprise. Usually when she's here she has juice. She's used to him saying things to her in quite a grown-up way, but this is different: this really is as if she's another grown-up.

"I'm having one," he says.

She finds her voice, and it comes out hoarse as if she's got a cold. But then that sounds grown-up too. "Yes please."

He makes two cups of coffee, and takes it over to the little table between the armchairs. "Shall we have it here?" he says politely: so she gets up and goes over and sits down with him and drinks the coffee.

"People sometimes say nasty, upsetting things without meaning to," he says, sitting back and crossing his legs. "But they're still nasty and upsetting. When I was young someone once said I looked like a little mole. Perhaps because I was dark and short-sighted. They didn't mean any harm saying that, I'm sure. They probably even meant it in a nice way. But I was upset about it for a long time. I didn't want to look like a little mole: I thought everyone would think it and laugh behind my back."

She can't help stealing a look at him now he's said this, to see if he looks like a mole. He doesn't; but she's sure he knows what just went through her mind. He smiles a little.

"Did Donna upset you?"

"Yes."

"Do you think she meant to?"

"I don't know. Don't think so."

"Tell me what she did."

"I can't tell you about it."

"Why not?"

She clenches her lips and shakes her head.

"You know I won't tell anyone else about it. You know that, don't you? It's strictly secret, whatever you choose to tell me."

"It's rude," she says, and then stops because she can feel something inside, like the turning of a key in a lock.

"That's all right. I don't mind. If it's something rude that Donna did or said, you can tell me. I'll know it's not you, that you're just telling me about it."

"She . . . she showed me a dirty picture."

"Yes? What was it?"

"It was out of a magazine. It was a lady with no clothes on showing her thing."

"I see. Had you seen anything like that before?"

"Not really like that." Her cheeks feel as if they're on fire. "Only the ones in newspapers and things like that."

"Yes, I see. But this picture was much ruder than those? Because of what you could see?"

She nods.

"That must have been surprising for you. Have you done anything at school to do with that? What adult bodies are like, and what they do?"

"Sort of," she says. "I mean, I know in a way. About how babies get made and everything."

"Did your mummy and daddy tell you anything about that?"

"Some. And there was Daddy's books. I mean, I sort of know, but . . . " She doesn't hate him any more: she just hopes he won't hate her for what she's going to say, think her a disgusting little girl. "Donna said that I would look like that lady in the picture and I would have to have a man's willy put up me and it would hurt and I'd bleed and I don't want to, I don't want to but she says you have to . . . "

Now it's unlocked and she cries. It doesn't last as long as she thought, but it makes her chest hurt terribly.

"Donna's the same age as you, isn't she?" Dr Kaufman says when she's finished.

"Yes."

"Well, though she might pretend to or think she does, she doesn't really know about these things."

"It's true, though, isn't it?"

"It's not all true. For one thing, you don't have to do that. Some people do it when they're grown up, some don't. But it isn't a thing you have to do."

369

"Why do they do it then?"

"People have sex because they want to. Usually because they love each other, and when they're grown up they have a strong feeling that makes them want to show that love by having sex. The first time a woman does it, it sometimes hurts a bit because it's new, like a new tooth coming through, but not always. But it isn't a bad thing, or dirty. If Donna said it was, she's wrong, and being silly."

"But she said it's what happens, and it's horrible and it's like what they did to my mummy and that was a bad thing, and I can't stop thinking about it . . . "

"Carol. Carol, listen to me. That isn't the same thing."

"It is the same. Why is it different?"

"Because it's about what you choose to do. What did you have for dinner today?"

She doesn't understand.

"What did Aunt Jean give you for dinner?"

"Spaghetti."

"And you liked it? You liked having that for dinner?"

370

She nods.

"So that was nice. But suppose you hadn't been hungry, and didn't want spaghetti. And suppose Aunt Jean didn't take any notice, and made you eat the spaghetti, pushed it in your mouth and made you swallow it until you were sick? She wouldn't do that, of course. But suppose she did. That would be bad, wouldn't it? Bad and cruel?"

"Yes."

"But it's eating spaghetti just the same. Yet there's a difference. It's the difference between wanting to and not wanting to. It's the same with sex. If a lady wants to do it, that's good because it's her choice. If she doesn't, and a man does it to her, it's bad and cruel. Do you see?"

"Yes . . . But I won't ever want to do it."

"Well, that's up to you. It's not a thing you need to worry about or think about. But don't think it's rude or dirty to talk about these things, because it isn't. Is that what you felt?"

She nods.

"You felt ashamed?"

"Yes."

"It's nothing to be ashamed about. Though I'm sure it might feel embarrassing and awkward. It doesn't matter. As long as you know you can tell me if you want to. There might be some things about sex that you might prefer to talk to a lady about, some time, rather than a man. perhaps Aunt Jean or somebody else That's all right. As long as you know that if there's anything you want to say to me, you can say it. It doesn't matter if it seems silly or bad or whatever. If you want to tell me, I'll listen. Always."

17

"I'M sorry about this," Carol said as soon as Dr Kaufman opened the door.

"Don't be." He took the chain off the door, opened it wide. "Come in, you must be soaked."

The rain had begun as drizzle that Friday morning, had increased to a steady downpour by about half-past four when she made her desperate phone call to Dr Kaufman asking if she could come to see him, and by the time her train had pulled into Liverpool Street had become a torrent of monsoon intensity. Just the short walk from the Tube station to Dr Kaufman's house off the King's Road had left her drenched, her hair plastered to her head like a skullcap. She had come without an umbrella or even a proper coat: only now did she take account of the fact.

"I'd better take my shoes off," she

stammered, "I'll get water all over your floor — "

"Fuck the floor," Dr Kaufman said crisply. "Come in, get warm, and get on the outside of a large vodka."

Dr Kaufman was sybaritic about warmth. The heat in his sitting room made the blood tingle in her cheeks, and when she drank the vodka he gave her she felt as if she were pleasantly on fire. Here on his home ground he had shed the dark glasses, but there was nothing noticeably different about his eyes except a slight discolouration. He moved easily about, pouring himself a drink, turning down the radio, switching on a table lamp. The room was uterine in its comfort, with nothing of the bachelor pad about it — at least, none of the frigid neatness that was the real mark of the bachelor pad. One wall, where the fireplace was, was completely covered in bookshelves. The others were crowded with prints and several fierce Indonesian masks, and a six-foot carved totem stood in one corner. There were two low comfortable sofas, strewn with cushions and partly covered with richly patterned throwovers, and a

374

thick Chinese rug. The coffee table was given over to glasses and bottles of spirits. It was all just as she remembered it, except that the TV that used to stand by the hi-fi was gone.

Dr Kaufman didn't speak until she had finished her drink. Then he only said, "Have you eaten?"

"Sandwich on the train," she lied.

"We'll have something later," he said, pouring her another. "Go on. If your stomach's empty, all the better, it'll hit you quicker."

"I'm so sorry . . . springing up on you like this," she said, running a hand through her wet hair. There was such reassurance in this room, and in his presence, so sane and civilized. Yet she felt the reassurance only, as it were, at one remove. This wasn't a refuge, and it wasn't the hope of a refuge that had brought her running here as soon as the working week was over.

"Do you feel ready to tell me about it yet?" he said, sitting down on the sofa opposite her.

"I don't know where to begin," she said, and it seemed the truth. Everything that had happened in the past few weeks had been internal: she had not spoken a word of it to anyone. There was a mass of words dammed up inside her, and she hardly dared to make the breach, feared she would babble and yell.

"Is it something to do with this *déjà vu* you told me about?" he said. "Or rather, which you didn't tell me about."

"Yes. But it isn't that really. I mean I'm not coming to you with one of the old problems that I used to — God, you must be sick of it, I mean look at me, turning up like this and you were supposed to have finished with me years ago. I'm just so sorry . . . " Amazingly, she found she was crying — amazingly, because she had had not the slightest inkling that it was about to happen. She fumbled for a tissue, wretchedly embarrassed. She hadn't cried in front of Dr Kaufman since she was a child.

"Carol. I don't 'finish with' my friends," he said; and then as she howled louder, "Sorry, I should have remembered that saying something nice only makes a person cry harder. Pull yourself together, for God's sake. How's that?"

She half laughed, half sobbed, wiped her face with a tissue. "That's better," she said.

"Whatever it is, it's probably not insoluble," he said. "I doubt whether that's what you want to hear just now, and I don't mean to diminish it at all. What I am saying is, you've overcome every obstacle so far. It doesn't mean the obstacles will stop. Nobody can be stable all the time. Doesn't matter if you take a few steps back as long as you're going in the right general direction. And other platitudes like that. No, come on, describe. Have you been dreaming again? Suffering from insomnia? Crises of confidence?"

"All of those, in a way," she said. "But that's what I — I mean, if it was just that I could handle it. But it isn't something inside my head. It's something out there and I don't know what to do about it." She took the refilled glass he gave her, noticing with a passing pang the way he had to grope for her hand and then place the glass in it. She sipped, trying in her mind to place the events of the last weeks in sequence and context, to give coherence to what had seemed at the time to unfold with the illogical but relentless purposefulness of a nightmare. "You're right about the *déjà vu*, it was that that started it. It was a child in my class, Ben Yeomans. I kept getting the feeling that I knew him from somewhere — that I'd seen him before. But not in a casual way, the feeling of familiarity was just too strong. And too — unpleasant. It made me uneasy. I started having disturbed nights. Flashbacks."

"Flashbacks to what? To when you were a child?"

"To fifteen years ago."

"Specifically?"

"Specifically."

He was very still, listening. "Right."

"Then . . . I met Ben's parents. It was at their house. He got into a bit of trouble on a school trip and I felt I was partly to blame and so I went round there to apologize. Their names are Geoff and Elaine. They're from London, they moved out to Dunmarket after they were married. He's a painter and decorator. Ben's their only child. They're about thirty, maybe thirty-two. They're nice people. When I happened to mention this repair that needed doing in my flat Geoff came round to do it. And this week I was invited to Ben's birthday party and I stayed for drinks afterwards . . . " She gulped at her drink, her fingertips white as they gripped the glass. "And all this time the feeling of — of recognition, the feeling of familiarity, the flashbacks, they've got worse. And now I know why. Ben takes after his father, and I've seen his father before. When he was much younger. Fifteen years younger."

The radio, tuned to a classical station on a low volume, decorated the silence that followed with filigrees of harpsichord music. Dr Kaufman pressed the remote on the arm of his chair and turned it off.

"This is serious stuff, Carol," he said thoughtfully. "God. Have you told anyone else?"

"No."

"Are you going to?"

She shrugged: all she knew was that she had felt herself driven to breaking point by her predicament, and her thoughts had flown straight to Dr Kaufman; her conscious will seemed hardly involved at all.

"Jean?" he said.

"It's different. Not her, but her situation. She's starting a new life. I don't want to drag her back there . . . God knows, I don't want to go back myself."

"No . . . So. Do you want me to tell you you're wrong?"

"I don't know. Maybe."

"Because I can if you like. I could say this is a stress-related delusion and that it was bound to happen eventually. I could tell you authoritatively that it's all in the mind and you should go home and not worry about it. Do you want me to do that?"

"Oh yes, of course, I want that. That would be great. But it's not going to happen. Because I know it isn't true. I'm certain of — of what my senses tell me about this. Maybe I don't know exactly how the process is working, but it's real. It's recognition."

"Which literally means knowing again. Yes. I remember you saying to me that you'd know those youths again if you ever saw them. And now you're telling me it's happened. With one of them at any rate."

"Yes. And I know it sounds crazy."

"You don't know anything of the kind, because it doesn't. I know you, Carol: I trust your mind, even if you don't. And I can't tell you how the process works, except to say that nothing ever dies. The film in our brains is made of imperishable stock. You've probably heard the story of the Finnish teenager who started singing a song in medieval English under hypnosis. Cue the claims that she was Chaucer's wife in a previous life or some such. The truth was far more remarkable: she'd seen that song written down, just once, when she was idly leafing through a book on the history of music. She couldn't even remember doing so, it was a glimpse, the work of a moment. But the brain is endlessly greedy. It doesn't turn anything down." He picked up the vodka bottle, held it an inch from his face to see how much remained, then poured another glass. "It's all in there. Like I've said before, every single experience in your life is stored away. And theoretically it's all retrievable. Just needs the right trigger, the right nudge. Proust's madeleine, unlocking the past. Your case is slightly different, of course."

"Is it?"

"Your past wasn't locked away. When I first saw you I expected complete trauma syndrome — not being able to remember anything about your ordeal. Perhaps unfortunately for you, you remembered practically everything. There was no merciful obliteration, except in some visual detail — your parents, the state of the house — "

"Some of that's come back lately too," she said. "I had a clear memory of seeing graffiti on the wall, and the word 'cunts'. I'm sure I didn't have that before."

"That's interesting. What about the dreams? Are they of those events?"

"No. The old bird dream."

"So we're not talking about having to dig anything up. We're talking about — well, simple recognition. But obviously it's not simple with something like this. The memory that's being jogged concerns an extremely horrifying and traumatic event, and so it's all hedged about with emotional landmines and tripwires. You're going to be — confused, disoriented, with objectivity out of the question. Naturally feelings of hurt and vengefulness will be revived. Which gives it a very similar appearance to your imagination running away with you — or hysterical paranoia."

She was bewildered. "Is that what you think it really is?"

"No, of course not." Dr Kaufman smiled. "I'm on your side, Carol. I'm saying this to forearm you in case you hear it again, from the police, when you tell them about it." He cocked his head in the direction of her silence. "That's what you're going to do, isn't it?"

"I don't know. I mean, yes, that's the obvious course, but . . . There's a part of me that just disbelieves it. I mean, I'm certain of it in my mind, but there's some sort of moral sense that just says, Oh no, it can't be. This is — an ordinary family, an ordinary man."

"Well, it doesn't necessarily follow. There are plenty of unsolved crimes, serious ones, which means there are plenty of murderers and rapists walking around. And they must appear ordinary, or else they would have been rumbled. But OK, what do we know about this man? You think he was one of the four who broke into your parents' house. We've got the strong evidence that he could be, because you recognize him. Is there any strong evidence that he couldn't be? Apart from the fact that he lives an ordinary adult married life?"

"Not really. I've tried to find out about him, about his past, about his character, but there's only so much you can do without coming out and saying it. He's from London, he doesn't seem to have any family, his past is pretty well a mystery except that it doesn't seem to have been too savoury. His wife, Elaine, is really nice, I like her a lot, and so that goes against it. I mean, I can't imagine, if he's a monster like that, how on earth . . . "

"Well, I won't talk about 'the banality of evil', because it's become banal in itself. Are you frightened when he's around?"

"Yes," she said promptly, surprising herself. "Yes, I . . . now I come to think of it, when I've been with them I do feel fear, though he seems OK with his family and you don't get any feeling that he's a violent husband or anything. And the other day I actually felt frightened with Ben. It was that that turned the balance for me. He went into this wild destructive fit and I couldn't control him, had to report him to the head which I didn't like doing. He was tremendously sorry after and in a way he was provoked, but all the same . . . what I saw in that boy in that moment, in his eyes and in his look and even his movements . . . Well, I'd seen it before. That's all I can say. I'd seen it before."

A clock on the mantelshelf struck the hour: that too was new, Carol noticed. Dr Kaufman listened to it, then said, "You're staying?"

"I can get the last train at nine — "

"No point. You'd only have to come back in the morning, to see the police. Won't you?"

All at once something that was like relief, yet far more intense and positive than that word suggested, came over Carol: it left her without words for some moments, feeling as if her heart had swollen like a football.

"Yes," she said, almost gasping. "Yes, that's right. Thank you, I'd love to stay if I could."

"The spare room's made up. We'll eat soon. Tomorrow I'll call the police at Lavender Hill. I'm not sure whether Detective Inspector Lennard is still there, I think he must be near retirement age now — anyhow, we'll see. The point is, the file on your parents' murder was never closed. I know Lennard took it personally to heart that he never cracked it. There's no reason why they shouldn't reopen the inquiry. And as you say, there's only so much you can find out yourself about this man, and it's not wise for you to carry on trying. It should be taken out of your hands."

"There is one reason. Why they shouldn't reopen the inquiry." She swallowed the last of her drink. "They might not believe me."

"Very possibly. That's why I'm going to come with you and give it as my professional opinion that you're not a paranoid fantasist entertaining wild suspicions about every man you meet — if it comes to that. I don't think it will, but I think you'll have to be prepared for some scepticism. But you want it resolved, don't you? Isn't that the heart of the matter?"

"It is," she said. "Oh God, it is because — because I just can't go on like this."

18

FIFTEEN years ago the police had dealt with her as gently as they knew how. Though she had been central to their investigation, and had been questioned more times than she could remember, she had no recollection of having to go to a police station. They had come to her at the hospital, at Aunt Jean's, at Dr Kaufman's office. Later she had felt an appropriate gratitude for this handling, whilst realizing that it was partly due to the failure of the investigation. She had never been called upon to identify a suspect: no case in which her testimony was required had ever come to court. Success would have forced them to remove the kid gloves; as it was, the investigation was completely roadblocked, and while she continued to be visited by police officers, the visits probably contained an element of desperate propitiation, and a reminder to themselves of what they were dealing with. She remembered that Uncle Keith, enraged by a report of some enormous police operation to catch a dealer in stolen birds' eggs, had once stormed down to the police station and demanded to know what the hell they were playing at and when they were going to give his wife and niece justice: but for her, it had all been a remote world from which human figures like Detective Inspector Lennard would periodically emerge to ask her the same questions or just to talk to her, sadly, as if they wanted her to give them some comfort or reassurance they couldn't find.

And yet, strangely, when she entered the police station next morning with Dr Kaufmann it was like walking into an old school or a former home.

Maybe it was the institutional smell of the place, because that was the smell of fifteen years ago: the overused, crowded, polish-and-disinfectant smell of the hospital and of the new school she had had to go to once the press got on to her old one. Or perhaps it was the alarmingly purposeful atmosphere created by the posters, the ringing telephones, the unglamorous and stifling-looking uniforms — all belonging to that other dimension possessed by life and largely, blissfully ignored: the dimension that had broken into her family home fifteen years ago and run riot. It was the dimension of disaster and mortality, of blood and bones, where the shattered pieces of normality had to be picked up and cobbled together. It was the dimension known to ambulance drivers and firemen and rescue workers and nurses and doctors, and to police officers; and it was known to Carol.

It was only as she waited at the glassed-in reception desk with Dr Kaufman that Carol realized how far she had come since that time: how complete had been the rebuilding, allowing her to join the ranks of other people for whom that dimension was a distant abstraction, embodied only in news reports and in the candied form of fiction. She had left it behind . . . but all the time it had been here, waiting for her.

"Kaufman, K-A-U-F . . . Consultant in child psychology at St Thomas's

Hospital and . . . Look, I telephoned, we have an appointment, Chief Superintendent Lennard knows who we are . . . "

The deadpan obstructiveness of the desk sergeant seemed to Carol a bad sign. She stared bleakly at a poster showing a still from a bank security camera, a gunman in a balaclava helmet frozen as he retreated to the door. October 10. Not long ago. Fresh and urgent. A detective in shirt sleeves, young and almost ridiculously handsome, hurried through the reception area carrying a box file. The glance he gave her seemed to reproach her. They were busy, their concerns immediate: they dealt in reality, and a fear went through her that she was coming to them empty-handed.

It wasn't so, of course; and the sense of relief that had overwhelmed her when Dr Kaufman counselled the decision that in her heart of hearts she had already taken was still with her. This was right, the one right thing to do. Yet it was a fearful thing too, not something she could embrace gladly. It wasn't just the inevitable revival of old agonies: it was more complex than that, including a fear that it might turn out to be a meaningless exercise and the contrary fear that she might set in motion tremendous changes in the lives of all concerned.

Luckily she found room in this turmoil for a deep gratitude to Dr Kaufman. His robustness cleared the way for her and kept her sane. And he was a powerful ally to have, as was shown when Chief Superintendent Roy Lennard himself came through to greet them, waving the desk sergeant away.

"Dr Kaufman, how do you do? It's been a long time." Lennard gave her a quizzical and slightly surprised look: she felt he was mentally adjusting an old image. "And Miss Halstead. It's been even longer. I'm glad to see you. Come on through to my office."

As Detective Inspector Lennard, this man had been Senior Investigating Officer in the case of the murder of Alan and Hilary Mitcheson, and at one time had been at the head of seventy officers from several Metropolitan divisions. She knew this from those bitter, frustrated enquiries of Uncle Keith's, which had eventually produced icily polite written replies in which the CID had informed him in detail just what the hell they were playing at. The compilation of a special databank: the technical expertise of the Metropolitan Police Forensic Science Laboratory as well as the Home Office laboratory at Aldermaston: psychological profiling; all this plus the unswerving dedication of Lennard, who even Uncle Keith had ultimately to admit had made the case something of a personal quest and who later spoke publicly of his extreme disappointment at the way the investigation had turned out; all this, and no good.

There had been forensic evidence; but forensic evidence, Carol now knew, was not a bloodhound that led you baying to its quarry. It was what gave prosecution lawyers a case; but there had to be a suspect to begin with. First catch your hare.

For the first time, Carol found her heart quickening with a savage triumph at the thought of one of these hares being possibly, finally caught. Till now the idea of identifying one of her parents' killers had only produced anxiety, denial, bewilderment, and the pain of dreadful memory. It was perhaps the sight of Lennard's face that caused this new, harsher feeling: remembering him as a big, ruddy, tweedy man who looked as if he could lift haybales with one hand, she saw how much he had aged and shrunk and could not help suspecting that there would have been fewer lines on his cheeks if it hadn't been for that decisive failure fifteen years ago. It would be good to give him what had so achingly eluded him.

She pushed away the thought of the alternative — that she might only be leading him to more disappointment and frustration, and herself to God knew where.

"Sorry it's so hot in here. Having problems with the heating. It just blasts out all the time no matter what you do with the thermostat. Do sit down. You were lucky to catch me, actually. I shall be away on leave for two weeks starting Monday."

He watched with a frown as Carol helped guide Dr Kaufman to a seat. Plainly he didn't know about the psychiatrist's illness, and he seemed to regret the briskness with which he had spoken.

"That's if I take it, of course," he said, propping his elbows on the desk and his chin on his hands. "I'm a bit resistant to the idea, what with my retirement coming up. I fancy I shall have more leisure than I'll know what to do with . . . Well! I must say it is good to see you, Miss Halstead. I recognize you now, though at first . . . You still live locally?"

"No. Suffolk. I'm teaching there."

"Really? That's good, that's — marvellous." His eyes lingered on her a moment, and again she saw the struggle, the shift from memory to perception. "Congratulations. Well, I'm very curious to know what this is all about. Something about the — " he glanced at Carol, ran a big liver-spotted hand across his grizzled moustache — "the Mitcheson case, you say. Is it some journalist digging it up? We can soon have a word, Miss Halstead, if you're being hassled. I know what those ghouls are like, if there's nothing new — "

"It's nothing like that," Carol said. "It's . . . that case. My parents. It's still open, isn't it? The file or whatever?"

"It was an unsolved crime," Lennard said, a little stiffly, sitting back and folding his arms. "They don't have a sell-by date."

"Well, I think I've got . . . " For some reason — perhaps the severity of this pine-panelled airless office and something unexpectedly severe about Lennard — she fell back on a legalistic phrase. "I've got some new evidence."

The change in him was remarkable. He had looked old, jaded, managerial, pens and pencils set fussily out on his desk as if they were all he had to concern himself with. Now he sat forward and his eyes were bright as a bird's. "Tell me."

She told, keeping her eyes fixed not on Chief Superintendent Lennard but on a calendar on the wall. It showed scenes of Scotland and she wondered whether he were Scottish: there was no trace of it in his accent, as there had always been in her father's, but something about him suggested Scotland to her somehow:

a touch of feistiness, a certain granite solidity.

Integrity too; of that she had never had any doubt. When she was old enough to understand such things she heard that there had been some pressure on him over his failure with the Mitcheson case, which had been well publicized; but from what she remembered of him and knew of him she had never entertained any doubts about his capabilities. He was even, in a curious way, one more victim of what had happened that night.

She was able to detach herself from her narration like this because she had rehearsed it many times in a mostly sleepless night in Dr Kaufman's spare bed. And also because this thing was simply part of her now, bone of her bone and flesh of her flesh. It didn't require any effort to bring it out: it was participating in normal everyday life that needed an effort.

Dr Kaufman had advised her to tell it simply and fully, as she had told it to him, and not to attempt to rationalize it or tidy it up or make less of it. She could see him out of the corner of her eye, closely attending what she said and ready, she knew, to pounce in and support her if the policeman should raise an objection at any point. But Lennard heard her out without interjecting a word. He didn't even nod: he didn't even move his eyes from her face.

And when she had finished he didn't speak to her. He sat back with his hands behind his head and said, "Dr Kaufman, you were closely involved, of course, with this case."

"I first saw Carol in hospital the day after her parents' death," Dr Kaufman said. "I began therapy with her shortly afterwards."

"And — let me get this right — Miss Mitcheson, Halstead I should say, has been your patient ever since then?"

"She's been a friend ever since then," Dr Kaufman rapped out. "I continued to see Carol regularly for informal counselling for some time after the initial therapy, at least until she was past primary school age, and I remained on hand for any problems that she might have after that. I'm sure you'll understand there's no quick fix for a trauma such as that. And as grown-up people we still get on, as you can see. I've occasionally given her some good advice and she's done the same for me."

"Yes, I see. I just wondered — "

"Whether her word's not to be trusted because she's a screwball, well, no, take it from me. Carol is a schoolteacher, Superintendent. They used to allow nutcases to be teachers, in fact in my day it was mandatory, but not now. She's one of those members of the community who are asked to write references, like doctors and policemen."

"You mustn't misunderstand me — "

"You mustn't misunderstand me either," Carol said. "I'm not doing this for fun. It might be a terrible thing to say but I don't *want* to bring all this back, I'm like anybody else, I want life to be easy and no hassles. And if I could just dismiss this thing out of hand and forget about it I would, gladly. But that's not going to happen."

Lennard studied her for a few moments. He nodded, though noncommittally.

"I do need to know," he said, "how you can be sure."

"You know me, don't you? Yet you haven't seen me since I was a child. You didn't quite know me at first. If you'd sat opposite me on the train or something, it might not have registered consciously, but it would have niggled at you, wouldn't it? You'd have thought, I know that person from somewhere."

"I dare say, yes. But I saw a good deal of you when you were a child, Miss Halstead. I talked to you many times. All I'm saying is this case is slightly different — "

"You've heard the expression 'Never forget a face', haven't you?" Carol said. "Well, that's how it is with me and those — those youths. I know I only saw them briefly. But it's stayed with me." Her breathing was short and she was sticky with perspiration, but she didn't quite realize how upset she was becoming. "Something like that doesn't fade away. You might even want it to but it won't. Perhaps you don't remember what — "

"I remember the details of this case perfectly," Lennard said, and there was a sudden barely controlled stridency in his voice. "I was exclusively occupied with

400

it for the best part of a year and I was damn well haunted by it for a long time afterwards. I also remember you, Miss Halstead. I remember having to keep asking you questions when you looked like a little — piece of suffering, that's all, nothing else to you, just suffering, and I remember how that felt, believe me. I remember what kept me going was the thought that soon it wouldn't be you I was questioning, it would be those bastards. I was going to get each of them in a room and . . . oh God yes, I was going to question them all right. I agree, I entirely agree there are some things you never forget. What I saw in that house was one of them. I was hoping that when we got the bastards, that would help. But maybe it wouldn't. Who knows?"

He looked sour and even hostile; but that, Carol knew, was a ready cover for defensiveness.

"I'm sure," Carol said. "I'm sure as I can be that I've identified one of those — " her use of his own word was a reconciling gesture, a hand extended through the fog of bitterness and guilt — "those bastards."

"It's not that I don't believe you," Lennard said in a lower tone. "Let's just say I want to believe you so much that it makes me a bit wary. I want to believe you so much it hurts."

"What are the legal chances," Dr Kaufman said, "if this identification's correct? Could there be a successful prosecution after all this time?"

"Yes." Lennard was bullish. "Yes and yes. If you point us to one of the scum who did that, we'll nail him to it. Fifteen years ago or fifty years, it doesn't matter to me." He picked up the phone on his desk. "Yep, Les, have you got a minute? Right. No," he said turning to Carol, "don't get me wrong. When I say you've got to be sure, I mean you've got to be prepared for what happens afterwards. If this pans out, then you're really — well, you're starting something. That's all."

"Or finishing something," Carol said.

There was a knock and a plump, fortyish man with a baby face and what Carol could only call period hair, crinkled like crepe paper, came softly in.

"Detective Inspector Lesley Munt," Lennard said. "Les, you remember the

Mitcheson murders? Clapham, fifteen years ago. You were a DC at the time."

"I know of them," Munt said carefully. "I wasn't on the case."

"No, you are now. This is Carol Halstead, Carol Mitcheson as was. Surviving witness. You remember that part?"

Munt nodded, looking at Carol. He had slightly bulbous eyes that didn't seem to blink.

"We've got a possible suspect," Lennard said. "Miss Halstead believes she can identify a man known to her as one of the individuals still wanted in connection with these crimes. After talking at length to Miss Halstead I've decided we should follow it up."

Munt nodded again, bland and unsurprised.

"Dunmarket, Suffolk. I'll get on to the local constabulary and tell them to expect you."

"When?"

"When you've thoroughly acquainted yourself with the file. I'll go through it with you."

Carol had supposed, and hoped, that Lennard would be personally involved. It must have shown in her look, because he gave her a faint smile and said, "You needn't worry about Les. He'll do the business, I can assure you of that. We'll find out what we need to know, Miss Halstead. I haven't said thank you, have I? I'll say it now. And now I'd advise you to go home and forget about it as far as you can. That's when you've done one more thing for me. I need a couple of addresses. Yours first, please, and phone number, so we can get in touch."

Carol told him.

"And," Lennard said, writing, "the gentleman in question, please."

Carol glanced at Dr Kaufman. He must have picked up the slight movement of her head, because he smiled and nodded.

"Geoff Yeomans," she said.

19

CAROL returned to Dunmarket on Sunday morning.

She was welcome to stay till the last train in the evening, Dr Kaufman said; but she felt she had imposed enough, and she knew that he valued his privacy. She was, besides, hardly good company. The previous evening he had tried to take her out of herself: they had gone for dinner at a place by the river in Chelsea where he had talked tirelessly, wittily and vivaciously about every subject under the sun except the one that was on her mind.

"Look," he said at last, "it's like the man said. You've done your bit for now. They have their own way of dealing with these things. Just let them get on with it."

She had no choice, of course; and it was that very helplessness that replaced her feeling of relief with a new tension and frustration. She would be better off at home, and alone: fortunately Dr Kaufman was the very person to understand this.

He was also, perhaps, the person to answer the question that gnawed at her all Saturday night, and which she finally asked him just before she said goodbye.

"Why on earth do I feel guilty?"

"Because you feel like a snitch, maybe," he said. "Nobody likes going to the police, it's natural. And also there's probably a bit of doubt. Say one per cent?"

"Less."

"Well, even that. A less-than-one-per-cent doubt that you might be wrong and you're putting an innocent man through an ordeal of interrogation by the police about something of which he knows nothing."

Carol flinched inside. Sometimes Dr Kaufman's directness could be more painful than bracing.

"Well, I shouldn't let that worry you even if it was the case. They don't use the rack and the thumbscrews now."

"True," she said; but she knew that they didn't need to.

406

Taking the Tube to Liverpool Street, she wished she had driven down to London. Night driving on a Friday in London, in torrential rain, in her then frantic state of mind, had appeared not only unappealing but dangerous; but now she felt oddly conspicuous and uncomfortable in public and longed for that mobile privacy that was the car. The business of driving, too, would have occupied her mind, which was all too free to twist and chew and hurt itself like a caged animal.

She discovered another trace of guilt within herself, too: she had spent the weekend in London without seeing Aunt Jean, a thing she would never normally have done. Her general unfitness for company excused it — even leaving aside the fact that she wanted to keep Jean out of all this, untouched and untroubled. And there was the matter of Brendan, besides: she really didn't feel that she could drop in unannounced now that he lived there.

It felt strange, but it would be best, she decided, if Jean simply didn't know she had come down this weekend. Maybe she could know about it later: maybe she would have to, now that the file bearing her dead sister and brother-in-law's names had been reopened. For now all Carol wanted to do was slink quietly home and hide away.

And then she saw Brendan.

The Tube train had stopped at the Embankment, and she was idly watching the passengers disembarking and moving off down the platform when she spotted Brendan amongst them. Unmistakable — the ambling, reined-in gait, the cropped hair, the designer workshirt. He must have been on the same train as her. There was time only for a moment's relief that he hadn't been in the same carriage, and then he turned his head and looked into her eyes.

The doors closed, and the train began to move. Brendan stood still on the platform, looking at her through the window; and then as the train pulled away he lifted his hand and smiled. It was a wry sort of smile, as if she were a schoolchild spotted bunking off. He was out of sight before she could wave a hand in return; and so she had to leave in abeyance the question of whether she had even wanted to.

Saw Carol today. Didn't know she was coming down to London this weekend, did you?

Thinking of this, Carol was brought face to face with what she had tried to deny: her simple dislike of that man. She must dislike him very much, in fact, because she was immediately picturing the subtle use he would make of that. His drift would be thus — I'm as nice as pie to her. No good: she starts acting differently towards you without giving me a chance. Obviously doesn't want you to have a life without her. You must be hurt. Lean on me; make your choice.

Yes, Carol could see it. A trivial thing, no doubt, compared to the great and terrible thing that had taken over her life now. But somehow it didn't seem so: it seemed all of a piece with it.

A can of worms.

She remembered Ben using the phrase in class. Opening up a can of worms . . . Well, she had certainly done that; but the image suggested to her nothing so innocuous as the wriggly cartoony worms of Ben's drawing. The image that filled her mind was grim and foreboding, and the worms were the kind that ate you away.

★ ★ ★

"I'm just saying that maybe it's not a good idea to keep pestering the police like that."

Aunt Jean's voice.

Carol, tiptoeing across the landing to use the toilet, pauses outside Aunt Jean and Uncle Keith's door and listens.

She shouldn't, she knows — but there can't be any harm in it. It's the mention of the police that catches her attention. Even now, three years after, a sudden hope sometimes rises up in her again. The hope that the police have got them: that it will all be settled.

Dr Kaufman says it's probably best not to keep thinking of it, and she thinks he's probably right. Still, it's there. It's different sort of hope now — more grown-up. In the early days she had a secret fear that if the boys weren't caught they would come and get her the way

410

they got her mother and father. That's gone now: childish. Instead her ears prick up at the mention of the police because it would be right if those boys were caught. It would be — the word flashes on her mind now — justice.

"They need bloody pestering." Uncle Keith's voice, grumpy — unusual for him. "It was taken in broad daylight, for God's sake. I saw the guy getting into it. Is that such a tough nut to crack?"

"Keith, I don't know how many cars get stolen in London every day, but I wouldn't be surprised if it's hundreds. You've got to remember it's — it's not that big a deal."

Oh. It's just the car again. She breathes out her disappointment; but continues to listen, because it's odd hearing Uncle Keith talk like this. He's normally so calm.

"I know it isn't. I accept that. It's just their bloody smug offish attitude that gets me. What do we pay them for, if not to solve crimes? They make out they're doing you a big favour just by looking into it."

"I know." Aunt Jean sighs. "I know

411

what you mean. But I just don't thin.
it's any good pressing them."

"Maybe. Or maybe I didn't press then
enough. Last time."

A moment's pause.

"You did all you could," Aunt Jea
says slowly, "and the police did all the
could."

"Did they? I don't know. It just go
me to thinking when I was down at tha
damn cop shop today — all these pen
pushers, all this snotty obstructive blood
stupidity . . . Is it any wonder they neve
caught them? Did they even try?"

"You know they did." Jean's voic
sounds tired, or perhaps unhappy. "Yo
know the lengths they went to. The las
time I saw that Mr Lennard he wa
practically on the verge of tears becaus
he couldn't tell me what I wanted t
hear."

"Four youths. Four. And Mr Plo
couldn't find one of them. They mus
have been covered in blood, you know
whoever it was must have had that muc.
evidence plainly written all over them an
I can't — "

"Sssh." Sharply. "I know that. Yo

412

don't have to tell me that, Keith."

"No . . . I'm sorry. But sometimes it comes back and I just get so angry . . . "

"I get angry too. All the time. It never goes away. I look at Carol sometimes and I see Hilary in her face and I feel such anger that I could . . . well, I could kill. But it's not the police I feel angry at. Not them."

"No . . . maybe it's the same with me. Maybe it's better than thinking about — those people. Thinking about them still being around. Scot-free. Perhaps even — " he gives a short, bitter laugh — "happy. How do you handle that?"

"You don't. You can't. It isn't possible. So you just have to go on. That's why I'm asking you not to say anything about this when Carol's around. She's going forward, Keith. Slowly but surely. And I want her to carry on going forward. Otherwise those people destroyed her too. I want there to be a day for Carol when it's all gone. Without her even knowing it."

"I know. You're right. But I can't help wanting another day for her — the day when she watches those bastards go down *for life. But no, you're right."*

Carol tiptoes on to her bedroom, her face flaming because she has heard herself talked about, and snuggles down into bed.

She tries not to think about what she's heard. But she can't help it: can't help thinking that though Aunt Jean is right, Uncle Keith is right too.

20

IT wasn't meant to happen, which probably indicated that it was one of those things that were meant to happen.

She got back to Dunmarket in the early afternoon of Sunday. The rain had cleared and the town was roofed with a pearly sky straight out of Constable, the kind that really did occur in this part of Suffolk. People had come out of doors to stroll in the mild air, and the playing field next to Stour Court was crowded with both children and adults, throwing Frisbees, walking dogs, even sitting on the grass to read and sip Coke just as if it were summer.

But Carol, literally and horribly, didn't know what to do.

Tomorrow should at least be negotiable: she had work, and teaching must focus even the most anxiously burdened mind. But she simply did not know how she was going to get through the time until then.

Each single minute that passed was an exhausting ordeal of thinking and trying not to think, of wondering and trying not to wonder. Desperate to know what would happen, utterly unable to influence or hurry the happening — that was the rock and the hard place between which Carol found herself, and from which Martin extricated her.

At least for a time. It could be no more than that, just now, and though nothing was said she felt that somehow he understood it. She not only wanted but needed to be taken out of herself, and the need must have been apparent to him. He did it, and seemed content to be her instrument of forgetting; with only slight hints that he would want to be more than that when the time came.

He telephoned her about five. It was ostensibly about the staff meeting he had missed last week. They dropped the pretence after about a minute.

"I rang you yesterday, actually," he said.

"I've been away this weekend," she said.

"Nowhere nice, by the sound of it."

"No. Not really . . . "

"Can you, stroke, do you want to, stroke, would it do any good to talk about it?"

"No."

"Can you, stroke, do you want to, stroke, would it do any good to meet over a drink and talk about something else entirely?"

"Yes." She pictured a pub: the lurking, hiding feeling was still with her, and vetoed the idea. And her own four walls were intolerable: Geoff Yeomans had left his image imprinted here. "Can I come over to you?"

"You surely can," he said, after a mere instant's pause of surprise. "Just give me a few moments to club the rats into submission."

Martin's flat was at the top of an oddly truncated, shabby-genteel Victorian villa on Ipswich Road, the busy main road that led out of Dunmarket to rich brown farmland and ultimately to the county town. Though he played up to the school myth of him as the slob of the world, there turned out to be as much truth to this as to most myths. The place wasn't elegant, but the basic structure of the flat ensured that: the window-frames were in an advanced state of decay, there was a plethora of old paintwork capable of being cleaned only by enslaved housemaids, and the kitchen was divided from the sitting room by a weird remnant of the 1950s, a fixed screen of teak-effect twirls.

"I see you're admiring my period feature," Martin said of it soon after he let her in. "It's a fantasy, isn't it? It makes me want to look like Laurence Harvey and drink espresso from a chrome-legged coffee table whilst listening to Julie London on a gramophone with fins."

"I should have spiked heels and a bouffant," she said. "And bare arms with those really sharp elbows."

The living room was undeniably a mess, but the mess consisted of jumble rather than dirt. There was one overstuffed bookcase, and the rest of the books were stacked about the floor in little islands that she had to step carefully between. The table was unusable for any practical purpose, being covered from end to end with more books and papers and letters and coffee cups and, she noticed, a small child's toys. The portable TV was balanced on a pile of newspapers, and he shifted another great heap of them to give her room to sit down.

"I buy them and don't get round to reading them," he said, "but I will. I want to find out how that war in Vietnam turns out." He snatched up a tie from the back of the chair and after a moment's hesitation stuffed it in his pocket. "People always say, 'Sorry about the mess,' even when the place is like some show home for anal retentives, so I don't know what that leaves me to say. How about, 'Sorry about the appalling, den-like, all-too-revealing and unrelenting squalor'?"

"I like it," Carol said. She did: with the wind booming at the high windows, it reminded her of a ship's cabin or a lighthouse. She could imagine Martin too, with his big sloppy robustness, his all-weather clothes, his slightly craggy face with the puckered lines around the eyes, as something like a lighthouse keeper, solitary and a little outlandish. "It's lived-in."

"It's that all right," he said; but he seemed pleased in a faintly embarrassed way. "Good to see you, by the way. Stay as long as you like, don't say you really must be going unless you mean it, fall into reflective silence whenever you feel like it without thinking you're being rude, and the loo's through there. That's the formalities over, what do you want to drink? There's spirits, there's beer, there's — oh, there's everything really, even wine in one of those boxes and how do they get the wine in there is what I want to know."

"I like those boxes. You can't tell how much you've had."

"Like that, is it?"

"No, not really. I'm fine. And thanks for — having me round. How are you doing?"

He laughed at that. "I'm very well, thank you. Hope you're the same. Don't you just hate it when you get an answer to that question? When you say, 'How are you?' to somebody and they proceed to tell you about their lumbago and how they couldn't get to sleep the other night and they're going to have their wisdom teeth out next week. I don't know why we ask really, it must come from the days of the plague or something. If they said they'd got the sneezes you ran all the way home and put a poultice on your chest. Or drank it or whatever you did with a poultice. Boxy wine, then? It's white, that's all I know about it. Well, it's not white at all, it's a sort of transparent yellowy colour." He fetched the wine and glasses and a four-pack of beer from the kitchen, perched them on a heap of large books. "Coffee-table books, use them like a coffee-table. I should know what a poultice is. Children's books when I was a kid were full of them. You know those very worthy children's historical novels you used to get. Kids called Simkin and Tamsin romping around Tudor England and helping to put Edward the Whatever on the throne. All that carefully researched detail, possets and sackbuts and linsey-woolsey stomachers. You literally didn't know what the hell was going on, it might as well have been Japanese. Hence a mystified generation. I say this hypocritically, because I look at children's novels now and wish for the old days. They're such downers now. Any parent who hasn't got terminal cancer has to be an abuser. What are you reading to your lot this term?"

"Oh, *The Lion, The Witch and The Wardrobe*. Very trad. They seem to like it."

"I tried *Professor Branestawn* on mine, but I think they found it a bit fey." Martin cracked a beer-can. "Just help yourself to that wine. Keep on siphoning. Fill up while you can. There won't be any at Chris's do next week."

"What's that? Oh yes!" She vaguely remembered Chris Bryce coming up to her in the staff room and inviting her to an anniversary party at his house. Next week: again that dark, inconceivable impossibility. "There won't be any drink?"

"Not drink drink. Well, there wasn't last time. Just juice, would you believe. No crisps either. Just some sort of home-made things like wood chippings. They had the kids there as well. On account of kids being present at all adult celebrations in the East et cetera. Poor sprogs were bored out of their brains. Bitch, aren't I?"

"I don't think so. Well, maybe. I don't care. You make me laugh."

"But you're not laughing," he said, regarding her gently, quizzically.

"I'm laughing inside."

"As opposed to crying inside."

She shook her head.

"That's the last time I'm going to press, by the way," he said, getting up and hunting through a pile of vinyl LPs. "God, I don't know where I stand with these. First I was embarrassed because I hadn't moved up to cassettes, then I was embarrassed because I hadn't moved up to CDs, and then I was embarrassed because it suddenly became trendy to have vinyl records and it looked like affectation — "

"Martin."

"Carol?"

She didn't know how to say it. "It's good to see you."

He frowned, crouching. "Er, didn't we already do this bit?"

"You're the — the one person in the world I wanted to see tonight."

He thought. "Not counting Mel Gibson?"

"Counting him as well."

"How about Brad Pitt? God, isn't that sickening, even his name's cool and butch. Why couldn't I have had monosyllables for my name? I don't know, maybe my parents couldn't afford them . . . The same goes for me, you know. Vice versa, ipso fatso. And not just tonight. And counting Julia Roberts and Michelle Pfeiffer and all those."

"Cindy Crawford?"

"And Michael Crawford and Joan Crawford come to that . . . How about Tom Cruise? Damn it, he's got mono-syllables too — "

"Shut up, Martin. Put some music on." Just as she was laughing for the first time in what seemed years she had a vivid mental image of Elaine on Ben's birthday. Geoff at the bar. *Put some music on* . . . Geoff's wolfish smile and wagging head . . .

Ben. He loved his father: it was plain to see. Was she about to destroy an innocent eight-year-old's world? She shuddered and gulped at her wine, and then a tough voice spoke up inside her.

Your eight-year-old world was destroyed. Remember that.

Martin looked up from the ramshackle stereo.

"You cold, Carol?"

"Not with this," she said, raising her glass, and then turning the gesture into a toast. He leaned over and clinked his glass against hers.

"Here's to juice and wood chippings," he said.

"And poultices and possets."

Their eyes met and held for a significant extra second. The idea of his putting his arms around her became present then, simply in the room with them like the music that started up from the crackling speaker. It was enough simply to acknowledge it: there was no necessity to feel anything about it.

They talked: they ranged far and wide. The drink went down, the wind rattled at the rickety windows, the record played itself out and they hardly noticed. At one stage he showed her a photograph of his daughter, a thin pretty girl with reddish hair that, Carol thought, must come from her mother. The photograph was put away in a drawer.

"You don't have it up?"

"No. I know what she looks like." He was silent a few moments, and then spoke of his parents' home when he was a child in Stockport. "Always framed photographs of me and my brothers everywhere. Like a family shrine. Should be nice, I suppose, but it gives me the creeps to think of it. Good parents, though. Got me *Look and Learn* every week because I was bright. Remember *Look and Learn*? 'Great Moments in History' and 'The Church's Year'. My dad would put on a suit for parents' evening. You don't have to suck up to those old grammar-school fossils, Dad, I used to think, all angry and frustrated. He was doing it for me, of course. Ay-yi-yi, one of the many things you realize too late."

When she avoided the subject, didn't respond with experiences of her own, there was no problem. He leapt over these gaps to something else, taking her with him. And this was everything she had hoped. The wine and Martin kept it all at a distance, saved her temporarily. She knew it couldn't last: it was like a ride in an aeroplane, you simply couldn't stay up there for ever.

But that didn't make it unimportant — or irresponsible. When she kissed him she was drunk, she was seeking solace and distraction and comfort, and she was aware that ugly tomorrows beckoned which probably made this seem sweeter; but she also knew what she was doing. This was a place she would have come to by another road. It didn't matter that the road that had brought her here was dark and left her travel-sore. It was also a place she would have wanted to stay in, explore, enjoy at leisure — bring her whole self to, in fact; and if she couldn't yet, didn't know when or if she would be able to, she could only hope he understood as much as he seemed to.

The bedroom was tiny, which made the bed look huge and obvious in a way that slightly abashed her.

"It's a long time since I've done this," she said.

"Well, they say it's like riding a bike. Did you bring your cycle clips with you?"

They also said that laughter was inimical to passion: she didn't find it so, indeed was startled at her own tumultuous response. She was afraid afterwards that she had shouted out, and as she lay with her head in his neck and with a not unpleasant renewal of shyness stealing over her she said, "Your neighbours downstairs, are they — you know, can they hear?"

"There's just one very refined deaf old lady. She's got a thing about Benjamin Britten, skipping off to America when the war started. Says he should have been shot by a firing squad when he came back . . . There's a thing I want to say."

She reached up and touched his lips. "You don't have to."

"No?"

"I feel it anyway."

"I feel . . . hugely happy."

"So do I."

She felt him look down at her. His fingers paused on her shoulder.

"I wish I could fix it. That happiness. So you could have it all the time."

"Bit impractical."

"Oh, I don't know . . . we could nip into the store cupboard at break. I do mean it, though. You're not — happy. Whatever it is, I want to help with it."

"I know you do. You're kind, Martin." She kissed him.

"Well, I'm going to be unkind now and put you on the spot. I'm not asking you to let me in. I'm asking if you will let me in, some time." He listened to her silence, and then said, "Sorry, unfair."

"No. No, it's not."

"Did you say I was patient as well as kind?"

"No."

"Damn, thought you did. Well, I am. So don't worry: forget about it."

She wanted to, yet in a way she wanted to let him in too. The trouble was, it wasn't a very nice place. It was dark; and she feared it was about to get darker.

21

MONDAY and Tuesday passed, somehow.

Their plain normality was such that Carol began to wonder whether her visit to London, the police station, Chief Superintendent Lennard, Detective Inspector Munt, the calendar with scenes of Scotland, the restaurant by the river, were all the deceptively real details of a dream; just another manifestation like the déjà vu and the nausea and the flashbacks, inconclusive, born of pain, not to be trusted.

On Monday evening Dr Kaufman rang to ask if there were any news, and promised to get on to Lennard if they heard nothing soon. Later in the evening Aunt Jean rang. She was pleasant and friendly and mentioned nothing about Brendan's having seen Carol on the Tube.

At work she and Martin behaved, and probably appeared, much as they always did, though she couldn't escape a feeling that the new development between them was written all over her as if on a sandwich board.

In class she hid behind the efficient shield of Miss Halstead. It worked — always excepting, of course, the presence in the class of Ben Yeomans. He was all long-faced and apparently genuine regret for his astonishing outburst last week. His gemstone eyes followed her everywhere. Presumably he interpreted the way she distanced herself from him as a sign of her continuing displeasure. In fact she hardly knew what she felt, except that this was the only way she could keep going, and that being around him in this everyday fashion was the most intolerable part of an intolerable situation.

For she still liked the boy: what she had seen in him last week hadn't destroyed that. Whatever else it had done.

On Tuesday afternoon she came home to Stour Court to see a car she didn't recognize parked outside the block. A man was sitting in it.

"Miss Halstead."

He was out of the car as soon as she

had stepped out of hers. It was DI Munt, bland and plump and expressionless. He was wearing a zip-up windcheater, and as he came over to her she thought randomly how easy it would be to pass him unseeingly in the street, never suspecting for a moment that he was a senior policeman and that rapists and murderers were his business.

"I — I didn't know you were here," she said stupidly.

"Uh-huh. I'd like to talk to you, if I may." He turned his pale eyes in the direction of the block. "Inside?"

There was no reason for her to be afraid of him, but she was — or afraid of what he brought. It wasn't only the stairs that left her breathing fast and heavily when she ushered him into the flat.

"I've just come from the police station," he said, taking up a position stolidly in the middle of the living room. "Newmarket Road, is it?"

"That's right." She stared, trying to read him. "Oh — have a seat."

"Thanks." He gave a cursory glance round, as if he knew the place well already and were merely reminding himself. "I've just been on the phone to Chief Superintendent Lennard and he said I should come and see you."

He left a pause, which bewildered her: she wondered if she were supposed to thank him.

"Have you — what have you got to tell me?"

DI Munt sighed. "Just that we're grateful for your help but it appears your identification was mistaken. The individual in question has been interviewed at Newmarket Road police station by myself and we've made thorough inquiries into the matter. We shan't be needing to talk to this individual again and, er, as far as we can see there's no further action that we can take in this regard."

He didn't seem to mind her stare: he just coolly looked back at her.

"This can't be right," she said, finding her voice.

"I don't quite follow."

"You — you can't have . . . You say you've talked to him? You've looked into him, his background, his — "

"Our inquiries were very thorough and we shan't require this gentleman's help any further. Superintendent Lennard told me to tell you not to worry about it any more and, er . . . " He sucked his teeth. "No harm done, as it were."

Carol felt as if her heart had stopped and given out: there seemed to be no pulse inside her at all.

"You can't have got the right man," she said. "There's a mistake . . . Geoff Yeomans? Arch Street?"

"The gentleman you informed us about, yes. You must understand — "

"I don't understand," she said, clenched and trembling. "If this is some sort of — attempt to fob me off, I certainly don't understand. Did you really interview him? Did you really take this seriously? Because I — "

"I was about to say," Munt said, raising his voice, "that you must understand our position in this. That we can't give details of our inquiries to a member of the public. Even when that member of the public is a . . . witness involved in the investigation. However — " he waved her to silence — "as I say, I've been on to my superior in this and he feels that under these special circumstances you should be informed of what's happened. I must emphasize that what I'm going to tell you now is confidential. Mr Lennard's letting it pass as a favour to you."

He took out a notebook and leafed through it for what seemed several minutes. There must be lots of things in there, Carol thought, again with that almost detached randomness: lots of other cases, other inquiries. This thing that had taken over her life was quite small, even insignificant.

She found that she was sitting down, with no consciousness of having done so.

"The crime in question took place at 15 Clanvowe Street, London SW4 in the early hours of 20 December 1981," Munt said droningly. "The gentleman you identified as being one of the perpetrators was at that period living in a juvenile detention centre situated near Billericay in Essex. This was a closed residential centre from which the inmates were denied egress without special permission. Our interview with the gentleman has confirmed this, as have the records of the establishment in question."

There must be something wrong with her brain: it just wouldn't take in what he was telling her. It was as if her mind had become shell-like, impenetrable.

Except to what it wanted to hear.

"It couldn't have been him, Miss Halstead," Munt said, flipping the notebook shut. "It all checks out. He was miles away that night, and banged up in a place where security was pretty tight. I'm sorry."

The slight relaxing of his forensic manner nudged her into speech. "But — but not necessarily. I mean maybe he — "

"Maybe nothing. Believe me, Miss Halstead, we've taken this very seriously indeed. My governor had a strong feeling about it and he had me give it the works. We've thoroughly explored the possibility of him slipping out of that place around that time, perhaps even undetected. It has happened. But it just won't wash. Look, don't let this worry you. As it happens your feeling wasn't so far off. I shouldn't be telling you this, but the gentleman is known to the police, as the phrase has it. Some breaking and entering offences, quite a few years ago. I found out he'd got that sort of form from the computer before I came down here and that made me all the more keen to talk to him. I didn't know about his juvenile record then, it doesn't show on the computer. But once he'd told me that and once I'd checked it out, well . . . " He shrugged. "That's it. You've heard the expression 'cast-iron alibi'. There's no such thing, of course, but this is about as near as it gets." He stood up and offered her a smile. "I should put it out of your mind right now. There's no harm done. You made a mistake, that's all."

22

*N*O *harm done. You made a mistake, that's all.*
No harm done.

There was no analysing the feeling with which she dully repeated these words in her head after Munt had gone. The mixture of disbelief and doubt and perplexity and apprehension was beyond her power to disentangle. All that came to mind was an image: of coming suddenly to the edge of a cliff and looking helplessly down into a bottomless gorge.

Well, nothing has changed. The killers were never identified before this happened and they're still not now. Nothing's changed: you're in exactly the same position as you were in, say, a year or two years ago. And you were fine then.

She tried to tell herself this, tried to hammer it in like a multiplication table; but it was whistling in the dark of the feeblest kind.

Everything had changed.

Her belief in her self — all the mental and emotional security that you took for granted as naturally as the earth beneath your feet and that was just as vital: that had changed with DI Munt's deadpan revelations, and she scarcely dared to inspect it to see what the damage was.

And as for the Yeomans family — well, she feared there must be damage there too. She had put an innocent man through an ordeal of interrogation, of suspicion of a dreadful crime . . . and it seemed that she had inadvertently raked up a past that she doubted the current Geoff Yeomans, proud husband and father and householder, would care to be reminded of.

A can of worms. And they were still crawling destructively around. God only knew what the final result would be. And to add the crowning touch to her wretched confusion, something else was beating like a steady drum inside her, the one thing that remained, madly, unchanged despite the topsy-turvy revolution of the past few minutes: *I was sure. I was so sure.*

The telephone rang.

She stared at it through several rings: half consciously she was readying herself for some new mind-twisting shock. At last, her hands feeling cold and numb, she picked up the receiver.

It was Dr Kaufman.

"Carol? Are you OK? I've just spoken to Lennard. I wondered if — "

"Yes," she said. "I've heard. The other one came to see me. Inspector Munt." She struggled for words that would not come. "It — it was nice of him to let me know."

There was a pause on the other end.

"I can come down," Dr Kaufman said. "I can come down to you now if you want. Say the word."

The kindness, sudden, unexpected, unsurprising, was like a blow to the heart.

"No, no," she said, "I wouldn't dream of it. Thank you — but I think I've been quite enough of a pain and — and general prat-arse just lately as it is."

"Balls. Listen, Lennard was just as let down as you are by the whole thing. You're not alone, Carol. I can't emphasize that enough. And if you let this knock you back, after you've come so far, I shall be extremely pissed at you. I mean it. If you're down, I want you back up pronto. You made a mistake. This is human. This is normal. Believe it. It is most definitely not evidence of anything wrong with you."

"I was wrong, though. I was wrong about Geoff Yeomans when I was sure and . . . and I can't truly say that I feel any less sure now, deep down. So why would I feel that? Why would it happen in the first place?"

"Resemblance," Dr Kaufman said readily. "People look like other people, uncannily so in some cases. Apparently I have a double who's a toilet attendant at Waterloo station. Of course you're not going to be able to just shrug and say oh well, that's that. This was too big. But that doesn't mean you can't let it go, and soon, and without getting screwed up by it. I do appreciate that it doesn't seem like that just now. It will. Trust me."

"I do. I always have." On the verge of adding *But can I trust myself?* she stopped: it was too self-pitying. "Thanks again."

"Any time you need to see me, you know where my doorstep is. Just turn up on it. Promise me that?"

"OK. But I'll be fine, really." There was a loud knocking at the door: she wondered if it were Martin and simultaneously wondered what she would say to him, how she could present any sort of normal facsimile of herself to his affectionately observant eyes. "I'd better go — there's someone at the door."

"All right. Remember what I said. I'll call you later and nag you some more."

The loud knocking came again. She hurried to open the door, picturing it to be Martin and faintly annoyed at this insistence.

Geoff Yeomans stood there, glaring down at her. There were dots of white paint in his hair and her first bizarre impression was that he had gone grey overnight.

"I want a word," he said.

He was past her and in the flat before she could reply.

So this was it, she thought: at the back

of her mind since Munt had left had been an entirely selfish dread of the next time she would see Geoff Yeomans, and now there was even an element of relief that it had come so soon.

In the living room he turned to face her, hands jammed in the pockets of his plaid jacket. His skin looked pallid and there was a crease between his eyebrows, as if he were in pain.

"You'll never guess where I've been all day," he said.

She couldn't answer him.

"I'll tell you, shall I? I've been down the cop shop. Being grilled as if I was some sort of frigging villain. They fetched me from work, right in front of my boss. Well, that bastard did anyway. The one who's just come out of here. Oh yeah," he said at her look, "I followed him, too right I did. Once they let me out I stayed outside that cop shop and waited. I wanted to see who it could be in this little town who's fucking me about — getting some high-grade copper on to me all the way from the Met and trying to pin something on me that I didn't do. Funny, I didn't think

I'd got any enemies round here, but I mean it must be *somebody* who knows me, *somebody* must have said something because the filth don't suddenly pull you in for *nothing* after all *this time* . . . "

He was shouting, but it wasn't the volume that was alarming so much as the hectoring, half-reasonable tone. And the stillness. He didn't wave his arms about: the only thing that moved was his mouth, while his eyes bored into hers.

"They wouldn't tell me about it, of course. Wouldn't say where it was that they got this so-called information. All I know is somewhere got broken into and somebody got killed years ago, fifteen frigging years ago, and suddenly I'm in the frame for it, I mean, that's *terrific*, imagine getting dragged away from your ordinary working day and having that shoved in your face . . . " All at once he took a single step forward, and the slight action was as startling as if he had lunged at her. "It was you, wasn't it?"

Carol flinched. It occurred to her that she might lie: that she might deny it all, say she didn't know what he was talking about; that he was even half hoping, in some strange way, that she would do so — simply because he was old-fashioned and wished to believe the best of ladies and schoolteachers.

And she couldn't do it. It would simply be another kink in the tangle that surrounded her, perhaps the final one that put it past unravelling.

As it happened, her silence was enough.

"Well," he said, his lip curling in a kind of triumphant disgust. "God only knows what you think you're playing at. What have I done to you, eh? Can you at least tell me that? Because that was not a nice thing I just went through, lady. I don't suppose you've ever had the police grilling you, have you? Helping them with their inquiries, as they put it. As a matter of fact I have. I don't pretend I'm a saint and it was a long time ago and I sure as hell didn't want to go back there. Was that it? Eh? You dig something up on me and decide to drop me in it again? Is that the sort of fucking screwed-up busybody you are?"

"I made a mistake," she burst out. "I'm sorry — I'm really sorry, but I honestly made a mistake, I thought . . . I thought I knew you from a long time ago and — "

"You made a mistake all right. You made one big frigging mistake. I just hope you don't make another one because I'll tell you something, lady, you are dangerous. If you get your kicks going around fingering people to the pigs for something they didn't do then you've got a problem."

"I've told you, I'm sorry. I didn't know it would . . . turn out like this, I never meant — "

"You're cracked. That's about the size of it. I'm trying to feel sorry for you but — " he coughed out a sardonic laugh — "I can't quite manage it somehow. Well, I hope you're satisfied, anyway. I feel like ten kinds of shit, if that's what you wanted."

"So do I," she said. "You can believe that or not. I can't make you believe it but it's true. I didn't mean this to happen."

"No? What was meant to happen, then? I'm supposed to be banged up right now, yeah? Isn't that it?" He gave her a narrow-eyed, even cool look; then it was as if a switch were tripped inside him again and he moved towards her, barking, "What do you think you're playing at? I've got myself a good job and a family and I've worked hard to get here and now look! What do you reckon my boss is going to think? How do I know the filth aren't going to pick me up for something else? Soon get a reputation in a town like this. Soon have you down as a bad'un. And all down to you. Thanks a fucking — "

His right hand came out of his pocket: it swung back in a fist. For perhaps two seconds he was about to hit her, two seconds in which her mind didn't know whether to scream, to duck, to hit back — or merely to accept what at a deep level did not surprise her in the slightest.

And then his arm went down, slowly and jerkily, as if an invisible hand were pulling it. He made a noise in his throat as if he were going to spit and pushed past her to the door.

"I'm not having my son mixed up with you any more," he said, pausing in the hall, but not looking at her. "I shall get on to the school and make a complaint. Have him moved to another class." He yanked open the door. "They can't all be like you, can they?"

23

NEXT day Macleish called her into his office at lunchtime.

"Sit down, Carol. I've been meaning to have a chat with you for some time, just informally. See how you're getting along."

There was something about Macleish's office that made it impossible to be fair to him. You wouldn't mind him being such a pompous man if it weren't for the framed photograph of himself smirking at some heads' conference or the framed degree certificates that immediately made you think they must be phony; you wouldn't mind him being such an ignorant man if it weren't for the small bookcase and the new-looking books with conspicuous paper markers in them that immediately made you think he'd never read a word of them.

She didn't know what to expect, but curiously she wasn't afraid. She was just a blank sheet, ready to be written on.

Macleish sat down behind his desk and turned his chair to the side, presenting his acid profile against the window. "So, Carol," he said to the wall, "any problems that you need to talk to me about?"

"I don't think so," she said. "None that I can't handle, anyway."

He turned his head and gave her a drab yellow smile.

"I do wish you'd be frank with me, Carol. I like to think of my staff as a family, as you know. I don't think a happy family should have secrets. Now what's the problem with Ben Yeomans?"

"I . . . Ben's doing very well."

"I had his father on the telephone to me first thing this morning," Macleish said, crossing his arms with a flourish. "Apparently he wants young Ben moved to another class. He doesn't want you teaching him any more. I must confess Mr Yeomans was rather incoherent. I tried to ascertain in what way he found you unsatisfactory as a teacher for Ben. All I could gather was that he didn't trust you, in his words. The disagreement seems to be one that originates outside of school. Would that be the case?"

"Yes. There was . . . I have met Mr Yeomans outside school, and there has been a personal disagreement. It was very unfortunate and I'm sorry that it happened, most of all on Ben's account because . . . it shouldn't affect his schooling in this way and I regret that deeply."

Macleish studied her for a moment, like a crocodile in the shallows.

"This is a small community, Carol. Teachers and parents will inevitably rub shoulders in a way they wouldn't in a large town or city. One accepts that and one accepts that it may lead to the personal getting mixed up with the professional. One also *expects* — " he unleashed the smile again, his eyes hooded and dangerous — "that one's staff have the sense to see this, and to be appropriately careful in their behaviour. Their first concern is the teaching of their pupils. They should see that nothing should get in the way of this. Clearly you haven't. Obviously you need to be told, Carol, though you shouldn't: don't get involved socially with the parents of your class. They should know you, certainly, be able to approach you and talk freely with you about anything that concerns their child's schooling. But they should know you only as a teacher. This should have been plain to you when you entered the profession, and I find it disappointing that I'm having to remind you of it."

"I'm sorry," Carol said. Part of her was stinging and mortified at this, because teaching, and being a teacher, was so important to her: but another part of her was quite calm and detached. "I made a bad mistake, and it won't happen again."

"Mr Yeomans was quite abusive on the phone, and I can't say I'm favourably impressed by the man. Arch Street, isn't it? Mm."

Carol didn't want snobbery as an ally. "They're a very nice family," she said. "I just feel badly about this for Ben's sake. He's settled in well and . . . " She hesitated: did she herself want to go on teaching Ben now? She couldn't tell. There were no certainties in her life any more, just a mass of unanswerable questions. "I don't want his schooling upset."

"A pity you didn't think about that before. You don't have to tell me what the precise nature of this disagreement was, of course, Carol, but it might be helpful if I knew."

"If I don't have to tell you, Mr Macleish," she said carefully, "then I'd rather not."

He blinked at her, then took a fountain pen from his desk, unscrewed it and inspected the nib. The fountain pen was very Macleish. A pointless messy impractical archaism that was meant to look posh and just looked cheesy. Probably he had a cravat and a decanter at home, she thought with absent maliciousness.

"It's easy to become over-confident in a job like this, Carol," he said. "To feel you know it all. Even in your probationary period. I wouldn't want you to fall into that trap."

"I'll try not to."

"Please do." He laid the pen down and turning round to the desk pulled some papers towards him. "I'm not going to take any action in regard to Ben Yeomans yet. I think it possible that Mr Yeomans might reconsider after a little cooling-off period. He was very . . . emotional this morning. If he remains insistent, then we'll have Ben moved after half-term next week. Well, you'll be wanting your lunch, I dare say."

Carol stood up. Her hand was on the door handle when Macleish spoke again.

"It's fortunate that Mr Yeomans didn't ask for his son to be moved to another school," he said, bent over his papers. "That really would have been serious. I think perhaps we should count ourselves lucky."

She went out. There was no doubt that 'we' meant 'you'.

24

HER class played her up that afternoon, more than they had ever done before. Just as in Macleish's office, the part of her where her professional pride lived reacted smartly to this, while another part remained aloof and removed from it all: almost as if it had ceased to matter.

Always in her mind, of course, were the events of yesterday: what they meant and what they didn't mean, their significance, their repercussions. But all they did was revolve. They formed no pattern: it was as if there were a piece missing. It was as if she were waiting for something.

And then, when school was over, she went out to the car park and saw Elaine Yeomans waiting by the gates.

Elaine waved a hand. Carol went to her.

"I've sent Benny to play at his friend's. I need to talk to you." Elaine's face, normally so full of expression, was unreadable. She had on a long mohair scarf, thrown over her shoulder with a certain dash: it made her look stylish and composed.

"I know," Carol said.

"It's cold." Elaine stamped her feet. "Do you fancy a cup of tea?"

There was a tea shop called the Earthenware a short distance from the school. It adjoined a shop called Where on Earth that sold joss sticks and tarot cards and the sort of clothes that you wouldn't find in the High Street. Both halves were favourite haunts of the town's senior school students, and all but one of the tables in The Earthenware were filled by blazered sleek-headed groups, all trying to outdo each other in outspoken casualness. The age when adulthood was seen to consist of being blasé about everything: how wrong could you be, Carol thought.

Their table was tiny and their seats so close together that their knees almost touched. This seemed decidedly inappropriate and awkward under the circumstances, but Elaine didn't seem troubled by it, merely remarking, "Gets busy in here, doesn't it? They must make a bomb, the prices they charge."

The waitress took their order for two teas, and Elaine lit a cigarette.

"At least they let you smoke in here. You know there's no-smoking pubs now? They'll be banning people farting next . . . " She blew out smoke and frowned at the lace tablecloth. "Geoff got sacked."

"Oh God."

"I know. That's what he said. Or words to that effect. Listen, I'm not entirely sure what this is all about. I'm not sure whether I'm supposed to be throttling you or throttling Geoff or throttling Geoff's boss or . . . All I know is they had him down the police station yesterday. Trying to pin something on him, he reckons. And that it was you who pointed the finger."

Carol nodded, drew a deep breath. "It . . . I can explain."

"Well, I'm sure you can. I wish somebody would, anyway."

"Why did he get the sack?" Carol said before she could go on: fearing she knew the answer.

"He was at work when this copper fetched him yesterday. So obviously his boss wants to know what it's all about and why the police are so interested in him." Elaine drummed her fingers on the table. "Geoff's got a bit of a temper. As far as I can gather his boss had him up on the carpet today and got so niggly about it that Geoff — well, snapped, I suppose. Turns out he's been in trouble with the law for being a tealeaf. Even did a year inside, before I knew him. This was news to me, by the way. But the police brought it all up again, apparently. And there's his boss nagging and nagging at him wanting to know what the police had to say and — he went and told him." Elaine sighed and closed her eyes. "Which I can just see him doing, I'm afraid."

"They can't sack you for that, can they?"

"They can if you hide it. When he applied for that job he was supposed to reveal details of any previous convictions. And he didn't. Geoff's a decorator. He goes into people's houses. You've got to be able to trust somebody in that position, haven't you?"

"Oh God."

Elaine looked at her unhappily. "Well, you've got to understand what Geoff's boss is like as well. Not an easy sort of bloke. He's an elder in some sort of funny church and probably a Freemason and God knows what else. Probably best mates with the Chief of Police, so I wouldn't have been surprised if it had come out eventually anyway. Course, you can imagine what Geoff's saying — that if he'd put it down on his application form that he'd been inside they'd never have given him the job in the first place. Which I suppose is true but . . . oh, I don't know what to think."

"Where is he now?"

"At home. Pouring beer down his neck and ranting and raving." Elaine gave her a straight look. "And saying it's all your fault."

"I'm so sorry. Isn't there any chance of him getting his job back?"

"Dunno. He's got a temper, and there's no telling what he might have said to his boss in that state."

"Maybe I could see his boss — talk to him . . . "

"Well, this is precisely it, you see. I still haven't got it quite straight where you come in or what you reckoned he'd done. And whether I should be tipping this tea over your head."

Carol liked Elaine: it was this simple fact that stood out from the guilt and pain and confusion she was feeling and made her decide, instantly, that she should tell her. It was a big decision, because she had never told it before. The people who knew, like Dr Kaufman and Aunt Jean and Superintendent Lennard, had been involved from the start, when she was Carol Mitcheson. As Carol Halstead, she had never let it out.

"When I was eight," she said, "my parents were killed. Some people — four teenage boys — broke into the house one night and . . . and stabbed them to death. I hid and they didn't find me. But I saw them. I got a good look at them and . . . Well, anyhow, the police never caught them."

Elaine's round eyes had grown rounder. A long stem of ash formed on the tip of her cigarette and at last fell gently on to the tablecloth.

"Oh my God," she said blankly, as if reading the words off a card, "oh my God oh my God."

"What can I say?" Carol shrugged. Her words came out haltingly, painfully. "They were never caught and the years went by and I grew up and qualified to be a teacher and came here ... But I always remembered — I *thought* I remembered — what those youths looked like and that if I ever saw any of them again I would know them. And then I met Geoff and — well, it was Ben really, there was something about the face and I was sure, I mean I was so sure, this is what you've got to understand, Elaine, this isn't a thing I would have done lightly, it wasn't a thing I wanted to happen and I would never have gone to the police if I hadn't been so sure and yet — yet I was wrong and the whole thing's just like a nightmare and I'm so sorry, I can't begin to — "

"Hey, hey." Elaine touched her hand. "Ssh. It's all right."

"It's not, though, is it? I've lost your husband his job."

"Well . . . " Elaine looked in perplexity

461

at her cigarette, as if she couldn't imagine where it had come from. "There is that. But, you know, it's a job. There are — bigger things in life."

"I've never told anyone this before."

"I don't suppose you would, really."

"My parents' name was Mitcheson. My father was a doctor. You might remember, it was in the papers a lot at the time."

"It rings a bell . . . My God," Elaine said again, and then speaking with a sort of wince, "Where did you hide?"

"There was a boxed-in fireplace. I got behind there."

"Jesus." Elaine looked at her tea. "I wish this was something stronger . . . And you thought — you thought it was my Geoff — "

"I know it sounds awful. It was just this strong feeling that I recognized him, I mean it wasn't anything to do with him as such . . . " She remembered the thick fist poised in the air, about to swing towards her, and how there had been no surprise in her as she awaited it: and wondered just how true that was. "So I told the police that — I thought

462

I'd recognized one of those youths from years ago. I just had to tell them: my mind couldn't rest."

"And they took you seriously," Elaine said. "Obviously."

"They went into it thoroughly. That's why they — had Geoff in for questioning. But it turns out it couldn't possibly have been him because . . . well, he couldn't have been there at that time. Definitely."

"Mm. That's another little surprise he gave me. In some sort of borstal when he was a lad. Oh, I don't mind, I mean in a way I don't blame him for wanting to put it all behind him, but I can't help feeling miffed that he felt he couldn't tell me."

"I suppose he wanted to start afresh with you."

"Well, he did: he's never been in any trouble since we got married. Christ . . . I can just hear my mum and dad saying, 'I told you so.' Well, like I say, I always had him down as a rough diamond. I can't say I like being kept in the dark but it doesn't alter my feelings about him, you know . . . He came and had a go at you, didn't he?"

"A bit."

"A lot, if I know him. He's wild at you, you know that. I couldn't stop him ringing the school this morning. He wants Ben moved to another class."

"I know. The head told me."

"Well, we can maybe sort that out."

"Do you still want me as Ben's teacher?"

"Ben thinks the world of you. I don't really know what to do. What you've told me . . . I mean, I could tell Geoff, if you want. Get it through to him that you didn't exactly do it for fun."

"Would it change things?"

"Well, it doesn't change the fact that you thought he was one of those people. I can't see him getting his head round that the state he's in." Elaine lit another cigarette, touched her own cheek with tentative fingers. "I reckon this bloody eczema's flaring up again . . . He wouldn't have done something like that, you know. Killing someone. No way. I know the guy. He hasn't got the . . . It's not in him. You just know, don't you? When you know someone really well. Being a bit of a bad lad when he was young, all right, I can believe that. But not the other."

"No." Carol felt helpless. "I'm sorry."

"What a mess. Well, I'm starting to understand. He's a proud man in his way. It's having all this stuff dragged up and thrown back in his face, that's what he can't handle. I'm with him there. It seems bloody unfair. But then . . . " she sighed and pulled a face, "I don't suppose it's been much fun for you either, so where does it leave us?"

"In a mess. As you say."

Elaine stirred her tea thoughtfully. "He keeps saying he's finished. I'm afraid there is some truth in that. You know what towns like this are like. Word soon gets round. I wouldn't put it past that boss of his to be on to every employer in Suffolk saying, "Watch out for Geoff Yeomans, he's a wrong 'un."

"I will talk to him. Geoff's boss. I might be able to do something. What's his name?"

"Ernest Evert, he's in Ipswich. But I doubt you'll do any good. Geoff didn't declare his criminal record and there's nothing that can change that. And I'm afraid he'd go spare at the thought of you — well, getting involved in his business any more. Look, it's not the end of the world. I'm working and, well, who knows, this might be a blessing in disguise. Geoff's always going on about starting up on his own account. Maybe he can do that. Or maybe a builder'll take him on, he knows plenty of them. We'll get through it somehow . . . Do you want me to tell him? You know — what you told me?"

"I don't know . . . if you think it would help . . . "

Something must have shown in her face — some uncertainty. She could only hope that what didn't show was its true nature. Because the hard, irrational, intuitive core of her heart still wasn't convinced that she could have been mistaken.

"Well, we'll see," Elaine said. "But whatever happens, I promise I won't tell another soul. And I do keep my promises."

"Thanks."

Elaine drained her tea, leaving a crescent of frosty lipstick on the rim

466

of the cup. "You must have been pretty strong," she said.

"I . . . had good friends."

Elaine shrugged on her coat and smiled at her, a pretty, tired smile.

"Maybe you still have," she said.

25

CAROL had kept Martin at a gentle arm's length since Sunday. He had been patient about it, and seemed to accept it as part of their unspoken contract. But when he phoned on Wednesday evening and asked if he could come over, he wouldn't be put off. Probably he discerned that her defences were weak and that she wanted him in spite of herself.

But once she had put down the phone and actually pictured his arrival, she suffered a mild sort of panic. In essence she couldn't comprehend why he should want to see her. What was there to see? All she consisted of just now was a bundle of flailing thoughts that barely held together.

Thoughts above all about the Yeomans family and what she had done to them. That was the foreground; the dark and foreboding background, where the sort of person she was and the havoc she might be capable of wreaking on herself and others was luridly sketched, was scarcely to be looked at yet except in appalled glimpses.

Dr Kaufman would say she was overreacting, no doubt: but Dr Kaufman didn't know everything. He didn't yet know the disastrous result of her mistake, for one. And for all his prescience, he didn't know — couldn't know — what this episode said about her. Resemblance, he said: but suppose there was no resemblance? Suppose the *déjà vu* and the uneasy feeling of familiarity and the recurring dreams had no referable cause, were a manifestation without an object? Suppose she began having creeping suspicions about every man of Geoff's age she ever met?

Neurotic, hysterical, deluded, unstable, paranoid, obsessive: the words buzzed around her like teasing bees. She felt that if she were not mad already, they would make her so. But something else kept them at bay — paradoxically, because it was the one thing that should have put the tin hat on the whole business and sent her gibbering round the bend. It was that feeling of certainty, totally resistant to the explosive facts that should have blown it away.

I *was sure. I was so sure.*

It simply didn't make any sense. And yet that gut feeling was the strongest thing she had. It was a backbone, though it shouldn't have been. Maybe that was what it was that got crazy people up in the morning. The Martians weren't really coming to get them, but if they stopped believing it, they folded.

She switched on the TV to find Arnold Schwarzenegger and Danny DeVito in *Twins*, and a thought occurred to her that made her laugh out loud, sickly and mirthlessly. Maybe that was it. Maybe she should pick up the phone and call Geoff Yeomans and say, "Hello, Geoff. Sorry about screwing up your life, but anyway I just had a thought — have you got a twin brother?"

The empty laughter kept jolting through her for some time, but it had finally gone by the time Martin knocked on the door. Instead, she let him in and then found herself bursting into tears that felt just as strained and hollow and empty as the laughter had been.

Martin had brought a bottle and a bunch of flowers, and he tossed them willy-nilly on the settee and took her in his arms. He seemed, if anything, grimly satisfied that this had come. He let her howl and when she had done steered her to a chair and sat on the arm of it.

"Here," he said, producing paper tissues. "Go on, they're clean. I've always got pocketfuls of them. I have a pathological fear of being caught short and going into a public convenience and finding an empty cardboard tube in the loo. This is true, actually." He stroked her hair; then withdrew his hand quickly, as if he feared the gesture could seem condescending. "Macleish?"

"What?" She had all but forgotten about that.

"I heard you had an appointment with humbug today. He's a worm, but he can be a bastard too. What was the complaint? Was he pissed off that you hadn't got a map on your classroom wall showing the British Empire in red? Or

is it that the kids like you instead o
trembling in fear every time you look a
them?"

"Oh . . . it was something and nothing."

He folded his arms, scrutinizing her
"More like something."

"It wasn't Macleish. He was just, oh
you know, his usual self. I'm all right
let's forget it. Let's have a drink."

"No." He didn't move. "Carol. You'r
not all right. Look, I thought you and
me had a thing going on. Or even a
thang, which is better. And when you
have a thang, shouldn't you be able to
talk? You know, freely. Unburden and
unbutton. I know it all sounds rather
gooey and Californian, but it does fee
good sometimes."

"I know," she said. "I'm sorry. But
sometimes it feels good to just forget
about things as well. And that's all I
want to do just now. All right?"

"No good," he said. "I can't just
pretend I'm not seeing this. You look
terrible, Carol."

"The silver-tongued cavalier."

"I want to help."

"You can't. Anyway, there isn't anything

to — to help with, so let's just forget it, eh?"

"Is this me?" His eyes had gone very slightly hard. He made a gesture of mock appeal. "Is this just me, or did I think there was something pretty important and good and nice between us?"

"Yes. But I told you I needed just a bit of space, just for now, and you said — "

"Fuck what I said. I want in, Carol." And as she shook her head, more in utter weariness of spirit than denial, he went on, "Being a mysterious and tantalizing enigma can get to be a bit of a drag after a while, you know."

She withdrew from him, hurt. "Is that what you think?"

"Yes. No. Oh God, cut out my tongue . . . Look, is this a way of saying you want out? Is that it? I want in and you want out?"

"No. I just want us to go on as we were — you know, not heavy, having a laugh . . . "

"I'm not laughing," he said. "How can I feel like laughing when you keep shutting me out like this?"

If she had been in better fettle — if she had been, in a word, herself — she might have been able to explain to him that she wasn't shutting him out: that what she wanted was to shut him away from this dismal thing that had overtaken her life, keep him separate from it because he was the one good thing in her view, the one untouched element and too precious to her to be contaminated by it. But she felt too confused and oppressed to begin to explain, knowing that the explanation would have to include everything; and that accusation of deliberate mysteriousness had really cut her, in a place where she bled.

"I asked you over so that we could have a nice time," she said, "not this."

"I see. Well, of course, you must tell me when I overstep my limits."

"You just have."

There was no last word, and she didn' see him go.

26

"STEPHEN Stone."
　　"Yes, Miss Halstead."
　　"Michael Swales."
"Yes, Miss Halstead."
"Lisa Underwood."
"Yes, Miss Halstead."
"Ben Yeomans."

No answer. Carol looked up from the register.

"Anybody seen Ben? Thomas, you usually call for him in the mornings, don't you?"

"Nobody was answering the door this morning, Mrs Halstead," said Thomas, a bright but forgetful boy who could never remember that she was a Miss and not a Mrs.

"Oh. Did you call around your usual time?"

"Yes, Mrs Halstead. About ten past."

"Oh," Carol said again. She looked down at the register. Ben's attendance record was complete. "Oh well, perhaps

475

they all over-slept."

She didn't like the look of this. If Geoff insisted on Ben being moved to another class, she would just have to accept it. But keeping the boy away from school altogether just wasn't on; it was making Ben suffer for no reason. He wasn't patient with concepts he couldn't grasp straight away and they were at a crucial stage of some new number work.

But Elaine had spoken yesterday as if she thought she could talk Geoff round, on the matter of Ben's schooling at least. Of course, it all depended just how overbearing Geoff could be. Elaine said he had been drinking. Perhaps there had been some sort of crashing all-night row . . . But even in that case you would expect the child to be packed off to school in the morning.

"All right, folks, let's have you down to the hall. Quick sticks. Take those gloves off, Michelle, it's not that cold."

"I'm freezing, Miss Halstead . . . "

"Well, you'll have to move around a bit faster, won't you? Chop chop."

Martin was leading his class ahead of her in the corridor. At the doors to the hall he paused, waiting for her.

"Sorry," he said sideways.

"It's all right," she said. "I'm sorry too."

It was said, but it lacked the last degree of conviction. It was no more than a declaration: much more would be needed, and she wasn't sure she had the resources just now.

The children filed into the hall, noisy, autumn-bronchial. Half term couldn't come too soon for everyone, Carol thought. She studied her class whilst Tony Plumb attacked the upright piano and Macleish led the singing from the stage, dressed in one of his characteristic suits, suits that looked designed to be worn whilst reading the novels of Sir Walter Scott with a plate of dry biscuits. She looked at their heads, neatly groomed heads and tatty heads, ribbons and slides and soft barbered necks; at their guileless eyes, their gracefully awkward stance, their fiddling, restless, intelligent little hands. Thirty of them, or twenty-nine today: a lot of young lives, in each of which she played a central part, and exerted an influence that could hardly be overestimated.

A big responsibility: was she fit for it? She posed herself the question seriously, not in luxuriant despondency. Because if there were any hesitation about her answer, then she must grab herself by the scruff of the neck and *make* herself fit. Toughen up. For their sakes.

This predicament she found herself in was pretty horrible, no doubt. It had called into question her most basic certainties: had caused her to revisit, or be revisited by, a past that was full of pain and horror and that it had been her life's work to liberate herself from; and had led her, indirectly and unwittingly, to damage innocent people's lives.

All true enough. But she was here; she was on her feet. If the possibility of making the life for herself and others that she had aspired to appeared crisscrossed with shadow just now, she must remember that there had been darkness before, and she had come through it. Maybe she should regard what had just happened in a different light, view it as something complementary to the sale of her parents' house in

Clapham — a healthful severing of the past. Maybe all these years she had been clinging to the hope, at some profoundly unconscious level, of seeing her parents' killers brought to justice; and now she had a stern lesson. It wasn't going to happen — so let it go. A lesson such as that was bound to be painful, but it might also be crucially liberating.

And whatever happened, these twenty-nine (or thirty) children must come first. It was a sophistry to say that she wouldn't let what was happening to her touch them. Of course it would touch them: every moment of absent-mindedness, every wavering of her concentration, every diminution of her patience would have its effect.

So it was a choice: be a teacher, or not. Win through, or let those animals of fifteen years ago have the victory.

Put like that, it was no contest.

She went back to her class in good heart. They had TV before break — the nature series with the gulping, crooning Californian presenter. "Watch how the alligator turruns the eggs," he breathed earnestly, sounding as if he were conducting a role-play session in group therapy. "That fearsome mouth can be so *gennul*."

She remembered the way Ben's face would twinkle with amusement at that voice, and wondered again what was going on at the Yeomanses' house. This business needed to be talked through, she thought. If her continuing to be Ben's teacher were definitely out of the question, then she wanted a say in where he was to be moved to — in other words, she wanted him in Martin's class and not Mrs Juby's. This wasn't favouritism — if she had her way she wouldn't let any child near Mrs Juby, because the woman couldn't teach a duck to swim. If her own association with Ben was to end, she still wanted the best for him.

It occurred to her that Ben's absence might be his own choice. If he had listened to his father's version, he might decide he didn't want to go to Miss Halstead's class any more — and she knew he could be pretty strong-willed. But she couldn't quite believe that, because of Elaine. Elaine had as near declared herself Carol's ally as was possible in the circumstances: she was certainly the voice of reason in the whole business. And Carol had a strong feeling that Ben was closer to his mother than to his father.

Well, there was one way of finding out. Still feeling resolute and practical, she used the staff-room phone at break.

There was no answer at the Yeomanses' house. She dialled again to be sure and let it ring a score of times before putting the phone down.

"Problems?" Diane said, seeing her expression.

"Oh, just one of my class off school. He was fine yesterday, I just wondered . . . "

"I've got six of my lot off at the moment. My doctor says there's a tummy-bug going round. It's probably that."

"Yes, probably."

"It's irresponsible of doctors to talk about these bugs," Mrs Juby said, stomping past. "Once the children hear about it, they all pretend to have it."

"And school's such *fun* too," said Martin, who was in an armchair with his back to them. "Why ever would they

481

want to bunk off? They could spend the whole day in a nice warm classroom learning about *dragons*."

If it was an illness that was keeping Ben away, it was a diplomatic one, Carol was sure of that. For the rest of the morning session she put the question on the back burner, and by lunchtime it had simmered to a decision.

It was a decision taken in the spirit of the new determined mood that was on her. Face everything: hide from nothing. It was the only way.

She avoided Martin, who seemed to be lingering about the staffroom door waiting for her (yes, that would be faced in its turn too) and headed for her car.

In a small town like this it was probable that she would bump into Geoff Yeomans at some point in any case, so why wait? Even if she were setting herself up for another tirade of abuse, it would surely clear the air. At the very least they would know where they stood.

She turned into Arch Street and parked outside the Yeomanses' house. Geoff's van was parked in the drive. She thrust down the tremor of nerves the sight of it gave her: thrust down too the thought

I was sure I was so sure

that rose like a bubble to the surface of her mind, and walked up to the front door.

It was answered on the second knock. Not Geoff, nor Ben, nor Elaine. A youngish woman with a mane of dyed hair the colour of an aubergine. Carol recognized her as one of the neighbours who had been at Ben's birthday party.

"Oh, hello, I wondered if — Geoff or Elaine was in."

The woman gave her a strange, dramatic look. She glanced behind her into the house, then stepped out, pulling the door to behind her.

"There's been a bit of trouble," she said in a husky, artificially hushed voice. "You're little Ben's teacher, aren't you?"

"Yes, he didn't come to school today, and I wondered if everything was all right."

The woman shook her head, her black-rimmed eyes huge and solemn.

"No. Everything's not all right, I'm afraid." She lowered her voice to an urgent whisper, glancing back at the house. "That's why the kiddie didn't go to school. Geoff's dead."

Carol took a step backwards, just as if the woman had hit her in the face. The gravel path seemed to ripple under her feet, like a rug lifted by the wind.

"Yes," she heard the woman say, distantly, as if from the end of a long tunnel. "Unbelievable, isn't it? Elaine's in a right state and the kiddie . . . It was last night. Well, the small hours of this morning, I think. Apparently he hit the booze something chronic last night and then before he crashed out he must of took a load of tablets. Elaine woke up about half two and took a look at him because she was worried, you know, and there he was — well . . . They took him to hospital but it was no good. Thirty-one years old, can you believe that? Thirty-one. Apparently he'd just lost his job and, you know, he got depressed. He was always a bit of a drinker, it's like he didn't know when to stop, do you know what I mean, and then he'd get really down but still . . . you don't expect that, do you? Thirty-one. That's all he was . . . "

Carol reeled away towards her car,

hearing her own voice saying something, something that sounded, amazingly, quite sensible and coherent about how sorry she was and wouldn't intrude . . .

Amazingly, because all her mind contained was a single thought, turning there like a vicious blade.

Killer.

That was the thought. *Killer.*

And so she was right after all. She had looked into the eyes of a killer quite recently. As recently as this morning, in her own mirror.

27

BEN did not return to school the next day, which was Friday; and the next week was half term. Just the one day to get through, and Carol got through it, she supposed. It didn't mean anything.

She waited for rumour to ignite, but there was nothing. The tragic news went round the school as just that: a piece of tragic news. There was nothing to link her to it. Macleish knew that there had been a quarrel between Carol and Mr Yeomans, but no more. That she was connected with the loss of his job was known only to herself and Elaine.

Even there the connection was tenuous, viewed in a certain light. You could say that it was his temper that had lost him his job, or his initial dishonesty in failing to declare his previous convictions. You could say that, coolly. Dispassionately. Carol tried saying it thus to herself, as an experiment. It felt like dirt.

Martin rang her on Friday evening, but she had next to nothing to say to him.

On Saturday the local evening paper carried a short report on Geoff Yeomans' death. It confirmed pretty much what Carol had learnt from the neighbour. Geoff had been drinking heavily most of the day and all night; and before going to bed, unknown to his wife, had swallowed half a bottle of paracetamols. When Mrs Yeomans found he was not breathing he was rushed to Ipswich General Hospital but attempts to revive him were unsuccessful.

Carol stayed in her flat, cleaning it. She took down the net curtains and washed them. She washed the walls. She scrubbed the oven and defrosted the fridge. She scoured the bathroom and treated the drains with Jeyes. She cleaned the windows. She hoovered the carpets and when she had done that, got down on her knees and picked up by hand any specks that she had missed. She bleached her coffee mugs. She stood on a chair to clean the coving round her ceilings. She dusted the lampshades, using a make-up brush to get into each pleat. And when she had done all that she looked round in a sort of hungry desperation for something else.

All she could come up with were the door handles and letterbox, which were brass-effect if not actually brass. But they would require a proper metal polish, and she didn't have any. To get some would mean going out.

She braved it. There was a minimart about two hundred yards from Stour Court and she hurried there, head down, and bought some metal polish and got back to the flat with it and slammed the door behind her and stood there panting and guiltily triumphant, like a secret drinker with her morning bottle of sherry.

She took a long time over the door handles and the letterbox, but of course they were finished eventually. And when they were, she sat and looked at the telephone.

She got as far as the first digit of Elaine Yeomans' number before putting the receiver down.

Perhaps she should just get in the car and go over to Arch Street and see

Elaine. She tried to picture it: tried to picture Elaine answering the door, perhaps with Ben at her side. Elaine's face, Ben's face. Looking into hers.

No. It seemed like the worst thing she could possibly do — but that wasn't saying much.

Her mind turned to Martin, to Aunt Jean, to Dr Kaufman: most of all to the latter. Because he was, after all, the official repairman when it came to things like this. Someone had died and you felt indirectly, if not directly responsible and no amount of self-admonition or self-analysis or clear thinking or logical thinking or lateral thinking or any kind of thinking could rid you of that feeling: what else should you do but consult a psychiatrist?

It was tempting: it was too tempting. You could only lean on people so much.

"I do know what it's like, you see," she said to the telephone. "To be robbed of your father as a child. It's . . . well, it's beyond you. You just don't see why."

She wrote a letter to Elaine that night. She said she was sorry. This was, the songs would have you believe, the hardest word; actually it was extremely cheap, probably the cheapest word around. You said it when you brushed against someone in the street. You said it when a husband and father had died in despair.

That was his decision.

Something severe and unsentimental — perhaps a distilled essence of Dr Kaufman — hovered over her shoulder as she wrote, putting in remarks like this.

Suicide means killing yourself. By its very nature it is not something one person can do to another. Write your condolences by all means. But spare the sackcloth and ashes. We are what we are.

She listened, but didn't listen. She told Elaine, in the letter, that she felt responsible. She asked if there were anything she could do, willingly setting herself up for the classic riposte that she had done enough.

I was sure. I was so sure. She wondered if she should put that in the letter: after all, it was still there, a just-discernible pulse inside her. But really it was the sort of thing that wouldn't mean much to anybody else; and she couldn't even say what it meant to her any more.

Besides, where did that excuse lead? Did she mean that if her identification had been correct, then everything would have been all right? If that had been the case, there would have been an arrest, a trial . . . again, a husband and father taken away.

Except of course that would have been different. She wouldn't have felt a qualm: even in this state, she knew that.

Pointless to think about. There was only what was.

She wrote that she was sorry again, put the letter in an envelope, sealed it and addressed it. Her writing didn't look like her own at all, she noticed: she wouldn't have recognized it.

Re-cognize: literally, to know again.

Carol had begun to doubt whether she had ever really known in the first place.

She ventured out to post the letter. Her neighbour, the one who apparently dined off sugar, caught her on the way back into the block and began to say something. Carol actually, physically fled from her into her flat.

She went to bed in a smell of bleach

and disinfectant, and had a dream that was entirely new.

In it she was back in the house in Clapham. It was that very same December night: the Christmas tree was up in the living room, the manuscript her mother was working on was by her chair, the same film was on TV. But things turned out differently. Eight-year-old Carol Mitcheson went to bed, and then there was a dream elision and her father was gently waking her and saying with a smile, "I got them. Come and see."

She went with him, putting on her dressing gown and slippers, for it was still the middle of the night. He led her downstairs, past the living room where the Christmas tree glittered, down to the ground floor where her mother was in the kitchen, making a pot of tea: she smiled too.

"In here," her father said, "I got them in here," and he showed her the door of the walk-in pantry. There was a shiny padlock on it that she had never seen before; and in the centre of the door, just about at the level of her eyes, there was a round hole, like a peephole.

"Have a look," her father said. "You just have a look at them. And then we'll ring the police to take them away."

And Carol Mitcheson found she didn't want to look: she didn't want to put her eye to that peephole, not at all. But her father and mother looked so eager and happy that she decided she had better look, just to please them.

She put her eye to the peephole. It was all dark: she couldn't see anything. But wait —

Carol Halstead woke up.

The relief of waking cradled her for a few moments; and then memory flooded in and she lay back, covering her face with her hands.

And for the first time, she had this thought: *I should have died that night too.*

Wretchedness like this, she discovered, was not dramatic. It did not fall into paragraphs or swell to a climax, or dissolve into oblivion. It just continued. People with more enthusiasm for than understanding of psychopathology would have said she was having a breakdown, meaning the conjunction of apathy with leisure. It was nothing so convenient. Sunday followed Saturday, and Carol went on living. No messages came through from Scotty in the engine room saying that they were losing power and the switchboards were about to go kaput. All the agonies she felt were felt keenly, sanely, and as it were mundanely. *I can't go on* was just a phrase. Simply by saying it you disproved it.

Nothing was going to happen inside her to change this or bring it to a head, it seemed: life just didn't work like that. And in the same way, she didn't dare to place her hope in outside intervention — but it happened, none the less.

Elaine Yeomans phoned her on Monday morning.

"I got your letter," she said. "Thanks for writing."

There was nothing to be read into her voice: it merely sounded a little flat, as if she had a slight cold.

"Oh . . . I'm glad you got it," Carol said, and bit her lip. "How are you — how are you coping?"

"Oh, you know. Coping, really." Elaine

drew a deep breath, which sounded as loud as thunder on the phone line. "The funeral's tomorrow. At St Botolph's. Eleven o'clock. Will you come?"

"Do you want me to?"

"Yes," Elaine said, in a vague way, as if she were thinking of something else, and then: "My parents are coming down."

"Oh, are they?"

"Uh-huh . . . God, I'm going to need somebody to talk to."

" . . . Me?"

"You."

28

ST Botolph's was a modest, pretty little church, more like an oast house in shape, down by The Leas with the river close at hand. On the day of the funeral the dank November cloud broke and there were gentle gleams off the water, a feeling of lucid calm in the air. In this mild and domesticated setting the funeral cars arriving outside the church, the soberly dressed mourners, the floral wreaths all gave the impression of some dignified, decent, thoughtful ritual, more reflective than desolating.

Even the sight of the coffin did not disturb this impression. It seemed more like an appropriate and well-fashioned prop than a thing of death. It was only when Carol, seated near the back of the church, saw the small unnaturally neat figure of Ben walking beside his mother to the front that something went through her like a stroke upon iron, cold and reverberating.

In the same pew she saw a middle-aged couple whom she took to be Elaine's parents. The woman wore a fur hat and a coat with a fur collar. From time to time she gave a slow, faintly disdainful glance round the church and then looked at her watch, as if the occasion were a dull party at which she had to put in an appearance.

Ben was turning up his face to whisper something to his mother. He looked pale, hollow-eyed, but not tearful. When Carol experienced a flicker of *déjà vu* at the sight of his profile she merely felt weary with herself.

Yes, those features are familiar. He takes after his father. And his father's dead.

The service was taken by a woman minister, tall and thin and toothy, with wild hair and a sing-song nasal voice: like a vicar only more so, Carol thought. She spoke of Geoff's virtues as a husband and father, then made a rambling, half-absurd comparison between being a painter and decorator and living a holy life. The fur-hatted woman sniffed in a dutiful way: Elaine and Ben were silent, their heads bowed. Ben's ears looked huge and red, as if they were stinging.

It was all over quite soon. The pallbearers, ancient men who looked far too weak and unsteady for their job, hoisted the coffin with surprising ease, and the mourners filed out.

Ben lifted his eyes to Carol's as he walked past. Something kindled there: she could almost suppose it was gratitude to her for coming.

If only he knew, she thought, and then stopped herself. Enough of that. Elaine had asked her to come: Elaine wanted to see her. Let that suffice, for now.

It was not far to the cemetery. This place too had the pleasantness of small size and semi-rural setting: one could fancy here that death was a rare event. Carol kept at a discreet distance through the burial ceremony. Near her a blackbird pecked companionably in the grass. Finding a worm at last it tugged and tugged, altering its position with a flutter, straining and bracing: it was as if the worm had incredible strength. When the bird finally pulled the worm clear it gave it a sharp fling against the ground, as if in cruel, matador-like triumph.

When it was time for the mourners to file past the grave Carol made sure she was last in line. The minister stood close by the hole with a faint serene smile on her face, as if it were her handiwork. Carol just glanced in. The tarpaulined sides of the grave gave it something of the look of an unmade bed.

"All went off quite well, I think," the minister murmured, and Carol hadn't the slightest idea how to reply. She turned, and found Elaine beside her.

She looked tired, and the flaring of her eczema made her face appear pitiably exposed and vulnerable. But her eyes were dry, and the characteristic liveliness had dimmed rather than left them.

"Can you come back to the house?" she said.

"Yes, I — I can do."

"Give it a little while. Say about one." She moved away to where her parents were waiting with Ben.

Carol hung around a while, looking at the wreaths. Her own was there amongst them. There were not many: she remembered that Geoff had no family. She noticed a large one in the shape of a Bible bearing the card, 'With deepest sympathy, from all at Ernest Evert P'ting and D'rating.' For the first time it occurred to her that she might not be the only one suffering pangs of guilt over this death.

When she drew up outside the house in Arch Road she was surprised to see no other cars there. But she'd left it till well after one; she couldn't be too early.

She knocked, and the door was opened almost immediately, as if her knock had been eagerly awaited.

"Come on in," Elaine said. She had changed out of the dark suit she had been wearing into a pullover and jeans. "Thanks for coming."

There was no one in the house except Ben, who was sitting in front of the TV and looked up with a murmured "Hello" when Carol came in. There were a few sympathy cards standing on the mantelpiece.

"Sorry — am I early?" Carol said.

"What? Oh no, I didn't want to have people back. Funerals are bad enough without that bloody farce." Fetching a bottle of whisky from behind the bar, she gave Carol a straight look. "And no, not even my mum and dad. Especially not them. They're driving straight back to London this afternoon. Oh, I don't know, I suppose they mean well . . . but sod it, no they don't. I've had them since yesterday morning and it's just been — well, they switch from one snidey innuendo to another. One minute I'm well rid of him and the next minute it's something like this was bound to happen and the next it's why couldn't I have married someone else and not put them through this . . . Well, I got a bit ratty with them. I suppose I shouldn't have, but — oh, who gives a stuff?" She held up the whisky bottle. "Are you going to have a drink? Because I am."

"All right," Carol said, after a moment's hesitation.

"It's OK, you know, I'm not going to embarrass you with floods of boozy tears. I've done all that and it's finished with. Benny, are you all right?" Elaine went over and stroked his hair. "Do you want a Coke or anything?"

Ben shook his head.

"You just going to watch your video, yeah? All right, sweetheart. We'll go down this end so we won't talk over the top of it and spoil it, all right?"

She led Carol through the dividing archway to the dining area.

"I got him *101 Dalmatians*," she said, sitting down at the table. "I think he's . . . sort of wanting to like it."

"How is he?" Carol said.

"Ben's a toughie. But he's not stupid. So it's half and half really. You can tell yourself things like, Well, he's young, he'll get over it — but there's no knowing, really." She poured two generous measures of the whiskey, handed one to Carol. "People do, of course. You did, didn't you?"

"Yes. I suppose I did."

"Maybe you could . . . talk to him about that some time. I don't mean now. You know — some time when he's back at school. Just give him an idea that you know what he's going through."

Suddenly Carol couldn't look at her. She frowned into her untouched whisky and said with difficulty, "I shouldn't be here."

"I asked you to come."

"Why?"

Elaine didn't answer. She tossed back her whisky, wincing, and refilled her glass. Carol glanced over at Ben. He was watching the TV with his chin in his hands, though it was hard to tell how much he was taking in.

"I didn't mean to sound hard — you know, about not having people back," Elaine said. "It's just such a lot of stupid hypocrisy. Especially with the way it happened. You know, I said to him more than once that he'd kill himself with his drinking. Funny how things turn out, isn't it? Apparently the dose he took might not have been enough on its own, but the combination was." Elaine swallowed down the second whisky and shuddered. "I'd been feeling angry with him before. For not telling me about his past, him thinking I — wouldn't like him or something because of it. Hiding. And you know, I've still been feeling angry since. A job, for Christ's sake. And being an ex-con. He told me more about that, that night: it was old grannies he pinched off. Nasty. But Christ, you can live with

503

things, you can carry on. Look at you."

"That's . . . oh, Elaine, that's not a comparison you should make. It's not right, I feel — "

"I know, you feel responsible." Elaine sighed. "Look, as far as I'm concerned, that little secret of his was bound to come out sooner or later. It was like a bomb, it was going to go off. It doesn't alter me feeling — just angry and disappointed. He chickened out. I tried to explain to him, that night. About what happened to you, how you hadn't exactly gone to the police just for the hell of it . . . Anyway, there was no getting through to him. He was away." She grimaced. "What a way to go."

"I'm just so sorry."

"Me too. I did love him. Here, drink up, I'm beating you." She sloshed more whisky into Carol's glass. "Yes, I loved him, you know the way you do. I think I fibbed to you, though. That day in the café when you told me — what it was you thought he'd done. I went all defensive. No chance, I said, not my Geoff. And that's because there was a little tiny bit of me that thought: Maybe he did. So I sat on it. But it was there."

Carol stared at her, frozen. "What are you trying to say?"

"I don't know. Not that he did do it, I mean, it seems like that's not a possibility anyway, just because of where he was at the time. I can't even see him doing it when I . . . think about it. It was just something in the gut that wasn't totally surprised when you said it." Elaine lit a cigarette, her hands quite steady. "Geoff could be violent. Oh, it wasn't often, and he never touched Ben as far as I know. But it doesn't have to be often, does it? Once is enough to . . . show you. When he was wild he was . . . well, wild. No trusting him. I threatened to leave him last time. It seemed to knock him back a bit." She shrugged. "Who knows? Most of the time you knew where you were with him, but he had a side . . . They say a leopard can't change his spots, don't they?"

Carol had only had a few sips of the whisky, but it seemed to be going straight to her head: the sensation wasn't unwelcome. Everything Elaine said seemed large and vivid and surprising.

Taking another sip and feeling the burning at her stomach wall, she realized she hadn't eaten properly for days.

"Did he get like that — the night it happened?"

"No. Too far gone. I had seen him that bad before — I wanted to say that to you. It wasn't totally unknown. I remember when he got in a pickle over a debt he owed somebody — some half-dodgy deal he got into, buying a load of so-called cheap building gear. He was going spare then, saying he'd ruined us. He wasn't very good with money really, though I can't talk. Maybe it was because he never had any."

"How are things going to be for you? You know — practically?"

"There's nothing in the bank, but Geoff had insurance. My mum and dad have, ahem, let it be known that I can turn to them for help. As long as I don't mind them saying, 'I told you so,' over and over again, no doubt. I can probably ask for more hours at work — they've given me leave for now, and . . . I don't know. I haven't really thought about it. But no," she said with an angry shake of her head, "that's another lie that people always come out with. Of course you think about it. Maybe it's wrong, but it's the truth — what comes into your mind practically straight away is how the hell you're going to manage, what's going to become of you — all the selfish stuff. Terrible, eh?" She jabbed out her cigarette in an overflowing ashtray. "Had Geoff's boss on the phone this morning, saying he was so sorry he couldn't make it to the funeral. Enough to make you sick he was, creeping and crawling."

Carol sat back and regarded her nakedly. "Like me with that letter?"

"If that's in your head," Elaine said, "I don't suppose I can get it out. But look, I'm sitting here with you now, aren't I? I wouldn't have been able to talk like this to anyone else. Jackie next door, she's been great, but it's all — oh, I don't know — smothering stuff. Keeps talking to me in this whisper and — " Elaine gave a weak laugh — "and patting my hair, would you believe, which I don't like. I don't know about you but I do not like having another grown woman patting my hair. I feel like you don't judge. Except yourself, maybe. And like I say, what you told me about — the thing that happened to you: that puts everything in a different light, somehow. We're sort of in the same boat."

"Oh, no. It was years ago. I'm over it."

Raising her glass to her lips, Elaine looked at her over the rim of it. "Are you?"

Carol hesitated: then, "Yes," she said, "it was a long time ago."

"It must stay with you, though. I mean — like the business with Geoff. That shows it comes back."

Carol shrugged helplessly. "All I can say is that never happened before and I still don't understand it and — yes, things come back. I suppose because it was never resolved. So in that way time doesn't work for you like they say it does. But the grief and the loss — time does soften that. Miserable old cliché, doesn't deserve to be true, but it is."

"For kids too?" Elaine said. "Benny?"

Carol nodded. "It's like you said, he's — " An unwanted memory of Ben screaming and pounding at Stephen

Stone's cringing head with his fists intruded, and nearly threw her off what she was going to say. "He's a toughie, mentally I mean. Just now he's getting on with the business of accepting that it's happened. Probably there'll be a lot of questions later, bitterness maybe. It's something about wanting to know the why and wherefore: you think there'll be an answer and that'll settle everything. Maybe us teachers are to blame for making them think that."

"What's up, doc?" Elaine said, as Ben got up and came over to them. "Is your video finished already?"

"No," he said, standing close to her. "I paused it."

"Come here." Elaine gave him a hug. "Paused it, eh? Well, you would *paws* it when it's *101 Dalmatians*, wouldn't you? Blimey, I wonder how many paws that would make in that film?"

"Four hundred and four," Ben said promptly, leaning against her. "But there's some more because there's this sheepdog called Colonel and there's a cat called Sergeant Tibbs."

"Is there? I bet it's good. I shall have

to watch it with you later, eh?"

"The book's really good as well," Carol said, as Ben's very solemn, very dark eyes turned to her. "We could have that as our afternoon story next term."

Ben murmured something in his mother's ear.

"Shall you stay in Miss Halstead's class?" Elaine said. "Well, you can, duck. No reason why not. Do you want to?"

Ben nodded.

"Thanks, Ben," Carol said. "I'm glad."

"It doesn't mean everything's going to change, you know," Elaine said, her arm round his shoulder. "It means you and me will have to look after each other, but we'll do that, won't we, the pair of us? And there's your teacher as well. That's three — the Three Musketeers. So we'll be all right — won't we?"

29

CAROL saw Elaine every day that week.

It was no deliberate policy on her part. Elaine's behaviour to her on the day of the funeral had done much to dull the lacerating edge of her guilt; but complete absolution could not come so easily, and she didn't think it should. It certainly wasn't her intention to seek it by an ostentatious befriending of the woman on whose life she still felt she had been an indirectly destructive influence.

But Elaine made the overtures: Elaine made it plain that she needed a friend and that Carol was the person who fitted the bill. Perhaps in her bereavement she was clinging to the nearest solidity that offered itself: Carol was a landmark in the void and she stuck close to her. No doubt the fact that her family consisted only of an unsympathetic and distant mother and father played a part too. And it was undeniably true that there had been confidences between them — sparks struck out of the cruellest and hardest of circumstances, but confidences none the less. In a strange way they were extremely close.

Carol was far from rejecting these overtures. She was glad, from a purely selfish point of view, to have the burden of guilt partly lifted from her; glad to be able to help; glad of an occupation for a mind that had existed in a sort of static frenzy; and also, she simply liked Elaine.

But she knew it wasn't enough: that knowledge never wavered for a moment. And throughout those days of half term, that knowledge began to take shape: she felt it narrowing to a point. She was going to have to do something. It was no use trying to regard what had happened to her as merely an episode, to be shrugged off as a temporary aberration and forgotten. That wasn't going to work. If the past had something to say to her, she was going to have to do more than listen: the communication would have to be more than one way. She couldn't live a life of unfinished business. To go forward, she would have to go back.

The realization of this need was more important for now than the precise details of how she would go about it. But a signpost to her direction came in the shape of a letter from the family solicitors in London. It was a polite enquiry as to whether she still possessed a set of keys for her parents' house in Clapham. The buyers, who had begun renovating the property, weren't demanding their return — just seeking to establish the whereabouts of any extant set of keys before the locks were changed.

She did possess a set of keys. They were in an old jewel box at the back of her wardrobe, together with a few documents of her parents' and some jewellery that had belonged to her mother. Aunt Jean had placed them there when she had helped her move to Dunmarket, and there they had remained, as firmly out of sight and out of mind as it was possible to be. But she thought of them now.

In the meantime, she helped Elaine. It was mostly a matter of moral support. Elaine had much to do. She had appointments with her own solicitors, with the building society who were their mortgage lenders, with the bank and the insurance company, with the Department of Social Security, and with the family doctor who wanted to see both her and Ben and who advised her, incredibly, that sleeping tablets were all very well but she would feel better if she stopped smoking.

It was plainly a tiring and frustrating business and Carol was glad that she could help — by ferrying them around Dunmarket and to Ipswich, by being on hand to lend a sympathetic ear as well as to stay with Ben while his mother was swallowed up by yet another strip-lit carpet-tiled office. Once or twice on these occasions she tried gently talking to him about his feelings, trying to discover whether he was coping as well as he appeared; but she could get little out of him and she soon gave it up, feeling it was meddlesome of her. One thing she knew about Ben was that he was only open when he wanted to be: once the shutters went up, you were out and couldn't even hope to peep in.

"How come they all turn into these megabitches as soon as they get behind some bloody office furniture?" Elaine exploded after one such encounter, slamming the car door. "The next one who says in that whingey way, "I'm not with you," I shall ram her bloody mouse down her throat. I don't like women in these situations, I really don't. Men are drongos but I hate to say it, they're better at dealing with the public. Women seem to get this *tone*. Like a constipated duck. God, I need a drink. No, forget I said that. Let's just go home and have a nice cup of tea and a cry. Please, I mean. Sorry. Treating you like the chauffeur."

"So what did the megabitch have to say?" Carol said, working the car with difficulty into the traffic flow of the High Street.

"Oh, the same again. Can't take any action on that until they've heard directly from the insurance company. Ring them then, I says. I'm not authorized to do that, she says. I'm afraid my hands are tied, Mrs Yeomans. Well, if we get in arrears, we get in arrears. I'll just say ask that cow in the cast-iron knickers about it."

Carol hesitated for something like a minute before saying, "You know, if there's any help I can give you that way . . . say the word."

Elaine looked at her in surprise. "What, on a teacher's pay? That would be very nice of me, wouldn't it? Dig you into debt for the hell of it. Nice one."

"Well, I'm going to be getting a lump sum soon," Carol said carefully. "My . . . parents' house has finally been sold, you see. So there'll be that money."

She didn't take her eyes off the road, but she could feel Elaine's gaze on her.

"Oh," Elaine said at last. "You mean the house where . . . ?"

Carol nodded. "If it would help tide you over. Whatever."

"I don't know what to say. Except — no. And thanks. Thanks a million, but we'll be all right."

"It isn't that I'm trying to — "

"I know what you're trying to do. You're trying to help. Because you're a friend. And as a friend I'm saying I couldn't possibly. I can say it straight like that because you *are* a friend, in fact I feel like I've known you for years. But really, we'll be all right."

"Well. It's up to you."

"You've helped a lot anyway. In fact it's all been a bit one-sided, hasn't it?"

"Eh?"

"You helping me. It's not as if you haven't got problems of your own — "

"Oh Lord, no, nothing really."

"I don't think so. Not from what you told me. I'm not sure how I can help but . . . I'd like to."

"Thanks. But I'm fine."

Elaine said nothing more, and it seemed the subject had been dropped. They came to Arch Street, and Carol accepted her invitation to come in for a cup of tea. Ben asked if he could go and call round for Thomas.

"Course you can, matey," Elaine said. "Make sure you're back for teatime." When he had gone she raised her eyebrows at Carol. "That's the first time. Do you think he'll be all right?"

"Best to let him go. He's probably trying to find his routine again, see if it makes him feel better."

"Yes . . . It's difficult to tell with Benny, isn't it? He's come into my bed a couple of times, I've seen him crying on the quiet once or twice . . . but still, you can't quite tell with him. Don't know who he takes after." Clearing a space on the cluttered kitchen table for the teapot, she brushed aside a pair of men's driving gloves. Her eyes met Carol's. "I'm going to have to do something about all this," she said.

"Where do you start?" Carol said, with a glance around. There were so many things directly suggestive of Geoff: everything from a set of flightless darts in a leather case to an oily handprint on one of the kitchen cupboards.

"Somewhere," Elaine said. "Start with the basics, I suppose. His clothes. It's got to be done. It's either that or end up like some loopy Miss Havisham character, with everything like a shrine. I dare say some charity or other would take them. It's going to feel really shitty doing it but where's the alternative? You can't live in the past, can you? Probably that makes me sound really hard. But I've got to make a choice, you know? Forward or backwards. And there's Ben to think of. He's got his whole life ahead of him."

"What about the house? Would you think of moving?"

"Maybe. But — we had some good times here. Ben's settled with his friends and his school and there's my job. Of course, the place has got . . . it's got Geoff all over it," she said with a deep breath. "But so has everything, once you've been married to someone like that. I'll see him every time I look at Ben."

"You're brave," Carol said.

"I don't know about that. Either you lie down or you get up." Elaine handed Carol a mug of tea and sat down at the table opposite her. "Anyway, would you call yourself brave? With what you went through?"

"No."

"Well, you were. Or you were a survivor. That's the same thing. You survived. That's what I want to do. Maybe I could learn from you."

Carol sipped at her tea. "I don't know about that."

"How do you mean?"

"Well, I thought I'd survived, as you say. Left it all behind. And then look what happened."

"What did the police think about it all? I mean, they must have taken you seriously — questioning Geoff like that."

Carol winced. "Yes, they did. I suppose they have to. That case was never solved and it's a bit of a black mark against them. And I was the only witness. In a way they've got to listen to me. I suppose after fifteen years of stalemate one more false lead isn't any big deal, to them at least."

"But it is to you?"

"I hate not being certain of anything. And even though those youths were never caught I had this certainty that I saw them and I would never forget them. Now . . . it's like that's been taken away."

"Perhaps you don't remember as well as you thought. I mean, can you picture what you saw in your head? Like a photographic-memory sort of thing?"

Carol spread out her hands. "I just don't know any more. That's what I need to find out somehow. Or else there's never going to be an end to it."

"Can't they hypnotize people to remember things like that?"

"I did try hypnotism when I was younger. But some people are better hypnotic subjects than others, and it just wasn't very successful with me. Anyway, as far as the police and the doctors could make out, it wasn't as if there were any major blanks in my memory. It didn't seem as if I'd blacked anything out. But now . . . I'm not so sure."

"So." Elaine put down her mug and faced her squarely. "What are you going to do?"

Carol returned her look quizzically.

"Like I say, it's been all me. We've got me sorted, as far as practical things go. I'm going to make a start on Geoff's things. But you've got to do something, haven't you? You can't just leave it. There must have been a reason for what happened lately. Something must have brought it all back. I don't reckon you're the sort to sit on your hands any more than I am. So. What's it to be?"

Carol shifted, thinking. Though the posing of the question was new, she found that in the past week she had already travelled a long way down the road to an answer; and it was with a sense of completing the last steps that she said, "Well, I suppose it's like you said. You have to start with the basics. Like you with Geoff's clothes. You're prepared to tackle that, aren't you?"

"Got to be done. It'll be hell, all the memories and everything, but I can't run away from it."

Carol nodded. "Probably I've been running away without realizing it. Well, I think it's me who should be learning from you. I think I should start with the basics. Go back to the beginning. Because that's the one place I've never been back to."

Elaine, an unlit cigarette in her mouth, stared wide-eyed at her.

"I've never been back to the place where it happened. Never even been near it. My aunt adopted me and brought me up and my parents' stuff was disposed of and the house was let and that was it: I never even went near that part of London again. So in a way something has been blanked out. It happened in that place — which is why they kept me away from it at first, and why I kept myself away from it later on. That's the place where the memories come from." She picked up Elaine's lighter and lit the cigarette that still dangled from her mouth. "So that's the place I've got to go back to. See if it's got anything to say to me."

Though she spoke plainly, even casually, her feelings were far from casual at this prospect. Indeed, even a few months ago the notion of returning to her parents' house would have been unthinkable; and her mind still could not grope at the thorny idea without trembling and pain. Strangely enough, actually articulating it helped her. It was easier to say out loud than to think privately.

Elaine's eyes never left Carol's face. "God," she said. "Can you do that?"

"I've got a key," Carol said. "Unless they've changed the locks already, I should be able to get into the house. It's Sunday tomorrow, I doubt whether the builders will be there."

"But I mean . . . can you? Face it, I mean?"

A profound coldness crept over Carol, as if she were going to be ill; and there was a voice somewhere saying, no, turn away, forget it. But she didn't think much of that voice: she didn't think it was the voice of the heart or instinctive wisdom or anything of that kind. It was, she felt, a little mundane undistinguished voice that probably did more continuous harm than the wildest of impulses: the voice that counselled you to stay in bed instead of getting up, to ignore that credit card slip, to forget about that hurtful remark you made, to pretend that life was long and easy instead of short and difficult.

"I don't know," she said at last. "I'll have to see when I get there; but I hope so. It's like you said, you either lie down or get up."

Elaine let out a soft whistle. "You're going to go tomorrow?"

"No time like the present," Carol said. Grasp the nettle. Strike while the iron's hot. Time and tide wait for no man. It was strange how moments of crisis blew the dust off clichés. They came up like new. They were primal, and belonged to primal situations.

Primal: relating to beginnings. Words grew sharp and bright too. Everything was narrowing to a point. She could only hope that that point would not impale her.

"How are you going to get down there?" Elaine said.

"Oh, drive, I suppose."

"Not on your own."

For a moment Carol didn't understand what she was saying. Then she saw, and shook her head.

"No, no. Don't even think of it."

"Why not? You've been with me. It means a lot. Just to have that company, somebody backing you up."

"I — I couldn't ask you to — "

"You don't have to. I'm asking you. Just look at it like I'm being selfish: I would only have been floating around this weekend, brooding. A trip out would do Benny good too. So you'd be doing us a favour, if you can put up with us coming along for the ride. Plus you'll have somebody there for . . . well, support if you need it. But that's just an optional extra. What do you say? I mean . . . " She suddenly looked uncomfortable. "Unless it's something you really want to do on your own. Sorry. I can be a bossy devil."

"I wouldn't call it that." Carol reached out and squeezed her hand. The gesture, though spontaneous, was a little out of place between them, and they acknowledged it with a laugh.

"Yes, then?" Elaine said.

"Yes, then."

30

CAROL made two phone calls that night.

The first was to Dr Kaufman, and was intended as a sort of pre-emptive strike. For she knew, without the slightest doubt, that Dr Kaufman would not approve of what she intended to do. He would condemn it in the strongest terms and use the strongest reasoning to dissuade her. He did not approve of self-help strategies: "self-abuse books", he called those slim uplifting volumes that seemed to fill half the shelves in bookshops now. Moreover, to tell him what she was going to do would be to reveal her own deception, for she had presented herself during the course of several phone calls since Inspector Munt's bombshell as very much what Dr Kaufman counselled her to be — philosophical about her mistake, hanging tough, putting the whole business behind her and getting on with life. Which she wasn't; but it seemed necessary to hide it and necessary most of all to give him no hint that she was preparing a confrontation with her past. So, conscious of her duplicity, guilty about it, but driven by an urgency that brushed the guilt aside, she made an upbeat, chirpy and lying phone call, telling him that she was going to the coast with some friends tomorrow after a lot of thinking had convinced her, in effect, that life was too short to worry and that, as he had told her, serendipity ruled.

He seemed pleased, and told her to go for it. Of course, she thought afterwards, he wasn't a psychologist for nothing, and maybe saw through the spurious *joie de vivre*, but no matter. The main thing was that he could have no inkling of what she was planning to do.

The second phone call was to Aunt Jean. There was a simpler motivation behind this — she rang, as she often rang, to give her loving greetings to her aunt and ask after her — but a touch of the same deception entered it too. She wanted Jean to have no hint of her plan either. So she dialled and prepared to tell the same story of a trip to the coast.

It didn't turn out quite as she thought. Aunt Jean wasn't there, and it was Brendan who answered.

"No, she's just popped over to see a friend. Was there any message?"

"Oh — not really. I just rang to say hello, you know . . . "

"Uh-huh." Brendan, in his nerveless way, did not trouble to fill in phone silences.

"So anyway, er, how are you both?"

"Fine. Been doing a bit of work in the kitchen this week, taking up those old tiles. Don't know how Jean's managed to put up with them for so long. It's funny you should ring, actually: we were thinking of driving up to see you tomorrow."

"Tomorrow?" She was stunned for a moment: there was an attentive silence on the other end of the phone. "Oh — well, that would have been great, only tomorrow I'm — I've got roped into going over to the coast with some friends, well, some of the people I work with, sort of a day out and er, I don't think I can get out of it really."

"Oh, right. That's a shame." His voice was almost expressionless.

"Yes, it is, isn't it? . . . Only, you know what it's like when they're people you work with and you've made a promise, it's — it's difficult . . . "

"Sure. I understand. No problem. Well, some other time, maybe."

"Yes, that'd be great. Sorry about that."

"Uh-huh. Well, I'll tell Jean you rang, anyway."

"Yes — give her my love, won't you?"

Was that satisfaction she had detected there? she thought after she had put down the phone. She was afraid she knew what her excuse must have sounded like — especially after her last visit to London when he had spotted her on the Tube. She could hardly have handed him more ammunition.

Yet even the knowledge that she had laid up trouble for herself by her deception, perhaps to the extent of causing a rift between herself and the person she loved most in the world, did not move her from her decision. Her life was in a state of suspension:

everything but this one crucial matter had to be placed on hold. It didn't mean these other things were unimportant. On the contrary: she wanted to give their importance their full due, and that she could not do until this disabling tension at the centre of her life had been resolved. She had to deal with the past so that she could give her heart to the present and the future. It was something of this that she needed to, but could not convey to Martin when he phoned her that night.

"It's me. Are we talking?"

"Well, it sounds as if we are. Are you OK?"

"Fine. I've had Lucy this week, which is partly why . . . you know. And partly not. How have you been?"

"OK. I've been . . . trying to help out with Elaine Yeomans, and Ben. You know."

"Oh, right. How are they coping?"

"Not bad. It's hard to tell with Ben, he can be quite a reserved kid."

"What the hell was that arsehole playing at, anyway?"

"I . . . I think he was depressed. He lost his job."

"Big deal. Join the three million. Oh, I don't mean to sound hard. It just gets my goat. As if there isn't enough waste in the world . . . So you didn't make Chris's party?"

"No."

"Me neither. I don't, actually, care to be anywhere that you're not. Am I allowed to say that?"

"Yes," she said. "You're mad, but . . . thank you."

"Meet me tomorrow."

The sound of his voice, the thought of him, touched her and hurt her; but there was no room for it, not yet. "Tomorrow I can't," she said. "I'm sorry, but — I'm going to be away tomorrow."

She heard him draw in a breath. "I wish you'd tell me," he said.

" . . . I can't."

"I mean tell me yes or no! Oh God. I'm ranting and raving again, look, I'm sorry. I'll see you at school Monday." He was gone.

Call him back? She debated it. But she was afraid that somehow her resolve would be sapped, her concentration deflected.

She left it, and went early to bed, having arranged to pick up Elaine and Ben at ten the next morning.

When the bird nightmare woke her around three, dragging her gasping up from sleep like a cruelly hooked fish, she felt no diminution of her purpose. In fact, her rendezvous with the past could hardly come soon enough.

31

READY for the off at quarter to ten the next morning, Carol found that her car wouldn't start. For some time this simply stupefied her. Things like this didn't happen. When you had some great undertaking in view, lesser matters were supposed to bow down in supplication. The world was meant to be obliging at such times.

Then she was angry: incandescent. She thumped the dashboard, hurting her hand. She got out, flung up the bonnet more as a satisfyingly violent gesture than to any purpose: her mechanical knowledge ended with the oil and water.

A car was pulling into the parking area with a beep on the horn. Fearing patronizing male assistance, she slammed the bonnet down and jumped back in the car, deciding to give it one more try; if it was no good, stealing someone else's occurred to her as a not entirely absurd alternative.

And this time the engine caught and purred just as if nothing had been wrong. She rode her luck and pulled out, and only as she was making the turn out of the parking area did she who it was in the other car: Martin.

He had his window down and was shouting to her.

"Carol! Wait! Carol, please! Stop hiding from me, for God's sake . . . !"

Breathing a desperate apology, she accelerated away.

She couldn't let anything else deflect her from her course, she simply couldn't. The thought flitted across her mind that she should have told Martin from the beginning, but she dismissed it. It was too late now, and besides out of concern for her he might have tried to stop her, and then she would really have had to blow him out.

It was better this way.

Elaine and Ben were waiting for her, and came out as soon as she drew up outside the house.

"Nice day for it anyway," Elaine said, climbing into the passenger seat while Ben got in the back. "You're still . . . you know?"

"Yup."

"All right then. Lay on Macduff." Elaine leant back to place a shopping-bag on the seat next to Ben. "I brought a few goodies to keep us going. Light refreshments. Now don't you go and snaffle 'em all, Benjamino Yamani, d'you hear?"

"Have you ever been to London, Ben?" Carol said.

"Once."

"A visit to grannie dearest," Elaine said. "Not an experience to be repeated. She gave me a bell last night, bless her. Kept saying about how I was still young and I should remember that."

Carol glanced at her face as they pulled away. "Meaning . . . ?"

"Meaning just what it sounds like, I think. Plenty more fish in the sea, go out and land yourself a respectable one this time. Oh God." She waved a hand, her lips tight. "Let's forget about it."

The day was cold but limpidly bright and still: one of those days that, cropping up in the midst of wintry dankness and rain, can have a more refreshing impact on the spirit than the highest pitch of summer. Though the country through which they drove was bare, the high East Anglian light found unsuspected beauties in it: there was a pleasing geometry in the clean-cut lines of the furrows in the fields, and there was a fascination and satisfaction, like that of an anatomical drawing, in the revealed shapes of the naked trees. As Elaine had hoped, the drive seemed to act like a tonic on Ben, who by degrees lost his withdrawn and listless look and began to sit forward, pointing out things he saw. A couple of pheasants, looking, as they always did, as if they belonged on a table-mat rather than in reality; a tractor on the skyline, oddly slow and clumsy and appearing scarcely more up-to-date than the Suffolk punches it had replaced; a glider glittering in the sky like a crucifix; a sign to a place called incomprehensibly Dog's Leg Farm. Elaine seemed to relax too, like a slackened string. She joked with Ben, laid bets with him on the colour of the next car they would pass, hummed odd snatches of a tune; and from time to time would give Carol a keen, thoughtful glance and say simply, "All right?"

"Never better," Carol said. A long way from the truth, but she felt better than she had done for weeks, and that in itself was like being lifted to a high place. She was forcing herself to think of one thing at a time, in a way that reminded her of writing her name in her books as a small child: *Carol Mitcheson, 15 Clanvowe Street, Clapham, London SW4, England, The United Kingdom, Europe, The World, The Universe.* Because first came getting to London: concentrate on that. Then, negotiating London and crossing the river and getting to Clapham: concentrate on that. Then, find Clanvowe Street. Then, number fifteen. Then . . .

I'll cross that bridge when I come to it.

Again, the cliché was entirely apt. Because entering that house again for the first time in fifteen years would indeed be crossing a bridge, and she had literally no idea of what she would find on the other side.

The traffic was manageable as they

came into the city. Still, she needed to concentrate, and Elaine recognizing this chatted to Ben, who was drinking in everything he saw.

"Mum, Mum, what's that man?" he cried as they came through the Sunday streets of Tottenham. "Him in that big black hat."

"A Jew," Elaine said. "They dress like that if they're, what is it, Orthodox. Really strict and religious."

"Here, it said Highbury, is that where Arsenal play?"

"I think so."

"Arsenal are rubbish."

"Are they indeed? I wouldn't know, but I wouldn't shout about it round here if I was you."

Carol concentrated on the road, thinking, not thinking. So far, it could be an ordinary journey, a visit to Aunt Jean. The point of no return was not yet. Let it come.

London unwrapped itself before them, a series of tight onion-like layers, suddenly opening out into expansiveness as they came to the river. Ben bobbed from one end of the back seat to the other, goggling.

"Mum, where's this? Is this London Bridge?"

"It is indeed," Elaine said. "Don't worry, it's not falling down. Look down there, that's where the Tower is, see? That's where they used to put you years ago if you were a traitor."

The cool sunlight semaphored from the river, seeming to hold out an invitation, a promise of grandeur and significance. Life, complex and dramatic and worthwhile: come and take it. So Carol felt it, and knew that what she was doing was right: knew that there was no possibility of accepting that invitation until . . .

Until what? What exactly was she counting on? She examined herself, trying to put her finger on the answer. All she could say was that she was seeking completeness. It might be that to return to the scene of the murders would trigger memories, of whatever kind, that would bring completeness to her picture of that night. It might be that the house would trigger nothing at all, and force her to reconcile herself to the fact that she would never know more than she knew now; but that too would be a form of completeness. After that, she would have done everything she possibly could to exorcise the demons of the past, and the rest would be up to her.

Both alternatives were fearful in their way: there was no choosing between them. The only way to go on was to go on. Concentrate. Take each mile, each yard, each foot as it came: the miles and yards and feet that were steadily diminishing, the sum being subtracted, the gap closing. Drawing her to the house that had been the locus of her destiny — just as something, fifteen years ago, had drawn those four youths to it through the night-time streets, drawn them there to pitch their stakes of nightmare brutality. The work of minutes, and everlasting.

"Mum, why's it called the Elephant and Castle?"

"Now you're asking. That means I don't know. You'll have to ask Miss Halstead when she can think a minute."

"There was a pub here with the sign of an elephant and castle," Carol said automatically. "Apparently because they dug up the skeleton of an elephant round here years ago. Which might have been an elephant that was brought over by the Romans hundreds of years ago. That's one story, anyway."

Kennington Park Road. A few minutes from Aunt Jean's house: all she had to do was signal, make a turn, go and visit Aunt Jean, introduce Elaine and Ben, go back to Dunmarket afterwards: simple. It was just a physical action, it didn't even involve changing her mind.

She carried on.

"Clapham High Street," Ben read out. "Is that where we're going?"

"Yes, that way," Carol said. She glanced quickly over her shoulder, met Ben's interested, enigmatic eyes. "I want to have a look at the house where I used to live."

★ ★ ★

With a blanket wrapped round her, she goes up into the police lady's arms. The police lady isn't very big, but she scoops her up as easily as Daddy does.

The police lady inches the blanket up

over her eyes, which makes it dark. That's all right, it's good, like her hidey-hole.

She feels herself going downstairs. It's like she's floating. And then suddenly it's cold and noisy and a bright blue light comes even through the blanket.

"We're just going to take you to the hospital, pet. Make sure you're all right."

Peeping out, she wonders where she is for a moment. There are all flashing blue lights and policemen and an ambulance and a sort of ribbon going all the way round. It looks a bit like her street, yet so different.

It must be though, because there's the number fifteen behind her, on the front door. And it's going away, they're taking her through the little front gate, away from her home.

32

CAROL stood outside the little gate, looking up at her old home. The street was a puzzle: it wasn't familiar. Pebbledash, loft conversions, new double glazing had changed its features, and though the structure must remain the same she somehow couldn't see past the surface detail. It might as well have been a different street.

But the house, now: that was different. Or rather, it wasn't different. It was known in the fibres of her, familiar as a mole on the skin, familiar as the taste of milk and the sensation of hunger and the drawing in of breath. It looked ancient, antediluvian, the oldest and first thing in the world.

It was the same.

The changes in its features meant nothing. The door was black that used to be blue: the brass numerals had been replaced with plastic ones: there were several doorbells where there used to be one. And instead of curtains and blinds there was plastic sheeting at the windows, and a sign stood in the little front garden: 'Another quality development by HAYWOOD CARTER, Wandsworth.' But it made no difference.

It was, simply and unalterably, home.

Where the heart is, thought Carol; and suffered a sensation as if she had been painlessly flayed, every nerve of her nakedly revealed, everything that she was and everything that was her suddenly exposed to the world and at its incomprehensible mercy.

She had parked her car next to the skip outside, and Elaine and Ben were still hovering near it, watching her quietly. At last Carol turned.

"Well," she said, and her voice sounded as small and tinny in her ears as a voice down a phone line, "this is the place."

Elaine, nudging Ben forward, came and stood beside her, looking up at the tall closed house.

"We'll come in with you," she said. Her breath steamed a little: it was colder here.

"You don't have to. I won't be long."

"You don't know that. Come on."

Carol opened the gate, went up to the door. Getting out the keys, her fingers trembled and she dropped them.

Ben stooped and picked them up and handed them to her. The cold air had made his cheeks glow, and his eyes looked as round and black as a bird's, with almost no white at all.

"Thanks, Ben," she said. She got her hands under control, and opened the door.

Somehow she had expected a stale smell, a smell of lost years gusting out, like the opening of an ancient tomb. Instead the smell that greeted her as she stepped into the hall was fresh and curiously positive. It was paint and builder's size and new timber: it had nothing of the past in it at all.

She paused on the threshold, wondering if the developers had rigged up some sort of alarm in case of squatters. But there was no sound, only that murmurous emptiness, like an echo in the making, that a house without furniture produces.

"Big place," Elaine said from behind her: just, it seemed, as a reassuring reminder that she was with her.

Carol went forward. Her sense of expectancy was such that she found herself treading with an exaggerated slowness and balance, like a ballet dancer.

To her left, the coat closet and downstairs toilet. Wellingtons went in there, she thought; and there always used to be a calendar hanging opposite the loo, something her father got free from pharmaceutical companies. And woodlice, that used to crawl from tiny cracks in the plaster near the floor.

It was all as clear as yesterday — yet she had no sense of revelation or recovery, even though as far as she knew she had not thought of these things since she had lived here as a child. They were just memories that she came across: fragments.

Weren't such places supposed to look smaller when you revisited them as an adult? It all seemed so big and cold. Perhaps it was because there was no furniture in it.

Or perhaps because there was nothing in it: nothing at all.

She walked down the passage beside the stairs to the dining-room door. It had been stripped prior to repainting, and the handle had been removed. She pushed it open and went in, hearing Elaine murmur behind her, "Come on, Benny. Stay with me."

The dining room was a large uncurtained space. The carpet had been taken up, leaving a bare floor that made it seem more like a garage than part of a house.

She struggled. The table used to be there, by the window. Pine, she thought: or wouldn't that have been before pine came in? She recalled accidentally making a mark on it with a knitting needle, and trying to cover it with a place-mat . . .

Another fragment: picked up, looked at, tossed aside.

The kitchen: always very much the centre of her parents' house. She stared, trying to think of her family in here, talking, laughing, dinner bubbling on the hob . . . But it was just a kitchen. The cooker didn't look familiar: the stainless-steel sink looked pretty old, but it suggested nothing one way or another.

A washing machine stood where she thought, possibly, the fridge had once been: some fluff-caked bits of machinery were sticking out of the front, just as if it had exploded.

She turned, hastily, nearly bumping into Elaine.

"Looks like they're giving it a proper facelift," Elaine said, looking closely into her face.

"Yes," Carol said. "Yes, it's — it's quite different."

She went to the foot of the stairs, and looked up the stairwell; but the perspective lacked that yawning dread that she had felt in Aunt Jean's house. She cleared her throat, and the sound came flatly back to her from the upper regions of the house.

Carol put her foot on the first stair, and something registered.

The stair carpet: it was different. This was a plain cheap blue. The stair carpet back then had borne a hectic pattern of red flowers. Her parents had hated it, but it covered every stair and landing of a three-storey house and the cost and trouble of replacing it had caused them to postpone the project indefinitely.

Of course, it would have been taken up, after that night. Because of the blood.

She climbed up to the first floor, staring at the dull puce matt that covered the landing walls. Graffiti here, or hereabouts, dark red and sticky. Remember . . . ?

She remembered, but the remembering was a conscious act: no reinforcements came to its aid from these lifeless bricks and mortar. It stole upon her that the very idea was absurd, a poetic conceit.

Elaine and Ben were following her, their footsteps creaking on the stairs.

"Here, it's all safe, this place, isn't it?" Elaine said. "I mean nothing's going to give way?"

"I think it's all structurally sound," Carol said. "They sold it as that, anyway."

Sound as a bell. Houses, perhaps, were stronger than people, adapted to new lives, shed the dead past like a skin.

She entered a room on the first floor, her boots clomping on the bare boards. The room had been the living room. Over there was where the TV had stood — you

550

could still see the aerial point in the wall — and round about here, somewhere in reach of that electrical socket, the Christmas tree.

She closed her eyes.

And for the first time, there was memory, memory that was not hauled up from stock but fresh, hurled at her like a bleeding slice of meat.

Running down here in her slippers to use the phone to call the police. Seeing the Christmas tree knocked over and the baubles shattered and aching at the sight even though the sights she had just seen upstairs were so much worse and the way the smashed baubles looked like eggshells so that you almost expected yolk to come out of them . . .

"Here." Elaine was touching her arm. She held up the shopping bag. "I brought a drop of something warming. Do you want one?"

"Oh — thanks. In a minute. I'll just . . . go upstairs first."

Upstairs: a fragment of the past had unwittingly slipped from her mouth. Upstairs, back then, always meant the top floor. The first floor was upstairs, of course, but nobody in the family referred to it like that.

She patted Ben's shoulder as she went to the door. He was being very good, quietly looking around him, his hands dug into the pockets of his anorak. It must be boring for him.

"Was this your house?" he said.

"Yes," she said, "when I was about your age," yet even now she couldn't feel it as a physical fact. It was like looking at a photo of yourself as a newborn baby. It was the same individual, it couldn't be any other, but try as you might you couldn't establish any real continuity between your adult self and those tiny fingers and doll-like eyes: the gulf was too wide, the metamorphosis too complete.

Yes, she had been here before, but as a different person. And Geoff Yeomans? Could there have been some hole in his alibi that the police hadn't spotted — could he have been here too, on a December night fifteen years ago?

She hadn't really entertained the question, even when Elaine had confided in her about his violence, and her own less than total belief in him: she simply hadn't been able to pick up the pieces of what had been so effectively demolished by the deadpan words of DI Munt. It wasn't that she believed the police and the authorities to be infallible, she had just been prepared to accept, at that low point, her own fallibility — had accepted it almost to the point of despair.

Now, after a blank glance into the room that had been her mother's study, she climbed the stairs to the top floor and made herself tackle the idea that Geoff Yeomans had been one of those youths after all. And his death? Was it possible that he could live with that secret all those years, and then suddenly not be able to live with it any more?

Possible, if the secret seemed to be on the point of coming out. Simply the mere reappearance of such a past, even if it posed no direct threat, might have been enough to send him over the edge if he had really remade himself in the meantime. She ought to know that.

She halted on the top landing. It was colder here. It always was, and she recalled her father joking about the fallacy of hot air rising; but one could easily fancy that the drop in temperature had another cause.

Because this was the place. There to the left, the bedroom that had been her parents', the place of the savagery and screaming; here, in the middle of the landing, the place where her father had gone down at last beneath a hail of bloody knives; there to the right, her own bedroom, where she had hidden and seen.

For the first time she pictured that from the youths' point of view: the child's bedroom with the teddy bears and shelves of books and the hamster cage, the boarded-up fireplace stuck about with drawings. And there, somewhere in the middle, a peephole and a glistening, blinking eye.

She wondered what would have happened if they had seen that eye.

"You all right?"

Elaine was beside her: she seemed to have picked up on some extra significance in her stillness.

"Yes. I'm fine." Her eyes turned slowly around, feeling heavy in their sockets, taking in the dingy magnolia paintwork, the cobwebby square that was the entrance to the loft, the landing window still hung with an oblong of frowsty net curtain, the two stripped doors standing ajar. The place where nightmare and memory met. The place where she had seen four youths who might as well have materialized from hell and disappeared back there as soon as their amusement was over.

Flitting shapes. Swish of jeans and excited giggly breathing. Narrow young heads in movement, flash of teeth.

Carol closed her eyes. No picture formed, nothing at least with any more definition or detail than the blurred snapshots she had carried in her head for fifteen years. Something came though: there was a deepening of impression in one aspect of the memory.

Glee. That was the word. The skulking, flitting, laughing shapes gave off a feeling of glee in what they were doing. The atmosphere of that night, its slaughterous hilarity, returned to her like a sudden stench, making her recoil.

She opened her eyes and went forward

to the door of her parents' bedroom. And as if in gentle benediction, a sweet clean scent met her.

She looked in. The old fitted cupboards had been dismantled by the builders, and there was a stack of creamy new timber in the middle of the floor, placed on a piece of polythene sheeting. The builders had left a couple of sweet wrappers and a newspaper, folded open at a half-finished crossword.

Impossible to picture horrors here. Carol breathed out a little sigh. Because she didn't want this blank filled in: didn't want the second-hand memory of finding her mother in here turned into an intolerable blast of first-hand recollection. Let it remain like something she had been told, not something she had lived.

"I won't be long now," she said to Elaine, crossing the landing to the door of her own room.

She didn't know what she expected to find now: in a way she had gone past expectancy, and the sheer riddle of the past occupied her, its nearness and remoteness, the way it could touch and not touch. Maybe that was why the ghost was so often used as a metaphor for the past — it looked real but it wasn't tangible, lacked some crucial dimension.

Carol walked into the room that had been her bedroom and the scene of the most powerful influence on her whole life, and didn't recognize it.

After a shocked moment she realized that even now some atavistic part of her had expected the room to bear signs of her occupancy. Because, she supposed, she was alive: she at least hadn't been erased from the record. And that same part of her, whilst accepting that the rest of the house would in the nature of things be transformed, had clung to a vision of this room as forever the bedroom of eight-year-old Carol Mitcheson.

Someone else had lived here: that was the one impression that immediately swarmed in on her. The place was redolent of other lives. Probably several tenants had passed through, called the room home for a while, moved on. The bare carpet was imprinted with lines and marks like hieroglyphs telling the room's story. Four round depressions like the spots on a dice spoke of the little metal legs of a stacking hi-fi as eloquently as if the equipment still stood there. Clean squares and rectangles on the browning walls suggested the posters that had occupied them. There even seemed to be a faint smell of bedsit cookery.

And the boarded-up fireplace where she had hidden might never have existed. The chimney breast was still there and the mantelshelf, but the fireplace had long ago been bricked up and plastered over and painted and made as flush with the rest of the wall as possible. The feature had been obliterated.

And it was absurd to be surprised by this. What had been in this room fifteen years ago had been a fortuitous, temporary patch-up in the process of renovation that her parents had been planning — as temporary as that pile of timber in the next room. Yet somehow it struck Carol like the apparently glancing blow that finally fells a boxer. She stared about, and stared again; and could see nothing.

She suddenly felt weak and almost faint. There was nothing in the room to sit down on: she simply folded up and sat down heavily on the floor, her head in her hands.

After a moment she felt a nudge. She lifted her head. Elaine had sat down near her, and had taken a Thermos flask from her shopping-bag.

"Here," she said, holding it out. "Go on, it'll take the chill off."

Carol accepted the flask gratefully, and poured out a cupful of what looked and smelt like strong tea mixed with something stronger.

"Brandy," Elaine said. "I know it's not the answer, but it makes you forget the question. Benny?" She passed her son a carton of juice with a straw.

"Thanks for this," Carol said, drinking, feeling the heat of the brandy hit her throat and then, both fiercely and comfortingly, her stomach. "And . . . thanks for coming with me."

Elaine shook her head. "This was your room?"

Carol looked around. "Yes," she said. "It might as well not have been."

"Ben," Elaine said, "do you want to go and have a look round on your own? We won't be long."

Ben, sucking noisily on his juice, ambled obediently out of the room.

"I'm sorry," Carol said, leaning back against the wall, feeling abominably tired, "dragging you all this way."

"No good?" Elaine said, sitting with her arms clasped round her knees, watching her.

Carol shook her head. "Perhaps I've been watching too many thrillers," she said. "Where somebody goes back to a place where something happened and it all — comes back to them." She found her tongue slurring a little: the brandy must be strong. And she had missed breakfast that morning. Remembering herself, she held out the Thermos cup. "Sorry — I'm pigging this."

"After you," Elaine said with a slight shake of the head. "You need it."

Carol drank again, then leant her head back: the hard wall felt remarkably comfortable. She closed her eyes for a moment; then opened them with a jerk. Actually almost nodded off there. The stuff really must be strong.

Elaine was regarding her with bright dry interest.

"Feeling better?" she said.

"Sort of," Carol said. She felt soothed, but almost to the point of numbness: there was a dull tingle in her hands and feet, as if she had been lying awkwardly in bed.

"Anything come back yet? There must be something. Try and picture it." Elaine cocked her head and pointed. "Now the bed would be over there somewhere. And the hamster cage, just there to the side of it. Yeah?"

Carol blinked at her. This brandy really had gone to her head: she couldn't for the life of her remember when she had told Elaine about the hamster. Yet she must have done.

"Yes, that would be the bed just there," Elaine said, with a thoughtful look. "One of them pissed on it, didn't he? Stood up on your bed and pissed on it. What a meanie."

"How . . . " Carol's voice sounded hollow in her ears. The numbness had deepened, and seemed to leave her no sensation except for a pure, helpless, childlike bewilderment. "How did you know? Did I — tell you?"

"I know it all, matey," Elaine said with a faint rueful smile. "Your dad — they stuck a knife right up his jacksy when they'd finished with him, didn't they? And they tied your mum to the bed and rammed a Coke bottle up her. Those nice fluted bottles, you don't get them any more. Oh, and they slashed her throat and I do believe the blood went so high it hit the ceiling. And poor old Mr Hamster got stomped on."

Carol found that her head was shaking from side to side, without her volition.

"No," she said, and it came out long, like a record on the wrong speed, *Noo-oo*. "That was never, the police, it never got out, the press . . . didn't . . . "

The words took so much out of her. She had to stop, drag up the slow drowsy breaths that seemed to come from somewhere deep inside a body that had grown huge and dinosaur-sluggish. The room was spinning, but somehow the trim, spry, pretty figure of Elaine sitting in the middle of it didn't move: her image, smiling, was quite still and clear. Diamond-sharp, in fact.

"No, of course it wasn't in the papers,"

Elaine said. "I bet they'd have liked to get hold of it. I mean it was pretty juicy, wasn't it? Oh yes, and they left graffiti on the walls written in blood. Used the end of a scarf for that, by the way."

Understanding rose like a slow tide against the numb walls of Carol's mind. "Geoff," she mumbled. "Geoff . . . he told you. He was — he was here after all . . . Jesus . . . "

"Geoff didn't tell me," Elaine said. "I told Geoff." And she gave Carol her cock-eyed, droll, impish smile.

The tide of understanding sank again. And then it rose with a roar and Carol moaned as she struggled against it, tried vainly to resist the flood about to overwhelm her. "You — you couldn't know, you . . . "

"Blimey O'Riley, aren't you there yet?" Elaine said. "Put it this way. Who do you think Ben takes after most — Geoff?" She tilted her perky profile. "Or me?"

Carol's mouth fell open. She believed that she was screaming, but all that came out was a rattling sound.

"Hooray," Elaine said, shifting her haunches a little. "God, my bum's gone to sleep. Yes, duck, I was there. Here, rather. It all looks just the same to me, which is a weird feeling really. Four teenage boys, the papers said, didn't they? One of them very young, apparently. That was your description, and I can understand it in a way. I was a bit of a tomboy in those days. Kept my hair dead short and never wore a skirt, mainly because I thought my legs were skinny. And I think I must have been seventeen or even eighteen before I got any tits to speak of. Fifteen, I was as flat as a pancake. So it was an understandable mistake, really." She winked. "I'll let you off."

The tide was over her now but she managed to let out a drowning cry. "I don't believe . . . you couldn't . . . "

"Oh, you know what you're like when you're young. You don't care, do you? You're irresponsible. I was gobsmacked that we never got caught but there you are — just lucky, I suppose. I should just sit back if I were you, Carol, because you're not going to be able to get up. You've got some very strong tablets inside you and they'll put you to sleep pretty soon. Courtesy of one of my old grannies at the home. They get more prescriptions than you can count so it's pretty easy to cream a few off."

Beyond the tide Carol discerned another wave coming her way, dark and engulfing, and terror thumped at her chest with great slow strokes. "You've . . . oh God you . . . "

"Yes, it should finish you off, what you've taken. I mean, I don't know, I'm no chemist, it might just turn you into a veggieburger, if somebody finds you in time. I shouldn't worry about it, I don't think it'll hurt. Yes, it's funny how life turns out, isn't it? I had no idea, of course, that you were the one whose mum and dad we topped all those years ago, not until you told me about it in the café that time and then I thought hello, I do believe . . . You know, I wonder if you *had* recognized that one of the baddies was a girl, whether the coppers would have believed you? Because there's a bit of a reversed sexism thing going on there, isn't there? You know, if you're a woman you're supposed to be all nurturing and caring and what have you. I must admit I fell for it a bit myself, after I met Geoff. Gave it a go, the mumsy aprony bit. It has got its nice side, actually, I'm not knocking it. But like I say, I was a right tomboy back then. I liked knocking around with lads. Bad lads especially, but you do, don't you? There's this sort of attraction to the dodgy characters your parents wouldn't like. There were three I used to hang around with in particular. Tell you their names if you like: Andy Barnwell, Mick Griers, and Stan Finding. I don't think his real name was Stan, it was like a nickname, but I couldn't tell you what his real first name was. And my maiden name was Armstrong. There. That's what you've been wanting to know, right? Whodunit. That's whodunit." Elaine took out a cigarette and lit it. "Usdunit."

Death was coming for her. The guttering flame of consciousness that was Carol looked for horror in this knowledge. But the horror of the words she was hearing blocked everything else from view.

"I'd been drinking with the lads that

night," Elaine said, blowing out smoke with satisfaction. "Just cider and stuff like that, arsing around. We'd tried to crash this party over Wandsworth way but they wouldn't let us in. Then Andy went looking for some mate of his over this way who he reckoned he could get some dope from. It was all rubbish, I reckon. This is the thing, you see. We weren't actually on anything that night, like the papers kept trying to hint: oh, they must be on glue or acid or whatever. We weren't. We were just a bit pissed and bored and looking for something to do. Now a week or two before, we'd come across this old wino kipping down in an underpass one night and something, I don't know what, just made us decide to set light to him. So we did. We watched him burn, flapping about and trying to put himself out et cetera, and it was so comical. I mean it was — it was good fun, I can't really describe it. And so that night we started egging each other to do something really daring and way out and . . . that was it, really. It was a spree sort of thing. We got carried away in here, like being at the fair. You know what you're doing, that's what's so good about it. You're not out of your head or anything; it's just pure enjoyment. That's what annoys me about these hunters, when you see them on TV and they go on about it being traditional and it keeps down the number of foxes and what have you: why can't they just come out and say they enjoy killing things? Well, anyway, we did it, and then some noise spooked us and we legged it to Stan's car and went home. I'll admit we were all a bit worried afterwards. But nobody cottoned on. I think it might have been because of who we were and where we came from. I mean there was me in a rather naice part of Wimbledon and *my* parents didn't know half of what I got up to simply because they didn't like to think about it. They knew I didn't keep staying round a friend's to watch late-night films, for Christ's sake, but there, people believe what they want to believe, don't they? Like the other three — they were a bit rebellious but they were from perfectly ordinary respectable backgrounds. Mick was actually from Twickenham. I can tell you one thing though. My parents certainly didn't have the faintest idea but Stan's must have. Because he was the one who took charge of our clothes, you know, the ones with the blood and stuff on them. He burnt some in a bonfire and some actually got washed in his mum's washing machine. I mean, they must have had some inkling, mustn't they? But people cover up when it's family, I suppose." She looked closely at Carol, then leaned forward and snapped her fingers. "Hey, still with us?"

Carol tried to move. It was with some vastly remote idea of getting up and shambling over to Elaine and strangling her with her bare hands. All that happened was that she swayed forward and a groaning sound came out of her mouth.

"Anyway," Elaine said, tapping her cigarette ash into her handbag, "there it is. So it turns out you were nearly right after all. Poor old Geoff. I mean, I could have told you he hadn't got the oomph for anything like that. He was really going spare that night after the police gave him a grilling. Let's face it, he wasn't the brightest spark in the world and I think he'd half started to believe that he *had* done it. I just couldn't calm him down. There he was swilling the booze down and ranting and raving and I just thought, well, I'd better tell him. Put him out of his misery sort of thing. I mean, it had just come out about the naughty things he'd got up to, and like I say he was no saint, so it didn't seem a big deal. And I must admit I was curious to see what he'd say. *Well.* He really couldn't handle it. He went bananas. But I was his wife and the mother of his kid and he did love me and . . . oh, he was in a right state. So he just kept boozing as per. Drank himself pie-eyed and crashed out maundering on about how we'd have to get it sorted. Well, that I really didn't like the sound of. I mean, he was what you might call drunk and incapable just now, but once he'd sobered up . . . So I hoisted him up and fed him some soluble painkillers; well, a lot, actually. He didn't know what he was doing, he just thought I was giving him something for the hangover. Swallowed the lot and crashed out again. Bye-bye,

Geoff. I did like him, love him really, but I suppose I misjudged him and I couldn't take any chances. You have to be careful," she said, extinguishing her cigarette by dropping it into the flask. "This is the secret of life. We went a bit loopy here that night, but I made sure we were pretty careful as well. Don't know what became of the others, by the way. We drifted apart: people do, don't they? Probably selling insurance or something now. Being careful, that's the secret. It doesn't meant being boring. Far from it. If you're careful, then you can have all the fun you like. I've settled down a bit nowadays but I can still be a bit of a beggar when the fancy takes me. Like my job — there's a lot of scope there, if you're careful. Old dears are always hurting themselves and popping off so as long as you cover your tracks who's to know? This is what I've been trying to teach Ben, little by little. I want him to be able to have fun too."

Carol made a retching sound that she had thought would be a yell, and somehow lurched upwards to a kneeling position: then swayed there, straining for a strength that would not come.

"Ooh," Elaine said with mild interest, "well done. Yes, like I say, I've been teaching Benny. Just small stuff, with his pets and so on. But he's a quick learner as you know. It'll be interesting to see how he turns out." Elaine looked at her watch. "Speaking of Benjamino, where is he? It's time we were getting home. There's a train from Liverpool Street at half two."

Getting up she took the cup from Carol's nerveless hand, fixed it to the Thermos, and put it in the shopping bag. She adjusted the strap of her handbag on her shoulder, looking neutrally down at Carol.

"I thought I'd better put you out of your misery, you see. You might not have cottoned on but then again you might and like I say, you can't be too careful. The state you've been in lately, I don't think anybody's going to be too surprised at you topping yourself. Especially here where it all happened. Just one of those tragic things. You'll conk out soon, so don't worry."

Elaine went smartly to the door; then

turned and said, "Oh, by the way, I think your mum knew I was a girl. I could sort of see it in her eyes at one point." She waved, and went out, calling, "Ben! Benny!"

The tide was right over Carol's head. She felt the proximity of death, somewhere at hand, an intruder in the house.

She toppled forward, and found that her hands came out and hit the floor, holding her up. Just.

She concentrated her whole dwindling being on her knees. With an effort that seemed to grind her joints to powder, she moved them, first one, then the other.

Hands next. Slide the enormous, stone-heavy appendages forward across the carpet. One. Two.

On all fours, like a monstrous dream-dog, Carol crawled across the room towards the door.

"Ben! Where are you, duck?" Elaine's voice, still the one diamond-sharp sound amidst the roaring susurrus in her head.

Carol crept through the doorway of her old bedroom: it was like passing beneath some giant arch, a vast dwarfing structure of the ancient world. She began to cross the endless desert that was the landing.

"Ben! Time to go . . . "

The banisters loomed up before her, the pillars of a temple. She put out her great unwieldy hands, grasped them. Tried to pull herself up.

No. She was all weight, no muscle. Her body was going to sleep.

Pressing her huge face between the banisters, she opened her jaw and shouted down the stairwell.

"Help . . . help me . . . please . . . "

The voice was little more than breath. Her sluggish lump of a tongue quivered and was still.

Her eyes looked down. The varnished base of the banisters was thick with plaster-dust. She brought down one thick finger and, taking in death, began to write in the dust.

E . . . L . . . A . . .

The mammoth labour was not completed. Suddenly a suedebooted foot was there in front of her blurring eyes, and rubbing the letters out.

"That's a bit silly," came Elaine's voice, from a great height above her, while the booted leg moved backwards and forwards, obliterating the name, removing it from history.

Almost casually, the toe of the boot stamped down on Carol's fingers, killing them: then Elaine moved away a little, disregarding her, and leant out over the banister.

"Benny!" Elaine shouted down the stairwell, a touch of impatience in her voice now, her whole upper body craning out over the banister. "Ben, come here!"

And then there was a sudden surprising image of swiftness imprinted on Carol's dimming mind. The image was of Ben, laughing and mischievous, darting out from the room behind her — her parents' old room. "Boo, Mum!" he cried as he ran out, hands outstretched, perhaps to tickle, to pinch . . . The *perhaps* fell away like an echo as Ben collided with his mother, still bent over the banister.

The banister cracked like a fence being kicked in and the suede boots lifted in the air and Elaine went over, squealing, grasping.

With a last reflex Carol's huge left hand reached out, grabbing the seat of

Ben's jeans, tugging him back.

The squeal did not diminish. It stayed just below the level of Carol's head. She looked down, and into the eyes of Elaine. She was dangling above the yawning stairwell, gripping on to the broken banisters, which protruded into the air at a ninety-degree angle like a bundle of stakes.

"Ben! Ben, help me! Help me, Ben!"

Elaine's voice went up like a train whistle as she dangled and twirled, the suede boots kicking in emptiness. Carol turned her colossal head to see Ben standing beside her, looking down at his mother.

And then for a few lucid moments Carol was once again a primary schoolteacher trying to read the expression of one of her pupils. And the primary schoolteacher couldn't decide. Couldn't decide whether he stood there, motionless, gazing down, because he was paralysed with fear: or whether what glinted in his deep brown eyes was a passionate yet utterly clinical fascination.

"Ben! Help me! Ben . . . "

The last cry was a wail, with something

both frustrated and resigned in it. Elaine lost her grip and plunged down the stairwell like a shot bird.

"Ben," said Carol, looking up at him: making the very same appeal, and wholly unknowing, as her eyes closed, whether in her case he would extend or deny his mercy.

33

"THERE was a man here earlier, wasn't there?" Carol said, blinking sleepily at Aunt Jean.

"Yes. Superintendent Lennard. He said he'd come back later. How are you feeling?"

"Bit sick."

Aunt Jean stroked her hair back from her forehead. "They said that'll pass. You're going to be fine. Do you remember much of what happened?"

Carol licked her dry lips, her eyes roaming over the high ward ceiling.

"I remember everything," she said.

Jean gave her a painful smile and squeezed her hand. "Well, it's all over now."

"Where's Brendan?"

"He's at work. He'll be here later."

Brendan. She remembered everything, including Brendan rushing up the stairs, lifting her shoulders where she lay by the splintered banisters, shouting her back to consciousness.

"How did he . . . ? He came to the house. How . . . ?"

"Well, he was worried about you. He saw you earlier — driving down Kennington Park Road. It was the second time he'd seen you like that and something didn't seem right and so when he told me about it I . . . I was worried too and I told him. About what had happened to you. And when I mentioned the house being sold he said we should go down there." Jean swallowed with an effort. "The little boy was shouting through the letterbox — he couldn't get the door open. Brendan bashed it in and . . . "

Carol gripped her aunt's hand tightly.

"Like I say," Jean said, returning the pressure, "it's over now. I rang your Martin, by the way."

"Martin . . . " She remembered everything: everything that had happened in the house. The aftermath, the ambulance, the police, being brought to the hospital, being treated, was hazy, like a euphoric dream.

"You were a bit groggy at the time," Jean said. "But you gave me his number and said to ring him and say you were sorry. He seemed to understand, in fact he said he wanted to come down and see you straight away. I told him where you were. Was that right?"

Carol nodded. "That was right. Thanks, Jean."

She slept. There were no dreams. When she woke, the light on the ceiling had changed, and Chief Superintendent Lennard was beside the bed.

"Your aunt's just gone to get a cup of tea," he said. "How are you feeling?"

"Better. You were here earlier, weren't you?"

"I was. You talked to me, but you were a bit woozy. The nurse shooed me away after a while."

"Did I . . . tell you about it?"

"Yes, mostly." He took out a notebook. "You said you had some names. Can you remember them?"

"I remember everything," Carol said. "Andy Barnwell. Mick Griers. Stan Finding."

Lennard wrote busily. A furtive, almost

greedy look came into his eyes as he did so.

"Very nice," he said.

Carol struggled to sit up. Her stomach felt as if it had been wrung out like a dishcloth, and she was still a little dizzy. "She died, didn't she?"

"Yes. Her neck was broken."

Carol turned that over for a moment: found nothing, except a sense of ending.

Then she remembered something.

"What about Ben?"

"The little boy? He's OK. Remarkable really — very strong, very cool, hardly a tear. Poor little tyke. Father and mother both gone. Apparently his grandparents have taken charge of him: he even managed to give their name and address as soon as we picked him up. Remarkable little boy. But then," he added kindly as tears began to seep from Carol's eyelids, "he had a good teacher, didn't he?"

TO FIGHT THE WILD
Rod Ansell and Rachel Percy

Lost in uncharted Australian bush, Rod Ansell survived by hunting and trapping wild animals, improvising shelter and using all the bushman's skills he knew.

COROMANDEL
Pat Barr

India in the 1830s is a hot, uncomfortable place, where the East India Company still rules. Amelia and her new husband find themselves caught up in the animosities which seethe between the old order and the new.

THE SMALL PARTY
Lillian Beckwith

A frightening journey to safety begins for Ruth and her small party as their island is caught up in the dangers of armed insurrection.

THE WILDERNESS WALK
Sheila Bishop

Stifling unpleasant memories of a misbegotten romance in Cleave with Lord Francis Aubrey, Lavinia goes on holiday there with her sister. The two women are thrust into a romantic intrigue involving none other than Lord Francis.

THE RELUCTANT GUEST
Rosalind Brett

Ann Calvert went to spend a month on a South African farm with Theo Borland and his sister. They both proved to be different from her first idea of them, and there was Storr Peterson — the most disturbing man she had ever met.

ONE ENCHANTED SUMMER
Anne Tedlock Brooks

A tale of mystery and romance and a girl who found both during one enchanted summer.

CLOUD OVER MALVERTON
Nancy Buckingham

Dulcie soon realises that something is seriously wrong at Malverton, and when violence strikes she is horrified to find herself under suspicion of murder.

AFTER THOUGHTS
Max Bygraves

The Cockney entertainer tells stories of his East End childhood, of his RAF days, and his post-war showbusiness successes and friendships with fellow comedians.

MOONLIGHT
AND MARCH ROSES
D. Y. Cameron

Lynn's search to trace a missing girl takes her to Spain, where she meets Clive Hendon. While untangling the situation, she untangles her emotions and decides on her own future.